Praise ... **and her sizzling novels**

"With a distinct voice and fresh, complex characters, *Mine To Take* is a sexy, emotional read that gripped me from page one. I can't wait to see what Ashenden brings us next."
—Laurelin Paige, *New York Times* bestselling author

"A scintillating, heart-pounding love story. A dark, sinfully sexy hero with a tortured past. I loved it!"
—Opal Carew, *New York Times* bestselling author

"The sex is dirty-sweet, with a dark lick of dominance and the tantalizing potential of redemption, and an explosive ending provides the perfect closure to Gabe and Honor's story while setting up the next installment."
—*Publishers Weekly* (starred review) on *Mine To Take*

"Intriguingly dark and intensely compelling . . . explosive."
—*RT Book Reviews* on *Mine To Take* (Top Pick!)

"Powerfully suspenseful and, above all, sensual and meaningful . . . not to be missed."
—*RT Book Reviews* on *Make You Mine* (Top Pick!)

"Ms. Ashenden is an incredible storyteller."
—*Harlequin Junkies*

"Sexy and fun."
—*RT Book Reviews*

"Truly a roller coaster of a ride . . . well worth it."
—*Harlequin Junkies*

"Steamy."
—*Guilty Pleasures Book Reviews*

ALSO BY JACKIE ASHENDEN

The Tate Brothers

The Dangerous Billionaire

The Nine Circles series

Mine To Take
Make You Mine
You Are Mine
Kidnapped by the Billionaire
In Bed with the Billionaire

The Billionaire's Club e-book series

The Billion Dollar Bachelor
The Billion Dollar Bad Boy
The Billionaire Biker

Available by St. Martin's Press

THE WICKED BILLIONAIRE

JACKIE ASHENDEN

St. Martin's Paperbacks

This is a work of fiction. All of the characters, organizations, and events portrayed in this novel are either products of the author's imagination or are used fictitiously.

THE WICKED BILLIONAIRE

Copyright © 2017 by Jackie Ashenden.
Excerpt from *The Undercover Billionaire* Copyright © 2018 by Jackie Ashenden.

All rights reserved.

For information address St. Martin's Press, 175 Fifth Avenue, New York, NY 10010.

ISBN: 978-1-250-12281-0

Our books may be purchased in bulk for promotional, educational, or business use. Please contact your local bookseller or the Macmillan Corporate and Premium Sales Department at 1-800-221-7945, ext. 5442, or by e-mail at MacmillanSpecialMarkets@macmillan.com.

Printed in the United States of America

St. Martin's Paperbacks edition / October 2017

St. Martin's Paperbacks are published by St. Martin's Press, 175 Fifth Avenue, New York, NY 10010.

10 9 8 7 6 5 4 3 2 1

To Tess,
We have you. Kia Kaha

ACKNOWLEDGMENTS

Thanks to Monique and Helen, and the great team at SMP. Plus my own team of Maisey, Megan and Nicole. Also, to my readers. You keep me writing.

CHAPTER ONE

If there was one thing that Lucas Tate fervently wished it was that wherever his father had gone to after he'd died it was Hell and that he was currently burning in it.

It wasn't that Lucas hated his old man. That would assume some level of caring and Lucas had approximately zero level of caring. No, he felt nothing for the guy, and feeling nothing was pretty much Lucas's usual modus operandi.

But standing on a New York sidewalk, with the tiny ripped-up pieces of Noah Tate's last letter to him in his pocket, staring through the plate-glass window of the art gallery opposite, he almost felt the faintest stirrings of hate.

It wasn't because he was now one of the reluctant directors of the billion-dollar family company Tate Oil and Gas. And it wasn't because it was starting to look like he wasn't going to be able to get back to base and resume his career as one of the Navy's best SEAL snipers as quickly as he wanted to.

It was because of the woman standing in that gallery opposite, having what looked like an argument with someone else.

The woman who in his last letter to Lucas, his father had ordered him to protect.

If it had been any other woman Lucas probably would

have found someone else to do his father's dirty work for him, since he wasn't in the least bit sentimental about women in general. But it wasn't any other woman. It was Grace Riley, the widow of one of Lucas's fellow SEAL team members, Griffin Riley, a man who had once been the closest to a friend Lucas got and who had been killed in a terrorist operation in Europe some six months earlier.

A man who'd turned out to be a traitor, having been discovered supplying illegal experimental weaponry to international arms dealers, which was also the reason his widow currently needed protection.

It was a mess, a fucking mess, and if there was one thing Lucas hated more than any of the above it was messes.

He stared through the art gallery window at the woman inside, watching as she lifted a hand, making some emphatic gesture with it as she argued with the very well-dressed man standing opposite her and looking defensive.

Lucas had met Grace Riley on a number of occasions, at various ceremonies and other military gatherings, not to mention once up at the Tates' place in the Hamptons when Lucas had invited Griffin to one of Noah's infrequent summer garden parties. He'd also seen her a few times at her and Griffin's place, when he and Griffin had been on leave and Griffin asked him around for the odd barbecue or dinner.

Lucas didn't like her. In fact, every single time he met her he found himself thinking about exactly how much he didn't like her. It wasn't anything specific, there was just something about her that rubbed him the wrong way. She was opinionated and fiery and passionate in her views, and didn't hesitate to let people know all about whatever she was feeling at the time, all of which were traits he found extremely distasteful.

Nevertheless, for some completely inexplicable reason, whenever he was in her general vicinity he found himself drawn to her very much against his will, in a way he couldn't explain even to himself.

He still couldn't now.

Grace made another gesture, waving her hand, the many bracelets she wore sliding up her arm. The man she was arguing with took a step back as if he was slightly afraid of her.

No, Lucas really didn't understand his own fascination, because she wasn't beautiful. She wasn't even pretty. Not that beauty had ever been a big drawcard for him anyway, but Grace certainly didn't possess it. Her nose was far too long, her jaw too strong, and her chin too decisive for a start. Her hair was a pretty color, like fresh apricots, but it fell in long, frizzy untamed waves almost to her waist, and what with the scattering of freckles over her forehead and cheekbones, she kind of looked like Pippi Longstocking. And not in a good way.

Nevertheless, despite all of that, he had to admit there was something compelling about her all the same. Something he really couldn't put his finger on.

It had always annoyed him and now it looked like it was going to continue to annoy him.

Lucas closed his fingers around the pieces of that fucking letter he'd torn up three days earlier in Leo's Alehouse, the bar he'd met his brothers, Van and Wolf, in after scattering some of their father's ashes off the Brooklyn Bridge.

All three of them had gotten a letter each from their father, and if Van's and Wolf's letters had been anything like what was in the contents of his, Lucas couldn't blame them for the past three days of silence.

They were probably doing exactly what he was doing now, wondering what the fuck they were going to do. Not that there was any doubt in his mind about what *he* was going to do.

He respected Noah Tate, the man who'd adopted him and Wolf and Van from the St. Mary's Home for Boys all those years ago. But respect was the only emotion Lucas allowed himself. Certainly he felt nothing else for the guy.

So no, Lucas wasn't going to protect a woman he didn't particularly like for his foster-father. Lucas was going to protect her because this was a mission he'd been given and he'd never refused a mission yet. Plus she was a civilian and it wasn't her fault that her husband had been negotiating with a number of international arms dealers and apparently now owed those dealers a shitload of money. Money that he couldn't pay back because he was dead.

But Grace wasn't. And if Lucas's father's letter was correct those dealers would be coming to get that money from her.

Lucas couldn't let that happen, no matter how he felt about his erstwhile buddy or his foster-father. No matter how Lucas personally felt about her. Because if she couldn't give them their money they'd kill her, no two ways about it. Hell, they'd probably kill her anyway.

Lucas might have taken lives himself, all in the name of freedom, but he wasn't about to let an innocent civilian die. If she *was* innocent, that was. Maybe she'd known about Griffin's little deals? Then again, from what Griffin had told him about their marriage and from what he'd seen himself, he knew that wasn't likely.

There was only one thing Grace Riley cared about and that was her art. Everything else was just noise.

Across the road, Grace flung out her hand again, bracelets glittering in the dull winter light, then curled her hand around the long fall of her mermaid hair and shifted it over one shoulder in an unconscious, reflexive gesture.

Another thing he didn't like about her. Damn woman could never keep still.

A cold wind had started up, the gray sky above him lowering. Snow was in the air.

Lucas ignored all of it the way he ignored most things when he was on reconnaissance. Because that's what this was. Reconnaissance for a mission. Intelligence gathering on a target, Grace being his target. He'd been planning on visiting her anyway before he went back to base, simply to pay his respects and offer his condolences about Griffin, because it was the right thing to do. But then Lucas had gotten his father's letter and so the courtesy visit had instead turned into three days spent shadowing her, learning about her and her daily life. What she did, where she went. Where she lived. Where she worked. Who she associated with, the usual. All of it was all very mundane, nothing special.

She lived in a tiny apartment in the East Village with absolutely no security whatsoever, worked three nights a week in a local bar, and from the looks of her financial details—which he'd hacked with relative ease—she paid the extortionate rent with Griffin's military pension. She had a few friends whom she met once a month to drink and bitch with in a cafe near Central Park or called and texted with every few days—her phone records too had been relatively easy to hack—but she didn't have a boyfriend from the looks of things, which wasn't unsurprising considering she'd only been widowed recently. She had some family—her mother—but judging from those phone records, Grace had no contact with her whatsoever. The only other detail of note was that Grace spent most of her meager wages on art supplies. Typical struggling artist, in other words.

All up, it was a relatively boring life for a relatively boring female.

There were no signs she was being followed or anything

else suspicious, though, which was at least one blessing, since Lucas had been hoping to deal with anyone coming after her without her knowing. Dealing with her personally was something he wanted to avoid, especially when it would lead to painful explanations, messy scenes, and would probably further delay his return to base.

Interacting with people was not Lucas's favorite. Most particularly hysterical females, and if he could get away without actually having to explain to her that Griffin had been a traitorous asshole selling high-tech weaponry to people who shouldn't have it that would be good.

In the pocket of Lucas's motorcycle leathers, his phone buzzed with a text. He grabbed it and briefly glanced down at the screen. Of course it would be Van, his older brother, breaking the silence of the last three days. Lucas even suspected he knew what it was about too: being one of the directors for Tate Oil and Gas.

Problem was, he didn't give a shit about his father's company, had never been interested in it, and although he'd agreed to be a director, he didn't particularly want to have anything to do with it now, so he left the text unanswered and put his phone back in his pocket. Van could wait. Right now, Lucas had more important things to take care of.

Grace was now throwing both hands in the air in a dramatic gesture, the man she was arguing with slowly shaking his head in response. Clearly she was having trouble with something and maybe, given this was an art gallery and she was an artist, it had something to do with an exhibition or a potential exhibition.

Lucas went back over the information he'd managed to glean on her over the past couple of days. He couldn't recall that there had been anything in her phone records to do with this particular gallery or in her e-mails, though that didn't mean she didn't have something going on here.

She *was* having financial difficulties, though, as he could see from her last couple of bank statements. Basically all her money went on art supplies, which weren't cheap.

He narrowed his gaze as she pulled her hair over her shoulder in that reflexive movement again. Crazy woman What kind of person put art supplies over food and utility bills? The logical thing, if she was having money troubles, would have been to move out of New York and go somewhere much, much cheaper, not stay here.

Not that he cared. He didn't give a shit what she did with her money or her life for that matter. The only thing he cared about was that she kept her actual life, since it was pretty damn obvious she had no means to pay the people who were after her.

In fact, his initial response had been to doubt the veracity of his father's facts about Griffin, especially since the man was a friend and fellow SEAL and the accusations leveled at him were pretty fucking serious.

But the day after Lucas had gotten Noah's unexpected letter, an e-mail had arrived in his in-box with a heavily encrypted file attached. After running the decryption program suggested in the e-mail, Lucas had opened the file to find all sorts of financial information, photos, copies of e-mail conversations, copies of texts, and all about Griffin. Who'd apparently been recruited to work for a man called Cesare de Santis, the erstwhile owner of DS Corp, one of the country's biggest weapons designer and manufacturer, and who also just happened to be the Tate family's biggest enemy. Cesare and Noah had once been friends until it had all gone bad, and Noah had drummed it into each of his boys that one day Cesare would come for the Tates.

Certainly Cesare had come for Griffin. He'd been trying to get DS Corp experimental weapons onto the illegal arms market and had been paid very well for his efforts by Cesare de Santis himself. Until Griffin had been blown to bits by an unusually well-targeted missile strike.

Across the street, Grace made another emphatic gesture with her hand; then quite suddenly, as if she'd heard a sharp sound, she turned her head.

And Lucas found himself staring into a pair of intense amber eyes.

It had never happened before, a target seeing him before he was ready to reveal himself, and he couldn't think for the life of him what he'd done to give himself away.

And then as if being spotted weren't bad enough, Grace abruptly made things worse by starting toward the art gallery front door, leaving him in no doubt as to what she was going to do.

Shit.

She was coming to confront him.

Grace had been feeling an odd itch to the back of her neck for the past day or so, and the sensation had been aggravating her even before she'd gone to see Craig at his pretentious SoHo gallery. Then he'd refused to allow her to change the dates for her exhibition, which had only aggravated her further.

Not that she actually wanted to change the dates, it was just that she was having real difficulty with the final piece she was working on, the piece that would tie her entire exhibition together.

The piece she hadn't actually started yet, because she'd seemingly run out of inspiration.

Yeah, and that too had been aggravating. In fact, more than aggravating. Her lack of inspiration was anxiety making in the extreme and she was doing her best not to think about it, hoping that Craig would be at least a little understanding and move the dates to give her some breathing space.

Sadly, Craig was not understanding.

And that annoying prickle on the back of her neck was getting worse, like someone was watching her. Like she was being followed.

"I understand it's difficult," Craig was saying, condescending as always. "But the schedule is what it is. And it'll affect a whole lot of other artists as well, you do understand that, don't you?"

Momentarily forgetting her argument, she turned her head sharply, squinting through the big plate-glass windows of the gallery and studying the street outside. A steady stream of people went by, heavy traffic moving beyond them.

Then she spotted a tall figure, dressed in black motorcycle leathers and standing very still beside a streetlight. At first glance he looked like a bike courier, and there was nothing very suspicious about that, yet something kicked hard in her gut, an instinct she never questioned.

She squinted harder. His features were indistinct, but that instinct was telling her she knew him somehow. That he was familiar. And that quite definitely he was the one who'd been following her.

Griffin?

A jolt of electricity went through her and she had to stop herself from saying his name aloud, because of course it wasn't Griffin. He was dead and had been for six months, and if there was one thing this man wasn't it was her deceased husband. He was too tall, for one thing.

A thread of grief wound through her in the way it did whenever she thought of Griffin, bringing with it a flare of unreasonable anger at whoever the hell was standing out there, reminding her of things she didn't want to be reminded of. Clearly she needed to go out there, find out who it was and why he was following her, then give him a piece of her mind.

Craig was still going on about something, but Grace wasn't listening. Turning back to him, she held up a finger. "One second. I'll be right back."

Without waiting for a response she turned and headed straight for the gallery doors.

Outside the weather was being its usual crappy winter self, the wind whipping under the leather trench coat she'd found in a flea market the year before and cutting straight through the gold wrap dress that had been her thrift-store find the month before that.

Ignoring it, she strode straight out into the traffic, dodging a few cars and shrugging off the sound of car horns, still squinting at the tall, dark figure standing by the streetlight and trying to figure out who it might be, because she still couldn't quite make him out.

The man didn't move, simply stood there watching her come, and as she got closer his features became more and more distinct, arranging themselves into a familiar pattern.

Deep gold hair shorn close to his skull. Silver-blue eyes. A very singular, intensely masculine beauty. And cold. Cold as the icy wind that was whipping around her booted ankles right now.

Oh yeah, she knew him. You didn't forget a face like that.

It was Lucas Tate, one of Griffin's SEAL buddies and the most beautiful man she'd ever met.

Her anger melted away as quickly as it had come, replaced instead with a small shock of surprise. Because what the hell was Lucas Tate doing here?

He and Griffin had been good friends and Lucas had been included in a lot of the social gatherings she and Griffin had organized—or rather Griffin had organized, since she wasn't much of a socializer. Whatever, she'd never understood why Griffin had been Lucas's friend, because her husband had been warm and easygoing, a laid-back, chilled-out kind of guy, and Lucas was . . . none of those things. He was icy, emotionless, had apparently no sense of humor at all, and was a complete control freak. Basically the opposite of Griffin in just about every way.

At first she'd wondered whether the attraction for Griffin had been because Lucas was one of the Tate brothers, the adopted son of one of the country's richest and most powerful oil billionaires, and somehow Griffin had been dazzled by that. Except Lucas never talked about his family or flashed money around or, in fact, gave any sign that he even had much of a personality to start with.

Grace found him intensely uncomfortable to be around, not the least because not only was he cold, he was also the most physically perfect human being she'd ever met, a fact that her artist's soul found absolutely fascinating.

Then there was that other part of her, the free-spirited part, that always had the oddest urge to mess with him. Poke at him. He was like a frozen lake, all pristine white ice that she wanted to get on and skate across, cut great lines over, gouge holes in. Dig under to see what was underneath.

Probably more ice.

Yes, well, there was that. Though there had been times, once or twice, when she'd caught his silver-blue gaze on her and seen something else. Something that she thought might have been actual, honest to God emotion, though she couldn't imagine what it was and when she'd looked again it had gone.

Anyway, the last time she'd seen him had been at Griffin's funeral, where he'd offered her the world's stiffest sympathy speech before turning around and walking off before she'd been able to say a word.

"Lucas?" She came to a slow stop on the sidewalk right in front of him, shock still coursing through her. "This is a surprise. What are you doing here?" And then, remembering that prickling sensation on the back of her neck, she narrowed her gaze. "Have you been following me?"

He remained absolutely still, looking neither pleased nor particularly unhappy at seeing her, studying her with a detached kind of intensity, as if he were a scientist watching an experiment that he wasn't particularly invested in yet was curious about the results of anyway.

"How did you spot me?" His voice was as deep and cold as the arctic sea.

It sent chills through her, made her feel like someone had slipped an ice cube down her back.

Ugh, yes, now she remembered why she never liked it when he came round for dinner or joined Griffin for a beer sometimes on the weekends. That icy voice of his and his detached manner, coupled with the restlessness that seemed to grip her whenever he was near. A restlessness she could feel beginning to set in now.

She didn't like it. Not one bit.

Grace shifted on her feet, folding her arms across her chest, trying to ignore the familiar urge to simply stand there and stare at him like a teenage girl in front of a poster of her favorite pop star. "It wasn't hard. I looked out the window and there you were." She let out a breath and asked again, "What are you doing here?"

His heart-stoppingly beautiful features betrayed no emotion whatsoever, his jawline so perfect and sharp it was as if she might cut herself if she touched it. Not that she was going to touch it. He was like King Midas, except he didn't turn things into gold, he froze them solid instead.

"No one sees me if I don't want them to." He ignored her question completely, his gaze focusing on her like a laser beam. "How did you?"

Grace folded her arms tighter, resenting his stillness and the weird effect he always had on her. It was probably the way that he loomed over her, even though she wasn't standing all that close to him. She wasn't used to having men tower over her, since she was a good five nine in her bare feet and six foot in heels. Maybe it was all that black leather he was wearing, the way it molded to his long, leanly muscled body, making him seem big and powerful and somehow dangerous.

Ugh. She didn't like dangerous.

"Well, you can't have been trying that hard, because it wasn't very difficult," she muttered. "Also, it's not like there are a million guys hanging around in black leather watching me through the windows." She frowned at him. "And you didn't answer my question. You've been following me, haven't you?"

He didn't move and he didn't say anything, that focused stare of his taking in every inch of her, from the top of her head to the soles of her Victorian-style lace-up black boots. It was so dispassionate, as if she were a map he was studying, or a set of instructions he was trying to decipher.

It made her even more uncomfortable, which in turn made her even more annoyed.

She'd never been pretty and she knew it, and she was fine with it. But being in the presence of such a beautiful man, with those uncanny silver-blue eyes studying her so intently, she was suddenly very aware of every single one of her physical failings. Her long nose and big jaw. Her squinty eyes and her long frizzy hair. All the things her father had constantly picked on and that she was self-conscious about.

Yeah, she didn't appreciate that little reminder, that's for sure.

"Can you answer the question, please?" she said more sharply than she intended to, flinging out a hand to emphasize her point. The collection of gold, silver, and beaded bracelets jingled on her wrist. "Have you been following me?"

He didn't answer her question. Or, at least, not immediately, his icy gaze continuing to take her in without any hurry.

God, he was so still it made her feel like she needed to pace up and down, climb out of her skin, *do* something.

"What makes you think I'm following you?" he asked after a moment.

"Just a feeling."

His blond brows drew down. "A feeling?" He said the word like he had no idea what it meant and wasn't interested in knowing either.

But by this stage Grace had lost what little patience she had, and she'd never had much to start with. "It's something to do with Griffin, isn't it?" It had to be. Why else would his buddy be hanging around watching her?

Despite the progress she'd made over the last six months, as soon as she said the name a small needle of grief caught underneath her ribs.

Damn. Actually, she *didn't* want it to be about Griffin, because the last thing she felt like doing was discussing her dead husband with this icy statue currently masquerading as a man. Especially not when what she should be doing was getting out and finding inspiration for her last piece, so she could meet her deadline for the exhibition she had scheduled in Craig's gallery.

It had taken her months of calling and badgering to finally get him to agree to let her show, and even though she knew it was only because of some vague connection to her grandparents, she didn't care. It would be her very first exhibition, the realization of a dream.

Not that she was expecting to sell a lot of paintings, because God knew making it as an artist in Manhattan was next to impossible. It was the exhibition itself that was important, to show her grandparents they were right to have faith in her, as well as give the big middle finger to the memory of her father, who hadn't had any faith in her whatsoever.

Lucas's eyes narrowed slightly as if he knew exactly what the sound of her husband's name had done to her. Yet when he spoke, his voice was the same, devoid of anything even remotely sympathetic. Devoid of anything but ice. "Yes. Of course it's something to do with Griffin."

Great. Well, there went any hopes she had of not feeling crappy for at least one day.

She let out a breath. "Okay, can it wait till—"

"No," he cut her off without a second's hesitation. "It can't wait. I need to talk to you now, Grace."

CHAPTER TWO

Yeah, it was official. Lucas *really* didn't like Grace Riley.

She stood in front of him with her arms crossed over her flat chest, surprisingly tall for a woman and willowy with it, her amber eyes narrowed.

There was nothing about her that should have appealed to him, nothing at all. Yet that feeling that gripped him was the same one that gripped him whenever he'd visited Griffin and Grace happened to be there, the strange pull he had toward her.

She was . . . golden. And red. And orange. And pink. Like a flame or a sunset, with those eyes of hers and that long apricot hair, and the gold dress she was wearing that he could see between the edges of her leather coat. Gold across her cheeks and nose too, in the dusting of freckles across her pale, milky skin.

He didn't understand the feeling that tugged at him and he sure as hell didn't like the way she'd apparently spotted him so easily through the window of that art gallery. Targets did not see him if he didn't want to be seen. Yet apparently she had, and he found that deeply disquieting.

"What do you mean, you want to talk to me now?" Her voice too was oddly fascinating, all smoky and rough round the edges, and soft like worn velvet.

He didn't like that either and he definitely didn't want

to be having this conversation. But the choice had been taken out of his hands the moment she'd somehow seen him through the window.

Of course he could have gotten on his bike and ridden away before she'd come out to confront him, but Lucas had never run away from anything in his life and he wasn't about to start now.

"Now as in immediately." He glanced down the street, automatically checking for threats and finding nothing. "We need to go somewhere a little more private."

"Wait what?" She held out her hand yet again, her bracelets making a soft, silvery chiming sound as they moved on her narrow wrist. "I can't go anywhere now. I've got a meeting with the—"

"Now, Grace," Lucas said icily, his tone final and precise as a blade. He had no time for arguments, not when a life was at stake.

Her straight red-gold brows arrowed down in a scowl. "Excuse me?"

Christ. It had been a while since he'd had to deal with civilians and now he remembered why he preferred being in the forces. With his team, no one had to be polite. Everyone shut up and did what they were ordered to do and there were no goddamn arguments.

"Your life is in danger," he clarified. "Which means I do not have time to stand around on the sidewalk answering your questions."

Grace blinked rapidly. Her mouth opened, then shut again. Then she uncrossed her arms, put her hands up, and pushed back the mass of her hair, raking her fingers through it.

So soft . . .

What the fuck? Why was he thinking about her hair?

"My life is in danger?" Grace repeated blankly. "What the hell do you mean by that?"

Lucas dragged his gaze away from her hair and back to the street, scanning for a safer place to take her where they could talk that wasn't right out in the open.

A few doors down from the gallery he spotted what looked like a bar.

Excellent. That would do.

Grace was talking again, but he wasn't listening. Instead he reached out and slid his fingers around her elbow, gripping her. "Come with me," he said tersely before steering her in the direction of the bar.

He'd obviously caught her by surprise, because she went with him without hesitation. For a second. Then she stopped dead and he felt resistance travel the entire length of her body. "Hey. What the hell do you think you're doing?"

Yeah, he *really* wasn't a fan of civilians.

Keeping hold of an elbow so she didn't take it into her head to run or do anything else ridiculous, he said, "There's a bar down the street. We can go there and talk."

"But I don't want to go anywhere and talk. I need to go back to the art gallery and—"

Lucas ignored her, deciding to keep her moving, urging her subtly along with him. He kept up a surreptitious scan of their surroundings, noting vehicles and people hanging around, including the tops of the buildings, since most people didn't bother looking up and being up high was a strategic place to hide if you were planning on taking someone out.

"Lucas." Grace tried to pull her elbow out of his grip. "Let me the hell go."

Okay, this situation was not developing at all like he'd hoped. First, she'd spotted him, which she should never have been able to do, and second, she'd come out and straight-up confronted him. And now if he wasn't careful she was going to create a scene and draw attention, which he *definitely* did not want.

Stopping short, he turned and met her irritated gaze, not loosening his grip one iota. "Right now, you are a target," he said flatly. "And continuing to argue with me only makes you more of one."

"Yes, but—"

"I need to get us somewhere out of sight where I can tell you what's going on, okay? There's a bar just down the street and that's where I'm headed, so how about you keep quiet and let me get you to safety."

There was definite heat in her eyes, a hot amber glow, and her mouth had flattened into a line. Clearly she was not happy with the situation.

Well, that made two of them.

Finally, proving she wasn't entirely stupid, she said, "Okay, then. But this had better be good, because you're creeping me out."

He didn't answer, mainly because he didn't want to waste any more time being out on the street, turning instead toward the bar and moving her along with him.

You should let her go now.

Yes, he probably should. Somewhat reluctantly, and he couldn't figure out why he was reluctant when he shouldn't have any feeling about it either way, he released her arm. She stepped away from him, her hand half reaching to rub at the place he'd touched, then falling away as if she'd only just noticed herself doing it. There was color in her cheeks, pink and pretty, and she didn't look at him.

Strange. Why was she blushing? Not that it was relevant to the mission. At all.

Looking away from her, he kept his gaze ahead as they walked, continuing to scan the area for any potential threats. She kept pace with him, her long legs matching his stride easily. "So," she murmured. "Are we going to—"

"Not here. I'll tell you in the bar."

"I would really like it if you didn't interrupt me just once." There was an annoyed edge in her smoky voice.

"If you stopped talking I wouldn't have to interrupt you." He gave a guy across the street watching them from the doorway of a store a narrow glance.

Could he be a lookout?

"It's rude, you know that, right?"

The man looked away unhurriedly, which could have been a front, but Lucas didn't think so. Not given the way he was now eyeing a woman in a tiny dress with a certain amount of appreciation.

"I don't care if it's rude or not." They were approaching the bar now and Lucas stopped, pulling open the door for her. "When a life is at stake, polite is the last thing on my list of things to be."

She gave him an irritated glance but said nothing as she stepped into the bar. He followed her, letting the door shut behind them.

The bar was nothing special inside, paneled wooden walls, a few tables scattered around, and red vinyl bar stools pulled up to the bar itself. There was a TV in one corner playing a hockey game, with the usual number of drunk and loud patrons all sitting watching it.

Lucas headed to the rear of the bar and chose a table that gave him a good view of the door. Pulling out a chair, he gestured to Grace to sit down. "We're going to need to buy a drink. Do you want anything in particular?"

"Scotch on the rocks." Her gaze flickered. "Make it a double."

He wasn't really interested in drinking, but the barman wasn't going to let them sit there for nothing, so Lucas went to the bar and ordered the scotch, getting a beer for himself. Then he came back to the table and put the drinks down, taking the chair that had its back to the wall.

Grace leaned her elbows on the table, her hair falling

over one shoulder in a long silky curtain. "So what's the deal? Why are you here and why on earth are you telling me that my life is in danger?"

Lucas had a lot of patience. As he was a sniper, it was virtually his middle name. But now he found himself impatient at the pointlessness of the question. "I'm telling you that your life is in danger because it is," he said coldly. "Do you seriously I think I'd spend three days following you around if it wasn't?"

Her eyes widened. "So you *were* following me?"

There was no reason to deny it. "Yes, I was."

"But why?"

"Did you miss that part where I said your life was in danger or were you simply not listening?"

She scowled and reached for the tumbler full of scotch, taking a decent swallow before cradling it in her hands. "I think you'd better start from the beginning. Because yes, you've told me that twice, and yet I still have no idea what you're talking about."

Well, that suited him.

"Before Griffin died, he was selling weapons to arms dealers," Lucas said, seeing no need to beat about the bush. "In fact, when he died he was in the middle of an important deal. Money had exchanged hands, but Griffin hadn't arranged the shipment. Now the arms dealers involved are pissed because they paid a lot of money for nothing and they don't give a shit that Griffin's dead. As far as they're concerned, he's got their money and they want it back."

Grace's eyes had gotten very large. "Weapons?" she echoed faintly. "Arms dealers?"

Lucas stared at her, a small needle of irritation sliding beneath his skin. People normally listened attentively to what he had to say and he did not like having to repeat himself. Sure, this would come as a shock to her, but all the more reason for her to listen.

"Yes, weapons." He let none of his own opinions about his erstwhile friend being a traitor show in his tone, and not because he didn't have them. He just didn't want to get into that now, not with his widow. "Griffin was paid a lot of money by a man called Cesare de Santis to put some high-tech weaponry onto the black market. De Santis used to own DS Corp, a weapons-manufacturing company with some big government contracts, but he lost control of the company last year so I assume he was trying to earn himself a little cash selling weapons on the side."

Truth was, the news of Griffin's illegal business venture had come as a huge shock to Lucas, since laid-back Griffin Riley was the last man he would have picked to have gotten involved in the arms trade. Worse, he'd had no clue of his friend's illicit dealings. Griffin had been a solid friend, a decent guy, a great sailor, and even now Lucas couldn't imagine what had made Griffin think that working for de Santis was a good idea.

The only thing that made any sense was money, yet Lucas hadn't been under the impression that Griffin had been hard up. Though maybe it was just plain old greed. Growing up as the child of a very rich man, Lucas had certainly seen a lot of that in his father's social circle.

Grace had gone pale, her gaze shocked.

A kinder man might have given her some time to process what he'd just told her, but Lucas was not a kinder man. He was not a kind man, period. Kindness wasn't going to save her life, and besides, she needed to know what she was facing and the quicker the better.

"The important thing to know," he went on, "is that some very dangerous men want their money back and since you're Griffin's wife, they're probably going to try and get it from you."

Her face went even paler, her freckles standing out against the ashen color of her cheeks. Even her little reflexive movements had ceased, her whole body settling into the stillness of shock. "But . . . I don't have any money."

"That doesn't matter," he said implacably. "If you don't, they'll use you to try and get some from someone else."

She was clutching her tumbler very tightly, her finger-tips white. Her fingers were very long, very elegant, and he couldn't help noticing, though why he should notice he had no idea. "Use me how?"

"As a hostage."

"But . . . I don't. . . ."

"Even if you have no family members willing and able to pay for your safe return it won't matter to them. They want their money and they'll try and get it out of whoever they can."

"A hostage . . ." Grace blinked at him, rapidly. "I'm sorry, but that sounds . . . insane. Griffin would never, *ever* do anything like that, for a start. He loved his job. He loved serving his country. I can't imagine him . . . s-selling weapons for God's sake."

The color had crept back in her cheeks and clearly she was now in the process of denial. That was fine, he'd expected that.

Reaching into the pocket of his leathers, Lucas pulled out his phone and swiped across the screen, pulling up the text messages from the file that had been e-mailed to him.

He put the phone down on the table and pushed it toward her. "Take a look if you don't believe me."

Again she blinked, her reluctance obvious.

"They're text conversations, Grace." He made his tone hard, leaving her no room for hope that he might be wrong, because there was none. "Griffin was arranging secret meetings with several high-profile arms dealers. I also have photos of him making a delivery. And if that's not enough for you there are details from a couple of bank accounts that were in his name. Payments from various Swiss bank accounts. Large payments."

She didn't look at the phone. Instead she lifted the tumbler and drained it, then put it with exaggerated care back down on the table. "My husband is dead," she said quietly. "You know that, don't you?"

Lucas frowned at her, not really sure what her point was, since it was pretty fucking obvious that Griffin was dead. "Yes, of course I know that."

"It's been six months, Lucas. Only six months. And now you're telling me that he wasn't the hero I thought he was, that he was selling weapons to some dangerous people and now those people are coming after me. . . ." She shook her head and gave a small laugh. "It's . . . ridiculous. I'm sorry, but I haven't got time for any of this." She pushed her chair back and stood up. "Thanks for the drink, but I've got to get back to Craig and change the dates for my exhibition." Her mouth, wide and somehow fascinating, turned up in a faint smile. "It was nice to see you again."

Wait a second. She was leaving?

"Grace," he said patiently. "I don't think you quite understand what's going on here."

"Oh, I understand. Some people are coming to take me hostage or something. Well, thanks for the heads-up, but I'm sure I can deal with them myself." She was already turning toward the door to the bar, wrapping her black leather coat more firmly around herself. "I'll be sure to let you know if I run into any difficulties."

And before he could say another word, she started moving in the direction of the door.

Grace didn't want to stick around and hear another word, not one. None of it made any sense. She'd only just gotten her head around the fact that Griffin was dead and not simply away on deployment like he'd been for the past year, let alone that he'd been dealing in . . . weapons or whatever.

And then there was the fact that she was currently in danger from people who wanted to extort some money out of her. . . .

No, it was crazy. And so was Lucas Tate.

"Grace." The sound of his voice was cold, clear. Saying her name with so much authority that she found she'd stopped dead in her tracks before she was even conscious of doing so.

It was vaguely enraging. Because if there was one thing she couldn't stand it was being ordered around by arrogant assholes. She'd had enough of that growing up with a control freak father. She didn't need it from anyone else.

He hasn't actually ordered you to do anything, so how about you calm down?

Calm down? Why the hell did she need to calm down when she was perfectly calm already?

What she needed to do was keep on walking. Head straight out of the bar and go back to the gallery and see if she could talk Craig round. What she did *not* need was to go back and sit down and listen to more lies from crazy Lucas Tate.

Come on, that man is the opposite of crazy.

Grace swallowed, staring at the door. The back of her neck was itching like mad and she knew it was because Lucas Tate's icy gaze was currently boring a hole right through her. And as much as she didn't want to listen to what he had to say, she couldn't ignore the fact that not only was Lucas far too cold and logical to waste time lying to her, he also had no reason to.

Which makes it all true.

Fear gathered like a hard, round stone in the pit of her stomach, which she hated. So she did what she always did whenever she was afraid.

She turned around and confronted it.

Lucas was sitting at the table where she'd left him, leaning back in his chair with his arms folded. His tall, powerful figure was so still, that icy gaze of his unwavering as it met hers, his features betraying absolutely no emotion whatsoever.

Even now, even when he was turning her world upside down, his beauty struck her like an almost physical blow. He looked like some kind of stern warrior angel. All he needed was a pair of white wings and a flaming sword and he could have been a stand-in for the archangel Gabriel.

It made her want to throw something at him, mark him in some way, disturb that icy, perfect beauty.

"I know this is hard to hear," he said without inflection. "I know this is a shock. But I'm not a liar. Every word I said is true."

Dammit. She did *not* want to deal with this. Not now. She didn't have the time, let alone the emotional energy, not when she had a piece to finish for her exhibition.

That's really all you can think about? Your piece? When your dead husband was apparently dealing in illegal weapons and your life could be in danger?

Well, she only had Lucas's word about that. Not that she disbelieved him actually, it was just . . . crap.

"Sit down." He nodded at the chair she'd just vacated. "We need to figure out how we're going to deal with this."

Grace hated giving in, every part of her rebelling against doing exactly what he told her like a good little girl. Then again, she wasn't stupid either.

"Okay, fine." She shifted on her feet, then reached up to her hair, pulling it over one shoulder, the movement soothing. "We can deal with it tomorrow. I've got a few things I need to handle right now, and quite frankly, I'm going to need a bit of space to get my head around everything you've just told me. So how about—" She stopped dead as Lucas pushed his chair back and rose to his feet in a smooth, fluid movement. He skirted the table, coming toward her so fast he was suddenly right in front of her, looming over her, before she'd even had a chance to draw breath.

She instantly wanted to take a few steps back to put some distance between them, but there was no way she was going to give ground to him or let him know he'd surprised her, so she stayed where she was.

"What are you doing?" she demanded, still finding having to tilt her head back to look up into his face something of a novelty. Even with Griffin she didn't have to do that. When she was in her heels, she and Griffin were exactly the same height, and she'd always found that cute and reassuring.

She did not find that with Lucas. There was nothing cute or reassuring about him.

"I can't force you to sit down and talk if you don't want to." His tone was uninflected. "But I'm not letting you walk around unprotected either."

"What does that mean?"

"It means you're stuck with me until the men coming after you have been neutralized."

Grace lifted one hand to her temple, rubbing at it, feeling a vicious headache beginning to pulse behind her eyes. "Hang on, back up a second. Stuck with you?"

He glanced away from her, scanning around the bar as if he was checking for threats already. "You can continue doing whatever you're doing, but I'm not letting you out of my sight."

Wait, what? Not let her out of his sight? "I hope when you say that, you don't mean you're going to follow me around all day. Because if you are that's not going to work for me." Good God, she didn't want him following her. She didn't want him around, period. She had stuff to do, and besides, there was too much about him that made her uncomfortable. And all this . . . stuff with Griffin didn't make it any better.

Actually, now she thought about it, why would Lucas want to follow her anyway? What was he getting out of this? And how did he know about Griffin in the first place? Had Griffin told him?

Maybe you should *talk to him?*

Lucas glanced down at her. "I don't care whether it's going to work for you or not. I was told you needed protection and so I'm going to protect you."

"Yeah, and who told you that?"

One blond brow rose. "So you do want to know after all?"

She found herself coloring, which irritated her. "Fine. You can do what you like, but I have to get back to the art gallery." Without waiting for a response she turned and headed toward the bar's exit, not waiting to see if Lucas followed her. Pushing open the door, she stepped out onto the sidewalk, the icy wind whipping underneath her leather coat. But as she walked back to the art gallery, it wasn't the wind that made her shiver. That prickling sensation was needling at the back of her neck again and she didn't need to turn around to see what it was. She knew. He *was* following her.

Apparently, when he'd said he was sticking around he'd meant it.

Trying to ignore both the man and the sensation on the back of her neck, Grace approached the gallery door, only to find a small handwritten note stuck to it: *Back in an hour.*

Oh great. This day was getting better and better.

Again there was no sound behind her, but she knew Lucas had come to a stop. She could almost feel him, his presence dense and cold like a heap of snow caught in the bough of a tree, ready to fall on some poor unsuspecting person passing beneath it.

"I guess you don't want to wait an hour." His voice was smooth and deep, but she didn't miss the faint edge of sarcasm in it.

It did not help her mood any.

Grace turned and then wished she hadn't. Because he was standing pretty close behind her, his height making her feel weird again. As if she were being crowded against the gallery door. It made her want to reach out, put her hands to the broad expanse of black leather covering his chest, and give him a good shove.

Maybe you should. Maybe you should see if he's as cold as he looks.

The thought caught her by surprise, stealing her breath for a second, and her palms itched, the urge to do just that suddenly overwhelming.

As an artist she followed her instincts without question, her emotions the creative engine that powered her work. She followed them as a woman too, a rebellion against the repressive atmosphere of her childhood, when her father and his moods were the sun that everyone else revolved around.

But right now, there was something about that urge to touch Lucas that she didn't trust.

It seemed to belong to the same fascination she'd always had with him, the need to poke at him, ruffle him. Disturb that icy calm. See if it was a mask or whether it was true that he was completely frozen all the way through.

Not that she was interested in finding out. Not at all.

Grace shoved her hands into her armpits instead. "No," she said grumpily. "I don't want to wait an hour."

"Then we should go somewhere that isn't quite so

public." He glanced away from her again, up and down the street, obviously checking perimeters or whatever it was that soldiers like him did.

Aggravatingly, he seemed totally unconcerned by how close he was standing to her, which was annoying given the urge that had come over her. No, he just stood there, a wall of black leather and lean, hard muscle. God, even if she did try to shove him he probably wouldn't move. He'd simply keep standing like a big, dumb rock.

Something deep inside her twisted unexpectedly, a little flare of heat. Kind of the same feeling as she'd had when he'd taken her elbow, a rush of sensation completely out of proportion to the impersonal touch. She couldn't work out what it was, so she ignored it.

Are you sure you don't know?

Grace pushed the thought away. "We? *We* are not going anywhere. *I* am going home."

"You can go home, but like it or not, I'm coming with you."

"No, you're not."

He ignored her, his attention on the street. "If you're going to go you'd better go now."

"You're *not* coming with me." She didn't know why she was being so insistent. Perhaps it was the thought of him in her little apartment, the tiny, pokey one she'd been forced to move into after Griffin's death because she hadn't been able to afford anything more. The place was even too small for her, let alone Lucas as well, and even apart from the size, she had her art stuff scattered all around the living area because she'd had to give up her studio space.

The thought of him surveying the apartment with those cold eyes of his, taking in all the artwork she had leaning up against the walls, made her cringe.

But he didn't appear to be listening. He'd gone very still again, his focus on something down the street, and Grace became aware that there was a dangerous kind of tension gathering around him. A lethal energy that made the hairs on the back of her neck suddenly stand up.

Something was wrong, she could sense it. The stillness about him was different from what she'd seen before. The sort of stillness that settled just before an earthquake hit or a volcano exploded.

"What is it?" she blurted out before she could stop herself.

He turned his head so quickly it was a wonder he didn't have whiplash, his gaze meeting hers, the expression in it so intense she didn't know if it was icy cold or burning hot. "Don't speak. Don't say a fucking word. Stay calm and do what I tell you."

Then he reached out and, for the second time that day, curled his long fingers around her arm.

CHAPTER THREE

Grace stiffened, as he knew she would, but he had no time for that kind of bullshit. Down the end of the street he'd seen a guy hanging around a newsstand. At first Lucas thought he was some homeless person panhandling, but the man had been moving slowly closer toward where he and Grace stood, flashing glances in their direction.

And as if that hadn't been enough of a giveaway, years of experience were currently whispering in Lucas's ear that the guy was as sketchy as fuck and that Lucas needed to get Grace out of here.

He'd always listened to that whisper and he didn't question it now. If the guy was indeed a lookout then the first thing Lucas should have done was get rid of him. But sadly this was a public street and he didn't have his TAC-338 with him, plus the police didn't take kindly to murder. Which only left him with getting Grace away as soon as possible.

Her eyes had gone large and this time he could see fear glinting in them. Clearly she'd picked up on his tension and correctly interpreted it.

Good. She should be scared. Maybe if she was then she'd stay the hell quiet and let him do what he needed to do, which was extract her from the situation.

"My bike is across the street," he said. "So we're going to cross over to it and then I want you to get on the back."

She shifted, the muscles of her arm going tense where he held it. "What's happening? What do you see? Can I—"

"Just follow my instructions," he cut her off with finality. "I don't want us to draw attention, understand? I'll explain when we get there." He didn't wait for her to respond, he merely turned, tugging her with him, moving down the sidewalk a little way and then to the curb.

She didn't resist this time but kept turning her head as if she was trying to spot what was going on.

"Eyes forward," he ordered. "You start looking around like that then you're going to give us away."

She flashed him a glance that he couldn't interpret but did as she was told, thank Christ. He kept hold of her arm, not wanting to risk her pulling away and drawing attention, the leather of her coat soft beneath his fingertips. Her muscles remained tight as he waited for a break in the traffic before crossing the street.

The lookout he'd spotted earlier had paused to talk to someone, but the guy kept staring in his and Grace's direction, so he kept moving, walking unhurriedly, like he and Grace were going on an afternoon's stroll together.

He'd parked the big black Harley he preferred to ride not far away, letting Grace go as he paused to extract his helmet from his saddlebags. "Put this on," he instructed, handing it to her.

She blinked as she took it, glancing down at it, then at him. "What about you?"

"I only brought one with me."

"But—"

"Put it on, Grace. We need to get the hell out of here."

Her jaw tightened, but she did what he said, securing the strap of the fringed black leather purse she carried over one shoulder before jamming the helmet down on her head. Her hair looked incongruous sticking out from beneath the shiny black helmet, long pretty, red-gold strands blowing around in the cold wind as she awkwardly tried to get on the bike. He held out his hand to her automatically to help her, and she took it, equally automatically.

Once, at a barbecue Griffin had invited him to, Grace had handed him a beer and her fingers had brushed his. The contact hadn't been intentional, but as soon as he'd touched her skin he'd felt something pass right through him, a fine current like static electricity. He'd found it disturbing then and had made sure to keep his distance from her afterwards.

He should have remembered. Because as her long fingers closed around his, he felt the same thing happen again, that sharp, electric thrill passing over his skin. It was so unexpected and unwelcome, he almost dropped her hand.

She didn't react, still struggling with getting on the bike, and he couldn't help but notice the way her dress rode up as she tried to settle herself. Her legs were very long and slender, encased in black tights and strange old-fashioned-looking boots. In fact, her whole outfit was pretty strange, with a leather coat and the gold dress she wore underneath it. Thrift-store clothes probably, given the worn look of the coat and slightly frayed hem of the dress.

Grace either liked shopping at thrift stores, which, given her general Bohemian kind of vibe, was likely, or she didn't have much money. Or maybe it was both.

She had her head turned toward him now, her helmet obscuring her expression, and when she pulled her hand out of his he realized he'd been standing there staring at her a touch too long.

Christ. What the hell was he doing? This wasn't the time to be standing there, remembering barbecues of yesteryear and pondering her goddamn clothing choices.

Vaguely annoyed at himself, Lucas tugged his keys from his pocket, then got on the bike himself. "Hold on to me," he ordered tersely, jamming the key into the ignition and starting the bike. The engine roared into life, adrenaline flooding through him the way it always did whenever he heard the sound.

Lucas didn't allow himself many indulgences, it was too dangerous, as he'd learned to his cost. But riding his Harley was one of them. There was something about the speed, about the wind on his face, about the ground passing beneath him, that made him feel as close to free as he ever got.

Except it wasn't about freedom now. It was about getting Grace to safety.

Her hands settled uncertainly on his hips and thank fuck he was wearing leather, because the pressure of her palms had his heart skipping a beat.

Which never, *ever* happened. He had perfect physical control over himself. As one of the best snipers in the business, it was vital that he did. He could slow his heart rate down to thirty beats per minute, allowing him to squeeze the trigger in between heartbeats so he could get the perfect shot.

His heart did not race when he did not want it to and it most certainly never *skipped*.

Fuck's sake. He never let women get to him, not that any woman ever had. When he wanted sex he had it, choosing partners who liked being told what to do and who didn't mind him being in charge, and who expected nothing from him after it was over.

Sometimes even when he wanted sex, he denied himself purely to maintain that control. Refusing to let himself be at the mercy of his physical desires. Of any desires, quite frankly. He kept himself cold as ice and that was the way he liked it.

He didn't want that ice to be threatened simply because a woman he didn't even like put her hands on his hips.

Think of it as a test.

Actually, yes. That was the perfect way to think about it. The pull he felt around her, the fascination, the strange electricity of her touch, it was all merely a test of his control. Hell, he was good at tests. He tended to pass them all with flying colors and this one would be no different.

Ignoring the ridiculousness of his heartbeat, Lucas kicked up the bike stand and took off into the traffic, glancing in his wing mirror as he did so to check on the lookout. The guy had his head turned in their direction, watching them, and Lucas could see a frown on his face.

Good. Now to see if anyone followed them.

Grace's grip on him had firmed as he sped through the traffic, her body pressing up against his back as if she was afraid of falling off. The heat of her seeped through his motorcycle leathers, making his earlier vague annoyance gather even tighter. Her long legs were pressed to the outside of his, and if he concentrated hard he could feel another, deeper heat centered against his tailbone. The heat between her thighs—

Someone pulled out in front of him all of a sudden and he had to swerve to avoid them, cursing under his breath. Jesus, why the hell was he concentrating on the feel of her body when he should be concentrating on whether or not someone was following them?

As far as tests go, you're failing this one.

Fuck.

Lucas never had to force himself to concentrate on a task. So why the hell he kept getting distracted by Grace sitting behind him was anyone's guess.

But getting annoyed wasn't going to help, so he did what he normally did with all inconvenient emotions. He ignored it as through it weren't there.

Instead he went back to the plan he'd been formulating over the past three days of Grace Riley reconnaissance. Since taking out her potential attackers before she even realized she was in danger wasn't going to happen now, he needed to get her somewhere safe. Somewhere they wouldn't find her.

The most obvious place, not to mention the safest, was his own apartment in SoHo, which wasn't all that far away from the gallery she'd been visiting. Of course she probably wouldn't want to go there immediately and would probably be very unhappy if he took her there without her permission.

Still, if that was the safest place . . . Then again, gaining her trust was going to be important if he was going to protect her adequately, so maybe taking her back to her own apartment and explaining the situation better than he had in the bar was the best scenario.

Once he'd explained and she understood the reality of what was happening, she'd see the sense in going back to his place. Being at her apartment to start with would have the added bonus of her being able to gather some belongings together to take with her too. Women tended to like having their own stuff around them.

Satisfied with the plan, Lucas glanced in his wing mirror again, but there didn't appear to be anyone following them. Not that he expected anyone to. The fact that there was a lookout back near that art gallery told Lucas that whoever was after Grace already knew her movements. Which meant they also probably knew where she lived.

Going back to her apartment wasn't perhaps the best idea in that case, but he hadn't seen any threats in the area while he'd been following her, which meant either they didn't have someone watching the apartment or they were very, very good at evading Lucas's notice.

Whatever, Lucas wasn't planning on being at her

apartment long anyway. They'd go back to his place tonight and he could keep her there until he figured out what he was going to do about the people who were after her. Narrow down which asshole it was in particular for example.

The traffic from SoHo to the East Village was light and it didn't take them all that long until he was pulling up outside Grace's apartment building. He parked the bike and got off, reaching out to help her. But she ignored his hand completely, slipping off by herself, then getting rid of the helmet, her hair falling over her face as she did so. Her cheeks were flushed again and she didn't look at him as she shoved the helmet in his direction, turning toward the front door of the apartment building. She didn't wait for him either, moving quickly up the front steps and entering the code to get inside.

He narrowed his gaze after her. What was the problem now? Was she afraid? Because if so, he didn't blame her. Having arms dealers after you wasn't exactly a picnic. But it would be fine now he was here. He'd protect her. It was his job after all.

Keeping hold of the helmet, he strode after her, only just catching the door as she let it swing shut behind her, then following her over to a bank of elevators that looked like they hadn't been serviced in decades.

"Are you okay?" he asked as she jabbed the button several times.

"I'm fine." She was holding on to the strap of her purse with rather more force than was strictly necessary.

"You don't look fine."

"Well, obviously not. I've just been told that terrorists are after me because my husband was apparently a gunrunner. How fine would you be?"

"They're not terrorists and Griffin wasn't technically a gunrunner. He was—"

"I'm not interested in the technicalities, Lucas." She still wasn't looking at him, her gaze on the numbers above the elevator, currently counting down to the first floor. "All I'm interested in is getting home. Thanks for the ride, but I think I can take it from here."

She didn't want to look at him, not even a glimpse. Mainly because her whole body was buzzing with a strange kind of energy and she had no idea how to handle it. She'd thought getting on the back of that bike wouldn't be a problem. No, she hadn't particularly wanted to go with him when he'd taken her arm, but the tension that had gathered around him had somehow stolen her resistance. She had no doubt that he'd meant every word he'd said when he'd ordered her to be quiet and do as she was told, making her sense of self-preservation kick in and do exactly that.

Hell, she'd even kind of liked it as he'd steered her across the street as if he had complete and utter control of the situation and nothing would happen that he didn't want.

Normally, she hated it when someone else took charge—certainly Griffin never did—but there was something about Lucas's seriousness and the way he'd handled her that she'd found . . . reassuring almost. As if there was no question that she would trust him and that she could, completely.

Then there had been the bike. She'd never ridden a motorcycle, but she wasn't opposed to them per se, even though getting on the thing had been awkward as hell. Until he'd reached out and she'd grabbed his hand, and then things had suddenly gotten a whole lot more awkward.

Because that's when she'd felt it, that energy. Like a small, localized bolt of lightning had sizzled up her arm the moment his fingers had closed around hers. His hand had felt warm against her skin and the contrast with his icy manner was so extreme that she hadn't known how to take it.

And then it had gotten even worse, because then she'd had to hold on to him. She'd had to put her hands on his leather-clad hips and, as he'd taken off into the traffic, she'd had to press herself up against his back purely so she didn't fall off.

Then things had gotten *really* weird. And disturbing. Because in her mind he was cold and she'd expected holding on to him would be like holding on to a marble statue. Hard and stone-cold. Yet it wasn't.

He was hot, so freaking hot, all that heat soaking through his motorcycle leathers and into her. He was hard too—that much she *had* been right about—but it wasn't an unpleasant hardness at all. There was a solidity to him, a kind of athletic, muscular power that had her palms itching again, to touch him, see if he really was as muscular and solid as he felt.

The combination made her breath catch, made that energy sing through her. Made her feel restless in a way she hadn't experienced before. It was profoundly disturbing and she'd wanted to stop the bike and get off it and away from him as quickly as possible.

But she hadn't been able to. She was stuck there as they'd raced through the traffic, with her thighs spread on either side of his lean hips, the heat of him pressed right between her legs.

You know what you're feeling. Don't pretend you don't.

Grace swallowed and concentrated on the numbers above the elevator and not on the voice in her head. She didn't want to think about that, didn't want to feel it either, not for a guy like him. He was Griffin's friend, for God's sake, and anyway, he wasn't her type, end of story.

He didn't say anything, standing there in his characteristic still way, but she could feel his gaze on her all the same.

She tried to ignore it, muttering a silent prayer of thanks as the elevator chimed and the doors opened. "Thanks, Lucas," she said, stepping into the elevator and reaching for the button to close the doors. "Perhaps I'll see you around."

But he clearly wasn't getting her hint, because instead of turning around and walking away like she hoped, he stepped into the elevator with her, even going so far as to hit the button for her floor.

Her heartbeat began to race and she felt the strangest urge to bolt from the elevator car and try the stairs instead. Because when those doors closed, she would be trapped in this tiny space with . . . him.

Crap.

"I meant it, you know." She was annoyed to find that she'd moved to the back of the elevator car as if to put distance between them. "You don't have to come back to my apartment. In fact, I'd appreciate it if you didn't. I'm kind of not up for guests right now."

"I understand that." He made no move to leave, simply standing there as the doors shut. "But what you don't seem to understand is that your life is under serious threat. Believe me, I have no interest in coming to your apartment right now, but you're in danger, which means I'm not going anywhere until that danger has been neutralized."

The elevator jolted and began to rise, and Grace cursed silently in her head, because it was as bad as she'd thought. He seemed to fill up the entirety of the space with his tall, lean, rangy presence. And now it felt different from before. Now she knew how hot he was underneath all that leather and how hard. How back on his bike, with her hands on his hips and her pressed up against him, he'd felt like a man and not an icy-eyed statue or beautiful avenging angel.

For the first time too, she was aware of his scent, a fresh, clean kind of smell, with something warm underneath it, like leather or spice. It wasn't what she expected and she was appalled to find she liked it. Very much.

The energy moving restlessly around inside her seemed to intensify.

Grace leaned against the rear of the elevator, trying to look like she wasn't trying to put as much space between them as she could. "So what? You're just going to hang around like a bodyguard or something?"

"Pretty much." He was holding his helmet in one hand, his long fingers curled around the mouth guard, and she found herself staring at the small, white scars on them and wondering how he'd gotten them.

Jesus, she was going insane, wasn't she?

"What if I don't want you to?" She couldn't seem to keep the edge out of her voice. "Don't I get a say?"

"No." The word was flat and very cold, the chill in his gaze as he looked at her almost palpable. "Unless you want to die."

"You think I'm stupid, don't you?" She hadn't meant to say it, but it just came out, and then she wished she hadn't because it made it sound like she cared what he thought of her and she didn't. At all.

His blond brows drew down fractionally as if the question mystified him. "Stupid? No, I don't think you're stupid. What the hell makes you think that?"

Great. And now she *felt* stupid too.

"The way you're looking at me." A note of defensiveness had crept into her voice, which was irritating. "And the way you're talking to me like I'm a kid and ignoring everything I say."

The expression on his beautiful face didn't change. "Don't take it personally. I treat everyone that way."

Was that . . . a joke? She honestly couldn't tell.

"And how's that working out for you?" she snapped. "I bet you have a lot of friends."

"My team has no complaints."

"So there's basically nothing I can say that's going to get rid of you."

His gaze focused on her intently for a second. "I'm here to protect you, Grace. Why would you want to get rid of me?"

Heat began to rise into her cheeks and she had to glance away from him. That intent look was doing stupid things to her heartbeat that she really didn't appreciate. How annoying.

"The people after you are part of a massive arms ring," he went on in that implacable way he had. Like a glacier moving, slow and cold and indifferent. "They're not the kind of people you want to get on the wrong side of. Griffin took their money and now they want it back and they will do anything they can to get it. And if that means taking you hostage, then sending pieces of you back to our government in exchange for ransom money, then that's what they'll do."

The fear that had been sitting in her gut suddenly grew sharp frozen spines, digging into her.

"Thanks for that little image," she said, hoping her voice sounded sarcastic and steady and not all thin and weak. "I really needed to hear that."

"You *did* need to hear it." There was no sympathy at all in the words. "Because if you're not shit scared you should be."

Mercifully, at that moment the elevator chimed and came to a halt, the doors sliding open. Grace made a dash for the exit, only to be stopped in her tracks by Lucas's powerful arm blocking the doorway.

"Wait," he commanded, the deep, cold sound of his voice wrapping around her and making her go utterly still. "I need to check the hallway first."

He glanced out of the elevator, his arm holding the doors open. Then he stepped out and, keeping his hand on the doors, gave her a nod.

Grace swallowed, her heart rate not in any way slowing down.

Taking you hostage . . . Sending pieces of you . . .

She did *not* like the sound of that. Not at all. God, what kind of thing had Griffin gotten himself into? She couldn't understand it. He'd always been a good guy, kind and generous and caring. So what had possessed him to do . . . this?

Maybe you should be asking Lucas.

It was a conversation she didn't want to have. But it was starting to look like she was going to need to.

As she stepped out of the elevator, she turned automatically down the hallway toward her apartment. But again Lucas stepped in front of her. "I go first," he said shortly, and before she could say anything he carried on down the hallway ahead of her.

Grace didn't argue. Mainly because she was thinking that maybe he was right. That there *were* actually people after her. It was horrible to think and doubly so considering Griffin, but Lucas was taking this very, very seriously indeed and she couldn't ignore that.

So she said nothing, following Lucas's tall figure as he strode down the hallway, every line of him screaming lethal danger. Yeah, and that didn't do anything to stop the weird fizzing, vibrating feeling inside her. The way he moved, all fluid and utterly certain, like a predator totally at ease in its environment. She found it . . . fascinating.

Lucas stopped outside her apartment, which both irritated her and annoyed her, because it was now obvious that he had in fact been following her without her being aware of him. How else would he know where she lived?

"Key." He held out his hand toward her without looking, his attention on the door, examining it as if the secrets of the universe were embedded into the wood.

Grace scowled as she dug in her purse for her key. "I can unlock my own door, thanks."

"Not when I'm here, you're not." He didn't even glance at her, his palm still outstretched. He was blocking the door, and short of shoving him out of the way, she couldn't unlock it anyway, leaving her with no choice but to slap the key into his palm.

He took it without a word of thanks, putting it into the lock and turning it. He didn't open the door immediately. Instead he thrust the bike helmet into her hands, then reached around to grab something from the small of his back. Her heart almost stopped beating when she saw he was carrying a compact-looking pistol.

This is real. This is happening.

"Oh my God." It came out as a whisper, her voice all scratchy. "Are they actually in my apartment?" Stupid, but all she could think about was her paintings and the thousands of hours of work she'd put into them. And how if they were destroyed all that work would have been for nothing.

"The lock hasn't been tampered with," Lucas said coolly. "And there are no signs of forced entry. But I'm being cautious. You wait here."

For a second Grace felt a rush of gratefulness toward him. Because he was so calm, so cold, and if all this was real then cold and calm was exactly what she wanted. Like that moment out on the street, when he'd taken her arm and given her instructions. There was something very, very reassuring about how in control of the situation he was.

She said nothing as he raised his weapon and pulled

open the door, disappearing inside her apartment and closing the door after him.

Silence reigned for a long moment and she waited, staring at the closed door, her mouth dry, fear sitting in a small, hard lump in her gut.

Then abruptly the door was pulled open and Lucas's silver-blue gaze met hers. "All clear." He stood aside for her to enter, shifting his bike jacket to put away his weapon, then taking back his helmet from her.

Grace stepped inside.

It was a tiny apartment, just one room, with her bed pushed up against one wall and a small galley kitchen jammed against the opposite wall. Apart from a table, a couple of chairs, and a dresser, she had no other furniture. She didn't have room, not when her living space was entirely taken up by the giant canvases that she had propped against the walls, some stacked on top of one another to make way for the biggest canvas. The one that was entirely blank.

Grace had just dropped her purse beside the door when a shadow flickered by the window near her bed.

And suddenly a hard arm caught her around the waist and she found herself backed up against a wall, that same arm across her chest, pinning her there. Then six foot two of leather-clad male muscle blocked her vision as Lucas positioned himself right in front of her, every line of him drawn tense and alert.

"Don't move." His voice was iron and steel, his attention not on her but toward the window. "Don't even breathe."

CHAPTER FOUR

She was very still, which was good, and she didn't make a sound, which was even better. Looked like she was starting to take this seriously.

He kept his arm across her chest, holding her against the wall, every sense he had aimed toward the window where that shadow had flickered. It could have been anything, a bird probably, but it paid to always be alert to anything and everything. He didn't like surprises and most especially not when they concerned the lives of civilians.

He waited for a couple of moments, a couple of breaths, staring at the window, listening. But nothing happened.

A bird. That's all it was.

Turning back to Grace, he met her wide amber gaze. There was fear in it, but he didn't mind that. Fear was a healthy reaction to something like this and if she was afraid then she might more easily trust him.

Telling her the most likely scenario about what would happen to her if these assholes captured her the way he had in the elevator hadn't been the kindest move, but then as he'd already told himself, he wasn't here to be kind.

He was here to protect her and if that made her scared or uncomfortable then so be it. She had to know how serious this was. Because it was. Very fucking serious.

Grace blinked, then touched her tongue to her bottom

lip, and he found his attention drawn by the movement, oddly fascinated by the curve of that bottom lip. Her mouth was wide and full, lush almost.

His attention dropped lower, as though he couldn't stop himself, to the beat of her pulse at the base of her throat. It was fast and as he watched it got even faster, racing beneath her pale, freckle-dusted skin.

Why was that? Yes, this was scary for her, but he was here. He was keeping her safe. He wouldn't let her be hurt.

"You don't have to be afraid." He lifted his gaze back to hers, following an impulse he never normally followed. The impulse to give reassurance. "I won't let anyone harm you."

She blinked again, her lashes a reddish gold, her eyes the color of fall leaves. "W-what was that?"

"That shadow? Probably only a bird."

"Oh." She swallowed and he found his attention dropping to her throat again, watching the movement. "Are you sure it wasn't a plane?"

Her neck was very long, very elegant. In fact, now that he thought about it, everything about her was very long and very elegant. "No, it was definitely a bird."

"That was a joke." Her voice sounded faintly husky. "You know, bird, plane, Superman."

Why the fuck are you thinking about how elegant she is?

Good question and one he didn't have the answer to.

"It's not a very good one." He dragged his gaze from her throat. "At least, I'm not laughing."

Her reddish brows were slightly winged at the corners, becoming more pronounced as she frowned. "Do you ever laugh?"

"Not often." And he didn't. Humor, in his opinion, was overrated.

"Good to know." Grace looked pointedly down at his arm across her chest. "You can let me go now."

Yes, he really should. Especially as the danger had passed. Yet he found he almost didn't want to. He'd become quite conscious of her scent, a warm, dry, faintly sweet smell, like apple wood left out to dry under a hot sun. He liked it. It reminded him of the expeditions he used to go on with his brothers when they were kids, after they'd been adopted by Noah Tate and brought to his ranch in Wyoming. Where they'd go exploring on the trails of Shadow Peak, the mountain behind the ranch house. Some nights they'd camp out under the stars and build campfires, and when he pulled his clothes on the next morning the fabric would smell of woodsmoke.

Something strange shifted inside his chest, a kick of some emotion he didn't understand and didn't want to.

Better not to think of that stuff. Better not to think of the past at all.

He took his arm away from her and stood back, giving her some room. Trying not to see the flicker of relief that played over her features as she quickly moved past him, as if she couldn't wait to get away from him.

You scared her.

Well, yes. He knew he would have. But so? If she wasn't afraid she wouldn't take this seriously. And she had to. He was only going to give her ten minutes to gather her stuff together and then they were going to have to leave, because they couldn't stay here. That much he was already certain of.

He turned around, taking in the rest of her place.

It was tiny and pokey. The walls had been painted white, but that made no difference to the general gloom, not helped by the small window that looked out on to the wall of the building next door.

The lack of space wasn't helped by the mess lying around either. There were clothes thrown haphazardly over a dresser near the window, old coffee mugs, plates, and stacks of mail covering the small dining table. A pile of dog-eared paperbacks had been messily thrust aside, or possibly kicked, to make way for the series of huge canvases that leaned against the walls. Tubes and pots of paint, and brushes and sponges, and all kinds of other artistic paraphernalia were lying around untidily. A palette lay in the middle of the room, a brush lying not far away from it, as if someone had thrown both onto the floor in a fit of pique.

The whole place offended his neat, military soul and it was all he could do not to start organizing it for her. Instead he dumped the helmet on the table, then walked over to where one of the canvases stood to get a better look.

It was of a tall, powerful man, his back to the viewer, his head turned and showing a strong profile. There was something oppressive about the painting, and not simply in the colors she'd used, but in the way the man was standing with his hand in a fist as if he were about to punch someone with it, shadows lurking around him. The figure loomed large, taking up almost all of the canvas, a study in blacks and charcoals and grays.

Lucas frowned at it. He couldn't have said why the painting seemed menacing, but it did.

Vaguely uncomfortable, he looked at the canvas standing next to it.

Another male figure dominated the painting, but the sense of oppressiveness was lacking. In this painting the man was again standing with his back to the viewer, his hands on the rim of a bathroom sink. He was peering into a mirror in front of him, letting the viewer see his features.

It came as an odd jolt to realize that the man was Griffin.

Lucas stared at it, momentarily taken aback for reasons he couldn't have explained. His friend's mouth was turned up in his usual lopsided smile, as if he were looking at the viewer in the mirror and sharing a joke. The colors in this painting were muted and quiet, lots of blues and whites, and when Lucas leaned in to take a closer look he realized the paint was heavily textured, as if layers had been added over the top of one another, giving the colors a deeper, richer effect.

Then, quite suddenly, Grace was there, nearly shoving him out of the way as she gripped the frame of the canvas and lifted it, moving it over the one of the oppressive-looking man. Almost as if she didn't like Lucas looking at it.

"Excuse me," she muttered belatedly, bustling about and grabbing another painting, leaning it on top of the others.

He resisted the urge to tell her to stop what she was doing, that he wanted to have a look at the canvases, which was strange, since he'd never particularly appreciated art. Not that they had the time to stand about looking at paintings anyway, but there was a part of him that was curious about them. Mainly because she was the one who'd painted them.

Why does that matter?

Yeah, he didn't understand that part either.

"Get your stuff," he ordered instead. "We need to get out of here."

Grace stopped dead, still holding one of the massive canvases, and turned to him in surprise. "What? What do you mean we need to get out of here?"

"You can't stay here. It's not safe." And it wasn't. It only had two exits, both of which were easily accessed, which meant that all anyone needed to do to get her was make sure to put men on each one so she couldn't get out.

Plus he'd noticed when he'd checked out the place that the locks on the windows a child could have opened. Same with the one on the door.

The place was a death trap and she wasn't staying here. His apartment in SoHo was the most logical place to take her, but now he wasn't quite so sure. They'd had a lookout near the gallery, which meant they knew she had business in the area, and that made staying in SoHo problematic.

The best solution would be to take her out of the city entirely, but he couldn't do that. Not when he had to stick around for Van and do his duty by Tate Oil. Luckily, Lucas had another place, a place no one knew about in Greenwich Village. The best part about it was not only had he had it fitted out with the latest security measures, the place also couldn't be traced to him, since he'd made the owner a shell company he'd set up himself years earlier.

There was, of course, the option to take her to the Tate property upstate, where Noah employed a full complement of security staff, but Lucas had always liked to keep things simple. And the fewer people who knew where Grace was the better.

She was still staring at him as if he'd suddenly grown another head. "What do you mean I can't stay here?"

Lucas moved over to the window and glanced out, scanning the outside of the building and the tiny alleyway beside it. "Do I really need to keep repeating myself?"

"Yes, actually you damn well do." Carefully she leaned the painting against the others, then took a couple of steps over to the bed, undoing the belt of her leather coat and shrugging out of it. "I'm not going anywhere, okay? I can't leave my pieces here, for a start. Not when I have an exhibition in two weeks. And especially not when there's one piece still left to complete and I haven't started the damn thing yet." She threw the coat down on the bed, then raised her hands and pushed her fingers through her hair, comb-

ing through the long, apricot-colored strands. The movement made the silky fabric of her dress pull and tighten
over her chest, molding it to her willowy figure in a way
he found distracting.

She wasn't as flat chested as he'd thought. Her breasts
were small and high, the wrap dress emphasizing the curve
of her waist, the way she was standing making the fabric
part just a little on one thigh and giving him a glimpse
nearly to her hip. She wore black tights beneath it, but for
some reason his brain insisted on filtering out the black
nylon and replacing it with pale, milky skin dusted with
freckles.

Why are you looking at her like that?

Again another excellent fucking question, and again he
had no idea why he was looking at her like that. Perhaps
it was because he needed sex? Then again, he tried not to
need anything and he was very good at it, so it couldn't be
that. What was irritating was that he was getting distracted.
Actually, no, it was worse than that. He was *letting* himself get distracted.

Then just don't let it happen.

Okay. So he wouldn't. He was a goddamn sniper, the
best in the business, ice-cold, calm, and ruthless. He let
nothing affect him, nothing touch him. Nothing get in the
way of a mission, a kill. And he never let that mask drop.

In fact, he'd been wearing it so long it was now part
of him.

One plain redhead wasn't going to turn the machine
he'd made himself into back into a man again.

Lucas met her gaze. Held it. Made sure she saw exactly
how deep the ice inside him went. He wasn't here to be
kind. He was here to protect her and if that meant doing
things she wasn't going to like that was too bad. She'd have
to suck it up. "You know what I saw back there at the art
gallery?" He kept his tone even. "You know why we had

to leave in a hurry? There was a lookout on the street. Which means that they were following you. And if they followed you to the art gallery they almost certainly know where you live." She paled, but he went on. "And because you came out and confronted me, they now know that I'm involved too."

"Oh," she said faintly. "I didn't know. . . ."

"Of course you didn't. But whether you like it or not, they know I'm with you and they'll know who I am. Which means they'll also know that they need a better class of asshole if they're going to come after us. Now, all they need to take you is a couple of men, one on the door and one on the window, and probably another five to take me, but they could do it if they're smart. There are no other exits here, and if I go down there's no way for you to escape."

She folded her arms, bracelets chiming. "All apartments have doors and windows. I can't see how—"

"The idea is to not let them get near in the first place and, if the worst happens, always have an exit route. . . ." He paused to let that sink in. "There are no exit routes here."

Her jaw took on an obstinate cast and she shifted on her feet, obviously unhappy with the situation. "So where are you suggesting we go?"

"I have a place in the Village. I installed the security myself and it's very defensible. It's also untraceable to me, so they won't be able to find us if we're careful."

She shifted restlessly yet again, her arms dropping to her sides, those damn bracelets making that silvery noise. Then she lifted one hand and smoothed her hair over one shoulder.

The woman was in constant movement and it was starting to annoy the hell out of him. His threat senses, already getting twitchy the longer they stayed in the apartment, were now starting to kick into overdrive and the way she kept shifting and moving her hands was not making things any easier.

Weren't you supposed to be not *letting her get to you?*

He could feel his jaw getting tight, a whisper of impatience threading through him. He locked it down. Hard.

"I can't leave," she was saying, turning around to look at the canvases stacked against the walls. "I can't leave all this behind. My pieces, my paints, my brushes . . . everything."

Lucas ignored her, moving over to the window again, his threat senses pricking at him harder. Jesus, they needed to get out of here and the sooner the better. He had no illusions about his own abilities, no false modesty. He was one of the best there was, but even he was only one man and if they sent an army after Grace he was not going to be able to protect her in this shithole.

There was nothing outside, the alleyway clear, but that didn't mean there was no one there or no one watching.

Christ, they couldn't afford to wait any longer.

He turned back to the room, finding Grace's amber gaze on his. He met it. "We're leaving," he said with finality. "You have five minutes."

Five minutes? To gather together the work of a year? And how was she going to take her canvases, let along all her art gear?

The answer was, of course, simple. She couldn't. He was asking her to leave it all behind.

That cold, hard lump of fear hadn't gone away, but now it was joined by sharp, electrical surges of anger. Because no, just *no*. She wasn't going anywhere without her paintings.

Meeting his silver-blue stare, she lifted her chin. "I have a gallery showing in two weeks. Two. Weeks. And these?"

She threw out her hand at the canvases. "These are my exhibition pieces. I can't leave them here. I *won't* leave them here. They took me all year to complete and I'm not leaving all that work behind."

Lucas didn't even look at the canvases. "Your work doesn't matter," he said coldly. "Your life does."

The electrical surges became a jagged bolt of fury and she found herself taking a few steps toward him. "Don't you dare say that." She didn't bother to keep her temper out of her voice. "And don't be so goddamn dismissive. Don't you understand? My work *is* my life."

His icily perfect features didn't change, his complete lack of expression chilling. "So you're quite happy to die or be tortured for a piece of fabric with some paint on it?"

Her anger gathered tighter and so did her throat, an old and painful grief locking it. She hadn't had anyone dismiss her work so completely since she'd been thirteen and had finally gotten up the gumption to show her work to her father.

He'd been an artist himself, temperamental but brilliant, and as a kid she'd idolized him. But as the years had gone by and his paintings had failed to sell, he'd gotten bitter, turning that bitterness on her. He'd taken one look at her drawings and declared them talentless wastes of time and that she should try something she was good at. Not that she was good at anything at all, according to him.

"Yes," she snapped, starting to feel furious now. "I pretty much would."

"You have four minutes," Lucas said, infuriatingly calm. "If you haven't gotten your things together in that time I'm picking you up and carrying you out of here."

Her instinct was to take another step and get in his face, yell at him that she wasn't going anywhere and that if he laid a hand on her she was going to call the police. But she had a feeling that Lucas Tate, cool, calm, and logical, would simply let all her blustering roll right off him, pick her up anyway, and take her away whether she liked it or not.

It made her feel panicky.

Sucking in a breath, she forced herself to go for cool, just like him. "I need my pieces, Lucas." She struggled to keep her voice even. "Like I said, I have an exhibition in two weeks and it's important to me. It's an opportunity that took me a long time to get and I can't miss it." She swallowed, clenching her hands into fists. His face was expressionless, his perfect features giving her nothing back. The look in his eyes could have frozen fire and she knew he wasn't going to understand. He wasn't the kind of man who knew about dreams or passions. He wouldn't know what it was like to want something so bad it hurt. To spend years and years fighting for it and now to have it so close she could almost taste it. And yet she had no other option but to at least make an attempt to get through to him.

"It's my very first exhibition ever," she went on, enunciating each word. "It's been my dream to show my work as an artist since I could first hold a crayon. I've been working toward it for years and it's only now that I have something good enough to show." She met his icy stare, willing him to understand. "I can't leave these here. They're too important."

His gaze flickered toward the canvases, then back to her. "If it's that much of a big deal I'll get you some more canvases and paints. You can just paint some more."

She almost laughed. No, of course he wouldn't get it. Why had she thought he would? "I can't just 'paint some more.' It doesn't work that way. And even if it did I can't do the work of a year in two weeks. I have one piece left to finish and I don't know how I'm going to finish it as it is."

But Lucas just looked at her. "Three minutes."

Beneath her anger, the panic twisted, and she found

herself taking another step, so she was standing directly in front of him. Then before she could stop herself, she'd put out a hand and gripped the hem of his bike jacket, the stiff leather warm beneath her fingers. "Please, Lucas." She stared up into his eyes, light blue and silver, such a beautiful color and yet so icy. The color of a cloudless, cold, perfect winter's day. "My work *has* to come with me. It has to. I don't know what those people will do to it if they come here. I can't leave it behind."

He simply stood there, a wall of black leather. Immovable as a mountain and just as hard. His gaze didn't even flicker. "Two minutes."

Her throat closed. Jesus, why even bother? Her father had done all he could to crush her dreams of being an artist just like him, and since her mother did whatever he said, she hadn't helped. Even Grace's grandparents, who'd been the only ones to support her dreams of going to art college when she'd been younger, had backed down when push had come to shove. Griffin had appreciated her art, but he hadn't been terribly interested in it, and that had suited her, since all she'd wanted was to be left alone to create it.

All those people who hadn't understood . . . Why should Lucas be any different?

She could waste more time trying to convince him or create a huge scene and declare she wasn't going anywhere. But she knew what would happen if she did that, he'd do exactly what he said and pick her up and carry her out of the building over his shoulder. She would certainly survive that, but maybe her pride wouldn't.

No, as much as she hated to give in, her only option was to do what he said, grab her things and go with him. Maybe if she did that she could try convincing him to go back and get the canvases. Or hell, maybe he wouldn't watch her 24/7 and she could even go get them herself.

Grace let go of the leather of his jacket and turned away, trying to hide the slow acid drip of disappointment. It was always a mistake to let people know how much you cared and it was a trap she fell into every time. A mistake because of course they could use it against you later, use it as a way to manipulate you, get things from you. Yet she'd never learned the knack of hiding her emotions and then, when she'd gotten older, her own stubborn nature refused to make herself even try.

"Be quiet," her mother used to tell her when she was being too loud or too happy. Too angry, too sad. Too anything. "Your father's working. He doesn't like outbursts." And when she was little, she'd tried to be quiet. But as her father's bitterness had begun to color her life like a streak of black paint in pristine white, turning everything gray, she'd stopped being the good, quiet girl who kept herself under control all the time. She'd let herself be wild instead.

Sometimes that was a good thing, but more often than not it wasn't. Like now, for instance.

Now she couldn't get rid of the feeling that she was thirteen again, her dreams being crushed by yet another uncaring prick of a man.

Grabbing a bag, she threw some clothes into it, not even paying attention as to what they were. Then she went into the bathroom to grab her toothbrush, pausing only to sweep the few other toiletries, including her collection of nail polishes, into the bag as well.

Coming out again, she picked up the bag, then grabbed her purse. Forced herself to meet Lucas Tate's uncaring gaze, and this time she didn't bother trying to hide her fury. "I know you're trying to protect me. And I know you think my life is more important than my art. But without my art my life isn't worth living. Just remember that."

He gave her a long, cold stare and she had the impression

that the passionate words had simply bounced right off him. "Come with me then."

What did you expect? That he'd change his mind?

Of course not. Because no one ever did, not about her. She'd told Griffin she didn't want him to go away again, that she was tired of being alone, and he hadn't listened to her. He'd re-upped without even talking to her about it. And when her father had refused to accept her grandparents' offer to pay for art college for her, they hadn't argued.

Lucas was just another in a long line of people who hadn't given a shit.

The only one who cared enough about her was herself, which made this situation, where she was at the mercy of someone else's decisions, a fucking nightmare.

She didn't want to follow him. She wanted to scream at his leather-clad back and throw things. Or sit on the floor and refuse to move. Let him see if he could pick her up and carry her out of the building after all.

But she didn't do any of those things. She followed him silently back down the hallway to the elevator and then down to the first floor. And she followed him to where he'd parked his motorcycle, got on when he told her.

And when he told her to hang on to him, she did. Without a word. Feeling as if she'd betrayed herself somehow by giving in.

This time the ride wasn't exciting and she felt nothing at the other end, where he parked in an underground car park beneath a white building, then led her to the elevator. It was a much nicer elevator than the one in her own building and they went up to the top floor. But she didn't take much notice of that either.

When the doors opened and she stepped into a big echoing space, she kept her attention on the dark polished wooden floorboards beneath her feet. She didn't want to look around. She didn't care.

Except then she noticed the colors on the floor in front of her. Reds and blues and greens and golds. How strange. Looked like light through stained glass. She looked up to see where it was coming from and the breath caught in her throat.

She was standing in a long, vaulted space, with a high, dark-beamed ceiling overhead. The walls were white, providing a stark contrast to the dark floor and a perfect surface for the light coming through the massive stained-glass windows to the left of her. They reached high and wide, the ceiling and the wall down one end of the long gallery-like room cutting them off, which meant that the rooms beyond the one she stood in would have some of the window too, as must the floor above her.

The colors were exquisite, even in the dull gray light of a New York winter, and she couldn't help taking a few steps toward them, staring at them in wonder. It looked like a huge rose window of a church, with angels and other religious iconography all set in the glass.

The rest of the room was virtually empty, apart from a big white sectional couch and a couple of armchairs. There was no art on the walls and no rugs on the floor, it was as if the stained-glass window was all the color and life the room needed.

She could sense Lucas standing behind her, the silence coming from him heavy and dense, like a black hole sucking away all life and heat. She ignored him, staring instead at the rose window and the space around her.

It was beautiful, light. Airy. Simple and uncluttered. She had no idea spaces like this even existed, let alone that she could be standing in one of them. That it looked like she would be living in it.

Suddenly she ached for a brush in her hand. For her paints. For a blank canvas in front of her. Ached so badly it was almost pain. What would it be like to paint in a place like this? To have all this color and brightness in front of her and around her. It would be amazing. She could almost feel her soul uncurl, as if it had been stuffed into a small, dark box and was only now being set free.

How strange that a man as emotionless and uncaring as Lucas Tate would have a place so full of peace and light and beauty. It didn't make any sense. She would have picked some heavy, industrial-feeling place or one of those sleek, clean, shiny penthouses that only the very rich lived in.

He is *one of the very rich, don't forget that.*

She took a small, silent breath and tried to school her features, not wanting to give him the satisfaction of showing him how much she liked this place. Because no matter how lovely it was, she still didn't have her canvases. And he was still a complete bastard for not even understanding how very important they were to her.

"Bedrooms and a couple of bathrooms are up the stairs on your right," Lucas said, his voice toneless. "Kitchen is down the end of the gallery. I'll leave you to explore."

She turned around. "Why? Where are you going?"

To her surprise, she thought she saw something flicker through his sharp blue gaze. Something that looked awfully like emotion of some kind.

"Where do you think?" He raised one blond brow. "I'm going to get your fucking canvases."

CHAPTER FIVE

Lucas had no idea why he was bothering, because retrieving her canvases made no difference to the danger surrounding her. She was still under threat whether she had them or not, and going and getting them for her could blow their cover. It went against every instinct he had, not to mention all logic, to return to her apartment simply to get a few paintings.

And yet . . .

Her plain features had glowed when she'd told him how much they'd meant to her. How long she'd been working on them and how her exhibition was her dream. *Without my art my life isn't worth living. . . .*

He didn't understand that, not one bit. Life was so very precious and complex, and it could be taken away in an instant, less than an instant. How could a bunch of paintings *ever* be worth more than that? No, he didn't get it, so it was a bit of a fucking mystery as to why he'd told her he was going to get her paintings back.

Nevertheless, he was doing it, turning away and leaving her standing in the living area of the apartment, for some reason not wanting to see the look on her face. The unfurling expression of shock, then surprise, then sheer joy.

In fact, he hadn't been able to get out of there fast

enough, heading back down onto the street and taking his phone out of his pocket, putting a call through to one of the Tate family employees.

Yes, there was a van that could be put to good use and yes, there were a couple of other guys who could help. And most important, yes, they could do it immediately.

Lucas knew that going himself probably wasn't a good idea, since it would link him more completely with Grace if anyone was watching. Yet, again for reasons he couldn't explain, he didn't want a whole bunch of people handling those canvases without taking proper care of them.

It's almost like you give a shit what she thinks of you.

Lucas frowned as he put his helmet back on and got on the bike. Well, to a certain extent he did give a shit, because he needed her to trust him. But there had been a sharp sensation in his chest when he'd ignored her pleas back in her pokey little apartment and he didn't like it.

Any kind of sensation that destroyed his focus was bad, both for him and for the mission. So of course he had to deal with it. And if retrieving her canvases was one way of getting rid of that feeling then he'd do it.

Sounds like a great justification.

He dismissed the thought. It wasn't justification. It was ensuring the success of the mission, that's all.

An hour or so later, having successfully supervised the removal of the canvases, at the same time as keeping a lookout for potential eyes on the apartment, Lucas directed the van to take a zigzag route back to his Village apartment. He followed a couple of cars behind it on his bike, making sure there were no tails, before telling the guys to park it in the private car park underneath the apartment building.

He was fairly certain they'd managed to take out Grace's canvases without anyone spotting them, though it didn't help that the things were fucking huge and it was painfully obvious as they'd gotten them out of the apartment what they were doing. With any luck, though, anyone watching would think the van was simply transporting Grace's art somewhere and not actually taking them to her in her hiding place.

And even if they did, Lucas was certain that they wouldn't be able to get inside his apartment anyway. He had a state-of-the-art security system, plus a number of different, hidden exits that he could take her out of if anyone did happen, by some miracle, to find their way in.

You could also call your brothers to help.

Lucas shook away the thought as the men he'd employed unloaded the canvases. No, he didn't need his brothers' help nor did he want it. Van was a SEAL commander and a bossy bastard, and Lucas didn't want him sticking his oar in where it wasn't wanted. Lucas was in charge of this particular mission and he wanted to stay in charge, period. And as for Wolf, well, that asshole was far too volatile and Lucas did not do well with volatility. Especially when he was trying to protect a civilian.

No, he was going to handle this himself and that was just the way he liked it.

Dismissing the guys and their van, he got the paintings in the elevator himself and transported them up to the apartment. He didn't want anyone seeing where Grace was, and even though the guys were Tate employees, the fewer people who knew her position the better.

As he came back into the apartment carrying the painting of Griffin, Grace appeared at the top of the stairs that led up to the bedrooms. Her eyes went huge and her wide mouth turned up in a smile that he told himself had no effect on him whatsoever. She came hurtling down the stairs as he leaned the painting up against one of the walls, but he didn't wait for her to speak, turning and heading straight for the elevator again. "I'm getting the rest," he said shortly over his shoulder. "You can decide where you want to put them."

"Lucas, wait," she called after him.

But he didn't wait, letting the elevator doors shut behind him. She was probably going to be grateful to him and there was something about her gratitude he found unsettling. He wasn't doing this for her, anyway. This was all about the mission, end of story.

It took him half an hour to get all the paintings up from the car park, plus all her art paraphernalia that he'd also had the guys remove from the apartment. She was probably going to need something to do after all, since he didn't want her running around outside and giving away her position.

By the time he'd finished, dumping the lot in the main living area, Grace was already sorting through her paintings, leaning them up against the walls and looking at them, a crease between her red brows.

Now he'd had a chance to see all of them, he noticed they were all of men, some doing things, some merely sitting there. He really didn't get art, but looking at them, he could appreciate the time and the effort that must have gone into creating them, since nearly every single canvas was huge.

As Grace positioned the last one and stood back, Lucas narrowed his gaze at them. Great. His house was full of an army of painted dudes and he wasn't sure he liked it.

She turned, her face lighting up, and then she came toward him. And this time there was no avoiding her.

"Thank you," she said simply, and before he could move she stepped right up to him and flung her arms around him.

He wasn't a fan of surprise hugs or public displays of affection. In fact, he really didn't like anyone getting into his personal space at all, and certainly not without permission.

But there was nothing he could do as Grace's slim arms slid around his waist and she laid her apricot-colored head on his chest.

He froze, because he could feel it, that electrical charge making every nerve ending he had come alive. Her body was very warm, the press of it against his a delicate pressure he felt echo through him like a note through a tuning fork.

Fuck. What the hell was this shit?

His first instinct was to throw her off, but he couldn't do that, not without hurting her, and he couldn't push her away, for the same reason. All he could do was stand there as she hugged him, a part of himself he thought he had well under control somehow acutely aware of the softness of her breasts against his chest. Of the way her wealth of hair drifted over his arms. Of that dry, warm scent, like apple boughs, with something a little musky and intriguing beneath it.

"Thank you, Lucas," she murmured. "I don't know why you changed your mind, but I'm so glad you did."

He didn't know why he'd changed his mind either, but one thing he was sure of; she had to stop hugging him. Immediately.

Grace lifted her head and looked up at him, her lush mouth curving in a way that shouldn't have affected him, and yet somehow he couldn't drag his gaze from. For a second she merely smiled, a fascinating gold color glinting in the depths of her eyes. Then she blinked, pink flooding through her cheeks, and abruptly she let him go, backing away from him so fast she almost stumbled.

He stared at her. What the hell was that about? Oh, he got the hug business. Didn't like it, but he understood it.

Yet the way she'd released him? So quickly and so sudden? That, he *didn't* get. Not when he hadn't moved or even said a word. Then again, why he should be puzzling over it was anyone's guess. The main thing was, she'd let him go.

She turned away before he could say anything, moving over to where he'd dumped all her art stuff. "Anyway," she said as if resuming a story she'd been in the middle of telling. "I appreciate this. You've got no idea how much. I can't believe you got all my brushes and paints too."

He felt strangely overheated, which was odd, since he kept the temperature in the apartment at a steady sixty-eight degrees. Christ, he couldn't remember the last time he'd felt hot, or cold for that matter. Tuning out his physical discomforts was pretty much second nature, so it didn't make any sense for him to feel them now.

"Put them wherever you like," he said tersely, turning toward the stairs that led to the upper floor and the bathrooms. "I'm going to take a shower." Cold water was definitely what he needed. Or else a hard workout, *then* a cold shower.

Nothing like extreme physical activity to help him focus.

It wasn't a retreat. Not at all.

Grace might have said something, but he didn't wait to hear what it was, heading up the stairs, taking his phone out as he did so, contacting another employee to organize a delivery of a few necessities. He couldn't remember the last time he used this place, and even though he kept it well maintained with a housekeeper visiting once a month to air it out and clean, there was no food in the cupboards. Grace was clearly going to need to eat.

As he finished arranging a grocery delivery, Van's number came up on the screen for the second time that day, but Lucas hadn't answered it earlier and he didn't answer it now. His brother could wait. He had shit to do.

The apartment's gym was as high-specced as he could make it, the usual machines all present and accounted for. There was some workout gear in the cupboard, so he changed and began the punishing circuit that was his normal routine.

It helped. Somewhat.

But an hour and a half later, his muscles screaming, he could still feel the press of Grace's slight body against his, so he turned to his favorite apparatus. The one he used when he needed to let off some steam and couldn't get out on his bike. The punching bag.

Lacing a pair of boxing gloves tightly on his hands, he launched straight into it, each punch landing with a heavy thumping sound, the bag swinging on its chain.

Sweat poured down his back, his heartbeat thundering in his ears.

Years ago, after the incident with the stables that he tried never to think about, his adoptive father had told him that he needed an outlet for all the dangerous emotions that simmered and boiled inside him. That although controlling himself was what he needed to do, sometimes control wasn't enough. Sometimes he needed to do something with them, let them out in a safe way. For Lucas that had meant riding the nastiest, most vicious of the horses all over the trails in the mountains, galloping fast and hard till both man and horse were covered in sweat. Making sure all those terrible emotions were completely gone, the rage and the grief and the guilt, until he was empty, hollowed out. But sometimes it didn't work and then all that was left was to take his rifle and practice shooting at tin cans. That focused him like nothing else, everything narrowing to the target and his finger on the trigger, seeing how accurate he could get. It was like meditation.

When he was finally old enough to enlist, he didn't hesitate, applying for SEAL training as soon as he could, just like his older brother. It had been hard, brutal, and he'd enjoyed every second of it, loving the discipline involved, loving the way it had pushed him both mentally and physically. He'd graduated from the training with the best scores of anyone in the past five years, doing even better than Van. But he'd refused a command position, heading straight into sniper training. He needed the intense focus and mental discipline required of a sniper, and he didn't want to do anything else. He still didn't.

He landed another punch on the bag, the power of it shuddering through his arm, and as he did so felt awareness prickle at the back of his neck.

Crazy that he should be so conscious of her, even here, even as he was punching the shit out of the bag in front of him. Nevertheless, he was.

"Sorry to interrupt, but I have a question," Grace said quietly from the doorway.

He didn't look up, keeping his focus on the bag, drawing his arm back for another left hook. "What is it?"

"How did you find out? About Griffin, I mean?"

There wasn't any reason not to tell her. "My father died just over two weeks ago," he said flatly, "He left a letter for me. And a file that included the info I showed you on my phone, the photos, financials, text conversations." Lucas launched another hit on the bag, the emptiness inside him echoing with the sound of his fist against the heavy canvas. He'd felt nothing hearing the news that Noah had died and that hadn't changed. The old man hadn't given a shit about him and the feeling was mutual. "The letter said that you were in danger and that I had to protect you."

"Your father?" Grace's voice was full of shock. "But . . . how did he know?"

"No idea. The man Griffin was working for"—a right hook this time, to the side—"Cesare de Santis. Was Dad's enemy. I presume Dad was keeping tabs on his illegal activities."

"But why would your father care about me?" She sounded genuinely mystified. "I only met him once. That time you invited Griffin and me to that garden party."

Lucas didn't know why his father would take such special interest in one of his enemy's employees and the wife that employee left behind either. He'd spent the last week or so trying to puzzle out Noah Tate's motivations and still didn't understand why protecting Grace had been been so important.

"I don't know." Lucas launched another punch, the sound of his fist hitting the bag deeply satisfying in a way he'd always found impossible to describe. "It doesn't matter anyway. You're in danger, I'm protecting you. End of story."

She said nothing to that, but he knew she was still there, because that awareness of her was unfurling down his back like that electrical current had somehow moved and was now concentrated directly on his spine.

It was distracting. Which was the very opposite of what he was trying to do here.

Finally Lucas dropped his fists, his breathing slowing, but not that much because it took a lot for him to get breathless these days, and turned toward the doorway.

She had to leave. Now.

The moment Grace had pushed open the gym door, she knew she'd made a mistake.

Lucas, dressed in nothing but a pair of workout shorts and tank top, was standing in front of a punching bag, his fists driving into the canvas like jackhammers. His golden skin was gleaming with sweat, his tank sticking to his body, molding over the most incredible muscles she'd ever

seen in her life. He put even Griffin to shame and Griffin
had been pretty fit.

For a second all she'd been able to do was stand there
and stare at him. Unable to drag her gaze away from the
way the light coming through the windows lit him up,
made him glow. Made him look even more like that stern
warrior angel she'd imagined him to be—

No. That was wrong. He didn't look like a celestial being right now. Yes, he was still beautiful, but it was a different kind of beauty. Golden skin and deep gold hair, wide
shoulders and lean waist, powerful arms that drove his fists
into the bag with explosive strength. Muscled and sleek as
a great cat. It was a raw, animal kind of beauty now. Fierce
and strong and nothing like cold.

And maybe that was the worst part about it.

There was something about the way he hit the bag that
she couldn't quite put her finger on. His punches were
precise and yet there was a wildness to the energy around
him, a hot, violent energy. His lips were peeled back in a
grimace, his expressionless features drawn in tight, fierce
lines. As if the bag were the source of all evil and he was
trying to beat it to death with his fists.

That was the problem with extreme cold and extreme
heat. Sometimes it was difficult to tell them apart.

She'd stood there watching him, absolutely mesmerized, forgetting what she'd even come here to ask, so she'd
said the first thing that had entered her head, a question
about how he'd known about Griffin.

The explanation about his father seemed strange to her,
since although she'd met Noah and even had a nice five-
minute conversation about art with him, she couldn't even
begin to guess why he'd given his son the charge of protecting her. Even given Griffin's link with his enemy.

It seemed . . . strange.

That Lucas had simply accepted the responsibility without argument had also seemed strange. Then again, maybe not. He was a soldier—no, scratch that, he was Navy, which made him a sailor—and following orders was what a military man did.

You should probably get out of here now.

Lucas launched one more punch into the bag and she found herself watching the lithe grace of him, fluid and elegant, the flex and release of his muscles its own sensual poetry.

She still couldn't believe she'd put her arms around him out there and given him a hug. She'd just been filled by the most intense gratitude that he'd gone and rescued her canvases. That they weren't going to be left to be torn apart or destroyed by whoever was after her, because people could be so destructive after all. No, the canvases would be saved, because Lucas had decided to go get them for her and bring them here. And not only that, he'd brought all her art supplies with him.

For some reason, he'd changed his mind for her, and since he didn't seem to want to hear her thanks, she'd let him know in other ways. With a hug.

Except as soon as she'd put her arms around him she'd realized she'd done the wrong thing. He'd gone rigid in her arms, his muscles locking up tight, holding himself so still and stiff it had been like hugging a marble statue. And that antsy feeling that had gripped her in her apartment when he'd held her up against the wall had gripped her again. Restless and hot. Making her want to press her palms to the hard plane of his chest, push against it, test it. Peel away the black leather and see what he looked like underneath.

Which was wrong. Very, very wrong.

She hadn't been able to let go fast enough.

Over by the punching bag, Lucas let his fists drop and he turned toward the doorway. Despite the gleam of sweat on his skin, he wasn't even breathing hard. His eyes seemed to burn a very intense blue, as if punching the bag had gotten rid of all the ice in them.

"You should leave," he said shortly. "I need to finish my workout."

A wave of heat went through her, making her feel like her cheeks were on fire, though why she should be blushing so fiercely she had absolutely no idea.

"Sure, okay." She ran a distracted hand through her hair. "I just need to know . . . if there's anything I'm supposed to do."

"Stay inside."

"Stay inside? That's it?"

He raised a hand and wiped the back of it across his forehead. "I can't have you going outside and giving away the fact that you're here, so yeah, that's pretty much it."

Grace scowled. "But I've got a job to go to. Tonight in actual fact."

"Leave it to me. I'll handle it."

"What do you mean you'll handle it?"

"I mean, I'll be calling them to hand in your resignation."

He said the words like they meant nothing, as if it were no big deal to leave a job that was all that was standing between her and having to leave her little apartment. Her earlier gratitude suddenly drained away like water out of a cracked bucket.

"What?" She had a horrible feeling her voice had cracked just like that bucket had. "I can't resign!"

Lucas raised a blond brow as if he didn't like her tone. "I have no idea how long it's going take me to get those men off your tail and ensure your safety. And until that happens, you're not going anywhere."

Understanding began to sink through her. Of the reality of her situation and what it was going to mean. The past couple of hours had passed in such a blur she hadn't really had time to think about it, but now . . .

"But I can't resign," she repeated, quieter this time.

"Will they give you time off indefinitely then?"

She swallowed. "No."

"Then you have no option but to hand in your notice."

Grace opened her mouth. Then closed it, panic beginning to wind its fingers around her throat. This was all happening way, *way* too fast and she didn't like it.

"If I resign I have no money," she forced out. "And if I have no money I can't pay my rent. What the hell am I going to do?"

As per usual, his expression betrayed no reaction. "What about your housing allowance?"

"It's not enough. It only lasts a year, which means I only have it for another six months anyway." Her panic began to deepen.

When Griffin had been alive, his pay had been enough to keep them in modest comfort while she worked part-time in various different jobs, earning her the money to buy her art supplies. But now he was gone, her widow's pension and her own part-time earnings were barely enough to pay the bills, let alone buy any new paints.

She tried not to let it worry her, because if worse came to worst she could always work full-time in the bar. That would leave her no time to paint of course, but maybe it wouldn't be for long.

What didn't help was the memory of her childhood, of being poor, of being dragged from state to state as her father took on temporary, often seasonal work that barely paid enough for rent and food, let alone the art supplies he needed. "It'll all be worth it," he'd told her once, when she'd been small and had complained about not being able to get a new dress she'd liked. "Once Daddy sells a few more paintings." That had been before poverty and lack of success had made him bitter, had made him mean.

She didn't want that for herself now she was an adult, not the poverty or the meanness, but she'd put up with having no money if it meant she could prove him wrong about her work. That she *wasn't* a talentless waste of time.

"Get another job then," Lucas said dismissively. "It's not like there's a shortage of bars in Manhattan."

Grace stared at him, at the light running lovingly over his sweat-slick skin, highlighting all that perfect, sculpted muscle. The way his tank was sticking to him, she could see virtually every single one of his abs.

God, how could such a cold-hearted bastard be so damn beautiful? It was just so wrong.

He's not totally coldhearted. He got your canvases for you.

He had. Yet in one fell swoop, he'd just undone all the good feeling that had given her.

"And exactly how am I supposed to get another job when I can't leave this apartment?" she pointed out, struggling to keep her voice level. "Being here doesn't stop all my bills from coming in and needing to be paid."

He paused at that, giving her another intense blue glance. "Like I said, I'll handle it."

"How?"

"Leave that to me." He was already turning back to the bag, reaching out to steady its swing. "We'll talk about it later."

Grace swallowed as the panic tightened its fingers around her throat. She wanted to walk right over there and put herself between him and the bag, demand he tell her exactly what he meant by "handle it." But the shocks of the day were making her feel close to tears and all it would take was him being an asshole to her and she'd probably cry. Which would be a blow to her pride that she just couldn't bear. Besides, she'd already had more than enough upheaval for one day and a massive argument was the last thing she needed.

Instead she swallowed past the lump that had risen in her throat. "You're damn right we will," she said, making sure her voice sounded strong. "I'm sorry about your father, by the way."

The mention of his death had been so casual, she hadn't taken it in until a couple of minutes after Lucas had told her. But then, as she was starting to discover, that was Lucas. He made the close death of a family member sound like absolutely nothing.

Unless he wasn't actually that close to his father.

That could be true and she could relate. Then again, she wasn't curious enough to ask about it. Not in the slightest. That would no doubt uncover her own daddy issues, and she did *not* want to revisit those anytime soon.

Lucas only gave a short nod of acknowledgment before lowering his head and raising his fists, sending another jackhammer blow into the bag in front of him.

Grace debated raising a middle finger in his honor and then decided it wasn't worth it. Not when he wouldn't see it anyway.

Instead she lifted her chin, turned around, and walked out. Leaving him alone with his stupid damn punching bag.

CHAPTER SIX

Grace sat cross-legged on the floor in the middle of one of the empty upstairs rooms, staring at the canvas propped up against the wall in front of her. The room was probably meant to be a bedroom, but since there was no furniture in it, she'd turned into a makeshift studio instead.

It was large and white and very bare, but it was saved from complete austerity by the top of the huge rose window that had its center in the living area on the floor below.

Light came in through the stained glass, casting colors across the blank slate of the canvas. There were skylights above her too, letting in more light, though this wasn't as warm as the reds and golds of the stained glass. This was the usual winter gray, a hard, dull light that normally meant snow was in the offing.

She frowned at the canvas, fiddling with the brush she held in one hand. A brush she hadn't used yet, mainly because she had no freaking idea what she was going to paint. Just like she'd had no idea for the past couple of months.

It was a worry. The painting in front of her was supposed to tie the collection together, so she wanted it to be special. She wanted it to be powerful and strong and uplifting. A hopeful piece.

Actually, now that she thought about it, that could be the problem. She just didn't feel very hopeful. Or inspired. Or creative even.

What she felt was anxious and angry and afraid.

It was crazy, especially in this place that was so full of light and color, and deep silence and peace. Yet the feeling she'd had when she'd first stepped through the doors, the need to pick up her brush and create something beautiful, had gone and hadn't come back.

No great surprises there.

Well, no, not really. It was a little hard to be creative when a bunch of scary men were after you, essentially keeping you a prisoner. Sure, her cell was beautiful, but it was still a cell. She still couldn't go outside, see if she could find some inspiration in the city that pulsed with life beyond the walls of the apartment.

Lucas had also forbidden contact with friends and family, so she was essentially isolated as well. The family part she didn't care about, not now her grandparents had passed on and she hadn't spoken to her mother since she'd told Grace about her father's death two years ago. Not even when Griffin had died.

Oh, she understood why she had to remain incommunicado, but it was infuriating, because she wouldn't have minded contacting her friends. Lucas did allow her e-mails but only if they were sent to him first so he could forward them via some complicated means that would hide her IP address. Or something.

Normally, when she was painting and getting into it, she wouldn't have minded being cut off from everyone, since, much like her father, she hated to be disturbed when the creative juices were flowing.

But they weren't flowing now, and sitting here, in an echoing empty apartment, where no one but Lucas knew where she was, she felt her isolation acutely.

Over the past couple of days, in an effort to shake herself up, she'd explored her little prison, poking around in all the rooms, including peering out on to the rooftop terrace just off the kitchen, where there seemed to be lots of plants, an arrangement of couches, and a Jacuzzi. It was amazing. In fact, the whole place was amazing. Lucas had told her it had once been an old church that had been converted into a couple of apartments and that he owned the whole building, using the front apartment as a secret bolthole, the rear apartment he kept empty because apparently he didn't like having neighbors.

It was a pretty big place all up, especially compared to her pokey little apartment, and she had to admit she was enjoying the luxury of the soft bed in the room she'd chosen for her bedroom, plus the walk-in shower in the en suite bathroom. The kitchen too—clean white tile and stainless steel—was spectacular, not that she was the greatest cook or anything, but it sure made boiling an egg a nice experience.

Yet for all of that, after a couple of days she was starting to go a little stir-crazy.

Lucas himself wasn't around a lot. He came and went with seemingly no pattern and without telling her what he was doing. The first night she'd decided she didn't want to talk to him after all, feeling exhausted and out of sorts, so she'd chosen herself a bedroom and had fallen asleep pretty quickly.

The next day he was gone by the time she woke up, but food had miraculously appeared in the cupboards, so she'd made herself coffee and some breakfast and explored. She found he'd left instructions for how to work the TV in the TV room that led off the long gallery of the living area, plus how to operate the stereo and various other electronic items. There was a whole page on the complicated lock on the front door, which he'd then rendered utterly pointless by reminding her she couldn't go out anyway.

She hadn't watched TV, though. She'd spent the day positioning her paintings in her new studio. He'd arrived back soon after that, briefly informing her that he had, indeed, handed her resignation to her boss at the bar where she worked. He'd also paid another month's rent on her apartment, plus settled all her bills.

She'd blinked at him, too shocked to say anything, and by the time she'd gotten herself together enough to speak he'd left again.

She didn't quite know what to do with the fact that he'd paid her bills. Or with the way he'd told her what he'd done. So flat and final. Allowing her no opportunity for argument or protest, which she resented.

He wasn't doing it for charity's sake, she knew that. Or out of the goodness of his heart, she knew that too. He was doing it because the bills needed to be paid and she couldn't pay them herself because of the danger she was in. He was there to protect her from that danger, and that clearly included ensuring she didn't lose her apartment.

If he'd been a different kind of man that would have made her feel really good. But he was stone-cold Lucas Tate and it didn't make her feel good, it only made her feel weird.

Grace glared at the canvas in front of her, but her brain refused to focus on it. For some reason her mind kept revolving back over the past couple of days and the brief meetings she'd had with Lucas. Particularly the one where she'd seen him in the gym with the punching bag.

Yeah, that particular image she couldn't seem to get out of her head.

Him, sweat slicked and powerful. Launching blow after blow at the canvas bag, making it rock and swing on its chain. The fluid way he moved, the sheer physical power in each stroke. Full of hot violence and raw male strength.

Restlessness filled her, making her get to her feet and pace up and down in front of the canvas. How annoying that when she wanted some inspiration for her most vital work the only thing that came into her head was him.

She turned and went over to where she'd stacked all her art supplies, bending to pick up her drawing pad and a couple of pencils. Maybe if she sketched him that would get him out of her head, because God knew she didn't need him in there.

Moving back into the middle of the room, she sat down again and flicked the pad open to a blank page, then furiously began to draw. Which lasted all of five minutes before, frustrated, she ripped the page out, balled it up, and threw it over her shoulder. Then she started again.

A quarter of an hour later, a small pile of balled-up pages at her back, the image of Lucas Tate boxing looming as large in her head as ever, Grace finally cursed and tossed her pad to the side.

Getting to her feet, she prowled over to the stained-glass window and peered through it. Not that she could see anything much out of it. Muttering another curse, she turned and walked back to where her blank canvas was.

The painting she'd done of Griffin stood beside it, his lopsided smile and familiar dark eyes reflected in the mirror, making it look like he was sharing a joke with the viewer. When she'd painted him, she hadn't quite known what she was going to do with him. She'd simply followed her instinct. And it had turned out to be such a very Griffin moment. That smile. The amusement she'd managed to capture in his eyes.

Grief caught at her, making the cracks that ran through her heart ache.

She had loved him. Probably not in the way she should have, but it had been love nonetheless. She'd met him at a party a friend of hers had thrown and he'd been so nice to her. So kind. Warm and funny and chilled out. The interest he'd shown in her had been balm to her lonely soul, and the fact that he was the antithesis of her moody, temperamental father in every way only made him even more perfect.

"What were you doing?" she murmured into the silence, staring at the picture she'd painted of him. "And why? Did you ever think that this would happen? Did you ever stop to think about what it might mean for me?"

But she knew the answer to that. Of course he hadn't thought about it. Griffin never did. He was always a shoot-first-ask-questions-later kind of guy.

Then again, she'd never thought he'd have kept secrets from her either, but clearly he had.

She took a couple of steps up to the painting, Griffin's figure looming large above her. It had been nearly eighteen months since she'd seen him, the sound of his voice already becoming faint in her head. She tried to remember the last time he'd touched her that hadn't been the hug he'd given her before he'd gone off on his last deployment. Tried to remember the last time he'd kissed her, the last time they'd made love.

But she couldn't.

All she seemed to see in her head was Lucas Tate.

You're attracted to him.

No. Just no. She wasn't. He was beautiful, sure, and she admired that. But she was an artist; she was supposed to admire beauty. And it didn't mean she wanted to do anything more than look at him.

Besides, even if she was attracted to him she wasn't exactly going to go out there and do something about it. He wasn't her type for one thing, and for another, he was Griffin's friend. Plus there was the fact that beautiful men like him did *not* go for plain girls like her. They just didn't.

"Grace." Lucas's cold, deep voice came from behind her, making her start.

Fantastic. He would have to come and find her right when she was looking at the picture of her dead husband while trying to get *him* out of her stupid head.

Hoping she wasn't blushing like a teenage girl and yet knowing she was all the same, Grace didn't turn around. "What?" she asked crossly, staring at the picture of Griffin instead.

"You haven't been eating the fish I bought. Is there something wrong with it?"

He'd been studying her eating habits now? "No. I just don't like fish."

"Fine. I'll make sure I get something different in the way of meat then."

"You know, it might be an idea to actually ask me what I'd like *before* you go buying food. . . ." She paused, looking up at Griffin's dark eyes reflected in the mirror. "Or paying my rent. Or settling all my bills."

There was a silence.

"Your financial situation was a problem for you." Lucas's voice sounded closer. "So I solved it."

For some reason her heartbeat had gotten faster, which was intensely annoying. There was no reason for her to keep having this reaction around him and she still didn't even know why.

"You solved it without asking me if it was okay," she said, feeling stubborn. "And I would have appreciated you asking me first."

"You would have told me no, purely because you don't like being told what to do. Which wasn't solving the problem. What's this?"

Grace turned around in time to see that he'd picked up one of her balled-up pieces of paper and was opening it out. The piece of paper with the drawing of him on it.

Oh shit. Her failed drawings of him boxing were the very last things in the world that she wanted him to see.

"Give me that." Forgetting her annoyance, she lunged at him, trying to grab the offending piece of paper out of his hand. But he was too fast, holding it up out of her reach.

"Lucas." Her breath was coming faster and she could feel her skin starting to heat with embarrassment. She made another grab for the paper, but he only held it higher. "Give that to me." She starting to sound breathless now. "It's private."

Great. Now you've made a big deal out of it.

Ignoring her, Lucas spread the drawing out and stared down at it.

There was an intense, heavy silence.

The pencil she'd been holding creaked in her grip and she had to fight to loosen her hold before she broke it. He wouldn't have seen her drawings before. Even in the apartment she'd shared with Griffin, she hadn't hung any on the walls, keeping all her paintings in the studio space she rented.

She didn't much like people looking at her work, even though she knew she was going to have to get over that if she wanted to exhibit it, and she certainly didn't want this man to be the first to give her a critique.

"This is me." His voice sounded as blank as it normally did, yet when he looked up at her, all of a sudden there was something in his eyes she didn't recognize. It wasn't the thin layer of ice that made his stare so sharp and cold. It was something else. "This is me, isn't it?"

There was a demanding note in his voice, as if it was vitally important to him that he know.

Grace lifted her chin, determined not to let him see her

embarrassment or her sudden trepidation. She didn't care what he thought of it. It was just a stupid drawing that wasn't even very good anyway. "Yes," she said, meeting his gaze head on. "It is."

"Why?"

The question was as sharp as the crack of a whip, almost making her jump.

Irritated with herself and by the fact that she was letting this get to her, she held out her hand for the drawing. "Why did I draw you? Because I wanted to."

He didn't give it to her. Only kept staring at her, that thing she didn't understand flickering in his eyes. And despite herself, fascination started to stir inside her. She wanted to get closer, see what it was that lurked in the depths of his gaze. Because it was an emotion of some kind, that much she was sure of.

Luckily, at that moment he looked back down at the drawing again, his brows drawing together in a faint frown. He seemed almost mesmerized by it, which for some reason made the ridiculous reaction she had to him even worse.

Starting to get quite annoyed now, Grace made another swipe for her drawing and this time managed to snatch it out of his hands.

His head came up sharply, that stare of his sliding right through her, pinning her.

"It's nothing," she heard herself say, the words somehow spilling out like grain from a tear in a grain sack. "It's just a stupid doodle. It doesn't mean anything."

"If it didn't mean anything then why are there ten other pieces of paper all scattered around here?"

He'd counted them? Oh, crap.

"Because I couldn't get it right, okay?"

"Couldn't get what right?"

You and your beauty. Your heat. Your spark. Your

power. The contrasts of you that I can't stop thinking about.

But she couldn't say that to him, she just couldn't. "Your energy," she said instead, somewhat hesitantly. "There was an interesting . . . energy in the way you were hitting that punching bag that I wanted to see if I could capture."

His gaze went to the piece of paper she was holding in her hands. "What kind of energy?"

Grace bit her lip. She found it difficult talking about her paintings, mainly because half the time she didn't know herself what she was trying to capture until the painting itself had begun to take form. It was usually a feeling that sparked it, a feeling she wanted to explore. But she didn't really want to tell him that because first, he probably wouldn't understand, and second, the feelings he was sparking in her were not ones she wanted to tell him about.

She didn't even want to think about them herself.

"I'm not quite sure I can put it into words," she said, going for a half-truth as she looked down at the drawing herself. Lucas, standing there with his arm drawn back, ready to send another powerful punch to the bag, his body tense, his face fierce with concentration. "But it's something I've been exploring in my work for the past year or so."

"What something?"

She looked up at him.

He was standing not far away from her, dressed in a pair of worn jeans that clung to his lean hips, and a soft-looking black sweater, his bike jacket thrown over the top. Simple, casual clothes that only seemed to emphasize his intense, masculine beauty.

The still way he was standing in combination with that intense, focused stare was somehow completely fascinating, making her fingers itch to put pencil to paper and start drawing him. See if she could capture his intensity in stillness the way she hadn't been able to when he was in motion.

"What? You're suddenly interested in art now?" She couldn't quite keep the defensiveness out of her voice.

"I'm interested in anything that concerns me and you trying to draw me concerns me, obviously."

Letting out a breath, she balled up the paper again and let it drop onto the floor. She hadn't told anyone about the idea she'd been exploring with her paintings, not even Griffin. Not because she was embarrassed or anything, it was simply something she'd wanted to keep for herself. Yet now, with Lucas's icy stare fixed to hers, she started to feel self-conscious about it.

"I was thinking about the idea of a hero and what being a hero meant." She waved a hand at the paintings leaning against the walls. "All these guys are examples of everyday heroes and I liked the idea of exploring different aspects of heroism with each one."

His gaze flicked around the room, taking in the various canvases. The cop leaning against a streetlight, caught in a moment of quiet reflection. The firefighter shrugging on his jacket, his gaze directed upwards, a grim look on his face as if the particular job he was heading out to was a dangerous one. Griffin, her husband, looking in the mirror and sharing a joke . . .

Lucas's blue eyes pinned her again. "I'm not a hero, Grace. So why the fuck are you drawing me?"

He wasn't quite sure why the thought of her drawing him was quite so confronting. Or why he wanted to know her reasons for doing so. Yet he found himself pushing her about it all the same.

She was standing in a pool of light coming through a corner of the stained glass, the colors of the window turning her hair a brilliant red-gold and picking up the sheen in the silky fabric of the tunic-type thing she was wearing. There was so much color to her, the deep turquoise of her tunic contrasting with the drifts of her hair. Black leggings covered her long, slender legs and her feet were bare, her toenails painted in sparkly gold nail polish

She was all golds and reds and blues, an explosion of color, like a firework against a dead black sky.

He shouldn't have come up to find her, he knew that. He couldn't even think why he had, only that when he'd come in from yet another fruitless day of trying to find the people who were after her, he'd been inexplicably drawn up the stairs to the little room she'd claimed as a studio.

She'd been standing in front of that painting of Griffin, uncharacteristically still, her hair an apricot-colored frizzy waterfall that nearly reached the small of her back. And it had struck him that he had no idea why he was there, since he had nothing new to tell her. So he'd said the first thing that had come into his head—about fish of all the fucking things.

Then his obsessive neatness had kicked in as he'd spotted those balled-up pieces of paper on the floor and he'd had to pick one of them up, spreading it out to see what it was. And looked down to see himself captured in charcoal, about to deliver another hit to the punching bag.

A streak of heat had gone straight down his spine, the picture a shock for some reason. As if she'd revealed something about him he didn't want anyone else to see. Something deeply private and painful.

How she had seen that, let alone been able to put it on to paper, he didn't know. But he wanted to find out what the hell she thought she was doing, because he didn't want her doing it again. Most especially if it was something to do with all this hero crap. Because he wasn't a hero and he never had been.

"Look, if you don't want me to draw you then I won't."

She had a pencil in one hand and was turning it over and over with her fingers in a continuous movement. "I didn't know you'd—"

"That's not what I asked," he interrupted, in no mood for bullshit. "Answer the damn question. Why were you drawing me?"

Her eyes were the same color as extra fine single-malt Scotch whisky, a rich, luminous amber, and her fingers kept turning that fucking pencil over and over. And he wished he weren't so fucking aware of these tiny little details about her, because they were driving him crazy.

She let out a breath and abruptly stuck the pencil behind her ear. Her hands lifted in a "stop" gesture. She wasn't wearing so many bracelets today, he noticed. Just a couple of gold ones mixed with a blue beaded one and another with black beads.

"Okay, okay," she said quickly. "I don't know why you give a shit about why I'm drawing you, but I'll tell you. I need some inspiration for the final piece of my collection. The piece that's going to tie all this lot together." She threw out a hand toward the big canvas that had stayed blank for the past couple of days. "I need to finish it before the exhibition and I've been having trouble with starting. Drawing you was supposed to help me figure out what I'm going to do."

He frowned. "How does drawing me help?"

"It gets me thinking about what I might want to put on that canvas." She moved, bending to gather up the balls of paper she'd discarded, evidently all pictures of him that she hadn't liked. "The day you met me at the art gallery I'd been intending to go and find some inspiration. Just walk around the city and people-watch, that kind of thing. But obviously I can't do that now, so I have to take inspiration where I can find it."

Lucas thrust his hands into the pockets of his jeans, the

sharp needle of electricity he always felt around her sliding under his skin yet again.

Christ, why the hell was he asking her all these questions? Why the hell did it matter to him whether she drew him or not? It wasn't like he didn't have other things to do, after all. He should be contacting Van for a start, because it had been a good few days since Leo's Alehouse, where they'd received their last letters from their father, and as he'd been made director of Tate Oil and Gas along with his brothers, he probably should see what kind of corporate shit he had to do.

He also needed to text Wolf to find out what the fuck was up with him, since he'd been maintaining radio silence too. The way he'd left Leo's five days earlier, so abruptly and without any explanation, was a bit of a fucking worry, though Wolf would have gotten in touch if he'd needed help. At least, he should have.

Except Lucas found he wasn't in any real hurry to contact his brothers. He wanted to know more about these stupid goddamn paintings, which only slid that sharp little needle deeper

"Do you need to finish that painting?" His voice had an edge to it he couldn't seem to smooth out. "You've already got twelve of them. Surely that's enough."

Grace went over to the wastebasket in the corner, emptying all the paper into it, then she straightened and gave him a look that told him plainly he had no idea what he was talking about. "No," she said dryly. "I can't do that. And no, I can't explain why I can't. I'm . . . missing something from the series and I won't know what it is until I start painting."

Jesus. So this was a job she was starting blind. With no idea of what she was doing or what direction to take it in. It was the very antithesis of everything he did and he couldn't even begin to comprehend it.

"How can you not know?" he demanded, not sure why it was so vital she give him a reason other than the fact that every piece of information she gave him was information he could use to potentially protect her better.

She pulled her hair over one shoulder, and as she combed through it with her fingers he noticed her fingernails were painted too. Dark blue with tiny golden hearts.

Why the fuck are you noticing her fingernails?

He had no idea. He had no goddamn idea at all.

"I just don't," she said, as though it weren't a big deal at all. "It's a . . . feeling. That's as best as I can describe it. I just know that the series isn't done and that there's something I need to tie it all together. That will make it all make sense."

A feeling. Jesus Christ

"What do you need for inspiration?" he heard himself ask, even though it really didn't matter to him one way or the other.

She looked away, scanning around the room as if she was actually looking around for the answer to the question. Then her gaze came back to his all of a sudden. Her brows arrowed down as her eyes narrowed, her focus suddenly intent. "Actually," she said slowly. "I think I might need you."

Lucas wasn't often surprised, since being surprised tended to lead to being dead, especially while on a mission. But he was surprised now. He felt it like a splash of cold water.

He stiffened. "Me?"

She was moving toward him now, her stare intent in a way that was familiar to him. Mostly because it was the same stare he used himself when focusing on a target. Except she didn't have a rifle. She only had a pencil.

"Yes." She came even closer, staring up into his face,

her gaze running over him in a strangely impersonal way, as if he were one of her canvases. "Yes, I think it's got to be you." She moved to his left, still staring at him, and began to circle around behind him.

Instantly his hackles rose and he turned with her, years of instinct against showing anyone his back kicking in. "What are you doing?"

She stopped and blinked. "Oh, sorry. I was . . . looking." Her cheeks had gotten flushed and he realized she was standing quite close to him and that he could smell the dry, faintly apple scent of her. "Sorry. It's only that I've been looking for some inspiration for weeks now and you . . . might be it."

His hands itched to touch a long skein of hair that had fallen over one shoulder, see if it was as soft as it looked, and he knew if he moved even the slightest bit he'd do just that. So he kept himself very, very still and only asked, "Why me?"

She clasped her hands, her elegant fingers with their pretty nails lacing together. "Like I said. It's your energy. Plus . . ." She hesitated. "You're also the most beautiful man I've ever seen."

The words hit him strangely and, like everything to do with Grace Riley, he had no idea why. Yes, he was aware of his looks. Aware that they made both men and women stare at him. When he'd been a teenager he'd gotten a lot of attention from girls, and when he was older he'd gotten a lot of attention from women. Another man might have enjoyed the attention or even used it, but Lucas didn't. He ignored it. Because looks meant nothing. Less than nothing. His looks had nothing to do with how well he did his job and so they didn't matter to him in any way.

Except now, looking into Grace's eyes, big and golden, he felt something tighten inside him. An emotion he didn't recognize. "Looks are nothing." He kept his voice cold and even, ignoring the twist of feeling in his gut. "They don't mean anything."

"Spoken like someone who's never had a day's plainness in his entire life." The words were tart and he didn't miss the note of hurt in them.

Strange. Why would she be hurt by that?

"My looks don't affect my aim and that's all that matters to me." Why was he explaining himself? "And if they don't affect your ability to put paint on a canvas then they shouldn't matter to you too."

She flushed and glanced away. "Yes, well, we weren't talking about me. We were talking about you." She looked back at him. "You kind of owe me, you know."

"Owe you? I owe you for what?"

"For sticking me in this apartment and not letting me out."

Unfamiliar irritation twisted inside him. "We've already discussed this. It's for your protection."

"Yeah, I get it, I know. But you also made me resign from my job and then paid all my bills without asking."

No, he still didn't get why she was annoyed about that. The job, sure. But the bills? "I'll make it an IOU then, if that would make you happier about it." Not that he needed the money paid back to him. Not when he had the Tate billions at his disposal. But if she was going to be stubborn about it and cut off her long, elegant nose to spite her face then he wasn't going to argue.

Grace slid her pencil out from behind her ear, then lifted it to her mouth, taking the tip of it between small white teeth. "I don't want an IOU."

He couldn't seem to take his gaze off her mouth, the way her full, red lips closed around the pencil as she chewed on it meditatively.

"What do you want then?" His voice sounded thick to his own ears.

Grace chewed a second longer, then she took the pencil out of her mouth. "I want you to let me draw you."

CHAPTER SEVEN

Grace sat on the floor in the main living area of the apartment, letting the cold gray light of the winter afternoon filter through the stained glass of the large rose window, watching it become warm and golden as it stretched over her bare legs.

It was warm inside, mainly because she'd finally figured out how to jack up the heating. Apparently, Lucas liked it cold, no surprises there, though sadly for him, she didn't. Her own apartment had crappy heating, plus it was expensive, so the luxury of being somewhere warm was one she was going to enjoy while she could.

She tilted her head, examining the tiny flowers she'd drawn painstakingly with a toothpick on her toenails. Nail art was something she did when she wasn't inspired to paint or when she needed something mindless to do to calm her racing brain, and her brain had been racing a lot of late. Good thing she'd brought her small collection of nail polishes from her apartment, because she *really* needed to calm the hell down.

Picking up a clean toothpick, Grace dipped it into some gold polish and began to draw even tinier golden leaves on the stems of the small silver roses, trying to make her brain focus on that and not on Lucas Goddamn Tate.

She should never have asked him to pose for her. Never.

It was just that he'd kept pushing and pushing, wanting to know why she'd drawn him and then asking more questions about her painting. And of course it had been years since anyone had shown any interest in hearing about it, so she'd opened her big mouth and started going on about feelings and energy and . . and all kinds of ridiculous things.

Then he'd asked her what she needed for inspiration and she'd looked at him and it had hit her like a lightning bolt, the way it did sometimes. That what she needed was him. Not for her big painting, no, but he was in her head and the only way she could get him out was to draw him. And maybe once she had, she'd discover what it was that she *really* wanted to paint.

Asking him to pose for her had seemed like a good idea at the time. Except then he'd flatly refused, turned around, and walked out of the room without another word.

It had been so infuriating she'd thrown her pencil at his retreating back.

He'd stayed away from her the rest of the day, spending more time in his gym, and then had gone downstairs to the basement area of the apartment, doing God knows what, and no, she wasn't interested in finding out.

Today he was gone by the time she'd woken up—yet again—and she'd had the whole day to sit and stew. And maybe panic a bit, just quietly, in the privacy of her own head. Because the days were ticking by and she still hadn't started her painting and she had this exhibition coming up in two weeks—no, a week and a half now. Plus Lucas hadn't made any progress on tracking down the people after her—at least, that's what he'd told her—so she had no idea what was going to happen if they weren't found by the time her exhibition came around.

Presumably, he'd try to stop her from attending.

She scowled at the toenail she was currently painting.

If he did that she'd kick him in the nuts or dose his drink with sleeping tablets and run away.

And then maybe you'd get kidnapped and tortured? Good plan.

Her jaw tightened. Yes, okay, there was that. Lucas might be an infuriating dick—which was annoying—but she certainly felt safe here in the apartment with him around.

Still, she couldn't miss this exhibition. She wouldn't. This was what she'd been aiming for ever since her father had first taught her how to draw and she wasn't going to let it slip through her fingers just because a bunch of arms dealers were after her.

Oh yeah, and that was another thing to feel irritated and antsy about. Lucas had no information about why Griffin had been running illegal arms deals and kept telling her the whys didn't matter. Only the reality of the situation did, because it was the reality that needed to be handled. She'd disagreed, only to have him tell her that it was pointless having this discussion because he didn't know Griffin's motivation anyway and, now he was dead, they never would.

Yet that didn't stop Grace from wondering. It ate away at her, made her replay the last couple of years of their marriage, looking for some signs of what had made him think that selling Cesare de Santis's high-tech weapons was a good idea. Had it been about the money or had there been something more involved? Had he been angry? Or had he been forced? Had someone blackmailed him into it?

It was easier to think that he'd been forced than to think he'd made the decision himself. Especially when she couldn't help wondering whether it was something she'd done that had turned him into a traitor.

Well, it wasn't as if you were the best wife in the world, was it?

Her hand shook a little, disturbing the fine line she was drawing. Okay, so she hadn't been perfect, but they'd had a decent marriage, hadn't they? They'd gotten on well, had been comfortable in each other's company. Yes, he'd been away a lot, but that was part of being a military wife. She hadn't liked it, but she'd accepted it.

You didn't have a marriage. You had a friendship.

Irritated with the direction her thoughts were taking, Grace stared at her toes instead. Did they need anything else? Or maybe she should start again, with butterflies or something.

Or maybe you should be thinking about how you're going to solve your little inspiration problem.

Grace muttered a curse under her breath, because the sad fact was she had no idea. Her muse, when it came down to it, was a fickle creature and when it had fixated on someone it didn't want to change. Even if she weren't a prisoner in an admittedly luxurious Village apartment and weren't currently being chased by a gang of nasty people she wasn't sure she'd be able to find inspiration anywhere else. She knew herself too well; she wasn't going to be able to paint anything else until she'd managed to capture him.

She glared at her toes. How the hell was she going to get him to agree? What was his problem with doing it anyway? All he had to do was stand there, or sit there until she'd managed a quick sketch. That should be enough to get him out of her head.

The elevator chimed.

Speak of the devil.

Grace didn't look up, keeping her attention on her toes. "I hope you haven't brought me more fish. Or maybe you've found the arms-dealer assholes instead?"

There was silence, but that didn't mean anything.

Lucas could move soundlessly, like a ghost, and sometimes she didn't notice he was there until he spoke. It was unnerving.

A pair of heavy black boots appeared in her field of vision, just beyond her outstretched legs.

"Tracking down an international arms ring is proving somewhat difficult, so no, I haven't found them," he said. "What are you doing?"

"Painting my toenails with tiny silver roses."

"Why?"

"Because it helps with inspiration sometimes." She finally looked up, meeting his familiar cold blue gaze. "I have to find it somewhere, since I'm stuck here with a painting to finish."

From this angle, with her sitting on the floor, he was even more imposing than usual, towering over her like one of her canvases. He was in his black motorcycle leathers again today, which somehow only added to his air of cold, dark ruthlessness. A shaft of light from the windows lay across his face, blue and red and gold, and the contrast of that color with that darkness was . . . fascinating.

She could draw him like this, with her sitting on the floor, looking up. Capture that darkness somehow, because she knew it was there. She could sense it. . . .

The restless energy inside her began to coil tighter, the way it always did whenever he was around. Making her heart race and her breath catch.

"Can you stay just like that?" she said before she could stop herself.

He frowned, the minutest twitch of his brows, the angle making him look somehow saturnine. "Why?"

A dark angel, that's what he was. Not so much Gabriel now, but something much less heavenly and bright. If he'd suddenly grown a pair of soot black wings from his broad back she wouldn't have been at all surprised.

Her fingers crept for the drawing pad and pencil that were sitting on the floor beside her. "Just . . . don't move."

But he wasn't stupid, his sharp gaze picking up the movement toward her pencil. "I told you I wasn't going to let you draw me."

Grace glared at him. "Yeah, and I'm not going to be able to do anything else until I have."

"That's not my problem."

"I could make it your problem."

Lucas raised one brow skyward. "Oh really?" There was a world of scorn in the words and another whole universe of threat. And the way he stood there, with that raised brow, more beautiful than the devil himself, made her so desperate to put pencil to paper she could hardly stand it.

She stared up at him, meeting that brutally cold gaze, the energy inside her becoming sharp and electric. What was his problem with her drawing him? She didn't understand the issue. "What are you so afraid of?"

Emotion flared unexpectedly in his eyes, but it was gone too quickly for her to figure out what it was, leaving behind it nothing but ice crystals and frost.

"I'm not afraid." His deep, cold voice was expressionless.

Maybe he was, maybe he wasn't. Who could tell when he never betrayed any emotion at all? The world could explode right in front of him and he'd probably stare at it the way he was staring at her right now.

God, it made her want to . . . do something. Poke at him. Ruffle him up. Disturb that icy front of his. See if she could uncover the man she'd caught a glimpse of at the punching bag, all that intense heat and raw, vital energy. The very antithesis of this . . . cold, dark stillness.

Grace slowly leaned back on the heels of her hands and gave him a very direct look. "Then it won't matter to you whether I draw you or not, will it?"

He said nothing to that, but the tension gathering around him changed, pulled tighter, became somehow . . . dangerous.

Yeah, she had him there and they both knew it.

She smiled at him. Deliberately. "All I want is ten minutes. That's all. Ten minutes and then you're done."

He didn't speak, that flat intense stare on hers.

Normally, she was pretty good at reading people, but she had absolutely no idea what was going on inside that beautiful head of his. No idea what he was thinking, none at all.

And you want to know.

She kind of did. She wanted to know what had made him like this, so cold and hard and smooth, like that frozen lake. Because something had. Something had made him lock himself down so tight, nothing could ever escape.

"Ten minutes then," Lucas said coldly. "Time starts now."

She didn't hesitate. Instantly her pad and pencil were in her hand and she began to draw as if the entire point of her existence were this moment. Were to capture the stretch of his powerful body above her and the way the light fell over his face. The arch of his brow. The pure line of his nose. The slightly cruel cast of his sensual mouth. His strong jaw. The intensity of his gaze on her.

Her heartbeat began to pick up speed, the sound of her pencil moving across the paper filling the sudden, deep silence. It came so easily, so naturally, Lucas starting to appear on the paper as if by magic.

"So," she began. "I know you and Griffin were on different teams, but did you—"

"Don't talk."

"Why not? I like to talk while I'm drawing." She glanced up, noting the shadows over one side of his face and figuring out how she wanted to shade it, her pencil moving fast. "I hope that's okay."

"It's not."

She couldn't help grinning at the flat note in his voice, the thrill of creating something after weeks of not being able to like a fire in her blood. "What have you got against talking?"

"It's pointless noise. Only useful when it involves sharing important information." He stood as still as a statue and seemed completely comfortable with it. As if he could stand there all day and it wouldn't bother him.

But of course it probably wouldn't. Griffin had told her Lucas was a sniper, which meant he was used to being still. Used to being patient. So very, very patient—

Inexplicably, a chill raced down her spine, and she had to force herself to refocus. His eyes needed work. They were going to be important to get right, since how could she capture that thousand-yard stare otherwise?

She glanced up again, studying him. His lashes were thick and surprisingly dark for a blond guy. "Pointless noise, huh? You're kind of a downer, you know that?"

He betrayed no reaction. "If you're wanting to know how he died I presume they told you."

The words gave her a little shock, making her pencil jerk. Griffin, he meant, and of course they'd told her. He'd died in an assault on a terrorist stronghold in Eastern Europe somewhere. They hadn't given her details, but that was okay, she didn't need to know. The fact that he was dead was the important bit. How he'd died didn't matter.

"They did." She picked up an eraser and rubbed out the mistake. "And that wasn't what I was going to ask."

"Why did you marry him?"

Her pencil, currently shading around his jaw, stopped in the middle of the paper. "What?"

"Why did you marry him?" His expression gave nothing away as usual, but there was something flickering in his gaze she didn't understand.

"Because I loved him of course." For some reason the question made her uncomfortable, so she glanced back down on to her sketch instead. "That's usually why people get married."

"Why did you love him?" He said the words in the same way as he'd asked her the first morning whether she preferred tea or coffee.

The uncomfortable feeling inside her deepened. "That's kind of a personal question."

"I'm letting you draw me and you like to talk. That means I get to ask some questions."

"I didn't realize this was going to be a quid pro quo type of deal."

"Five minutes left."

Asshole. Not that it mattered anyway. It wasn't like it was a secret.

"I loved Griffin because he was a really lovely guy. A good person. Chilled out and relaxed. Easy to talk to, fun to be with. He was supportive of my art, didn't try to tell me what to do, that kind of thing." She glanced up, checking the angle of Lucas's head and avoiding that stare of his. "Why do you want to know?"

Lucas's gaze was steady. "Give-and-take, Grace. You're doing the drawing, I'm asking the questions."

Her jaw tightened and she looked back down at her pad, focusing on the lean, powerful lines of his body. Fine, if he didn't want her asking questions she wouldn't. But that didn't necessarily mean she had to give him any answers.

"What else do you want to know?" She drew the shape of his arm, the crook of his elbow, the long fingers pushed into the pockets of his bike leathers. "We had a good marriage and I was heartbroken when he died. Yes, I was faithful to him, and yes, he was faithful to me too."

"He wasn't happy."

Her pencil slowed, her heart shuddering painfully in her chest, a cold feeling spidering through her.

Of course he wasn't happy and you knew he wasn't. But you let it go because you didn't want to have to deal with it.

Her throat constricted and it was only through sheer force of will she kept her pencil moving. "You don't know that," she managed to say, which was, naturally, an admission in its own right.

"I do. He told me."

She flicked a glance up at his beautiful face, the cold feeling getting worse. "What did he say?"

Lucas's stare was inescapable. "He said that he thought there was something missing from your marriage and he wanted more."

You knew what was missing. You just hoped he wouldn't notice.

Grace tore her gaze away, that uncomfortable feeling a cold, hard lump in her gut. She'd told herself that their marriage was fine for a long time. Sure, it had become more a friendship than anything else in the last two years, she could admit to that. But she'd thought Griffin had been okay with it.

Clearly he hadn't been.

"The state of my marriage is really none of your business." She added some devil horns to his head, then began to give him those wings she'd been imagining earlier. "It's between me and Griffin. Actually, it's just me now that he's gone, and I don't really want to discuss it with you."

Lucas said nothing to that, and after another minute of silence he asked, "Time's up. Are you done?"

Grace shoved all the uncomfortable feelings away,

studying the drawing in her lap. The sketch was bare-bones, but she thought she'd managed to capture him better than she had from memory the day before, the powerful lines of his body, the arrogant angle of his head, the intense, focused stare of those blue eyes. . . . Though she was missing something. Like a tail and a pitchfork.

Suddenly she didn't want to sit at his feet like a supplicant any longer. Or no, not like a supplicant. She was more like an insect, studied and poked and prodded by some asshole looking at her through a microscope.

Lucas Tate being the asshole.

"Yes, I'm done." She got to her feet, tucking her drawing pad under her arm. "I'm done drawing and I think I'm pretty much done with you for the evening too."

She didn't wait to see his response. She simply turned on her heel and headed for the stairs.

Lucas watched as Grace made her way down the long stretch of the living room gallery, tall and straight, her hair drifting out behind her, leaving nail polish bottles and toothpicks all over his tidy floor. She wore some kind of pale purple floaty dress that shouldn't have gone with her apricot-colored hair and yet did, the skirt swirling around her long legs, making him ache for reasons he couldn't have described.

Bullshit. You know exactly how to describe them.

His jaw felt tight, every part of him tense.

He shouldn't have said those things to her, shouldn't have asked her about why she'd married Griffin, and he *really* shouldn't have told her that Griffin hadn't been happy. But he hadn't been able to stop himself.

She'd sat there curled up on the floor, her hand moving across the piece of paper without hesitation. As if she knew exactly how to capture him. Then those luminous amber eyes had run all over him and he'd felt like she was systematically stripping layers off him. It shouldn't have bothered him. It should have had no effect on him at all. But it had and he didn't know why.

Women looked at him all the time and he'd never felt the way he had when Grace had looked at him. Like a position he'd thought was secure had turned out to be way more exposed than he thought.

He hadn't liked it one bit and it had made him want to make her as uncomfortable as he was. Besides, she deserved it. Griffin *had* been unhappy.

Lucas had never asked questions or probed for details about his friend's marriage, Griffin had brought up the topic himself once or twice. From the sounds of it Grace had treated him more like a friend than a husband and Griffin had been getting frustrated at being constantly shoved aside while his wife directed her passion into her art rather than into him.

She's getting to you. She's getting under your skin.

Fuck, there was no denying it. She was.

Lucas ripped open his bike jacket and flung it over the back of the sectional couch near the big rose window.

Already he could feel the pull of her winding tight around him, making him want to go after her, ask her more questions, find out more about her.

Touch her—

No. Fuck, no. There would be no touching. He was stronger than that. Christ, he wasn't a goddamn Navy SEAL for nothing. His control was perfect and he wasn't going to lose it over one plain redhead.

Your friend's wife.

Yeah, and there was that to consider too. Griffin had been a military buddy and Lucas didn't have many friends. Shit, Griffin was probably Lucas's only friend, since Lucas didn't let himself get close to anyone.

"Christ, even sex is a problem," Griffin had told him

one night, after a few too many beers. "She doesn't even like me to touch her."

Lucas hadn't mentioned that to Grace, but it was something he hadn't forgotten. Because his fucking brain kept returning to it, going over it, examining it from different angles. Imagining what it would be like if *he* touched her. Would she like that? Would that fizz of electricity consume her or was it only him that felt it?

Lucas realized he was pacing up and down in front of the window like a crazy man. Jesus, what the fuck was wrong with him?

He made himself stop and go absolutely still, turning his mind inward. Breathing deeply, becoming motionless and silent, becoming part of the scenery, using some of the calming techniques he practiced when he was setting up a target.

His heartbeat slowed and he concentrated on it, letting the deep sound of it fill him.

Control. He was absolutely, perfectly in control.

The buzz of sexual hunger began to ebb, thank God, and he turned, striding down the long gallery of the living room, going past the stairs and into the kitchen. Moving over to the fridge, he pulled it open, took out a beer, then leaned against the stainless-steel kitchen counter and popped the tab.

Okay, so he had to focus. He'd gotten in touch with Van earlier that day at last, ignoring his demands for an explanation as to his silence, and, once Van had stopped giving him a lecture, agreed to a meeting with the Tate Oil board the next day. It wouldn't be a pleasant meeting. The three brothers had to tell the current board they were out of a job and that the Tates were now going to be running the company in their stead.

Lucas had accepted the position as one of the directors, but only because of his father's letter. Because as a director he'd have access to more resources that would help him in his mission to keep Grace safe. He certainly didn't intend for it to be permanent. He couldn't. He had to get back to base, get out in the field again. The demands of his military career were what he needed in order to maintain his control and his focus, not sitting behind a desk wearing a fucking suit. Sadly, his military career was going to have to wait until the company bullshit Van had roped him into and the situation with Grace had been dealt with.

The company stuff he could handle. It was tracking down who was after Grace that was the real issue. There were a number of players who could be responsible, but narrowing them down had proved to be surprisingly difficult. The file his father had e-mailed him had contained photos of Griffin with various different people and that had given Lucas a couple of names to start with, but whether it was just one asshole who was trying to recover his money from Grace or a few of them he didn't know.

Over the past couple of days, he'd discovered that Grace's apartment was being watched, as was Tate Oil. Both of which he'd expected. Since they'd been seen together, they were now linked, so it made sense that whoever was after her was now trying to find him too. Except they wouldn't find him.

Whenever he left the apartment, he made sure it was at different times and via different exits, so there was no pattern for anyone to latch on to. He had his features obscured with his bike helmet and then, once or twice, had taken the nondescript black sedan he kept for emergencies just like this one, in case anyone was looking for a bike.

He'd gotten in touch with a special Tate employee who had various useful contacts in the criminal underworld and who'd provided information to Lucas's father on a number of occasions. But even that guy had come up with nothing.

Whoever was gunning for Grace didn't want to be found.

Which meant Lucas was probably going to have to go with his next plan of action: take down one of the bastards doing the surveillance of Grace's apartment and ask him a few important questions.

It wasn't a step Lucas particularly wanted to take, since it would mean alerting whoever was doing this to the fact that he was investigating them—at least if he left any unlucky asshole he happened to question alive. Then again, there were ways around that, that didn't involve actual murder.

Still, he'd been hoping the Tate informant would have had more information for him and he could go direct, so to speak. Set up a meeting. Make like he was going to pay whichever bastard it was the money he was owed. Because he wasn't going to actually pay the pricks. He did, however, need a plan for what to do about them instead. Probably killing each and every one of them, plus their supporters, wasn't really the done thing in the middle of New York. More's the pity.

He lifted his beer to his mouth and took a swallow.

Christ, he needed to handle this, and quickly, because the sooner he solved Grace's little arms-dealer issue, the sooner he could get back to base and forget about her.

Isn't this supposed to be a test? And don't you pass all your tests?

Lucas took another sip of his beer, the liquid cold down the back of his throat. Yes, he passed all his tests. With flying colors. He'd just . . . had no idea this particular one would be so difficult.

Above his head he heard footsteps, and he stilled automatically, tuning all his senses into the sound. It was Grace, he could tell by the rhythm. She was moving down the hallway upstairs, in the direction of the bathroom. A few seconds later he heard the water pipes shudder into life as she turned on . . . the bath. Yes, it was the bath. She liked baths, he knew because he'd come into that bathroom a number of times to find vestiges of bubbles in the tub and a wet bath mat in front of it. He had no idea where she'd found bubble bath liquid because he sure as hell didn't have any, yet it looked like she was definitely indulging in bubble baths.

He made a mental note to get some more bath liquid for her. She was so . . . feminine. Bracelets and floaty dresses. Sparkly nail polish and bubble baths. Long, silky apricot-colored hair. And yet, as she'd sat on the floor at his feet, her hand moving across the paper had been bold and sure, drawing dark, thick lines on the pad.

He still didn't know why he'd let her draw him. Perhaps it had been the way she'd looked up at him and asked him if he was afraid. Like she knew something about himself that he didn't. It had been a challenge pure and simple, and he never turned down a challenge.

Above his head he heard her move back down the hallway, going into her bedroom, then back out again. Obviously preparing for her bath.

He took another sip of his beer, fighting the inexplicable urge to go and look at the drawing she'd done. Inexplicable because he didn't give a shit what that drawing looked like. Did he?

The sound of the bathroom door shutting came, and before he was even conscious of having made a decision he'd put the beer down on the counter and was moving, fast and soundlessly, out of the kitchen and up the stairs. He ducked into the room she was using as a studio, checking the corner where she kept her art supplies to see if he could spot her drawing pad. But it wasn't there.

He should have left it then, gone back downstairs and picked up his beer again, but he didn't. Moving down the hallway, he stopped at the entrance to her bedroom and glanced in.

She was such an untidy thing, the purple dress she'd been wearing thrown over the back of the armchair that sat in one corner, a small pile of what looked like lacy underwear on the floor beside it. The bag she'd brought with her was on the armchair itself, stuff spilling out of it.

He took a cautious step into the room, scanning around, unable to help himself.

There were four bedrooms in the apartment, but it was obvious why she'd chosen this one. The great rose window that was front and center in the living area below reached up into this room too, creating tall, high arched windows that let in bars of colored light over the white walls and dark wooden floor, over the heavy white linen of the bed-clothes.

She did like color, he knew that much, and she'd already talked to him on more than one occasion about how much she liked the stained glass too. He didn't much care about the window. He'd bought the building because it still looked like a church on the outside and he hoped people wouldn't think there were apartments on the inside. A bolt-hole was useless if it looked like a bolt-hole, after all.

He took another couple of steps, his gaze narrowing on one of the nightstands. The pad was sitting on the one closest to the window, a couple of pencils on top of the pad.

What the fuck are you doing? Sneaking around in her room like a fucking pervert?

Lucas ignored the voice in his head. He wanted to see the drawing and who cared why? He just wanted to and so he would.

Skirting around the side of the bed, he then stopped beside the nightstand and carefully moved the pencils to one side. Then he picked up the pad and began to leaf through it. There were lots of sketches in it, all of people.

A woman on a park bench trying to coax a bird closer with a piece of bread. A man lying on his back looking up at the sky. A teenager throwing a basketball through a hoop.

Simple sketches of people doing everyday things, and yet each drawing was full of movement and life. Even the ones that were more restful and contemplative seemed to leap off the page.

He knew nothing about art, nothing whatsoever, but he was pretty certain that what he was looking at was good. No, better than good. Amazing.

Flipping over a drawing of a group of teenagers sitting on some steps and laughing, he found himself looking down at a picture of what looked like the devil himself. Except this devil had *his* face.

Lucas stilled, staring at the sketch.

She'd drawn him from her point of view sitting on the floor, so he was looming over her. For some reason she'd given him some wings and devil's horns and there was a pitchfork held loosely in his fingers. A long, spiked tail curled over his shoulder.

But really, those were just details. It was his face he couldn't drag his gaze away from. That and the look in his eyes. Because somehow, even though his expression was cold and somehow menacing, she'd managed to capture heat in his gaze.

That discomfort he'd felt looking at the drawing of himself with the punching bag gripped him again. Like he'd been exposed or had something of himself stripped from him.

Jesus, had he given himself away? Had he somehow let slip his strange attraction to her? Did she know? Because he'd been looking straight at her as she'd drawn him. And if she'd seen that heat inside him—

There was a sudden movement near the doorway and Lucas became a statue.

Grace came into the room, humming to herself. She had one of his big white bath towels wrapped around her, her shoulders and most of her legs bare.

He was very good at being still, very good at blending into the background, and the area where he stood was shadowed. She didn't seem to notice him as she moved over to the armchair and bent to rummage around in that little bag of hers.

He should say something. Move. Tell her he was here. Yet he stayed exactly where he was, motionless. Watching her.

Her towel had started to slip, so she muttered a curse and straightened, pulling out the corner of the towel and unwrapping herself, holding the fabric straight out on either side of her, presumably to get it centered again.

It also gave him a front-row seat to her naked body.

Colored light fell over her, painting her milky pale skin with gold. She was dusted all over with freckles, even over the small high, round breasts and their pretty shell-pink nipples, and the light made it look like someone had sprinkled gold dust all over her.

His breath caught.

She was long and elegant, her waist a delicious curve and her hips narrow. The red-gold on her head matched the little thatch of curls between her slender thighs, and all he could think about was running his fingers through them to see if they were as soft as they looked. Or spreading them apart so he could see the delicate pink flesh beneath them.

The light fell on her hair too, catching the red-gold lights in it and setting it ablaze. Setting *her* ablaze. She burned like a flame in the white bedroom, red and gold and pink and orange, and all the colors in between.

He couldn't believe he'd ever thought she was plain. No, hers wasn't a conventional beauty, but she had it nonetheless. And it wasn't just her undeniably lovely body either. Her angular face, with its long nose and strong jaw, looked somehow as naked and vulnerable as she was underneath that towel. Not plain, not plain in the slightest, but unique and utterly compelling.

She was color and heat and flame, and he wanted her. Jesus Christ, he just fucking *wanted* her.

She was looking toward the window, a distant expression in her lovely amber eyes as she rewrapped the towel around herself, tucking the tail of it more securely between her breasts. And he could feel his cock getting hard, getting demanding, his pulse beating like the fucking march of doom in his head.

It would be so easy to close the distance between them. To pull away that towel and let him see that gorgeous body of hers again. To touch her, feel her silky skin under his fingertips. Take one of her nipples in his mouth, suckle hard on it, see if it tasted as sweet as they looked. Spread her thighs and—

Abruptly Grace blinked, her head turning slightly in his direction. Then her eyes went huge, open fear flashing across her face, her hands lifting to clutch at her towel. "Lucas?" Her voice was sharp and high.

Now you've scared her, you fucking tool. Perhaps you shouldn't have been standing in the corner of her bedroom watching her like a peeping tom.

Lust was beating at him like an out-of-control fire behind a closed door, heating him up, making it difficult to breathe. Making it difficult to stand there and not close that distance between them, put his hands on her.

Calm the fuck down.

But he couldn't. Somehow she'd lit a blaze inside him and he couldn't seem to put it out.

"Yes, it's me." He had to force himself to speak, and when the words came out it didn't even sound like him.

A wave of deep pink washed over her face. "What the
hell are you doing in my bedroom? Oh my God, did you
see—" She broke off, her eyes going even wider, because
he was moving, skirting around the bed, the decision made
before he'd fully thought about it.

"Lucas?" Her voice sounded uncertain.

But he didn't say a word, heading straight toward her.
She took a couple of quick steps back, yet he didn't stop
then either. He kept on coming until she hit the wall and
there was nowhere left for her to go.

What the fuck *do you think you're doing now?*

Grace's eyes had gone huge and he could see the panicked beat of her pulse at the base of her throat. He could
hear her breathing too, fast and hard, and the scent of her
was suddenly everywhere. Damp skin, all sweet and
musky, and that faint, tantalizing hint of apples.

He didn't know what he was doing. He didn't know
why he'd backed her up against the wall when what he
should have done was turn around and walk out. He didn't
know why he'd come into her fucking bedroom in the first
place, because he sure as shit didn't need to look at that
goddamn drawing.

But he'd done all those things and now she was here,
so achingly close, staring up at him with those whisky
eyes. And it wasn't fear in them, he saw that now. It was
something far worse than that.

"Lucas," she said again, shakily, and it wasn't a question.

And all he wanted to do was put his mouth over that
frantically beating pulse. Taste her skin. Pull away her
towel and lift one of those long legs up, wrap it around his
waist. Jerk down his zipper and get his cock out, sink into
her, feel her heat for himself . . .

Except to do that would admit defeat. Would be to fail
the test. Would be to acknowledge that somehow she'd

managed to do what no one else had ever done since he was thirteen: make him lose control.

He couldn't do that. It was a defeat he couldn't risk.

"What the fuck . . ." Carefully he placed one hand on the wall, then the other, on either side of her head. "Are you . . ." He leaned in close, staring into her eyes. "Doing to me?"

She blinked, her skin stained a deep rose pink, her mouth opening but no sound coming out. There were flames in her eyes, and when her gaze dipped to his mouth for a split second he knew there was no coming back from this.

Because, no, it wasn't fear in her eyes. It was the opposite.

She wanted him. And now this whole situation had become a thousand times worse.

"No," he said softly, coldly. "It will never happen."

Then he finally did what he should have done a good five minutes earlier. He pushed himself away from her and walked out of the room.

CHAPTER EIGHT

Grace wrapped her fingers around her hot coffee mug and glanced up at the clock on the wall of the kitchen. It was clean, minimalist, like everything else in the rest of Lucas's apartment. So much so that there weren't even any numbers on it. Still, looked more or less like it was 6:00 P.M. Far too late for coffee, but she didn't care. She needed it.

Raising the mug, she sipped, but the hot liquid did nothing to steady her. Lucas had been gone all day, and at first she'd been glad, because after that scene in her bedroom the afternoon before she didn't know if she wanted to see him.

Heat filled her at the memory, along with a painful embarrassment that made her put down her coffee mug and cover her face with her hands.

God, she'd been stupid. First of all she'd wandered into her bedroom to find an elastic to tie her hair back with, completely missing the fact that six foot two of pure male muscle was standing by the nightstand next to her bed. Then her stupid towel had slipped and she'd opened it up to rewrap herself and naturally she hadn't been wearing anything underneath it.

She couldn't quite think of what had made her aware of him, only that she'd turned her head and seen a male figure standing there. She'd gone instantly cold with fear even as a part of her told her that it was Lucas. Then he'd spoken, his voice strangely roughened, and then—

Grace swallowed, her throat abruptly dry.

Then he'd come at her, backing her up against the wall before she'd even known what had happened, his big, rangy body caging her in. Shocking her, because all that silver in his eyes had burned away, leaving an intense blue flame that felt like it was scorching her both inside and out.

"What the fuck . . . Are you . . . Doing to me?"

It had been like a veil had been ripped away. As if she were seeing him for the first time and what she saw wasn't ice but wildfire.

He burned and all she could think about was how desperately she wanted to burn with him. And of course he'd seen, because she'd never been able to hide her feelings.

"No. It will never happen."

She took another sip of her coffee, hoping it would make the shakiness inside her go away. But it didn't. Because she didn't need him to explain. She knew what he meant and part of her was still reeling from the fact that apparently this chemistry was mutual, that she'd somehow managed to affect him. Yet part of her had dropped away in an intense disappointment that even now she couldn't bring herself to accept.

But no, it was *good*. Yes, it was good that nothing would happen between them, because she didn't even know if she wanted that.

You don't know if you can handle him, you mean.

The breath escaped her in an explosive rush and she turned, putting the mug down on the counter and then leaning against it.

She'd never considered herself a particularly sexual person. Sex with Griffin had been pleasant and he'd always been a considerate lover, but she'd never felt like she would die if he didn't touch her. She'd missed his hugs but not the sex when he was on deployment. After all, she had a perfectly good vibrator when the mood took her and it didn't often take her.

So she didn't understand the ferocity of the hunger that had gripped her when Lucas had backed her against the wall. Didn't know where it had come from, only that it was linked to that buzzing, restless feeling she always felt around him. That he appeared to feel too.

Yeah, she didn't know what to do with that either. She didn't know what to do with any of it and she didn't mind admitting that facing him again after what had happened was going to be a problem.

Leaving the rest of her coffee, Grace pushed herself away from the counter. She really needed to go do something, such as start that last damn canvas, and to hell with the fact that she didn't know what she was going to paint. Maybe she just needed to get some paint on there, see what happened.

Or you could go and look at that sketch of him you did yesterday.

"No," she said aloud, just in case her stupid subconscious didn't hear. "No, I'm not going to do that." The last thing she needed was to feed the fire burning inside her, and she had a feeling that mooning around over that picture would make everything worse.

Draw him again. You want to.

Her hand closed in a fist, her nails digging into her palm, trying to ease the itch. No, she wasn't going to do that either, because again that wasn't helping. Maybe she should go stand in front of that picture of Griffin again, look at him. Remind herself of what she'd wanted when she was finally old enough to escape her father's reach: safety and stability. A person who would simply love her for who she was and didn't run her down or criticize her constantly. A person who let her do her own thing and who was supportive of her as an artist. That's what she'd wanted when she'd first come to New York and that's what she wanted now, even though she'd lost Griffin.

What she didn't want was a man like Lucas. Cold on the outside, burning hot inside. Controlling. Arrogant. Demanding. There were aspects of him that were so like her father it wasn't funny, and there was no way she was going to associate herself with a man like that again in a hurry. Basically, Lucas was the antithesis of everything she was looking for in life.

Why do you want him so badly then?

She had no idea. Maybe what she felt wasn't desire. Maybe she'd mistaken those feelings for something else. Easy enough to do when you'd never felt them before, after all. And he was such a goddamn irritating man that maybe it was simply dislike she felt for him. Yeah, perhaps that's all it was and she was getting all het up over nothing.

Liar.

At that moment, the sound of the elevator chiming came from down the end of the long gallery of the living area, and every muscle in Grace's body tensed.

He was back. Which meant she was going to have to face him, talk to him. Ugh, she'd probably have to look at him too and she really didn't want to do that. Alternatively she could just avoid him. . . .

Now you're not only a liar, you're a coward as well.

Shit.

Well, if she was going to escape upstairs she was going to have to come out of the kitchen anyway, so there was no point putting it off.

Straightening, she took a breath, then walked out into the living area.

And stopped.

Down the other end of the long gallery was Lucas. In a

suit. The dark color was the perfect foil for his short blond hair, while the tailoring set off his height, his broad shoulders, and his lean waist. He wore a plain white business shirt with it, but it was the tie that pulled everything together: It was exactly the same silver-blue as his eyes.

His long fingers were pulling at it as if the thing were strangling him, even though the expression on his face was the same as it always was. Hard. Cold. Except she knew for certain now that expression was a mask he wore.

A mask to hide the heat of the man beneath it.

Her breath caught, her pulse beginning to ratchet up.

His gaze came instantly to hers, his fingers pausing at the knot of his tie.

For a second something leapt in those fascinating eyes of his; then it was gone, leaving nothing but a rime of silver frost.

He said nothing, taking a step back and slowly sitting down on the white sectional sofa that stood before the great rose window stretching above him. Then he leaned back, putting one arm along the back of the sofa, the other resting on one powerful thigh. A relaxed posture, and yet there was nothing relaxed about him. He didn't stop looking at her, ice glittering in his eyes.

She wanted to draw him like this. Sitting relaxed, every line of his body still, yet the tension around him so tight it was like he was going to explode into movement at any second. Ice in his gaze and yet, beneath that, a deep, burning blue.

Where the fuck was her pencil and pad? Where had she left them?

"Can I draw you?" she burst out, all her earlier awkwardness at facing him dropping away. "Please? Another ten minutes, that's all. I promise."

Didn't you want to avoid him?

Yeah, she did, so why the hell she was now wanting to draw him she had no idea. Sometimes the demands of her creativity were incredibly inconvenient.

Once again, Lucas said nothing.

She didn't wait, though, racing upstairs to grab her pencil and pad from the nightstand in her bedroom, then racing back down again. He hadn't moved, sitting exactly as she'd left him, that intense gaze of his fixed to hers.

Grabbing a cushion off one of the nearby armchairs, Grace flung it down on the floor and sat on it cross-legged, her pad on her knees. And began.

As soon as her pencil moved across the paper she knew why she was drawing him. Because it was easier to look at him when she was creating, easier to push the feelings she didn't understand to one side and concentrate on capturing what she wanted in the sketch.

Because maybe if she kept on drawing him those hungry, intense feelings would be sated and finally go the hell away.

A dense, heavy silence fell that he made no move to break, and neither did she. Which was better, wasn't it? Sure, she liked to talk when she was drawing, but now all she could think about was how grateful she was for the silence.

But it wasn't a comfortable one. Not at all.

The minutes ticked by and Grace lost herself in the drawing in front of her, trying to capture the contrasts of him. His intensity. That razor-sharp quality that always surrounded him and all that lean, coiled strength.

Except . . . something wasn't quite right. She was trying to capture the duality of him, the differences between his relaxed pose and the edges of all the ice she saw in his gaze, yet he didn't look quite as relaxed as she wanted him to be.

What was the problem? Was it the tie? He'd been pulling at it earlier. Maybe if it was undone that would help, and also the top couple of buttons of his shirt.

"Can you undo your tie?" Her voice sounded strange in the heavy silence of the room, almost like an intrusion. She could feel herself flushing, much to her annoyance.

Lucas stayed exactly where he was. "Why?"

A shiver rippled over her skin, though she tried to ignore it. "Because I think it would help with the pose."

He tilted his head, keeping that flat, cold stare on her. It was dark outside, but the light from the streetlights outside filtered through the stained glass and cast colors over his stunningly beautiful features.

"You do it then," he said without inflection.

Grace blinked, the shiver becoming a sharp, electric thrill. "What do you mean?"

"I mean if you want my tie undone then you'll have to undo it yourself." Again there was no expression at all in the words and none on his face either. But the atmosphere had changed, electricity seething in the air between them.

Grace couldn't breathe all of a sudden, the intense hunger inside her stretching out, lazy and hot. All she knew was that she didn't want to go over there. Didn't want to get anywhere near him, because if she did . . . God, she had no idea what would happen.

She swallowed. "Why? Can't you do it yourself?"

He didn't reply, merely raised one blond brow.

There was no mistaking that look; it was a challenge, pure and simple.

Her heartbeat thumped loudly in her head, deafening her. Why did he want her to undo his tie? What was he getting out of it? Yesterday it had been like he was angry with her, demanding what it was that she'd done to him as if she'd done whatever it was on purpose, and then he'd told her nothing was going to happen. So what the hell was this about?

Part of her was very tempted to gather up her pencil and pad and retreat upstairs, leave him to his exasperating silence. Yet another part of her simply couldn't leave that challenge unanswered.

It would be a mistake.

Possibly it would. But then maybe this might be supposed to make her uncomfortable, make her stop drawing and retreat, chase her away somehow. If that was the case then there was no way she could let that happen. She couldn't let him win. She wouldn't.

"Fine," she said instead. "I'll undo your damn tie." And she put down her pad and pencil. Rose from her cushion. Moved over to the couch where he sat, her heartbeat getting louder and louder the closer she got to him, until she was standing right in front of him.

He didn't look away, not for one second, his gaze like a sword running straight through her, stealing any breath remaining in her lungs, which wasn't much. So cold and yet . . . was that anger she saw there? If so, why was he angry? Was it this situation with her or was it something else? Perhaps it had something to do with wherever he'd been to today, which clearly had been business related given the suit.

"Don't speak." His voice sounded flat. "If you're going to undo my tie do it now, because I'm not going to give you another chance."

Her curiosity twisted and briefly she debated pushing him about what he'd been up to. Then she decided it wasn't worth the effort, not given he might get up and leave, which would be intensely annoying, since she hadn't finished her drawing yet.

He was sitting back against the couch, making her have

to lean over him in order to start undoing his tie, and she thought he might sit forward to make it easier for her, but he didn't. He sat there, motionless, his long, hard body stretched out beneath her. And it didn't seem to matter that he was fully clothed, covered in crisp cotton and expertly tailored wool, she could still feel the heat of him radiating outward and into her. It made her breath catch and her hands shake as she reached for his tie, fumbling with the knot, trying not to brush against the smooth golden skin of his throat.

She couldn't bring herself to meet his gaze and maybe that was cowardly of her, but she just couldn't do it. She could feel the pressure of it, though, as if she were fathoms deep under the ocean, with the entire weight of the sea pressing down on her.

"When I was five I burned my house down," Lucas said suddenly, each word clear and precise and cold as crystal. "A neighbor was going to pass on one of their kids' old bikes to me, but my mother refused because she didn't like taking charity. So I took my father's cigarette lighter and set fire to the curtains in my room, because I was so angry with her. Then I ran out into the street and hid. I came out when I heard the sirens, and when I got to my house it was on fire, the whole thing burning. . . ." He paused and she realized she'd stopped trying to unknot the tie, barely aware of the cool silk beneath her fingertips. "They died," he went on. "My mother and my father, and since they had no other relatives, I had to go into care. I went to a boys home, which is where I found Sullivan and Wolf."

The blue silk of his tie was an intense color, with a sheen of silver. Though maybe that was the tears in her eyes.

"Lucas," she began, his name all husky.

"Keep going."

No denying that was an order, issued in that same hard,

flat voice, and since she had no idea why he was telling her this or even what to say herself, she obeyed. This time the silk slid easily and she was able to get the knot undone, pulling it away from his throat, exposing the pulse that beat just beneath the surface of his skin.

She could smell him, that fresh scent along with a note of something warmer and muskier underneath it, making her want to bend and put her mouth right *there*. Taste his skin. It was shocking to her, since she'd never, ever wanted to do that to a man before. But God, she wanted to do it to him.

Lucas remained very, very still, and as she watched, the beat of that pulse remained slow and steady. As if her nearness affected him not at all. It made her want to do . . . something to make it go faster, to push at him, make him as uncomfortable as she was, but after what he'd told her . . .

"I was adopted by Noah Tate when I was six and he took Wolf and Van and me out to his ranch in Wyoming." Lucas's gaze was a relentless, implacable blue. "He was a strict father and I clashed with him a lot. When I was thirteen I wanted him to buy me this new rifle developed by DS Corp. It was top-of-the-line and I was good at marksmanship already by that stage, and wanted a gun that was equal to my skills. But Dad said no. DS Corp was his enemy's company and he flatly refused."

She kept her gaze on Lucas's throat, trying not to breathe. Trying not to inhale that delicious scent of his. Trying not to ask all the questions that were suddenly in her head, because he was going somewhere with this and she wanted to know where that was.

Instead she watched his pulse, steady and sure. And it didn't falter, not even when she lifted her hands to undo the top button of his shirt.

"I was angry with him," Lucas went on inexorably. "I

loved shooting targets and he was always on us to improve our gun skills. The weapon was perfect for me, and even though it was expensive, he could afford it. I even offered to save up for it myself and buy it when I had the money, but he said no. So I found a box of matches and I took it out the back of one of the stable buildings, along with a couple of Dad's favorite shirts and his hunting knife, and I lit them all on fire."

She had to look at him then and she felt the impact of his gaze shudder through her, like she'd been hit over the head with a bat. Because all that heat inside him was blazing, as bright as the fires he kept lighting.

"The fire caught the stable building." His words were hard and cold, little pellets of ice like hail. "There were horses inside and they must have smelled the smoke, because they got frightened, started screaming. I tried to put out the fire myself, but I couldn't. It was too big and too hungry." He didn't even blink, staring straight at her. "I panicked and ran to get Dad and luckily they managed to get the horses out before they burned. But they couldn't save the stables. After that, Dad told me that if I didn't learn to control myself he was going to have to send me back to the orphanage. He said I was dangerous, volatile. That I had to learn how to distance myself, be detached, or else I might kill someone else one day."

Grace froze, unable to move. Unable to look away from the ferocity in his eyes. Her throat felt tight, a weight sitting heavy on her chest as if every word he'd spoken were a stone and all those stones were piled on top of her.

Had he told Griffin any of this? But she had a feeling she already knew the answer to that. No, he hadn't.

Unable to bear it, she tore her gaze away, staring down at the second button on his shirt. Just two and then she'd leave him alone. His skin was so close to her fingertips, so achingly close . . .

"Why are you telling me all of this?" she asked when he didn't speak.

There was a moment's silence.

"So you know why I said what I did yesterday. So you understand that I can't give you what you want, Grace. I can't *ever* give you what you want."

The words went down her back like a bolt of electricity and she lifted her gaze to his abruptly. "What makes you think I want anything from you at all?"

"The way you're looking at me. The way your hands are shaking right now, and the fact that your breathing is fast." The intensity of that blue stare was inescapable. "I know when a woman wants me, Grace. And you want me. Badly."

Anger lit in her eyes, he watched it bloom like the flames he'd once been fascinated with. Like the fire he'd once played with because it was beautiful. Because when he was a child it looked like the emotion that burned inside him too, hot and bright and alive.

But fire killed, as he of all people should know.

Christ, she was so fucking close to him, leaning over him, her hair drifting over her shoulders and glowing all the colors of the sunset. She was wearing that turquoise tunic today, the one that should have cooled her and didn't. The color only seemed to make her blaze even brighter.

Her amber eyes glowed, and he could still feel the heat from her fingertips, brushing so near to his bare skin and yet not quite touching. It made every muscle in his body gather tight against the need to reach out and bury his hands in that soft, silky hair, pull her down, and cover her wide, sensual mouth with his.

But he wasn't going to. And now she knew why.

He didn't like to tell his secrets to anyone—not even his brothers knew that he'd been the one to light the stable fire. They didn't know he'd burned down his family's house and killed his parents either. Noah had only known because he'd had Lucas's background investigated, but Lucas had never told his adoptive father himself.

Detachment. Distance. Control. That was how he'd lived his life after what had happened at the stables and he was happier for it. The wild swings of inexplicable emotion dampened, rage and pain and guilt blunted, muted. He didn't need those emotions anyway, and as for joy and happiness, well, they were overrated. Desire, though, that was different. That was harder to get a handle on, but he was trying.

He had no time to be distracted from his mission and especially not after what had happened today, when he and Van and Wolf had dealt with the board at Tate Oil and then, afterwards, the unexpected arrival of Van and their adoptive sister, Chloe, at Leo's Alehouse. Lucas hadn't even known Chloe was in New York, but it turned out that Van had brought her here from the ranch in Wyoming. Apparently, their father's enemy, Cesare de Santis, was after her for some reason and the Tate mansion on the Upper East Side was compromised, which meant Van needed to take her somewhere to hide her. The situation was serious, so Lucas had offered them his own SoHo apartment, since he was here with Grace. Van had been grateful, which in turn had reminded Lucas of the seriousness of his own situation too. Of the danger to Grace and how he really needed to get a handle on it. Deal with it, and fast, because the longer it went on, the longer he was going to have to remain here with her. The longer he was going to have to manage the intensity of the chemistry between them.

"You're an arrogant son of a bitch," Grace said, her lovely mouth flattening.

He ignored that, ignored the way his body was hardening in response to her nearness and that delicious, faintly apple scent. "And you're a liar."

Her gaze flickered and she straightened, drawing away from him. The movement pulled the silky fabric of her tunic tightly across her breasts, outlining the hard points of her nipples. Another giveaway.

"Not that it matters" he added. "I simply want you to be clear."

She stared at him for a long moment, then her gaze dropped to the open neck of his shirt. Slowly, she leaned over him again, more deliberate this time, her hair a scented curtain around them. Christ, what did she wash her hair with? It smelled of apples too.

You're thinking about the way her hair smells? What the fuck is wrong with you?

"Thanks for telling me all of that." She lifted those long, cool fingers, taking the cotton of his shirt between them. "And I'm sorry about your family. That must have been terrible, and I'm sorry about your foster father too." She slid the button out and he felt the electricity of her touch as her finger grazed lightly against the bare skin of his throat. It was the merest brush, yet he felt it move like lightning through him.

Her breath caught, the delicate flush in her cheeks deepening, making her freckles stand out. She hadn't meant to touch him, it was clear, yet when her gaze lifted to his there was nothing but challenge in her amber eyes. "But all of that doesn't give you the right to assume you know jack shit about me or what I want."

There was a roaring in his ears, his heart rate beginning to climb. She was leaning against his knees, her long, willowy body stretched out over his, and all it would take would be a small nudge and he'd have her over his lap. Then he'd take her down onto her back on the couch, crush her beneath him . . .

Jesus Christ, he was cold. And she was so fucking *hot*.

He stared back at her, unmoving, looking into her eyes because he couldn't bring himself to look away, reading challenge in them loud and clear.

Ah, yes. Like he'd challenged her to undo his tie, now she was giving that same challenge back to him. Fuck, what did she think he was going to do? Run away? Didn't she know that a man like him would *always* answer a challenge like that? And he'd fucking win too.

Yeah, and you should stop fucking panicking too. This is a test, remember? You're a goddamn SEAL. If the test isn't hard maybe you should join the Army instead.

That was true. Also, he wasn't thirteen anymore, battling a rage that seemed to have no end, a rage that didn't have anything to do with the gun he'd been denied but something else. Something he didn't understand and didn't have a name for.

He was stronger now. He'd been in perfect control of himself for years. He'd been on missions that had broken lesser men, and this woman, the widow of his best friend, wasn't going to make him lose it no matter how warm and elegant, no matter how smart or fascinating or downright desirable, she'd become to him.

He'd never been a weak man and he wasn't about to start now.

A test. . . . Time to make this test harder.

Lucas didn't say anything. Instead, keeping his gaze on hers, he lifted his hand, moving slowly so she could see what he was doing. With extreme deliberation, he pushed his fingers into her hair, curling them around the back of her fragile, beautifully shaped skull. The red-gold locks were as soft and silky as he'd imagined they'd be, softer even, and warm against his palm.

Her mouth opened soundlessly, her eyes going wide in shock.

She hadn't expected this, clearly.

Excellent. This would be a test for her too.

Keeping one hand on the back of her head, Lucas gently skimmed one finger across her cheekbone. She didn't speak, her breathing getting faster and faster, her small gasps audible in the dense silence of the apartment. Her eyes had gone black, only a thin rim of gold around the outside of them.

She looked . . . exposed, the vivid, compelling planes and angles of her face vulnerable.

Who else got to see her like this? Griffin, obviously, but Lucas was betting no one else ever had. Only him. The thought was vaguely satisfying.

He held her darkened gaze with his as he tightened his fingers on the back of her neck, drawing her down with aching slowness until at last—*at last*—her mouth was on his.

Electricity ran the entire length of his body, looking for a place to ground itself and finding nowhere, and it was only through sheer force of will that he managed to hold on to his control. To resist the urge to ravage that soft, vulnerable mouth, pull her to the floor, and get inside her any way he could.

His heart was racing and refused to slow, none of his usual exercises were working, the beat of it loud and insistent in his head. But he didn't stop what he was doing. He'd had harder tests than this in his training. One soft mouth wasn't going to get the better of him.

And it *was* soft. So fucking soft. And trembling slightly.

He began to explore the seam of her lips with his tongue. Gently, with care. Coaxing her to open to him.

She shook, a husky noise escaping the back of her throat as her mouth opened gradually to him.

So much *heat*. She tasted like coffee and something else, something sweet, and that heat was roaring up inside him, like a smoldering fire bursting into life with a breath of wind. No, scratch that. This was like someone had poured gasoline directly onto an open flame, turning it white-hot, bright and consuming.

If this is a test you're failing it.

No, he fucking wasn't. He could control this and he would.

Lucas made himself go very still, every muscle in his body tight, trying to force his heartbeat to slow the fuck down. At the same time, he began to kiss her with deliberate slowness, pushing his tongue into her mouth and exploring deeper, letting the flavor of her go straight to his head.

Testing himself. Testing her.

She trembled again, one hand coming down on the back of the couch near his shoulder while she put the other on the arm, as if she needed to lean against something for balance. But she didn't pull away, her mouth open and so damn sweet, and her hair was like the softest silk thread. She was leaning into him now, her body pressing against his legs, and the warm, musky smell of her was making his head swim. Then she touched her tongue to his, tentatively, as if she had no idea how to kiss, and he knew if this went on any longer he *was* going to fail this test, and spectacularly.

He began to pull away, gripping the back of her head when she tried to follow, holding her still until there was space between them and he was staring up into her eyes. They were smoky and dark, her cheeks deeply flushed, and she looked half-dazed. Her mouth was full and red and all he could think about was pulling her back down and kissing her again, harder, deeper.

But he didn't.

"Tell me again you don't want me, Grace," he said instead.

She stared at him, her breathing fast and shallow, and he could feel how she was shaking under his hand. Shock crossed her face and then a bright flash of pain.

Then before he could move, she jerked herself away from him and turned, fleeing the length of the room and disappearing up the stairs.

Lucas didn't go after her. He remained exactly where he was, his body tight, his cock hard as a fucking steel bar. It was a shitty thing to do to use a kiss like that against her, to merely prove a point, but there was no other way to do it. To test himself *and* her.

Of course she wanted him, and now he'd proved that to her. He'd also proved that his control was as rock solid as it ever had been. Sure, she pushed it, but he was master of himself. He could handle it.

He should have felt good about that, about passing his own little test, but he didn't. He felt like shit.

You shouldn't have used her. And now you've made the whole situation worse.

Maybe he had. Still, it had to be done. And now since he'd had a taste of her, perhaps he could concentrate on what he was supposed to be doing, which was finding out which assholes were after her and taking them out.

It all sounded good, but it was a long time before he got himself to move.

And the taste of her lingered in his head even longer.

He had a horrible feeling it wasn't ever going to go away.

CHAPTER NINE

Grace stood in front of her painting of Griffin, tears slipping down her cheeks, a thousand and one different emotions all tangling inside her and not a single one making any sense. Except maybe the grief and the guilt, she could understand those, but the anger? The regret and the hurt and the disappointment? No, she didn't get why she felt those.

She was alone in the apartment—again—but she didn't mind that. She didn't want to see Lucas or be around Lucas. She didn't even want to hear Lucas.

If he was gone he could stay gone, because she'd decided that she hated him. Quite literally hated him.

That kiss he'd given her had hurt in ways she'd never expected, a hurt that she was still feeling even now, a day later as she stood in front of the canvas of her husband.

A husband who'd never kissed her the way Lucas had kissed her. Who'd never made her aware of how hungry she was. Who'd never made her realize what she'd been missing all this time. Who'd never made her burn.

But she'd burned yesterday and she'd burned for Lucas. *He'd* been the one who'd made her realize what had been missing from her marriage. *He'd* been the one who'd made her hungry. And that's why she'd decided she hated him.

She hadn't wanted to know any of those things. Hadn't

wanted to feel any of those feelings. She'd been quite happy thinking of herself as relatively nonsexual, a woman who was much happier putting all her emotions and her passion into creating. She wasn't like her father, whose bitterness and anger at his artistic failure had played out in a string of affairs that her mother turned a complete blind eye to.

Yet the moment Lucas's mouth had touched hers, she'd been shown just what all those lovely little justifications were: lies.

He'd kissed her so slowly, so carefully. Tasting her like she was a fine wine, waking every sense she had into full aching awareness of what her body wanted, no matter what her head told her. Making her understand fully the depths of her own inexperience. Ripping away the comforting veil that she'd drawn over her own hungers and the relationship she'd had with Griffin. Showing her how completely different this was and, worse, what she'd been missing out on all this time.

What she'd been hungry for, for years, and yet never knowing.

Not to mention demonstrating how completely unprepared she was to handle a man like him.

Another tear rolled down her cheek, but she made no effort to brush it away.

Yeah, she hated him for showing her all these things. And most especially she was angry with him for turning all that intensity into a point he was proving, exposing her own desire for him, and making her run from the room like a scared virgin.

Asshole. Prick.

She didn't even know why she was crying, because she sure as hell didn't want to.

He showed you what you wanted. And then he took it away.

Yes, he had. He'd shown her everything in that deliberate, cold way, even as his mouth had give her a taste of the burning heat he kept so contained inside him. Made her realize how completely he saw through all her lies and her justifications, and that he knew she wanted him. Had recognized it even before she'd fully admitted it to herself, making her feel exposed and vulnerable. As if he'd been rummaging around in the depths of her soul while keeping himself safely locked away.

And even though he'd told her those things about himself—shocking things—she didn't make the mistake of thinking those were confessions or that they'd been given to her as precious secrets. No, they'd been all part of his point.

Not that she wanted his secrets anyway, asshole.

On the canvas in front of her, Griffin stared into the mirror, his mouth lifted in that achingly familiar lopsided smile. Sharing a joke. She was starting to think that maybe the joke was on her.

Abruptly she wished she had someone to talk to about this. Someone she could pour her heart out to or who could give her some advice. But she didn't. She had friends, but they weren't particularly close, and now her grandparents were dead, the only other family she had was her mother. And she hadn't spoken to her for years.

Did you ever have anyone to talk to?

That was a good question. Once, before he'd become mired in bitterness and anger, she used to tell her father everything. Back when she'd been small and his paintings had been selling and she'd still been his precious little girl. And after that had all gone bad and she'd left home before he could take out that bitterness on her with his fists, she'd been able to talk to Griffin. It had been part of the reason she'd been drawn to him, because he'd listened to her the way her father used to. But now Griffin was gone. . . .

She sniffed and belatedly wiped the tears away, trying to ignore the sudden sense of loneliness and the exhausted wrung-out feeling. She hadn't slept much the night before, tossing and turning in her bed, and right now the thought of taking a nap seemed like the perfect idea.

Except that blank canvas was still blank and she only had another week and a bit to go before her exhibition and if she didn't start soon she was never going to finish. And she was still stuck inside, in this damn apartment, unable to go out because of the choices her dead husband had made.

And because of Lucas Fucking Tate.

The anger that the tears had dampened flickered back into life, smoldering sullenly, getting hotter, leaping higher.

Her jaw tightened, her hands curling into fists. She turned sharply away from Griffin's painting and went to stand in front of the blank canvas instead, staring fiercely at it, her anger simmering like a pot of hot water on a stove.

That miraculous light from the stained glass was lying over the expanse of white, a brilliant splash of color, and she knew in that instant exactly what she wanted to paint.

Something had always been missing from this series of paintings and she'd had difficulty pinning down exactly what it was, hoping it would come to her in the end. Now she knew.

Lucas had told her he couldn't give her what she wanted, but he didn't need to give it to her. She could create it for herself, pour all that sharp, raw hunger onto the canvas in front of her. Bring it to life in a way that wouldn't involve him physically and that would finally get it out of her.

And perhaps once it was, she could finally kick this fascination with him once and for all.

Grace stalked over to the corner where she had all her art supplies and picked up a couple of brushes and a few tubes of paint. Taking them back to the canvas, she put them down, then lifted her hands to her hair and wound it in a tight knot, sticking a brush through the center of it to keep it in place. Then she picked up one of the tubes of paint.

Okay. It was time to start.

Time passed, she wasn't aware of how long.

She painted with brushes, with sponges, and with her hands, liking to get tactile with her colors, layering one shade on top of another, sometimes blending, sometimes smudging. Pouring out the tangle of emotions inside her onto the canvas, letting the art take her where it wanted to go.

After a while, she became aware of a loud, electronic buzzing sound that rang throughout the apartment, and it took her a minute or two to remember that it was the buzzer for the front door.

Crouched down before the canvas, Grace sat back on her heels and frowned. Who the hell was at the front door? No one knew they were here.

The sound rang again, more persistent this time.

She rose to her feet, irritated at being interrupted, and picked up a rag to wipe her hands on. Then she went out of the studio and started down the stairs, getting halfway before she remembered that anyone ringing the buzzer on Lucas's front door was unlikely to be anyone friendly.

Because, of course, she was currently being hunted by international arms dealers who wanted their money back.

The buzzing sound came a third time, making unease coil in her chest.

Okay, no need to panic. Lucas had told her not to let anyone in who wasn't him, so she wouldn't. She probably shouldn't answer the door either. Then again, maybe it was Lucas and he couldn't get in for some reason. The front door had a camera, though, which meant she could check to see who it was without giving away the fact that she was here at least.

The screen was in the entranceway by the elevator, the buzzing noise of the doorbell coming again as she approached. Trying to swallow past the icy knot of trepidation, Grace flicked on the screen.

A cop was standing on the doorstep.

She blinked, the knot untying itself and relief filling her. All right, so it was a cop, not some insane arms dealer bent on taking her hostage. She could cope with that.

Then that damn knot tied itself up again as she realized there was probably a reason there was a cop standing on Lucas's doorstep and it was unlikely to be anything good.

As if on cue the cop raised his hand and pressed the button yet again, glancing up at the camera as if he knew she was watching.

Her pulse began to get faster. God, what if something had happened to Lucas? What if he was hurt or worse? What if he wasn't coming back?

A peculiar feeling turned over inside her. Fear and a strange kind of grief, which was weird, since hadn't she decided she hated him?

She swallowed again. Lucas had been clear with his warnings. Don't open the door to anyone who wasn't him. Yet this was a cop and what if something was wrong? What if Lucas had had an accident on his bike?

Her hand was shaking as she lifted her finger and pressed the button on the intercom. "Yes?"

The cop was wearing mirrored aviator shades and she couldn't see his eyes as he stared up at the camera. "Afternoon, ma'am. Are you a relative of Mr. Lucas Tate?"

Oh God . . .

Fear slid icy fingers around her heart. "Why? What's wrong? Has something happened to him?"

"If you could just open the door, ma'am."

"Tell me what's happened first. Is he okay?"

"Open the door please, ma'am."

The fear squeezed tighter, making her go cold all over. "Has something happened to him? Is he hurt?"

"Please open the door, ma'am."

Her heartbeat was thudding, her breath getting shorter. "Do you have some ID?"

The cop reached into his pocket and pulled out a wallet, flipping it open and lifting it to the camera so she could see. It was enough for her. She lifted a shaking finger to the button that would unlock the door.

Then, so fast she barely had time to react, a shadow appeared behind the cop and a hand came down on his head in a hard, brutal blow. As the cop slumped, a powerful arm caught him around the waist, holding him upright, then another face appeared on the screen. Lucas.

Relief flooded through her, instinctive and strong, making her knees feel weak for a second. Then her brain kicked into gear. Did he just knock a cop out?

Lucas was staring at the camera, his beautiful face absolutely hard, reaching for the intercom button with the heel of his free hand, his long fingers wrapped around that lethal-looking gun of his. Then his cold, deep voice flooded through the apartment. "Open the fucking door, Grace."

She didn't bother questioning him, hitting the button that unlocked the door, then backing away from the elevator, her heartbeat going like a rocket in her chest.

A minute or so later, the elevator doors opened and Lucas stepped out, the unconscious cop in his arms.

Without a word he hauled the man over to the white couch, then dumped him on it without any ceremony at all. Then he lifted his head and looked at her. Lucas's face was a frozen mask, a thunderstorm in the air around him, gathering tight and dense and threatening. Making her want to back away from him.

"You were going to open the door, weren't you?" If his voice had been a razor it would have cut her to pieces where she stood. "What did I tell you about not opening the door to anyone?"

"He's a cop. I thought—"

"He's not a cop."

Grace tried to calm herself down and failed. "What? But he showed me some ID."

Lucas pulled something out of the pocket of his jeans and tossed it onto the couch beside the man's unconscious body. It was the cop's wallet. "The ID is fake."

"But how—"

"I saw this guy pull in a couple of yards up the street." Lucas's gaze glittered very blue. "He wasn't driving a cop car. So I followed him to be sure, and he came straight here. Then he asked about me by name and I knew he wasn't a cop. No one knows I live here. No one."

Reaction was beginning to set in, making her feel shaky. Jesus, she thought he'd been a real police officer. She'd been going to let him in.

Lucas's attention dipped to her hands and then he moved toward her, coming fast, leaving her no time to back away or avoid him. He took her fingers in his hands, looking down at them. "Are you okay? What's this on your fingers?"

The usual electricity sparked as soon as his skin touched hers, jangling her over-stressed nerves and making her jerk away from his touch. "It's nothing, only paint."

He didn't move away. Instead his eyes narrowed and, to her shock, he reached up and cupped her face between his hands, tilting her head back, his blue gaze roaming over her. "You've been crying. What's wrong?"

His palms were so warm against her cheeks, making her breath catch and her frantically racing heartbeat race even faster. "I haven't been crying."

He frowned. "Yes, you have. Your eyes are red."

Oh great. Just fucking wonderful. He *would* have to notice. "It's just grief, okay?" And it wasn't a lie. She'd been mourning Griffin and the marriage they should have had.

Lucas was silent a moment, his blond brows drawn down. Then he said quietly, "You've got paint on your cheek." His thumb moved, a light brush along her cheekbone, sending tiny sparks chasing over her skin.

She couldn't move. Couldn't even breathe. The heat of his hands and the sudden deep blue of his eyes held her motionless. Her awareness began to narrow, zeroing in on him, the rest of the world fading away. He was so tall, his body all hard, lean strength and lethal power, and for a second, standing so close to him, all she felt was safe. Protected. As if nothing could ever touch her as long as he was here.

Then the expression in his eyes changed and his hands dropped. He stepped away, putting some distance between them. "You stay here," he said curtly. "I need to deal with this asshole."

Her throat had gone tight and she could feel the imprint of Lucas's hands lingering on her skin, the warmth of his touch glowing there like a ray of sunshine. "Okay." The word sounded thick and husky. "What are you going to do with him?"

"Ask him a few questions." Lucas had gone back over to where the fake cop was laid out on the couch, still unconscious, and as Grace watched he bent and hauled the man up and over his shoulder in a stunning display of strength. "I've got a place in the basement I'm going to put him until he wakes up." Lucas went over to the elevator, moving as if he weren't carrying an unconscious man over one shoulder, and hit the button. As the doors opened, he gave her one brief intense glance. "Whatever you do, don't open the door to anyone else, understand?"

Then he stepped into the elevator and was gone.

Lucas was not happy.

He'd been out all day, leaving the apartment before Grace had woken up, because even though he was perfectly in control of himself, after that kiss the day before he'd thought it would be better if they both had some time apart.

After meeting with the Tate contact who'd been trying to track down the pricks after Grace and finding precisely nothing, he'd made his way back to the apartment, only to spot the fake cop heading in the same direction.

His military instinct had kicked in right then, telling him something wasn't right about the guy, and when the cop had gone straight to the front of the apartment building Lucas had *known* there was something not right about him. Especially when he'd then asked about Lucas by name.

Lucas hadn't thought twice. He'd acted. Simply stepping up behind the guy, knocking him out, and hauling him inside.

As the elevator made its way down to the basement, an emotion Lucas hadn't allowed himself to feel for years stirred inside him, heavy and slow, like an animal waking up from a long hibernation.

Fury.

Clever to dress up like a cop. Grace had been all ready to let this fucker in, no matter what Lucas had told her about strange people coming to the door. Though it wasn't entirely fair to be angry at her, not when she wouldn't have known the prick was a fake.

Christ, if he hadn't been here and she'd let that asshole

in they would have found her. They would have taken her. They would have *hurt* her.

Fury turned over and over inside him, twisting and tangling like a cut snake.

In fact, seeing red all over her fingers, he'd initially thought she'd been hurt somehow, and even though he'd told himself he was going to stay away from her, he hadn't been able to stop from going over to her and taking those long, slender fingers in his, wanting to check there was nothing wrong for himself. But it was fine, only paint like she'd said. Then he'd noticed her eyes were red, as if she'd been crying, and he'd stupidly taken her face between his palms, a tightness in his chest he couldn't get rid of. There had been fear in her eyes, he could see the lingering traces of it, and shock too, and she'd been a little pale, her freckles like tiny stars on her skin. A red stripe of paint stained one cheekbone and he hadn't been able to keep from stroking along it, wondering what she'd been painting and whether it was that last canvas she'd been so anxious about.

Fuck, everything about that moment had been wrong, especially given the situation and the fact that their cover looked like it had been blown. The very last thing he should have been concerned about was what she'd been painting or the fact that she looked like she'd been crying.

He'd had to force himself to let her go, to bring his attention back to the problem at hand. Which was the fact that these bastards had somehow tracked them to his apartment and had been trying to get in.

Lock it down, dick. You can't afford to lose control now.

Lucas gritted his teeth as the elevator chimed. Yeah, fuck, there was no reason to be this furious. Okay, so they'd somehow found his bolt-hole, but Grace was fine. Nothing had happened to her. And nothing would, because he was going to find out all he could from this asshole, then he'd keep him prisoner so it wouldn't get back to whoever had sent him here.

The doors opened and Lucas stepped out into the short hallway that led to his private shooting range. It was the perfect place to put assholes who should have known better than to come directly to his home and start trying to talk their way inside, because it was heavily soundproofed, not to mention that its locks were electronic and industrial-strength, so no one was going to get either in or out, not if he didn't want them to.

Lucas unlocked the door and stepped inside, hitting the lights. Then he dumped the fake cop onto the concrete floor before going into the small room off to the side that contained his personal armory, plus any other equipment a SEAL might need to keep himself in top condition. Finding some cable ties, he took them back over to where he'd left the fake cop and rolled him onto his stomach, securing his hands behind his back and tying his ankles together. Then he rolled the guy onto his back again and straightened, looking down at him.

Lucas had thought the prick's face was vaguely familiar and now he knew where he'd seen him before; he'd been one of the lookouts Lucas had spotted watching Tate Oil. So whoever was after Grace had managed to find Lucas's apartment and had obviously sent this asshole to check it out, which was a bit of a fucking worry, because no one had been more careful than Lucas about his movements to and from the apartment.

Did they know Grace was here for certain or were they still trying to find that out? And how the hell had they found the apartment in the first place? He'd been very, very certain he hadn't been tailed, so how had they known to come here?

Perhaps it was time to find out.

He reached for the gun he kept in a holster in the small of his back, pulling it out. Then he stuck the toe of his boot in the man's side. Hard.

The man groaned and his eyes opened, squinting at the harsh fluorescents.

"Who are you?" Lucas kept his voice clear and very, very cold. "And what the fuck are you doing here?"

The man blinked, focusing on Lucas. Then he let out a breath. "Wouldn't you like to know?"

Lucas casually extended his arm and aimed his SIG Sauer at the guy's arm. Then he fired.

The fake cop jerked, then bellowed, the sound of pain echoing off the concrete walls around them.

"Calm down," Lucas ordered flatly. "It was a clean shot through your upper arm. I even missed the muscle."

"You crazy fucker." The guy's teeth were bared, pain glittering in his eyes. "You think shooting me up is going to make me tell you anything?"

"I don't know, will it?" Lucas shifted the muzzle of his SIG down, to the man's left kneecap. "You know who I am. You know what I do. You probably even know my confirmed kill count. Which means you know that I'll shoot your kneecap off without a second's hesitation if you don't tell me what I want to hear. So, let's try this again. What the fuck are you doing here?"

The man panted, his gaze settling on the muzzle of the gun pointed at him. "They'll kill me if I tell you anything."

"And I'll kill you if you don't. *After* I've shot your kneecap off."

Fake Cop's features twisted. "Do it then. Better than what they'll do to me."

Fuck, this was the last thing he needed. A man with nothing to lose, who didn't give a shit about pain.

Lucas thought for a second, then he said, "Tell me what I want to know and I'll organize for the police to ready a nice safe jail cell for you. Or, I guess, you could try and take your chances on the run. I wonder how you'd do?" He tilted his head, holding the other man's gaze. "With your employers on your tail for fucking up and without a knee-cap." He shifted the muzzle of the SIG to the man's other leg. "Or maybe without two."

Fake Cop grimaced but said nothing. Blood was starting to pool under his arm, which was a nuisance. Especially if it made a mess and stained the concrete.

"By the way, you have ten seconds to answer," Lucas added, his patience running uncharacteristically low.

"Asshole," the man spat.

Lucas ignored him, keeping his gun aimed at the man's knee. "Seven seconds. Six, five, four, three—"

"Fuck, okay." Fake Cop heaved in a breath. "This address was given to me as a place to check out to see if the woman was here."

"Who gave you the address?" Lucas asked sharply. "How did they find it?"

"I don't fucking know how they found it. You think they tell me shit like that?" The man twisted onto his side, groaning slightly in pain. "The guy who gave it to me was Oliveira. That's the only name I know."

The name meant nothing to Lucas, but he filed it away for future reference. "Why are they looking for me?"

"Because you were seen with the woman." The man spat on the floor. "They know you were a friend of Riley's and they know you're protecting her."

"She's got nothing to do with that deal of Riley's."

The man lifted a shoulder. "They don't give a shit. They just want their money back."

"She doesn't have the money."

"Like I said. They don't care. If she doesn't have it then they'll use her to get it from someone who does."

Briefly Lucas debated whether putting a bullet through

the man's leg would help matters, then decided that was his fury talking. Besides, he was starting to have an inkling of an idea about how he could finish this once and for all.

At that moment, his phone began buzzing. Keeping his attention on his prisoner, Lucas grabbed it out of his pocket, then glanced down at the screen. It was Van. Shit. The timing was extremely crappy, but given what was going down with his brother right now, he couldn't afford to ignore the call.

Lucas hit the answer button. "What is it?"

Ten minutes later, the conversation with his brother having kicked him fully into military mode, Lucas did a brisk field dressing on his prisoner's arm, made sure he was safely tied up, then left him locked in the shooting range before heading to the elevator.

Lucas's idea and what he was going to do with the asshole would have to wait, since there was a crisis unfolding right now that concerned his adoptive sister, Chloe. All of the Tates—Chloe included—had always thought she was the blood daughter of Noah Tate. But it had turned out she was actually the daughter of their father's enemy, Cesare de Santis. And now he'd kidnapped her and Van, who was supposed to be protecting her, needed help with planning a rescue.

The revelation of Chloe's true parentage, not to mention that the de Santis bastard was also involved with all this shit that was happening with Griffin, did not help Lucas's mood. That guy needed taking down, which was clearly something Van and Wolf and he were going to have to address once this current crisis was out of the way.

Upstairs, he found Grace in the kitchen, leaning back against the counter with a cup of coffee held between her narrow paint-stained fingers. She straightened and put the cup down the instant he came in, the anxiety in her amber gaze fading, to be replaced by what looked like relief. Which was strange, since why the hell she'd be worried about him, especially after yesterday, he had no idea.

"What's happening?" She interlaced her fingers and clasped her hands to her chest, bracelets chiming. "What did that man say?"

She wore a white, paint-stained T-shirt and dark blue leggings with holes in them today, her hair in a knot on the top of her head and held there with what looked suspiciously like a paintbrush. There was nothing special about what she wore, nothing that should have made his heartbeat speed up. Nothing that should have made his breath get short and his muscles tighten.

But somehow the paint-smeared simplicity of the clothes only drew attention to her vivid face. To the way her skin seemed to glow in the fading light coming through the kitchen windows. To the white cotton stretched across her small, perfect tits and to the length of her legs in those ridiculous leggings.

There was paint on her cheek and on her fingers and for one intense, crazy moment, he wanted it on himself too. Wanted her to paint color all over his skin just to see what it would feel like. To have all her bright, vibrant energy touching him.

But even if he'd been able to have that there was no time now. And he wasn't able to have that in any case.

"I'll have to tell you later." His voice sounded stiff and harsh even to his own ears. "Right now I have to leave."

Her eyes widened, real fear chasing through them. "But what about that guy? What if anyone else shows up here?"

"He won't hurt you. He's locked up downstairs and there's no way he can get out." Lucas held her gaze. "Believe me, I wouldn't leave if I thought there was even the slightest risk to you. But my brother needs me and I have to go."

She blinked, then nodded, her throat moving as she swallowed. "Okay, but what about if anyone else comes?"

"They won't. They don't know you're here. That guy was sent as a reconnaissance, and since he's staying right where I put him, your location is not going to get back to them."

She gave another little nod, then let out a long breath, visibly trying to settle herself, and when she spoke again her voice was steadier. "And if anyone comes to the door?"

"You don't let them in. Even if it's the fucking President, understand?"

"Yes, I understand. . . ." She paused. "Do you have a spare gun or something? You know, just in case someone gets in?"

Jesus, was she serious? Yes, apparently she was.

He raised a brow. "Do you know how to use a gun?"

"No." Color rose in her cheeks. "But point and shoot, right?"

A sudden vision came to him, of Grace Riley in a paint-stained T-shirt and leggings, holding a gun and pointing it at some asshole's face, one long finger curled around the trigger.

Fucking hot.

A muscle in his jaw ticked and he shoved the vision away. Because it shouldn't be hot, yet his cock was definitely intrigued by the idea, and he had no time for that bullshit. "It's not quite that simple. If I had time I'd show you, but I don't, so don't worry about that now. Besides, no one can get in here. I made sure the place was like Fort Knox."

Her hands clasped tighter against her chest, but all she did was nod once again. "Okay. I'm sure it'll be fine in that case."

She was being brave, and he wanted to go over there, take her knotted hands between his, stroke them, make them relax, reassure her that it would be okay, and he didn't even know why. Because when had her feelings become important to him? When had they begun to matter? She was very alone, was Grace Riley. Only a few friends and a mother she never spoke to. A vibrant woman like Grace needed more than that . . .

Christ, he needed to get his head back in the game and not be standing there thinking about her.

Ignoring the urge to take her hands in his, he merely looked at her, hoping she'd read some reassurance in his gaze. "No one's going to hurt you, Grace. I promise."

She stared back at him for a long moment, the expression in her eyes unreadable. Then she glanced away. "Okay," she murmured simply.

He found that vaguely unsatisfying for some reason, but every second he spent here talking to Grace was another second he wasn't helping his brother, and right now that was more important, so he turned to go.

"Lucas."

He stopped in the doorway but didn't turn. "What?"

"Don't be too long."

CHAPTER TEN

Grace couldn't settle for the rest of the evening. There was a man locked up in the basement and Lucas wasn't here and she felt. . . . yeah, okay, she could admit it. She felt scared.

For the past couple of days, what with her painting and that damn kiss, she'd been ignoring the elephant in the room: namely that her husband had essentially been some kind of criminal and now some very, very bad people were after her.

And while she'd been so wrapped up in painting and fighting her attraction to Lucas, those people had been concentrating on tracking her down and now were very close to finding out where she was.

She didn't know what to do. She wanted to help Lucas in some way, but she had no idea how. It wasn't as if she were a highly trained military-type person with lethal skills or anything. She was only an artist who could wield a mean paintbrush, it was true. But short of stabbing someone with it, that really wasn't going to help.

As the evening crept by, she paced up and down in front of the big stained-glass window, her mind going around and around. Thinking about Lucas. Thinking about Griffin.

She should have paid more attention while they'd been married. He had so many secrets he'd kept from her, but she hadn't even noticed he had them. She hadn't even noticed his unhappiness. She'd been so caught up in her own stuff. With her art. With wanting to prove her father wrong, that she *wasn't* a talentless waste of time. That she was *good*.

Maybe if she hadn't been so single-minded, so blinkered by her creative urges, she might have seen what was going on with Griffin. That he was unhappy.

What would you have done if he was, though? Did you even care that much about your marriage?

That was an uncomfortable thought and one she didn't want in her head. It was wrong anyway. She'd loved Griffin and wanted to marry him. He'd been one of the few people who'd been supportive of her art and for that alone she would have done anything for him.

That's not the same as love.

Unease twisted inside her, making her turn away from the window. All this pacing around was doing her no favors and it wasn't helping Lucas. Then again, there wasn't anything else she could do to help Lucas except stay out of sight, so she might as well do something productive instead of brooding.

She went upstairs again and back into the studio, trying to lose herself in the painting, but for some reason it was hard work and she couldn't concentrate. She kept listening for strange noises and jumping at the sounds of sirens in the city outside. A part of her wanted to go down into the basement or wherever it was that Lucas was keeping the fake cop and ask him her own questions. But she knew that would be the height of stupidity, so she stayed where she was, dabbing paint on her canvas and trying to focus.

An hour later, Lucas arrived back and the muscles in her shoulders she didn't realize were tight abruptly relaxed. She came out of the studio, telling herself she wanted to make sure it was actually him and not some other strange man who'd somehow gotten access to the apartment, and it had nothing to do with the fact that she just wanted to see him.

He was heading toward the stairs when she appeared, halting at the bottom of them and looking up at her. His silver-blue gaze was as cold as it usually was, yet he scanned her from head to foot, sharp and focused as an X-ray machine. "You okay? Any problems?"

She shook her head. "Nope. All quiet here."

"Good."

"Everything okay with your brother?" No, she wouldn't ask for details. No, she wasn't curious.

"He's handling it." His gaze drifted over her again and a hot, shivery feeling cascaded through her. But all he said was, "I need to go visit our uninvited guest."

"Ah. Well, perhaps I could come and—"

"No. You're not going anywhere near him."

Grace didn't know whether to feel annoyed at Lucas's arrogance or flattered at his protectiveness. "I just thought I might be able to ask some things about Griffin."

"This guy won't know. He's a minor cog in a very big machine." Lucas turned away. "Leave this to me."

All of a sudden she didn't want him to go. "I thought we were going to talk about this."

He didn't even pause, heading back toward the elevator. "We will. Once I've managed to get some more info."

Grace swallowed, watching as he stepped into the elevator, battling the urge to simply straight up ask him to stay. But that would give away far too much and she wasn't ready to do that. So she said nothing as the doors closed, turning and going back to the studio.

She tried to get back into her work, but her concentration was shot, so she had a bath, then watched some TV. Lucas didn't appear and she didn't want it to look like she was simply hanging around waiting for him—even though she was—so she gave up and went to bed.

The next morning she slept in, and once again he wasn't around. There was a text on her phone waiting for her, telling her he'd gone out to help his brother again and he didn't know when he'd be back. Which was annoying, though she didn't know why, since it was easier to work when he wasn't around.

Irritated, she made herself a coffee, went back upstairs, and very purposefully flung herself into her work.

For some reason it was better today and she was able to concentrate, the feeling she wanted coursing through her as she began to apply the paint to the canvas. Lots of reds and oranges and golds. The colors of passion, of intensity. Of anger. Of lust . . .

A couple of hours passed.

Grace put her brush down and began to use her fingers, playing with the paint to get some texture, some movement, some life. Layering on more color as the feeling grew inside her, hot and electric.

The grief and the never-ending questions about Griffin faded. The threat to her life disappeared. There was only her and the hot current of emotion that flowed down her arms and came out through her fingers, into the paint. Onto the white space of the canvas.

More time passed, but she wasn't paying attention. And there came a moment when she sat back, considering the beginnings of the painting in front of her. There was something it needed, maybe. Blue. Silver-blue—

Abruptly the door to the studio banged open and it gave her a shock, making her jump, her heart in her throat.

Lucas stood on the threshold and there was the oddest look on his beautiful face. The air around his tall, powerful form was full of tension, like a thunderstorm about to break.

She blinked. If she hadn't known already what an icy, emotionless guy he was she might have thought that he was . . . angry.

There was no silver in his gaze at all. It was burning blue, like the night he'd kissed her, so full of intense heat it made her wonder how she'd ever thought of his eyes as cold.

Her mouth dried, her heartbeat accelerating as she slowly rose to her feet, her hands sticky with paint.

Something had happened. Something had finally affected him. What the hell had it been?

Lucas said nothing for one long, vibrating second, then he stalked toward her, holding something in his hand. His phone. "Look at this," he ordered brusquely, shoving the screen at her.

She held up her hands. "Not if you don't want paint all over it."

He bit off a curse, stabbed at the screen with his finger, then held it up so she could see. It was a short bit of video showing two people, one very tall man and a much smaller woman, standing together near what looked like the ice rink at Rockefeller Center. As she watched, the man reached out and took the woman's face between his palms, tilting her head back and covering her mouth with his in a passionate kiss. It was night, but the lights around the rink made the faces of the man and the woman clear, though Grace didn't recognize them. The video zoomed in, getting a close-up of that kiss, lingering on the couple in a way that made her uncomfortable. It was clearly a deeply private, passionate moment and not one meant for anyone else.

Lucas stabbed at the button again, stopping the video. The air of tension around him grew even tighter, that thunderstorm gathering around him gathering around her too. His gaze met hers and she felt the impact echo through her almost as a physical blow.

"I don't understand," she began, because she didn't. "Who are those—"

"My foster brother and my foster sister." His voice was utterly flat yet at the same time vibrating with a strange kind of intensity she'd never heard in it before. "He's screwing with her and he shouldn't. It's fucking wrong, that's what it is. Just fucking wrong." He turned away abruptly, and before Grace could speak he tossed the phone carelessly onto the floor, the glass screen cracking.

Her breath caught. Okay, so he really was angry. Angry enough that she could read it loud and clear on his normally expressionless face.

"Lucas," she began, then stopped as he rounded on her, the look in his eyes blazing.

"Van always does the right thing." There was a rough edge in his deep, cold voice. "He's the oldest, he's supposed to set a fucking example."

"Okay, I get that." She didn't, but her instinct was to try to calm him. He was agitated, every movement sharp and jerky, as if he didn't know what to do with himself.

"No," he snapped. "No you don't." Then his gaze was on hers again, intensifying, sharpening. "I deny myself. All the time, I deny myself." He took a step toward her. "I keep everything locked down, make sure nothing gets out. I want to do the right thing, Grace. I want to keep everyone safe."

She had no idea what he was talking about, but he was advancing on her, slowly stalking her, and it was purely instinct that had her backing away. The electricity coming off him was insane; he was virtually crackling with it, making the room seem very small and him seem very, very large.

"I know you do." She held up her hands, patting the air

as if that would help, a ridiculous movement. "Of course that's what you want."

"He's supposed to deny himself too. He can't just take what he wants." Lucas prowled closer and closer to her, forcing her backwards like a scared animal retreating from a much bigger predator.

"You're right, he can't," she babbled inanely, abruptly finding it difficult to breathe. "That's crazy."

"If he can't do the right thing what's the point of me even trying?" He took another few steps and she ran out of places to retreat to, her back hitting the wall. Yet Lucas didn't stop. "I'm fucking sick of denying myself. Sick of telling myself it's better if I don't want anything." His hands came down on either side of her head, his tall, powerful figure caging her, blocking out the rest of the room. The heat and intensity pouring off him were making her dizzy and she flung up her palms to hold him off, to keep him at a distance. They hit the hard wall of his chest, the paint on her hands staining the black fabric of the long-sleeved T-shirt he wore.

"Lucas," she said again, not quite sure what she wanted to say, only that he was far too close. Far too hot. Far too everything for her to cope with right now.

"Maybe it's time I stopped denying what I want." The words were full of a kind of rough, dark heat. "Maybe it's time for me to take it instead."

Grace struggled to get a breath. He was right in front of her and all the ice had dropped away from him, leaving him like a naked flame, hot and burning like a bonfire. God, she could feel how hot. Her palms where they rested on his chest felt scorched.

She trembled.

He didn't say anything else. And when she opened her mouth to speak, he simply bent and covered it with his own.

She forgot everything in that moment. His mysterious anger. The danger she was in. She even forgot about Griffin.

In that moment there was nothing but Lucas's kiss, so utterly different from the one he'd given her a few nights ago. That had been a slow kiss that tasted of denial. But this was something different. This was all about surrender to that crackling electricity, the volatile chemistry that occurred whenever they got close to each other.

It was scorching and it was raw, and at the touch of those beautiful lips on hers she ignited like the flame she was.

His tongue pushed into her mouth, arrogant and demanding, the hot slide of it making her gasp. She tipped her head back against the wall to deepen the angle, letting him take whatever he wanted, then taking in return. Exploring the heady, alcoholic flavor of him as the rest of the world fell away.

As everything fell away.

He pressed her against the wall, one hard denim-clad thigh thrusting between her legs at the same time as he thrust his tongue deeper into her mouth, and a soft, needy sound escaped her. She found herself kissing him back, frantic and feverish, tilting her hips so the tantalizingly firm muscle of his thigh pressed against her aching sex. Making her tremble even harder.

This was the storm front breaking. This was the hurricane. This was spark meeting dry tinder.

And she was desperate to lose herself in it, desperate to burn.

Her fingers curled into the fabric of his T-shirt, pulling him closer, the kiss getting hotter, hungrier, their breathing fast in the silence of the studio.

It wasn't enough. She wanted more than this. She felt like she was dying and only touching him could save her.

Letting go of his T-shirt, she slid her paint-stained fingers beneath the hem, feeling taut, hard muscle and smooth skin.

God, he felt like a work of art.

He bit off a curse as her fingers brushed over him, pulling back and jerking his T-shirt up and over his head. Then his mouth was back on hers and he was crushing her against the wall, blinding her with his heat, getting her drunk on the musky, masculine scent of him.

She couldn't stop herself from touching him, running her hands over his hot skin, tracing the sculpted corrugations of his abs, the hard planes of his chest, leaving streaks of red all over him, the paint getting everywhere. But she didn't care. She just didn't care. Not about anything but this. His kiss and his touch. The ache between her legs that was driving her insane.

She wanted him. She wanted him so desperately she was shaking.

"Lucas," she moaned against his mouth, unable to keep the need inside. "Lucas . . . *please* . . ."

He shifted his hands from the wall beside her head, and then they were all over her, sliding over the front of the old baggy T-shirt she wore when she painted, cupping her breasts through the cotton, his thumbs brushing over the achingly sensitive tips of her nipples, sending jolts of electricity through her. Making her pant. Then he pinched them and she groaned aloud, because it hurt and yet felt so damn good she almost melted in a puddle at his feet.

Then he shifted again, jerking her T-shirt up and off, tearing apart the cups of her bra and getting rid of the lacy fabric, baring her breasts. And then his hands were on them and he wasn't gentle. But she didn't want gentle. She wanted him as desperate and hungry as she was.

He stroked her, squeezed her aching flesh, pinching her nipples, his mouth leaving hers to trail down her neck in a series of small, precise bites that made her shudder and shake, a tree blown by the hurricane that was surrounding them.

She slid her hands up to his shoulders, her nails digging in, clutching him as his fingers moved to her hips, his hot, hard chest crushing her bare breasts as he forced her harder against the wall.

Someone was panting. Her. And she was moving helplessly, grinding herself against his thigh, wanting more friction, wanting to ease the terrible, relentless ache that gripped her.

He pulled away again, jerking her leggings down in a series of sharp movements, taking her panties with them, fabric tearing as he bared her completely. She shivered as the air whispered over her, wound so tight she knew she'd come as soon as he touched her. That was all it would take. One brush of his fingers between her legs and she was going to explode.

This is nothing *like it was with Griffin.*

The thought insinuated itself into her head, but then it was gone again almost instantly as Lucas's large, long-fingered hands clamped around her hips and she was being taken down onto the floor and pushed onto her back.

The bare floorboards were hard, but she barely felt them as his long, powerful body stretched over hers. She looked up into his beautiful face, shaking and shaking like she was in the grip of some fever.

And then her heart almost stopped, because his perfect features were drawn tight with hunger, fierce as a starving predator finally taking down its prey. The blue of his eyes was a gas flame, incinerating her, his hard, sculpted torso covered in smears of red, orange, and gold paint There was even some in his blond hair. Nothing remained of the ice-cold sniper, the emotionless, tightly controlled SEAL.

This man was all fire and she was fuel to the flame.

With one hand he jerked down the zipper of his jeans, and she tried to help, frantic to touch him, but he knocked her hand away. Then he was shoving her legs apart, his lean hips pushing between them, denim rubbing up against her inner thighs. Her breathing was wild, out of control, and she had to reach up to those broad, powerful shoulders again, needing to hold on to him, because she knew she was going to come apart. Any second now.

He reached down and she felt the blunt head of his cock pushing through the sensitive folds of her sex, hitting her clit, and she gasped like she'd taken a shock to the heart, the orgasm hovering right *there*.

His gaze was burning her alive, watching her intently as he rubbed himself against her, as if he knew how close she was and yet was deliberately holding the climax out of her reach. She heard herself start to plead, moving restlessly beneath him, near to screaming with frustration.

Then, just when she thought she couldn't stand it anymore, he was pushing against her, pushing into her, hard and hot and big, God, *so* big. And the orgasm was rolling over her before he was even halfway inside, flattening her beneath the weight of it, drawing a hoarse scream from her throat.

Lucas didn't stop. He kept pushing, stretching her, making her feel the burn of it, making her internal muscles clutch around him as if she were ready for more and not lying there overwhelmed by the most intense orgasm of her life. And then he made everything even more intense, gripping her hips and tilting them, sliding deeper, drawing another wordless sound from her, until he was seated as deep as he could get and she could feel him everywhere.

His breathing was hoarse, his skin shone with paint and sweat, the feral look on his face doing things to her, making her own hunger begin to ache again. Which should have been impossible, since she'd only been a one-orgasm-per-session kind of girl. But her body apparently didn't know that. And when he began to move, pulling out, then driving into her, hard and deep, and with fierce intent, the pull of another climax got even stronger.

"Lucas," she whispered raggedly. "Oh my God. . . ."

He said nothing, but the look on his face was savage, as if he were determined to wreck her, destroy her, and nothing was going to stop him. He began to thrust harder, his dog tags swinging in time with his movements and brushing against her breasts, and she found herself arching up into him, moving with him, her nails digging into the hard muscle of his shoulders. Relishing the slick slide of his cock in her sex.

Sounds escaped her, raw animal noises of pleasure as sensation wound like a clock spring inside her. So tight. Jesus Christ. When it released she was going to come apart.

Then he moved again, his hands gripping tightly to her hips, and suddenly she wasn't on the floor anymore but sitting in his lap while he remained buried deep inside her. His mouth was on hers as he yanked the paintbrush out of her hair, letting the mad, frizzy cloud of it uncurl over her shoulders, then the kiss turned savage as he flung the paintbrush away and resumed his grip on her hips, lifting her, then slamming her back down on his cock, his hips thrusting up as he did so. It made her as feral and savage as he was. She bit his lip hard, angling her hips so every time she sunk down on him, the base of his cock hit her clit.

Lucas growled, the sound electrifying, his fingers tangling in her hair and dragging her head back, exposing her throat. She gasped as he bit her, his teeth closing around the tendons at the side of her neck before moving farther down. A large, hot hand cupped one breast and then his mouth was on it, closing around one achingly sensitive nipple and sucking hard. She wailed, sliding her fingers down his back, scratching him as the pleasure became blinding, the pressure of the impending climax making her tremble.

Oh, she was going to scream when this one hit. He was going to annihilate her. He was going to leave her in pieces.

His mouth ravaged her breasts, sucking, teasing, biting. Releasing her hair, he resumed his grip on her hips, digging into the soft flesh. She was going to be left with bruises, she knew it. But that didn't matter, because he was lifting her up, then slamming her back down again, the sound of flesh meeting flesh and their frantic breathing an erotic soundtrack, the stunning heat of his body beneath her, inside her, making her feverish. Making her flame like a bonfire.

She was babbling, she could hear herself, helpless words spilling from her mouth under his and running together in a long stream.

PleaseLucasohGodpleasehardermorefasterdeeper.

She couldn't stop them, an earthquake beginning to tear her apart. And then he took his lips from hers and his hand slid between their straining, slippery bodies, his fingers finding her clit, circling, then pressing down at the same time as he thrust up. "Come, Gracie," he growled, his voice hot and rough, the voice of a stranger. "Fucking come for me."

And like her body had been holding out for precisely that command, the pressure released and she screamed, torn apart just like she thought she'd be.

Just as she hoped she'd be.

And as the pieces of her scattered in the air, she was dimly aware of him moving faster, and then came the sound of his own release, the guttural roar of it echoing in the room around them, his whole body stiffening under hers.

But she didn't have the strength to do anything more than wrap her arms around him and hold him tight as he came to pieces.

Just as she had.

Lucas turned his head into Grace's neck, feeling like a missile had exploded somewhere nearby and his head was still ringing from the blast. His pulse was thundering, his chest heaving like it was Hell Week back in Coronado. Shudders jolted him as if all his nerve endings had been hooked up to a power socket and someone kept flipping the switch, turning him off, then on again, over and over.

He could hear her panting, could feel the tight grip of her pussy around his cock, the ripples of her own orgasm wringing more sensation out of him.

It was agony. It was perfection.

Jesus . . . what had he done? What *the fuck* had he done?

He'd spent all morning helping Van rescue Chloe from Cesare de Santis's clutches and had been ready to finish that up and get back to Grace and their unwelcome visitor when he'd been called back with a curt request to take Chloe to the airport. Van wanted her out of the city and away from de Santis's clutches.

That had been fine. He didn't mind doing that. He didn't have the bond with her that Van had—she'd been far too young for him to really connect with, and besides, he didn't let himself connect with anyone anyway—yet he still felt protective toward her. She was his little foster sister, a Tate, and Tates stuck together.

Then he'd had orders from Van to drop her at Rockefeller Center instead of the airport—for what reason he'd had no idea—so he had. And not long after that, his phone had buzzed with yet another text from Van and there had been a video attached.

You'll see this eventually, Van had texted. *De Santis will post this everywhere very soon, but I wanted you to know first.*

A video of Van kissing Chloe.

The sight of that kiss had hit him like a brick to the side of his head.

His brother was supposed to be protecting her on orders of their father. His brother, the oldest, the Tate heir. His brother, the leader. Who'd been looking after him, then looking out for him, since he'd been five years old. Who was supposed to be above reproach. Who was supposed to set the example.

His brother who was screwing their foster sister.

Lucas didn't know why the sight of them had made him so furious. Sure, there was the fact that Van was meant to be keeping her safe and that did not mean fucking around with her, Lucas was pretty sure. Van was a lot older than her and way more experienced, and it was just plain wrong.

Van should have kept it in his pants and he hadn't. And in the end, it would be Chloe who'd end up getting hurt. She was young and innocent. She'd grown up in Wyoming and that was her home, whereas the Navy was Van's life. He wouldn't give that up for anyone, Lucas knew that for a fact.

But it wasn't until he'd gotten back to the apartment that he'd realized exactly why he was so pissed. It was because he too had a woman he was supposed to protect. A woman he'd been fighting his attraction to. Yet *he'd* been the good one, not Van. He'd been doing what he always did, keeping it locked down and under control.

Keeping everyone safe, like his father had taught him.

You can't let this anger of yours go again, Lucas. You can't let it control you. You have to control it, understand me? You don't want anyone else to get hurt, right?

So he had controlled it. And not just the anger, but everything else as well. He'd kept himself locked down.

Never letting himself want anything, never letting himself need anything. And that had worked and worked well, for years.

Until Grace. Until that fierce, inexplicable electricity that sizzled between them.

He'd never felt that before, not with anyone, and he hadn't liked it. Had tried to stay detached the way he always did. Because he knew what fire could do when it escaped. How it could burn and burn so hot, incinerating flesh, incinerating bone. Burning until there was nothing left but ash.

He didn't want that for Grace. It was dangerous to let that fire out for anyone, let alone a woman who was grieving and whose life was under threat.

So he'd decided to deny himself and he'd been good with that decision.

Yet he'd gone up the stairs to Grace's studio, not even sure why he was doing so, propelled by that anger at his brother, slamming open the door to find her crouched in front of that damn canvas. She had a paintbrush in her hair again, wearing a stained T-shirt and leggings, slender fingers covered in paint, and when she'd turned and looked at him her amber eyes had gone wide.

She'd never looked more desirable and he'd abruptly thought, *Fuck it. Why not?*

Why couldn't he have her? She wanted him, he knew that already, and shit, he'd been denying himself since he was thirteen years old. He'd pushed aside his own desires, ignored his own needs. Channeling everything into his career. Into the target at the other end of his rifle.

Yet it felt as if there was a pressure inside him, building and building like steam collecting against the lid of a pot of boiling water. And that if he didn't let that steam out somehow he was going to explode. Normally, when he felt like that he took his gun and shot targets, or rode his motorcycle way too fast on the freeway, or beat the shit out of a punching bag. But there was an asshole in his shooting range and his bike seemed like a poor substitute for what he actually wanted. And he really didn't want to hit anything.

Grace. He wanted her. He *wanted* her. And he'd been so good, telling himself he was stronger, that he was better. That he wasn't going to let his own desires rule him. But he was over it. He was done.

Deep inside he knew that he was simply looking for a reason to take her and that Van and Chloe were merely convenient excuses, but he wasn't going to listen to that noise anymore. He had to relieve the pressure somehow and he'd do it with her.

So he'd started walking toward her, backing her up against the wall, his cock hard and ready, his pulse going through the roof like he was twelve years old again, looking through the copies of his father's *Penthouse* magazines that Van had stolen.

He wanted her and he was going to fucking take what he wanted.

So he had. He'd gone completely feral. Taking her to the floor, all that pressure inside him escaping as he'd driven himself into the tight, wet heat of her body. He'd never felt so free. She'd been beneath him, her nails digging into his shoulders, begging and pleading, caught in the same madness as he was, and it was as if for the first time in years he was himself.

Which didn't make any sense to him yet nevertheless felt true.

Now Grace's grip on his shoulders loosened, her breathing getting slower. And he knew that the sensible thing to do since he'd released a bit of that pressure would be to get up and leave, put the fire that blazed between them back into the box it had escaped from. Pretend it was all over.

But it wasn't over. His cock was still hard, like he hadn't had the orgasm of his life, and the musky scent of sex and the soft drift of her hair over his bare shoulders were making him crazy.

Once was never going to be enough, not with Grace Riley.

She was heat and wildfire and sunlight. She was golden and glorious and *Christ* . . . He wanted her so badly. He wanted all that he could get. It would be a really bad move to indulge himself, but shit. . . . The spark had gotten out of that box and there was no putting it back in. All he could do was take his fill of her and hope it burned itself out.

She shifted on him, her hands sliding over his chest still slippery with paint. He lifted his head from her neck and met her gaze. Sitting in his lap, she was pretty much at eye level, her big amber eyes staring into his. She looked shell-shocked and not a little wrecked, which satisfied a very male part of him very much indeed.

He lifted a hand and slid it into the glory of her hair, cupping the back of her head. Then he kissed her again, sliding his tongue into her mouth, tasting coffee and sweetness and the heat that was all Grace. She responded to him without hesitation, kissing him back, giving a delicate little shudder as she did so that sent shocks through him.

Jesus, he'd never had a woman like this before. Never let himself go before. Basically because he'd never met anyone he'd wanted to let himself go with.

Grace, though, was different. She was so fucking *hot*. She'd burned the cold right out of him, gotten her color all over him—literally—and he simply couldn't bring himself to let her go.

He lifted his mouth from hers, keeping his fingers

wound tightly in her hair. "You want more?" His voice sounded roughened and cracked like he hadn't spoken in a hundred years. Or maybe a thousand.

"Yes." There was no hesitation in her at all, her own voice not sounding much better than his.

He didn't know he'd been hoping she'd say that until she did, sending a thread of sheer relief winding through him. He let his gaze drop down over her body, indulging himself totally, taking in all that bare skin covered in long smears of red and gold and orange paint. She should always be like this. Always be naked, covered in paint and sheened lightly with perspiration, her hair sticking to her forehead, her mouth red from his kisses.

"Are you sure?" He slid his hands around her and down, cupping her butt in his palms. "Because you'd better tell me right now if not."

"I want more." Her pretty little tits rose sharply as he squeezed the soft flesh in his hands and she inhaled, arching against him. "Please."

She was so responsive. So sensual. She'd opened her mouth to his as if she'd been waiting for his kiss for years and years. And then she'd put her hands on his chest and held on tight, her whole body trembling as he'd shoved his thigh between her legs, right up against the damp heat of her pussy. . . .

Time to get themselves into the shower, because as much as he loved wearing her colors, he wanted to taste every inch of her delectable naked body and he didn't particularly want to do it around a mouthful of paint.

Without a word he pulled out of her, some dim corner of his brain registering the fact that he hadn't worn a condom and that was obviously concerning. But he didn't want to think about it right now, so he didn't. Instead he rose to his feet with her in his arms and went down the hallway to the bathroom.

The shower was large and white tiled and he ran the water good and hot, getting off the rest of his clothing, then pulling her into the stall with him. At first she tried to touch him, running her artist's fingers all over his chest, but he gripped her wrists firmly and shook his head. "It's still my turn," he said brusquely before letting her go.

She made a pretty pout at that, which he ignored as he got himself a good handful of shower gel. Then he began to wash her, stroking the paint from her skin as he slid his hands all over her body. Stroking those small, perfect tits and rubbing his thumbs over her nipples, easing his hands down over the shivering plane of her stomach to the tangle of red-gold curls between her thighs. She trembled as he brushed his fingers over the slick folds of her pussy, finding her hard little clit and teasing it gently with a fingertip. She gasped, clutching at his arms, her hair hanging heavy and wet over her shoulders.

"Let me t-touch you," she whispered, shaking in his arms. "Please, Lucas."

"Why?" He circled her clit again. "Don't you like this?"

"I do, but I . . . really want to touch you."

"Too bad." He pressed down on that tight bundle of nerves, drawing another gasp from her. "It's still my turn."

He played with her for a while, watching, fascinated, the expressions of intense pleasure that played over her face in response to his touch. She was so unguarded, hiding nothing from him. It made his chest feel tight. Made him want to tell her she shouldn't be so open, so honest. Shouldn't make herself so vulnerable, and yet he liked that she was.

Was she like this with Griffin?

An odd feeling washed through him. It wasn't guilt. Sure, he'd felt drawn to Grace before Griffin had died, but he'd never done anything about it while his friend had been alive. And besides, Griffin wouldn't know. He was dead. No, this was something else. Something that felt like . . .

Jealousy.

No, that was ridiculous. He'd never been jealous in his life and he wasn't going to start now.

Ignoring the emotion, Lucas eased Grace back against the white tiles, then dropped to his knees in front of her. He wanted to taste her, tease her, drive her as crazy as she made him.

Make her forget every other man she's been with . . .

Lucas leaned forward and pressed his mouth to her stomach, tasting the water streaming over them and the faint, salty flavor of Grace herself. It was delicious, so he went lower, running his tongue down over her skin to the wet curls between her legs. She shivered, her fingertips coming to settle on the sides of his head, resting there lightly.

He could feel her tension, her muscles coiled tight as if she wasn't sure about what was going to happen. It made him wonder things about her. Things about her and Griffin. But he didn't want to be thinking about stuff like that, not when he was on his knees and that delicious little pussy was right in front of him.

So he gripped the tops of her thighs, gently spreading her open with his thumbs. Yet another tremble went through her and he loved that. Loved how fast and desperate her breathing had gotten in the steamy confines of the shower.

He leaned in, licking a path straight up the middle of her sex, getting a taste of all that salty wetness, the flavor exploding on his tongue and going straight to his head like a shot of the very best alcohol money could buy. He'd meant to tease her clit a bit more, make her moan, but he couldn't help himself, leaning in farther and pushing his tongue deep inside her.

The fingertips on either side of his head tightened and

she gasped yet again, her hips lifting against his mouth. Yet it wasn't enough, so he slid one hand around the back of her thigh, then down behind her knee, urging her leg up and over his shoulder. Opening her wider so he could taste her deeper.

"Lucas. . . ." His name was a desperate moan as she arched against the tiles, holding his head in a death grip as he worked her with his tongue, fucking her with it. "God . . . it's . . . I can't . . ."

But he wasn't listening. He was lost in her. In her salty/ sweet taste, in her heat. In the way her body shuddered and shook as she got close to the edge. In how badly he wanted her to scream his name as she went over it.

So he kept his mouth right where it was and brought his fingers into play. Stroking her clit, circling and teasing in time with the thrust of his tongue. And it didn't take very long before her whole body went stiff, and indeed, she screamed his name as the climax took her.

He was very tempted to push himself inside her right there in the shower, but he really needed a condom and there were some in the nightstand beside his bed. So he turned off the water and gathered her lax body up in his arms, stepping out of the shower with her. Then he dried them both off before carrying her down the hallway to his bedroom.

It was very plain and white, just how he liked it, the bed, a couple of nightstands, and a dresser the only furniture. He carried her over to the bed and laid her on the mattress, following her down onto it.

She put her arms over her head, spreading her legs for him as if he were a lover she'd known for years and was comfortable with instead of her husband's friend with whom she'd had an awkward relationship.

Another example of how she simply embraced what she felt without questioning, without restraint.

You could learn something from her.

He already had. He was embracing what he felt right now, in fact.

Reaching for the condoms in the nightstand, he took one out and got the packet open, rolling the latex down over his aching dick. Then he spread her thighs wider with his hands, pushing them as far apart as he could. She inhaled sharply as he did so and again he saw something that looked like uncertainty in her eyes. But he was too hard to wait, to think about what it was and what might have put it there, so he stretched himself over her, his hands on either side of her head, looking down into her eyes so all she saw was him.

Then, holding her gaze, he pushed inside her, going slowly this time, wanting to relish it and not gorge himself the way he had before. But she was so tight around him. So wet. So hot. Her pupils had dilated, looking black in the dim light of the room, and when she lifted her hands to him, trailing her fingertips over his chest, he was the one who shuddered.

It felt like she'd run them over his soul and it was too much. She was too hot. She was like holding a flame in his bare hands.

He thrust once, twice, then pulled out of her and flipped her over onto her front. Gently he took her wrists in his hands and drew them behind her, holding them in the small of her back with one hand. He couldn't have her touching him, not like that.

Keeping her wrists pinned, he wrapped his other arm around her waist and pulled her up onto her knees. She was shaking, her head turning to the side on the pillow. "Lucas . . ." Her voice sounded strained. "I don't know . . . I don't know if I can do this again."

He guided himself between her thighs, finding her slick flesh, sliding in deep, making her jerk against his hold, gasping. "You can." The words were guttural, torn from him. "You will."

Then he began to move, pulling his hips back and thrusting in, harder, faster, the pleasure beginning to build, annihilating.

She groaned. Her eyes had closed, her lashes resting on her deeply flushed cheeks, her mouth open. "I can't. . . ." It was a mere whisper. "I can't. . . ."

But of course she could. She'd come with him every step of the way since and she'd be with him now. He reached around with his free hand, putting it on her stomach and then sliding it down between her thighs, finding her clit and stroking, a slow back-and-forth that drew a hoarse scream from her.

And he kept moving, kept pushing in deep, lost in the heat of her pussy around him, in the pleasure that was ripping him apart. Kept touching her until she bucked and arched beneath him, screaming her climax into the pillow.

Only then did he let himself go, driving himself into her, faster, harder. And just before his own orgasm completely destroyed him, he had the oddest thought.

When he was young he'd thought Heaven was the wide-open spaces of Wyoming. Going camping with his brothers or shooting his new rifle. Then, after the stable fire, he'd never thought about it again, not even when he'd gotten older and joined the forces, facing death on the most desperate missions. But right now in this bed, buried deep in her heat, her cries in his ears, he thought that Heaven might be here, in this moment.

With Grace wrapped all around him.

CHAPTER ELEVEN

Grace opened her eyes to find herself lying on her back with a heavy male arm lying over her stomach. And she had a moment's disorientation thinking that the arm had to belong to Griffin, because she'd never slept with any other guy, so who else's could it be?

Then she realized that this wasn't her bedroom in the apartment she'd shared with Griffin, which meant the arm across her wasn't Griffin's. And anyway, Griffin was dead . . .

A sudden influx of memory caught at her. She'd been painting in her studio and then Lucas had come in and—

Oh God. *Lucas.*

She turned her head on the pillow and sure enough, the man lying next to her wasn't dark or built like a boxer. He was long and lean, and muscled like a panther. He was also blond, the gray winter light coming through the windows tipping his hair nearly silver, his beautiful face relaxed in sleep.

Shock moved slowly through her as memories of the night before began to filter through her consciousness. Of his mouth on her in the shower, the water streaming over her body as he'd tasted her, making the intense pleasure unfurl inside her. And then later, in his bed, on her knees with him behind her, holding her wrists in the small of her back as he'd thrust into her, his fingers between her thighs, playing her like an instrument made especially for him.

She hadn't thought he could possibly wring another orgasm from her, not after she'd had three already, and she'd told him so.

Apparently, she'd been wrong.

You've been wrong about a lot of things, haven't you?

Heat moved through her and she looked away from him, guilt and embarrassment following along in its wake.

Not only was it possible for her to have a fourth orgasm in a row, it was also completely possible for her to be so hungry for a man that she wanted him to give her another one. Preferably soon. Even right now.

She hadn't ever thought of herself as that type of woman. Not that it was bad, she'd just convinced herself that sex wasn't that big of a deal. Pleasant when it happened, but nothing to crave like she needed air to breathe.

Maybe you just weren't that type of woman with Griffin.

Her cheeks heated even further, guilt twisting inside her like an eel on the end of a fishing line. There was no denying it, she hadn't felt this way with Griffin, not even a bit of it. She'd liked him a lot, and when he'd died she'd felt the sorrow of it like an arrow in her chest. But . . . he'd never taken her down onto a hard wooden floor and made her scream. Nor had he knelt at her feet in the shower and licked her like an ice cream. He'd never taken her from behind either, and she had a horrible feeling that if he'd done any of those things she would have pushed him away. She would have said no.

But she hadn't said no to Lucas. She definitely hadn't treated him like a friend. She'd put her arms around his neck and kissed him back. She'd screamed his name. She'd let him do whatever he wanted to her.

You'd never say no to him.

The guilt inside her twisted tighter, another thread of unease twisting with it. If Lucas had come to her the way he had yesterday, while Griffin was still alive, would she still have given in as easily? Would she have been unable to say no then too?

She swallowed, not wanting to think about that.

Because you know the answer. Selfishness runs in your family, don't you know. . . .

Grace took a little breath. Maybe she should get out of bed, get some distance. That painting wasn't going to paint itself and she really needed to get back into it. But dammit, his arm was lying right across her, which was going to make leaving problematic if she didn't want to wake him up. . . .

Her heart raced, her body aching. She didn't want to think about Griffin, or her father, not right now. Not with Lucas so warm and so close, and fast asleep. And maybe this was a good time to just . . . look at him. See if she could figure out what it was about him that made her so desperate every time he was near.

Slowly, Grace eased his arm away from her and sat up, looking down at him. He was on his side, his blond head pillowed on his other arm, and the sheet had slipped down to his waist, leaving his magnificent torso bare.

Her breath caught. His body was beautiful, all hard-cut muscle and taut golden skin, marred here and there with the white scars of old injuries. His time in the military clearly hadn't been without incident, because she knew a bullet wound when she saw one; Griffin had had a couple himself.

On Lucas's shoulder she caught a glimpse of black lines, and closer inspection revealed the same tattoo of a skeletal frog that Griffin had had on his chest. SEAL ink. She couldn't stop herself from reaching out and tracing the outline of it, the heat of Lucas's skin burning against her fingertips as the look on his face the night before burned in her memory.

Savage. Feral. The look of a man who knew what he wanted and who was going to take it no matter what.

Her. He'd wanted her.

A shiver went through her, shaking her on a level that went deeper than merely physical. It was an earth tremor, shaking the entire foundation of who she was.

No one had ever wanted her the way Lucas had wanted her. Not with such passion. Not badly enough to cast aside the behavior of decades like a coat he'd been wearing and gotten sick of. Not badly enough that he'd looked at her like he'd die if he didn't get to touch her.

Griffin had never looked at her like that, not even when they'd first been married. Hell, if he had she would have run fast in the other direction anyway, because after years of her father's steadily worsening emotional storms Griffin's gentle, reassuring, and nondemanding interest had been exactly what she'd wanted. What she'd needed.

But after the night with Lucas, she had a horrible feeling that she'd been lying to herself for a long time.

You've been lying to Griffin too.

Yeah, and that didn't make her guilt any easier. Didn't make her want to stop touching Lucas either.

Her fingers slipped over his shoulder and she had the sudden intense urge to push him onto his back, so she did, pressing against his chest. He made a rough, sleepy noise and turned over obediently, flinging one hard, muscled arm above his head.

Grace wriggled closer to him, letting her gaze rove over him. Part of her wanted to take a moment to sketch him while he was asleep and unguarded, yet another part simply wanted to touch him. Because there was a very definite ridge pressing against the sheet where his groin was, making her cheeks feel hot and her breath get short. She curled her hand in the sheet and pulled it down over his narrow hips, then farther still until he was fully exposed. She stared, her fingers itching to touch the hard cock that jutted between his muscular thighs, which was just as beautiful as the rest of him.

Had she ever wanted to touch Griffin this way? No, she really hadn't. And it wasn't because Griffin hadn't been as handsome as Lucas, since Griffin had been handsome in his own way. Sure, there was an element in her attraction that was to do with Lucas's physical beauty, and definitely their intense physical chemistry was a part of it. But there was also something more there.

She'd always been drawn to his contrasts, to the glimpses of a different man beneath the icy mask he wore. And over the past few days, she'd been further drawn to him by the way she seemed to affect him. As if she got under his skin as badly as he got under hers.

That made her feel good. Gave her a sense of her own power, something she hadn't understood before. It was almost a revelation.

So, should she grab her sketch pad or simply keep on touching him?

Grace reached out and laid a hand on his ridged abdomen, letting his heat soak into her palms. Okay, she was going to keep on touching him, because she might not get the chance again, not like this. She slid her hand down and curled her fingers around the base of his cock, watching in fascination as he seemed to get even harder.

"I hope you're going to do something about that."

Grace nearly jumped, the sound of his deep voice unexpected. She flicked a glance up at him, meeting a pair of silver-blue eyes watching her from underneath thick gold-tipped lashes.

"Oh," she said stupidly. "Good morning."

"And good morning to you." He moved, too swiftly for

her to escape, and seconds later she found herself lying stretched out on top of him, hot, firm muscle beneath her, the hard ridge of his cock lying against her thigh.

She blinked down at him. "I thought you wanted me to do something about that."

"I do." He didn't smile, yet his expression was as relaxed as she'd ever seen it. "I wanted to see how you were this morning first."

She could feel herself blushing yet again. "I'm fine."

Lucas lifted his hands to her hair, sliding his fingers through it and pushing it back from her face, his gaze sharp. "Are you sure? I didn't go easy on you last night."

Oh great. Please don't say they were going to be having a discussion about this. "I'm sure."

"Are you sore? Did I hurt you?"

"No. Like I said, I'm fine."

Yet his blond brows drew down as if the answer didn't please him for some reason. "You're not fine. Talk to me, Grace."

Talking, wonderful.

She let out a breath. "Do we have to do this right now? It certainly seems like you don't." She gave her hips a little wiggle for good measure.

He didn't react, the idiot. "I can ignore that for as long as I need to, and yes, we have to do this right now. I don't want to hurt you, you know that. Which means I need to know you're okay."

Right, so he was being a gentleman and she was being a dick and letting her own unease with this situation get in the way. She definitely didn't want him to think that he'd hurt her.

"I really am okay," she said honestly, meeting his gaze. "And I'm only a little sore."

But that frown on his face didn't shift. "You seemed afraid last night. Did I scare you?"

She let out a breath. God, she did not want to get into this, because it would mean talking about Griffin and that was the last thing she wanted to talk about. But she had a feeling Lucas wasn't going to stop pushing until he'd gotten an answer out of her.

Hell, maybe she should be honest with him.

"Maybe," she admitted. "Maybe you did scare me a bit. But I'm not sure I want to discuss the reasons why now."

He ignored that, going straight for the jugular. "Because of Griffin, right?"

She looked away, all her muscles going stiff. "If we're going to talk about this, I'm really going to need some coffee." She tried to slip off him, only for his hands to grip her hips, holding her firmly right where she was.

"If you think I'm going to let you escape just because you're uncomfortable, you can think again." His voice was flat, the silver in his eyes glinting. "I know Griffin let you get away with it, but I'm not him, understand?"

She gave Lucas a glare. She wasn't escaping. She just . . . didn't want to have this conversation. And of course she knew he wasn't Griffin.

But she couldn't deny that Lucas was right. That had been a pattern she and Griffin had gotten into. He'd want to talk about something difficult and she wouldn't, so she'd escape into her studio so she didn't have to. And he let her.

Remind you of anyone?

The knowledge sat uneasily inside her, pricking at her, making her irritable. "I know you're not Griffin," she muttered.

"So tell me the truth then. Why were you afraid of me last night?"

Jesus, he was relentless.

"I was nervous." She looked down at the broad, muscular chest beneath her and the sprinkling of crisp blond hair on it. "I've only ever slept with two men in my life,

Griffin and you. And I guess I was a little out of my depth."

His fingers were resting on her hips and she felt his thumbs begin to move on her skin, a slow back-and-forth as if he was stroking her, soothing her. It made her unease, her embarrassment and guilt, feel less tight.

"Understandable," he said. "Especially if you've never done any of that before."

It wasn't a question and it made her look up at him, feeling oddly exposed and not a little defensive. "What makes you say that?"

The stroking thumbs stopped, his focus settling on her. "Because you were uncertain and hesitant, and there really wasn't any other explanation."

Uncertain and hesitant. Great.

Her jaw tightened and she looked back down at his chest again.

Only to have one long-fingered hand catch her under the chin and tilt her face up to look at him. "That wasn't a criticism," he said quietly. "You were everything I'd hoped for, Grace. Everything I wanted."

There was warmth inside her, making the other feelings start to fade, soothing the old hurts and stings, the scars left from her father's constant criticisms. And yes, from Griffin's apparent lack of passion too, though she knew that was something she'd encouraged.

It was silly to feel so good about a simple bit of praise, and yet she did. So she looked into Lucas's eyes and gave him the rest of it. "I was scared of this feeling as well. Of what happens when you touch me. It's like being shocked awake. I've never . . . wanted anyone the way I wanted you." She took a breath. "Not even Griffin."

A flame glittered in his eyes and she knew the confession had pleased him. "You're feeling guilty about it, aren't you?" he said.

She colored. "Is it really that obvious?"

"No. Only logical."

"You don't feel guilty?"

"Griffin is dead," he said bluntly. "Which means you're not married anymore and he won't know anyway. So no, I don't feel guilty."

She looked down at his chest again, her throat tight for some reason. Nice for him that it was so cut-and-dried.

"But then," Lucas went on, "I wasn't married to him."

Grace stared at the beat of his pulse at his throat. "I know what was missing in our marriage. It was this. It was what we did last night. And I didn't understand that until now."

Lucas said nothing for a long moment. His hands slid from her hips and up her back, then down again, long, caressing movements that had her wanting to arch into his touch like a cat. He was still hard, she could feel it against her thigh, yet it didn't seem to bother him.

When he spoke, it was quiet. "It wasn't your fault."

The words shocked her for some reason. "I know it wasn't."

"Do you?" The stroking hands on her back paused. "Look at me, Gracie."

Gracie . . .

Her father had once called her that and she'd hated it, so when Griffin had tried to she'd snapped at him. But hearing that old name in Lucas's deep voice : . . It was different.

Fucking come for me, Gracie.

Oh yeah. Very, very different.

She lifted her head uncertainly, meeting his gaze. "What?" She couldn't quite keep the defensiveness out of her voice. "I *know* it's not my fault. Griffin didn't seem to feel it either. In fact, he—"

"I've had a lot of women." The blue in Lucas's eyes was

beginning to burn out the silver. "And I've never felt anything like this for a single one of them."

Her breath caught. It shouldn't matter that he hadn't, it shouldn't. "Really?" The question sounded like she was begging for reassurance, and she regretted it the instant she'd said it.

His hands paused on her back, his gaze pinning her, making her lungs feel tight, as if he'd emptied all the air out of the room. "No. In fact, I felt it the moment I saw you, Grace."

The moment he'd seen her . . . Which had been when? That day when Griffin had finally earned his trident and she'd come to the graduation. He'd pulled her over to meet his friend Lucas Tate, and she'd taken one look into those icy blue eyes and instantly hated him.

Because you wanted him too.

"Why?" she couldn't help asking, some part of her unable to let this go. "I'm not beautiful. I'm not all that interesting. My career is just a series of part-time jobs I took purely to make money, and my art is my life. I haven't really done anything else."

Lucas's gaze was sharper than a scalpel, peeling her apart. "Who's that talking? I know it's not Griffin. He made some stupid choices in his life, but he wasn't into running people down, especially not his wife."

Her throat felt tight. "What do you mean?"

"I mean, you can't possibly believe all those things about yourself." The look in his eyes became even more intense. "You're beautiful. Why do you think I was standing there staring at you that day in your room? When you opened your towel? I couldn't take my eyes off you because you were just so fucking glorious."

Her mouth opened, but he clearly hadn't finished, continuing on. "And as for your goddamned career, aren't you already doing it? You're following your dream of being an artist and that takes guts and bravery and a shitload of determination. Don't you understand that?"

She blinked, her eyes filling with stupid tears even though the last thing she wanted to do was cry. But her wounded soul was soaking up the praise like a plant that had been starved of sunlight and she couldn't help it. "I know that," she croaked yet again, because she didn't know what else to say.

But Lucas shook his head. "Who was it, Grace? Who was it that did such a fucking number on you?"

She wanted to deny it, say that of course she didn't really think she was as pathetic as she'd made out. But the words that came out weren't denial at all. "Okay, fine. I guess it was my dad." She sighed. "I'm sure it'll come as no surprise to you that he was an artist too, and was actually a pretty good one. But he had these dreams of making it big that never happened, and that ended up making him bitter and just plain old mean." She glanced down at Lucas's chest, because it was easier to talk about this when she wasn't looking directly at him. "He was very temperamental and controlling. Used to get hypercritical when the work wasn't going well, and of course he'd take it out on me and Mom, since we were the closest targets." Her finger moved, tracing a pattern on his skin. "It's funny, when I was small he taught me how to draw, and he used to love that I took after him like that. But when I got older and things got tougher money-wise, and he couldn't sell his work . . . Well, he began to pick everything I did apart. Not just my work, but *everything*. How I was so untidy. How I was hopeless at math. How I was plain. How I was talentless and wouldn't amount to anything . . ." She stopped, the hurt of it still lurking inside her like a shard of glass she couldn't ever get out.

"He sounds like an asshole who didn't know a fucking thing he was talking about." Lucas's voice was hard, his hands settling on her hips once more, fingers pressing down as if he were trying to impress his conviction into her skin. "Did you tell Griffin anything about this?"

She lifted a shoulder. "He knew Dad was difficult, but . . . I never told him about the other stuff."

The silver was back in Lucas's eyes, glittering. "Why not? And is there more stuff?"

"I didn't tell him because I don't like talking about it." She still didn't. It brought up too many bad memories. Of feeling small and ugly and talentless as the brilliant father she'd once adored sneered at her drawings and made remarks about her plainness as if he'd never once tossed her and caught her in the air the way he'd done when she was small. Never once called her his pretty little sunset.

"What other stuff, Grace?"

She looked at him. "Why do you want to know all of this? Why does it matter to you? It's got nothing to do with last night."

"It matters to me because I don't like the idea of you basing your self-worth on some bullshit your asshole father told you."

"I'm not." She was sounding defensive now and she knew it. "I'm not that pathetic."

His fingers pressed down even harder on her. "Tell me about it, Gracie." Then he added, intensity burning in his voice, "I want to know about you. I want to know everything."

Grace's amber eyes widened and he wondered if he'd gone too far, said too much. But he hadn't been able to help himself. The hunger he'd felt the night before was still just as strong, just as relentless. And it wasn't purely physical anymore.

He'd woken up to find her cool fingers curled possessively around his cock and initially he'd thought there was nothing he wanted more than her hands on him and very possibly her mouth.

But first he'd wanted to check she was okay after last night, and things had gotten thorny after that. Or rather, not so thorny. He'd realized that although he wanted her hands on him, he also wanted to know why she'd gotten all embarrassed the moment he'd starting asking her questions. Why she'd been nervous when he'd dumped her on the bed the night before. What had been happening with Griffin . . .

Yes, all of it.

He wanted to know everything. And he especially wanted to know why her confidence was such a fragile, brittle thing that she'd thought the lack of passion in her marriage was her fault. Because it was clear to him that she did think that.

And yes, knowing that was more important than how hard his cock was and how badly he wanted her to do something about it. Sure, he'd lost it with her the night before, but now it was time to get that fucker under control.

Her lashes lowered, a red-gold veil over her amber eyes. "Okay, so what's to know? My dad was selfish and controlling, and everything that happened in our house revolved around him and his moods. Around him and his work." She let out a breath. "When he was painting Mom and I had to walk on eggshells so as not to disturb him, because if we did he'd yell and throw things, and blame us for taking him 'out of the zone.' When he wasn't painting he was angry and bitter. Drinking too much and tearing Mom to shreds about how she wasn't supportive enough. We were dirt poor because Dad was absolutely insistent that he support us as an artist. But because he barely sold enough to get by, even making the rent was an issue, let alone buying food." She was looking down at Lucas's chest the way she had before, tracing more patterns on his skin.

"Dad's parents were rich and they tried to offer us financial support, but Dad wouldn't take anything from them. He blamed them for not supporting his artist dreams back when he was a boy and I think shoving our poverty in their faces was some kind of twisted revenge." Her lashes quivered. "He hated that I wanted to be an artist like him. Once, when I was thirteen, I showed him something I'd been working on just for him. I so wanted him to like my work. He used to, when I was little. Used to be encouraging and patient, showing me how to explore my creativity. But that day . . ." She stopped and was silent for a moment. "That day, he took one look at my drawing, told me I was a talentless waste of time, then balled it up and tossed it in the fire."

Lucas felt his jaw get tight, the anger he always tried to keep inside himself suddenly burning hot.

This is why you shouldn't care, remember?

He wasn't caring. He was simply angry on her behalf, as anyone would be. Because he could see that this had hurt her, and badly.

"Like I said, he was an asshole." Lucas kept his voice hard, so she was in no doubt about how he felt about her prick of a father. "No decent father takes that kind of thing out on his kid."

Grace shifted, her beautiful hair trailing over his chest in a long fall of silk. "Yeah, he was kind of shitty. My grandparents offered to pay for art college for me when I was seventeen, but Dad refused. Told me—in front of them—that I wasn't good enough. That I didn't have the talent. God, I was so angry. I decided enough was enough after that, so I ran away, headed out west, and that's where I met Griffin."

Lucas slid his hands into her hair once again, wanting to touch it and tip her head back at the same time, so he could see her face. Because she kept looking down as if she was hiding and he didn't want her doing that with him.

He'd known she used to do that with Griffin, because he had always complained about it. About how whenever he wanted to talk about stuff, she withdrew. Shutting herself away in her studio and telling him she had to "work."

Well, she wasn't going to do that with him. He wanted to know what was going on with her and he wasn't going to stand for any withdrawing.

"Why didn't you tell Griffin any of this?" He curled his fingers in the soft, silky strands of her hair. "He would have wanted to know."

Her gaze met his, her lower lip full and red and strangely vulnerable. "If Griffin had really wanted to know, he would have come into my studio and made me tell him."

"Did you say that you didn't want to talk about it?"

She looked away. "Maybe I did. But Griffin never pushed. He didn't seem interested enough."

Ah, so that was it. She wanted to be chased and Griffin was not a chaser, that much Lucas did know. He'd complained a lot about how Grace shut him out, but it was clear that was only because he'd let her.

Her fingers traced yet another pattern on Lucas's chest. "I'm not sure I want to discuss my marriage with you, Lucas. It feels wrong right now."

It was either that or she was deflecting. Keeping him out the way she'd kept Griffin out.

Why do you want in?

Lucas shoved the thought away. Perhaps he should leave it for now. The weight of her soft, warm body was maddening and all it would take would be a slight shift of her hips and he could slide inside her.

"Anyway," she went on without waiting for a reply. "What about you? I should ask you whether you're okay too. After what went on with your brother and sister."

The question made him uneasy. No one had asked him if he was okay for a very, very long time and he didn't much like the way it made him feel.

He opened his mouth to tell her he was fine, but then his brain started firing. Van and Chloe. Cesare de Santis . . . Shit. He still had an unwanted guest in his shooting range whom he had to deal with.

Lucas had questioned the guy again the day before but hadn't managed to get any more out of him, which meant there was no point keeping him. And most especially not with Grace around.

Christ, and that was another thing to worry about. Whoever had sent the guy would still be waiting for a report and by now they would have realized something had gone wrong, since he hadn't come back. Which meant whoever it was would be alerted to this location.

Fuck. He really had to deal with this and ASAP.

You've got your own ways of dealing with unwanted questions too.

Lucas gritted his teeth and gently eased Grace off him, slipping out of the bed.

"Lucas?" There was surprise in her voice. "Where are you going?"

Moving over to his dresser, he began pulling out the drawers and finding clothes. "The guy in the basement needs to be dealt with; otherwise we're going to alert the pricks after you to the fact that you're here."

"Oh." There was a rustle of sheets behind him. "What are you going to do with him?"

Lucas began to dress in his basic off-duty uniform of jeans and a long-sleeved tee. A plan had begun to form itself in his mind, but he didn't want to tell Grace about it yet. Not until he'd managed to get the specifics nailed down.

Finishing dressing, he picked up his SIG from where

he'd left it on the dresser and tucked it into the waistband of his jeans.

"Lucas?" Grace said again. "You're . . . not going to kill him, are you?"

He turned.

She was sitting in his bed, the white sheet wrapped around her, the apricot cloud of her hair around her pale shoulders, her golden-brown eyes fixed worriedly on him. There was something vulnerable about the way she was sitting there, about the way she looked at him, that reached inside his chest and held on. Filling him once again with that need to reassure her.

He didn't question it, crossing to the bed and bending to take her vivid angular face between his palms. "No," he said. "I'm not. I've got something else in mind."

She searched his gaze and he could see the questions in her eyes. But the question she actually asked wasn't the one he was expecting. "Are we done? Is this over?"

He didn't need to ask her what she meant by that. "Do you want it to be?" He already knew the answer, but he wanted to hear it from her.

"No," she murmured. "No, I don't."

"Good." He bent and pressed a hard kiss to her mouth. "Because like I told you last night, I'm not done."

He didn't miss the relief in her eyes and it made him savagely glad, because he didn't know what he'd have done if she'd said she wanted it to be over. The spark he'd let out of the box would not go back inside it and he was pretty fucking sure it wasn't going to burn with anyone else.

It had to be Grace. Grace or no one.

"By the way," he added, as he remembered the thing he'd pushed to the back of his mind the night before. "You know we had unprotected sex last night, don't you?"

"Oh . . . uh . . . so we did." Color flooded her cheeks.

"Look, you don't need to worry. I got my last birth control injection just before Griffin died. It was six months ago, but the effects can last a while."

He wasn't worried, though. That was the strange part of it. "Okay. Well, I'm clean. I had my last health check a couple of months ago."

She was still blushing furiously. It was adorable. "Me too. Like I told you, I haven't been with anyone else."

Shit, and now he wanted to push her back against the sheets, lose himself in her, forget all about that asshole in his basement.

But he couldn't, settling for another hard kiss instead.

When he finally did get back down to the shooting range, the guy was furious at being cooped up. Furious enough that he ignored the food Lucas gave him and, apparently heedless of his own safety, started hurling curses.

Lucas was debating the merits of knocking the asshole out just to shut him up when his phone buzzed with a call. He almost expected it to be Van and was trying to decide whether or not he was going to accept it when he glanced down at the screen and saw it wasn't Van but Wolf, his younger brother.

Hitting the answer button, Lucas raised the phone to his ear, stepping out of the shooting range and out of earshot of his prisoner's curses. "What is it?" he asked curtly.

"Van send you that video?" Wolf asked without preamble.

"Yes. I saw it."

"What the fuck is going on? Did you know anything about this?" His brother sounded furious.

"No, of course I didn't."

"Jesus fucking Christ," Wolf muttered. "She's ten years younger than he is *and* our goddamn foster sister. And marrying her doesn't make it right."

Lucas stilled. "Marrying her? What do you mean?"

"You didn't see the front page of the paper today? It's splashed all over the fucking thing. Van is marrying Chloe and he's taking over as CEO of Tate Oil."

Lucas stared at the harsh brick wall in front of him. He was very rarely taken by surprise, but he couldn't deny the actual shock that pulsed through him now.

Feelings are like turning on a tap. You can't just turn them on to let one out, leaving the rest in the pipe. They all come out whether you want them to or not. . . .

The edges of his phone dug into his palms. "Explain," he demanded.

Wolf muttered another curse. "Read the fucking paper yourself."

"Give me the short version."

There must have been something in his voice that gave his shock away, because Wolf sighed. "Okay, I only know what I read and that was there's this video of Van and Chloe kissing circulating on the Net, but apparently it's not such a big deal because they've been lovers for a while and are actually getting married. Oh, and Van's getting out of the Navy and assuming control of Tate Oil."

"No," Lucas said, because Van hadn't mentioned a word of this to him, not during the entire course of rescuing Chloe. "That can't be right."

"It is, man. Read the fucking paper. It's all there in black and white."

"Van said nothing about it to me." The familiar anger was beginning to rise inside him, the anger he'd felt yesterday when he'd seen that video, and this time it came far more easily. Frighteningly easily. He tried to push it back. "I had no idea he was sleeping with Chloe."

"Yeah, well, too late now." Wolf's voice dropped, becoming even rougher and more gravelly than it normally was. "This is de Santis's fault. If Chloe hadn't been in danger this would never have happened. . . ." He paused. "We need to take that son of a bitch out."

Wolf wasn't wrong. Except Lucas couldn't spare any time to discuss that with his brother, not now. "And we will," he said coldly. "But right now, I've got my own situation to deal with."

"Yeah, yeah," Wolf muttered. "I hear you. Fuck, if you want to do something right you've got to do it yourself."

The call abruptly disconnected.

Lucas looked down at his phone, part of him tempted to call his brother straight back and demand he tell him what the hell he meant by that.

But a muffled curse sounded from behind the door to the shooting range, reminding Lucas that he didn't have time to dick around with his brother. He had some serious shit of his own to handle.

Pushing thoughts of both his brothers out of his head, Lucas shoved his phone in his pocket and went back into the shooting range. The fake cop was sitting on the floor, with his back to the wall, dried blood from where Lucas had shot him staining his uniform and his arm.

Lucas came over and stood right in front of him, staring down at the man. "You've got two choices," he said. "Either I call the cops and you get your own cell. Or you go back to your employers and deliver a message for me."

The guy's eyes narrowed. "Why the fuck would I do that for you?"

"Did I mention you had two choices? There's actually a third." Lucas drew his weapon and aimed the muzzle directly at the man's forehead, right between the eyes. "It's a bullet with your name on it."

The man's jaw tightened. "Like I said, you crazy fucker.

I'd rather die here than have to go back to them empty-handed."

"But you won't be empty-handed." Lucas tilted his head. "I want you to tell them that Grace Riley hasn't got their money." He allowed himself a slight smile that had nothing to do with amusement. "I do."

CHAPTER TWELVE

Grace ate a piece of bacon standing at the kitchen counter, her coffee mug steaming gently on the counter beside her plate.

Lucas had been down in the basement a long time and she was getting nervous. In fact, she was getting nervous about everything.

After he'd left to go deal with their prisoner, she'd slipped out of bed and had a shower, then dressed, her hands shaking as images from the night before kept playing out inside her head. Erotic images. They made her body heat, made the ache between her thighs get even more intense, and yet for some reason they also twisted the unease that had been growing inside her ever since she'd talked to Lucas about her father.

She still couldn't believe she'd let all that painful shit out, told Lucas all the things she'd never told Griffin. The things that hurt. That made her feel vulnerable. That made her feel as small and ugly and as talentless as her father had once told her she was.

But Lucas hadn't looked at her as if she were small and ugly and talentless. He'd looked at her with bright anger in his eyes and she'd known it was on her behalf. But that too had made her uncomfortable, as had talking about her reasons for not telling Griffin, and so she'd tried, belatedly, to protect herself.

Part of her had been glad when Lucas had suddenly remembered about the prisoner in the basement and had left, yet another part of her, the weak part of herself, had felt oddly let down. As if she'd wanted to spill her guts to Lucas completely. Tell him all about how alone she was. How sometimes at night, when she couldn't sleep and the darkness encroached, she would wonder whether her father had been right. That she was talentless, a pointless waste of space. And maybe, if she'd been different, he wouldn't have been so angry with her, so vicious and cruel. That maybe his lack of success and his subsequent anger, his bitterness, was somehow her fault.

Grace swallowed her bacon and picked up her coffee mug, and sipped staring sightlessly in font of her. Had she ever felt this nervous with Griffin? This unsure? She kind of had, since her experience with men had been limited. But it hadn't lasted long, since he'd been extremely kind to her.

Lucas was so different, though. He was like a bonfire. She wanted to get close enough to warm herself against the flames, but she was also terrified of getting burned.

He will consume you if you let him.

She shivered, the strange agitation getting worse. Perhaps she should push this aside for the moment and get some paint on that canvas, because standing around brooding wasn't going to get it finished any quicker.

As she turned toward the kitchen doorway, she heard the elevator doors open and her heartbeat started to race. Lucas was back. The needy part of her wanted to run to him, throw herself into his arms, but for reasons she didn't want to examine, she remained where she was and waited.

Eventually he appeared in the kitchen doorway, his gaze raking over her in a way that made her breath catch.

"Why aren't you upstairs and naked in my bed?" A thread of heat ran through his cold, cold voice, making her tremble a little.

"Coffee." She lifted her cup. "I needed it."

His gaze narrowed and she had the odd feeling that he'd seen right through her. Seen her agitation and knew exactly the reason for it.

"What did you do with our guest?" she asked, knowing she sounded tense yet unable to help it. "Fill me in."

"I let him go." Lucas moved toward her, coming fast, and she found herself backed up against the counter before she'd even had a chance to breathe. "I've got a plan for getting those assholes off your tail." He reached for the coffee mug she held in her fingers and took it off her, placing it on the counter instead; then he took her hand and slid it down over the front of his jeans and held it there. "But first, we were interrupted this morning and I'd like to continue where you left off."

He was already hard; she could feel him underneath her palm, heat burning through the denim. Her breath shivered in her throat and for some reason she couldn't look at him. "Why did you let him go?" she asked instead, concentrating on that because it was easier than the intense, desperate pull she felt deep inside her whenever Lucas was around.

"It's better if you don't know the details until I get some more information." The pressure of his hand increased, pressing her palm harder against his fly. "Don't worry. I've got it under control."

She focused on the beat of his pulse at his throat. It was steady and yet hers . . . Hers was racing the way it always did when he touched her. It made her afraid. Before he'd taken her to bed, their chemistry had been intoxicating and intriguing and she'd been so fascinated by how she'd managed to get under his skin that she hadn't thought about what would happen if they finally consummated the attraction between them.

Now they had and it had been . . . overwhelming. She'd never experienced passion like it before in her life. Never experienced such need. And then she'd started spilling her secrets to him, secrets she'd never even told her husband of three years, and it felt . . . too much. Too fast. Too everything.

Lucas let go of her hand, then gripped her chin, tilting her head back, and she found herself looking up into his razor-sharp gaze. "What's wrong? And don't tell me 'nothing.' "

Grace swallowed. "I don't . . . I can't—"

Abruptly he gripped her hips and lifted her up onto the counter, that intense blue gaze inches from hers. "You look scared. Why?"

She'd never been one to be afraid of emotional honesty and she didn't know why she was having trouble with it now. There shouldn't have been anything hard about telling him how she felt. Yet it was like she had to force the words out. "B-because I am," she began hesitantly. "This is . . . a lot for me. *You* are a lot for me. And this is going so fast and I've never felt this before, and I . . ." She trailed off, knowing she was sounding ridiculous and yet unable to explain it any better than that.

Lucas put his palms on either side of her hips and leaned against the counter. "This is just sex, Grace. There's nothing to be scared of."

Just sex. Did he really think that? Really and truly? Because it didn't feel that way to her. And maybe that's why it felt so frightening, why she felt so overwhelmed. She'd always been drawn to him, to the intensity that lived beneath the surface. And now the sex had made that pull even more compelling. She was fascinated by him, wanted to know him, and that terrified her.

"But that's the thing." She didn't want to reveal more, didn't want him to know how afraid she truly was. Yet he had to know before he drew her any deeper. "It isn't just sex. At least it isn't for me."

He stared fiercely at her. "What do you want?"

"I . . . don't know. I meant what I said, I want more of what we did last night. But . . . I'm afraid. . . ." She hesitated, then made herself go on. "I'm afraid of you. Of what you do to me. Of what I feel around you." *I don't want to give pieces of myself to someone. Someone who might not want them. Who might screw them up and toss them in the fire . . .*

Something in that hard, intense gaze softened, making her breath catch because she'd never seen that in his eyes before. "I would never hurt you, Gracie," he said quietly. "I've told you that."

"You might not mean to. But that doesn't mean you won't."

He didn't move, didn't look away, and she could see the heat in his eyes. Almost as if he was deliberately showing her. "I don't know what I can give you. Or what other assurances you want, because I can't offer you anything but what we have right now. And once this is over I'm heading back to base. . . ." He paused. "But . . . while I'm here, whatever you want, it's yours."

His honesty was inexplicably painful, especially since there was no way she wanted any kind of relationship with a man like Lucas Tate. She didn't want a relationship, period. Not so soon after Griffin's death. But at least Lucas was honest with her. At least she knew where she stood.

It was oddly freeing, made the strange agitation that had gripped her somehow less acute. Because now she knew, she could protect herself, couldn't she? She could have him and this crazy intensity without giving parts of herself away.

It's what you did with Griffin for years after all.

She didn't like that thought but knew it was true nevertheless. She hadn't given Griffin everything she was. For some reason she'd always held a part of herself back. So surely this thing with Lucas could be the same? She'd protected herself from even her own husband. She could keep herself safe from a guy who was mostly a stranger.

Tell yourself that. Give yourself all the excuses in the world. You just want him.

Of course she did. But she wouldn't fall for him. Not now she'd been warned.

Grace lifted her hand and touched his chest, ran her fingers down the hard plane of it, feeling his abs tighten as she brushed over them, reaching the waistband of his jeans. Then very deliberately she brought her palm back over the front of his fly, cupping him through the denim.

The blue in his eyes flared, his cock, still semi-hard, hardening even further. "Is that what you want?" he demanded, the dark thread of heat running through his voice. "Tell me."

"Yes. That's what I want."

"Be specific, Grace."

She swallowed. "I want your c-cock."

He didn't move. "Then take it."

She'd never asked for anything like this before. Never taken it because she couldn't help herself. Never thought she'd even want to. Griffin had asked her a couple of times if she'd use her mouth on him and she'd always refused, finding the idea vaguely unpleasant. He hadn't pushed and she'd been relieved. Yet at the same time there had been a small part of her hiding under that relief, a hurt, confused part that had found his easy acceptance painful.

Griffin had never demanded anything of her. He'd simply accepted her refusal as if it were no big deal. As if she what she had to offer wasn't good enough to argue for. . . .

But Lucas was different. She could see the demand in the hard, hot look in his eyes. He wouldn't let her refusal go without a fight.

Her breath caught as an idea wound its way through her head. What would happen if she *did* refuse? What would he do? Would he fight? Would he insist?

Her breathing began to get faster, her heartbeat beginning its usual spiral out of control. She couldn't actually bring herself to move her hand because that rigid warmth pressing against her palm was far too good, but she gave him a glance from beneath her lashes. "What if I don't?" Her voice had gone hoarse and shaky. "What if I just want to go back to my painting?"

The heat in his eyes seemed to build, getting hotter, more fierce. "Then I might have to insist."

There was an ache between her thighs, deep and wild. He was so big, so powerful. He was caging her on the counter, his hard body between her thighs. He wouldn't let her run. He wouldn't shrug his shoulders and turn away. He wanted her and he'd take her the way he had yesterday.

Her heartbeat pulsing loudly in her head, Grace tried to slip off the counter, not even understanding why she wanted to push this, but wanting to anyway.

Lucas's hands came down on her hips as soon as she moved, his grip unbelievably powerful. It made her breath get even shorter, panting almost. She loved the strength in that grip, how it could make her feel small and delicate and feminine. How it made her feel wanted.

She looked up into his face, the ache between her thighs getting demanding.

"You want me to chase you?" Lucas's voice was soft. "Because believe me, I will. I won't let you run. I'm a hunter and I'll hunt you down." His grip tightened, nearly painful now, that change coming over him again. Turning from ice man into a man of fire, blazing with desire, with passion. "I'm very patient, Gracie. I can wait forever, stay motionless for hours. Slow my heartbeat to thirty beats per minute in order to hit my target." Slowly, he leaned in close, intensity pouring off him, magnetic, compelling. "But not with you. My patience is very, very thin with you. So, how about you get on your knees before I lose it altogether."

Naturally, that insane part of her wanted to see what would happen if he lost it. But the pressure between her thighs, the hunger inside her, wouldn't be denied any longer, so she simply did what she was told and slipped off the counter to kneel on the hard wood of the kitchen floor in front of him.

He'd taken a step back to give her some room, but it didn't feel like she had any at all. His very presence seemed to take over every particle of the air around her, overwhelming her with him. His scent, his heat, the sheer force of him. It made her hands shake as she reached for the button on his jeans, fumbling to get it open. He said nothing, but she could tell he was looking at her, the pressure of his gaze like a heavy stone pressing down.

So far, it had been her who'd been the center of his attention. He hadn't let her touch him and that had been frustrating. Now, though, it was her turn and she wanted to make him as desperate, as bat-shit crazy, as he'd made her the night before. Make that vaunted patience of his slip through his fingers like water.

But she'd never done this before and she wanted to do it right so badly it scared her.

She couldn't stop the tremors in her hands as she spread open the denim of his jeans, staring at the hard length pressing against the cotton of his boxers. Her mouth watered, her breathing almost embarrassingly loud.

Part of her wanted him to simply take what he wanted

from her without her having to do anything, but he didn't move. He wasn't going to make her do this herself, was he?

He's obviously not impatient enough. Already you're failing.

No, shit, that was her dad talking. That was her father telling her she was useless. That she was talentless. That she couldn't do anything right.

"Grace." The sound of her name was a growl, harsh and guttural. "I don't want you to fucking stare at it. I want you to put it in your mouth."

His voice rolled over her, heat and desire, the edge of desperation, and that was all the kick she needed.

Hell, she was just going to do it. Trust herself. She'd already made him lose it the day before, dragged down onto the floor of the studio. She'd do it again, right here in the kitchen.

Her hands were steadier as she reached for the waistband of his underwear and pulled it down, taking him out. And as she'd already seen once before this morning, he was as beautiful here as he was everywhere else. Long and thick and perfect.

She took him in her hand, curling her fingers around him. His skin was unexpectedly soft and smooth, velvet over an iron bar. Another intriguing contrast. She ran her thumb up the length of his cock, the feel of him intoxicating.

"What did I say about my patience?" Lucas's voice was almost unrecognizable. "Stop playing and do as you're told."

"Hey," she said thickly. "It's my turn now, okay?" Leaning forward, she touched her tongue to him, tasting salt and something else, musky and delicious, and that too was intriguing. He shuddered, so she licked him again, swirling her tongue around the sensitive head. Then his hands were in her hair, holding her still, and his hips were moving, guiding her mouth to him insistently.

Looked like his famous patience had run out.

She kept her hand wrapped around the base of him and opened her mouth, letting that long, thick length slide in. The heat of him was astonishing and for a second she could only kneel there in amazement, because this was so much better than she thought it would be. He tasted . . . delicious and the harsh, raw sound of pleasure he made . . . God, it was so good.

Grace tightened her grip and gave an experimental suck, drawing another raw sound from him, his fingers curling painfully in her hair. So she did it again and again, taking him in deeper each time. His hips began to thrust, faster, harder, and she had to grip on to one muscular thigh to brace herself.

God, she hadn't realized how powerful this could be. How powerful it would make *her* feel. There was something about how vulnerable he was right in this moment, with his cock in her mouth, trusting her that she wouldn't cause him pain, because she could. So easily.

Grace tipped her head back and glanced up at him, wanting to see how she was affecting him. And was almost flattened by the sheer intensity of the expression in his eyes as her gaze met his.

He was staring down at her, his focus a laser beam of sharply channeled heat, passion, pleasure. Desire. As if she was the target he was aiming at and nothing would stop him from taking her down.

It was almost too much and she wanted to look away, but she couldn't. It was as if he'd hypnotized her. All she could do was kneel there as he thrust into her mouth, as she sucked him down, their gazes locked. Holding . . .

His hips moved faster, his hands in her hair painful, but

nothing on earth would have dragged her away in this moment.

"Grace," he said roughly. *"Grace."*

She tightened her grip, sucked harder, watching as the pleasure began to take him over, the lines of his face sharp with hunger. Then he stiffened, gripping her so tight pin-pricks of pain erupted all over her scalp. But she didn't care. All she could see was the pleasure twisting his beautiful features into something unguarded and utterly open, raw ecstasy.

You did that to him. You made him look like that.

She did. She had.

As the climax took him, she kept watching, his lips peeling back, a savage roar breaking from him. He didn't look away and she had the sudden sense that this was a part of him no one else ever saw. And that he was letting her see it. Deliberately.

Still think you can protect yourself from him?

She would.

She would have to.

"Keep still."

"I'm trying."

"If you move again you'll get polish on the couch cushions and then I *won't* be happy." Lucas frowned at the long, elegant foot that was currently sitting in his lap. Applying nail polish was a lot more difficult than it looked. Carefully he painted a little more of the sparkly gold polish on her nail, trying not to get it on her skin. Unfortunately, it appeared that Grace was ticklish and she kept jerking every time he took hold of her toe, which was not helping the application process.

"I kind of want to see you very unhappy," Grace said, shifting restlessly yet again. "Are you like the Hulk? Do you go green and rip your clothes?"

Lucas wrapped his fingers around her slender ankle to hold her still, frowning at a spot he'd missed. "What do you think?"

"I'm guessing not." She sighed. "How disappointing. I'd like to see you in ripped clothes."

"Make me get polish on my couch and maybe you will." He leaned forward and dipped the brush in the bottle on the coffee table in front of him, then applied a little more.

Her foot felt warm, the skin of her ankle smooth beneath his fingers, making the ever-present desire for her tighten inside him. But he was in no hurry to do anything about it quite yet, content to simply sit there and enjoy the feeling of her bare skin against his fingertips.

If someone had told him two weeks ago that he'd be sitting on a couch painting a woman's toenails he would have dismissed it as insanity. Yet here he was, sitting on a couch with Grace's foot in his lap, applying one of her favorite polishes. Apparently.

He still didn't know how he'd gotten here.

After she'd given him the world's best blow job, that sweet mouth nearly taking the top of his head off, he'd picked her up, carried her back upstairs, stripped her bare, spread her thighs, and proceeded to give her back every bit of what she'd given him. With interest.

Around the middle of the day, they'd both fallen asleep, waking again in the afternoon to sate themselves on each other again. Then Grace had decided it was time to eat, insisting that even though she couldn't cook, she could do a mean steak. He was used to cooking for himself and told her he'd handle it, but she ignored him, making him sit at the table in the kitchen while she bustled around making a salad and cooking the steak. She even forced him to open a bottle of wine, though he wasn't a drinker, and made him have one with her.

"Chill out," she'd told him as he'd gazed at the glass suspiciously. "One won't kill you."

Indeed, it hadn't. It was even nice to sip slowly at it, sitting and watching her move around the kitchen like she owned it, creating a meal with the same flair as she created pictures on a canvas.

He hadn't done that for . . . Shit, when was the last time he'd sat sipping wine while someone else cooked for him? He hadn't done that ever, probably. Even when he hadn't been on deployment, he'd spent his free time honing his skills. While some of the other guys had vacations, returning home to family and friends, he'd stayed on base. Van would always go back to the ranch when he was on leave, while Wolf tended to cut loose on trips to Vegas and various other party cities. But Lucas would stay and polish the skills he'd already spent years honing.

He didn't need vacations. He didn't need to cut loose. Griffin often told him he needed to relax more, but Lucas had ignored him. Fact was, he couldn't afford to relax. Absolute control, absolute focus, was what kept him sane, what kept all those powerful, impossible needs at bay.

So really, he shouldn't be sitting in a kitchen with Grace, drinking wine and listening to her chatter as she cooked him a steak. Couldn't be letting his guard down. But he did it anyway, because it made her happy.

He wasn't sure when making her happy had become important to him. Perhaps it had been earlier that morning, in the kitchen, when she'd looked up at him almost fearfully, telling him that she was scared of what was happening between them. That he could hurt her without meaning to.

Of course he could. He'd hurt people before, hadn't he? But he wouldn't if he kept himself in control of this, and if there was one thing he was very good at it was control.

As long as he kept every decision deliberate, it would work. Honesty too helped because it kept expectations realistic. He couldn't give her anything more than what was happening between them right now, but while he was here he'd give her everything he could. And he'd meant it.

The steak had been excellent and he'd told her so. And after they'd eaten, she'd confessed to an unexpected love of soccer and that there was a game on she really wanted to watch and would he mind. He'd never gotten into sports particularly, but he was happy enough to sit there while she watched it.

Especially watching her. She was vocal and passionate about the game, trying to explain to him the rules, all the while yelling at the TV when the ref made an apparent bad call. Lucas told her the game seemed to be more about rolling around on the ground pretending to be injured than it was about scoring goals, so she hit him with a cushion.

Then she got out her nail polishes, removing the tiny little roses she had on her toes in preparation for painting on something else. Given how distracted she was with the game, he wouldn't have been surprised if she got polish all over his white cushions, so he calmly took the bottle from her and took over himself.

It was surprisingly restful, giving him something to focus on, which he always liked to do. Though he could have done without her being ticklish, it had to be said.

"Why did you want to be a sniper?" she asked unexpectedly.

He didn't look up from what he was doing. "Aren't you supposed to be watching the game?"

"It's halftime. Come on, spill."

He raised his head and surveyed his handiwork. It would do. "I liked the discipline involved." He started on another toenail. "Both mental and physical. You have to be very focused, very patient, and very controlled. You also have to like being alone, which I do."

"Yeah, I get it. And I guess it's not a surprise about the control stuff given you're a major control freak."

He said nothing, since there was nothing for him to disagree with. He *was* a control freak and that was exactly the way he liked it.

Another long pause.

"How many people have you . . . um . . . you know." She sounded hesitant.

"Confirmed kills you mean?" No point in beating about the bush. "Just over two hundred."

"Oh."

Was that shock in her voice? It probably was, since people always were shocked when he told them. But then he saw no reason to lie to her. He was what he was, one of the best in the business.

Carefully he finished off the nail before dipping the brush in the polish and moving on to the next one. "It's war, Grace. I'm not there to put roses in the muzzles of people's guns. I'm there to take out the people I'm ordered to take out, to protect our forces. To protect civilians."

She'd gone still, and when he lifted his head briefly to look at her he found her pretty amber gaze staring back. He couldn't read the expression in it, but it wasn't horror or disgust, or any of the other emotions he'd seen in people's eyes when he answered their questions. Because they always asked questions. They always wanted to know how many people he'd killed.

"I know it's war. I mean, Griffin was a SEAL too. I just . . ." She stopped. "Is it hard to pull that trigger? Or do those people simply become targets to you?"

"The first time? It was difficult." He could still remember it. "There was a young guy strapped with explosive approaching a checkpoint. A kid, really. It crossed my mind that he was someone's son, someone's brother, and that taking him out wouldn't simply get rid of a threat but affect a whole lot of other people who cared about this guy. But he was going to kill people, people I knew, and since he was going to die anyway, I took the shot." He didn't add that afterwards he'd had to lower his rifle, get up, and walk around to stop himself from throwing up. "They became simply targets after that because I couldn't afford to make them into people. Hesitations cost lives and that's not why I was there. I was there to keep the body count down by taking out strategic targets, not make it any worse."

There was a strange expression on her face, as if he'd turned into someone she hadn't quite expected. "You're pretty lethal then."

He was and he wasn't going to pretend to be someone different or pretty it up for sensitive civilian feelings. Yes, he killed people, but like he'd already told her, it was war. And in war people died.

"That's what I'm paid for," he said flatly.

"That wasn't a judgment, Lucas. It's just . . . interesting. That you're this incredibly dangerous man and yet you're sitting on the couch painting my toenails." Color crept into her cheeks, her mouth curving. "I feel like I've tamed a wild beast or something."

He didn't know what it was about her expression that made his chest tighten. Maybe it was the note of satisfaction in her voice, as if she was pleased with herself. It almost dragged a smile from him.

Are you sure sitting here like this with her is a good idea?

Maybe it wasn't. But sitting here with her wasn't going to change what he was going to do after all this was over. He was still going back to base, no matter what happened.

Yes, he'd decided to take her, take everything, indulge himself totally in all the things he wanted that he never normally let himself have.

But afterwards, when this had burned itself out, he was going to walk away.

And hope he didn't leave a pile of ashes behind him.

He looked back down at what he was doing, taking her little toe between his fingers. Another shudder went through her and he heard the sound of a quickly stifled giggle.

This time he allowed himself a faint smile. "Keep still."

"I am, I am." She cleared her throat. "So, uh, how about teaching me to shoot?"

The nail on her toe was tiny and required a steady hand. Luckily, his was the steadiest in the business. "You don't need to learn to shoot. Not when I'm here."

"But what if I want to? What if these guys somehow manage to capture me?"

"They won't. I'll make sure of it."

"Oh come on. Wouldn't you want me to be prepared for every eventuality?"

He gave her a glance. "Why do you want to do that?"

A wicked little grin was playing around her lovely mouth, the amber of her eyes luminous. She was wearing that floaty lavender dress again and he happened to know that she didn't have anything else on underneath it. At least his cock remembered, hardening like Pavlov's fucking dog at the thought. "Hey, you're painting my toenails, so why can't I shoot your guns?"

Well, and why not? After all, she did have a point about being prepared. Yes, he was going to make sure she was nowhere near any danger that threatened, but it wouldn't hurt to give her a little training. Make sure she was able to defend herself should the worst happen.

It would give them both something to do until he heard

from that asshole he'd released back to the people who'd sent him anyway. He couldn't do anything until he knew who he was dealing with. Oliveira, the guy had said.

Lucas had sent the name to various contacts, including the Tate employee who was currently helping him with his investigations, but so far had gotten nothing concrete back. Whatever, he wasn't actually going to pay these assholes any money, but once he knew who they were, then he could devise a plan to take them out.

Or you could go straight to the source of the problem.

Cesare de Santis. The prick who'd started all of this by recruiting Griffin to be his salesman. Yeah, maybe he should.

"Okay, I'll teach you to shoot." He straightened up, put the brush back in the bottle, then released her ankle, keeping his hand open. "Other foot."

"Yay." Grace shifted, letting him take her unpainted foot. "Is it wrong that I'm excited about that?"

Hell, he could almost get excited about it, if only because it made her so happy.

Be careful. Caring is where it all starts to go wrong, remember?

Oh yes, he remembered. But he'd be able to turn it off when the time came. He'd have to.

Gripping on to her ankle, he leaned forward and grabbed the brush out of the pot, wiping it carefully before starting with her big toe. "It's not a game, Grace, remember that. You'd don't actually want to be in the situation of having to shoot a gun at someone."

"No, I know that." She sighed. "It's not only about wanting to shoot guns. I kind of want to help. I mean, I'm just sitting around here being the damsel in distress, which really isn't me."

"You have arms dealers after you. Protecting yourself from them alone isn't an option. If you were a guy I'd be suggesting the same thing I'm suggesting to you now, which is to stay here and let me handle it."

"Okay, okay. I hear you. I just wish I could do something. If I still had any of Griffin's stuff I'd offer to look through it, see if we could find something there, but I gave most of it to Goodwill and threw the rest away."

There was a thread of impatience in her voice, a hint of frustration. But then Grace wasn't a person who liked staying still. She was always moving, always doing something, and this enforced inaction wouldn't be easy for her.

"I thought you wanted to paint." He moved onto the next nail, laying down a smooth coat of polish. "Wasn't that the idea?"

"I do want to paint. But . . . I don't know. It feels wrong to do that when you're busy trying to save my life."

He flashed her a look. "I thought you had a deadline."

"Yes, I do, but—"

"I'll get rid of the arms dealers. You do the painting. That's more important, understand?"

For some reason she glanced away. "What makes you say that?"

He stared at her, puzzled. Should he really be the one pointing this out to her? When she'd made such a fuss about having her canvases in the first place?

"You don't think so?" he asked. "You told me this was your dream."

"It is." She shifted on the couch again and he had to tighten his grip on her ankle. "But I want to help you. I mean, this is kind of my fault."

"What?"

"Well, Griffin was my husband. If he hadn't been married to me and if he—"

"Bullshit. It was Griffin's decision. It's got nothing to do with you." He narrowed his gaze, watching her face as she crossed her arms over her chest, her jaw tight. Defensive.

And he had the sudden thought that perhaps this wasn't actually about Griffin at all.

She'd told him about the father she'd once adored, about the drawings he'd balled up and thrown in the fire. About how he'd criticized her, told her she was no good. And she was such a fighter, she wouldn't have taken that lying down. This exhibition, that collection upstairs, that was all part of proving him wrong, Lucas was sure of it.

And yet here she was, procrastinating on that last picture. The one she'd told him she *had* to finish before the exhibition date. Why wasn't she painting? Was she avoiding it?

"This is to do with your dad, isn't it?" he asked softly.

She blinked, her gaze flicking to his in surprise. "What? What about my dad?"

"I don't know. You tell me."

A scowl crossed her face. "This hasn't got anything to do with him."

"Really? So why haven't you finished that painting yet?"

"I . . ." She stopped and looked away yet again, her teeth sinking into her lower lip. "Maybe I'm not good enough."

But no, that didn't ring true. If she didn't think she was good enough she wouldn't be exhibiting in the first place, nor would she have a sizable collection of work already. No, something else was holding her back; he was sure of it.

"That's bullshit too. You know you're good enough." He kept his fingers wrapped around her ankle, pressed to her warm skin. "What's in your head, Gracie? What's stopping you?"

She kept her head turned away, her jaw tight. But he saw the slight tremble in her lower lip. "Sometimes I think . . . it's selfish of me." Her voice was husky. "Selfish to want to go after my dream. Especially after Dad basically destroyed all the relationships in his life going after his. He was such a selfish man, caused so much pain to so many people, and sometimes I think that . . . I'm heading down the same path."

Lucas kept his gaze on the lovely line of her profile, long nose and definite jaw. A strong, determined, stubborn profile. Conflicted and flawed, just as she was. Beautiful, just as she was. "No," he said quietly. "You're not selfish."

She shook her head. "How can you say that? After the way I treated Griffin—"

"Griffin made his own choices like your father made his. It's not your fault that your dad was a crappy parent."

Grace was silent a long moment, her face still averted. "He used to be so good to me, though." There was pain in her voice now. "He used to call me his little sunset. Used to tell me how proud he was of me. And then he changed, started telling me that I was plain, that I was useless, that I was a waste of time, and I . . ." She swallowed. "I still wonder if it was something I did. Something I said. That maybe I destroyed the relationship I had with him in some way."

Lucas's chest constricted, his own father's voice rattling around inside him, telling him things he didn't want to hear, terrible things. *You're dangerous. You need to control it. You don't want anyone else to get hurt . . . do you, Lucas?*

"No," he said, to her and to the doubts that echoed in his soul. "It's nothing you did. He was the one who let his own frustrations get to him and then put them on to you. He was the one who was destructive, Gracie. Not you."

Her throat moved and for a long moment she said nothing, blinking fiercely. Then slowly she turned back. "How do you know that, though?"

Wasn't it obvious?

Holding her gaze with his, he said, "I might not have known your dad, but I know you. Not as well as I want to, admittedly, but enough to know that destructive is the very last thing you are."

"But—"

"You told me that when you paint you let your feelings show you where to go, and from what I've seen of those paintings upstairs, it's nowhere selfish or mean. Nowhere destructive or petty. You create, Gracie. You don't destroy. Not like your dad." *Not like you.* But he didn't say that part. He kept that to himself.

Grace stared at him for a long moment and he thought he caught the sheen of tears in her eyes. "I actually do want to help you, you know."

"You can help me by finishing that damn painting. I risked my life for that fucking canvas." He let her see his faint smile. "And I want to see what you're going to put on it."

The tight look vanished from her face and she gave a reluctant laugh. "I thought you didn't like art."

It felt good to make her smile. It felt good to make *her* feel good. "I don't. . . ." He paused, remembering the paintings upstairs and wanting to be honest with her, because she deserved it. "But I have a feeling I could come to like yours."

Her smile became real then, slow and sweet, like the sun coming up after a very long and dark night, and he felt the ice in his soul begin to thaw. Then, without a word, she shifted her legs and moved toward him, kissing him hungrily.

The brush dropped from his hand, gold polish dripping on the couch cushions.

And he let it.

CHAPTER THIRTEEN

Sometime in the night Grace thought she heard someone cry out. Then a warm hand settled between her shoulder blades and someone whispered to her to go back to sleep, so she did.

Next thing she knew the room was bright and it was definitely morning. And the sheets next to her were empty and cold.

Okay, so Lucas was up. Which was disappointing. She'd been hoping for some lazy, sleepy good morning sex.

Hauling her hair back from her face, she took a bleary look around the room, then spotted the dress she'd been wearing the day before crumpled on the floor beside the bed. Reaching for it, she picked it up and slipped it over her head. Then she eased herself from between the sheets, shivering slightly at the cold floorboards on her warm feet.

Peeking first into the en suite bathroom to check if he was there—he wasn't—she went out into the hallway, only to hear the sound of his voice drifting up from downstairs.

Still half-asleep, she padded toward the top of the stairs and looked down into the long gallery.

Lucas was standing in front of the big rose window, his back to her, talking to someone on his phone. He wore nothing but a pair of jeans hanging low on his lean hips, and she took a moment to admire the width of his broad shoulders, the delicious lines of his lats and trapezius muscles. The tattoo of the skeletal frog on one shoulder looked dark as the morning light fell through the stained glass and over him, painting him in vivid colors.

Her heart clenched tight in her chest.

Last night had been the best. In fact, it might even have been the best night she'd ever had. Certainly it was better than anything she'd experienced since Griffin's death. Better than anything before that too.

She couldn't remember the last time she'd been so happy. Maybe when she'd gotten Craig to agree to the exhibition, but actually, on second thought, that maybe ran a close second.

No, cooking steak for Lucas, then watching soccer while he sat on the couch and painted her toes eclipsed even that. A lethal predator she'd somehow tamed enough to do something so intimate, so domestic.

Griffin had watched soccer with her, indulging her, since he was a baseball fan. But he'd never taken the bottle of polish off her and painted her toes for her. Oh sure, Lucas had told her it was because she was distracted and he didn't want polish on the cushions. But she had the sneaking suspicion he'd taken over because he'd wanted to and that he'd even enjoyed it.

He certainly hadn't been worried when she'd ended up naked and beneath him after what he'd told her about her about her father. About her paintings.

How he'd managed to guess it was that fear that was holding her back from her painting she had no idea. She hadn't even realized that was what had been going on herself. But as soon as he'd said the words the truth had slid through her like an ice cube dropped down her back, cold, unexpected, and very unwelcome.

She hadn't wanted to admit it, had wanted to deny it,

because she knew she wasn't like her father. She *knew*. Yet the look in Lucas's blue eyes, sharp as a scalpel, had cut her open, revealing the contents of her entire soul to him. To herself too. The truth she'd been trying to hide ever since she'd met him.

That she was just as selfish as her father was. That her art was more important to her than her relationships and that it was her fault her marriage had been crappy. That she hurt the people she should care about in the same way her father had hurt her and her mother.

She hadn't known what she'd expected Lucas to do with the knowledge, hurt her maybe, since that was what her father had done. But he hadn't. Instead he'd proved her wrong when she'd explained her painting process to him and she'd thought he hadn't understood. Turned out, he understood very well.

". . . you let your feelings show you where to go, and from what I've seen of those paintings upstairs, it's nowhere selfish or mean. Nowhere destructive or petty. You create, Gracie. You don't destroy."

She hadn't ever seen it like that. Hadn't ever seen her paintings as coming from somewhere good. Somewhere positive. Not when for years her art had always been associated with her father's destructive moods or his scorn, his lack of approval and her own anger.

It made her feel good about her own creativity. Like Lucas had somehow shown her how to free it from all those bad associations, all those bad feelings. Bad associations she hadn't even realized were there until now.

Her palm itched, ready for a paintbrush. But she didn't want to move yet. She wanted to stand there and watch Lucas for a moment, because he was so beautiful half-naked, talking on the phone, his voice so. . . . *cold*.

Something jolted through her. And she realized she

hadn't heard the ice he could inject into his voice for days now. Certainly the last couple of days there had been nothing but heat. Yet not now.

Who was he talking to?

She held her breath, listening.

"I don't care," Lucas was saying, every word an icicle. "I want your word that you'll leave the woman alone. She has nothing to do with this. . . ." A pause. "I have the money. You know who I am, you know I can pay." He stood very, very still, like a statue. "That's irrelevant. You want the money or not?"

Oh God, he was talking about her? Was he talking to the people who were after her? Who wanted the money that Griffin had taken from them?

He sounded like he'd been plunged into ice.

"I can get you cash in two days," he continued. "Take it or leave it." Without another word he lowered the phone, clearly disconnecting the call before sliding it back into the pocket of his jeans.

Then he folded his arms and stood silent and still, staring through the glass in front of him as if he were a thousand miles away and not right here in the same apartment as she was. As if he were staring through the sight of his rifle, watching his target move around, unaware that they were being watched. . . .

Grace swallowed, unable to drag her gaze away from him for some reason. The way he stood was so strong, so obdurate, like a marble statue on a Roman temple, beautiful and yet hard as stone. Able to withstand the weight of centuries, able to stand there for a thousand years without moving.

He's alone.

The thought hit her suddenly. Painfully. He *was* alone. Like those Roman statues, he watched the world move past

him without ever becoming part of it, playing the role of
the detached observer with that laser-sharp focus of his.

Griffin had told her once that Lucas didn't have friends,
that Griffin didn't even know why Lucas befriended him.
It seemed sad somehow. That this beautiful, dangerous
man seemed to have no one. Oh sure, he had his brothers,
but the way he talked about them . . . Were they close? He
hadn't even seemed that cut up about his father's death;
he'd kind of brushed it off.

Then again, that's what he did, wasn't it? He deliberately kept himself alone, deliberately kept himself closed
off, because of the way his family had died when he was
little.

Something wrapped sharp fingers around her heart and
for some reason it felt like grief. As he stood there in that
room, even with the colors all over his warm golden skin,
it suddenly came to her that for all the time they'd spent
together, she didn't really know him. She knew that he was
passionate, no matter how hard he pretended otherwise,
and that he hid it well. That he liked the mental and physical
discipline of being a sniper. That he liked being alone.

What else? Nothing. Whenever she'd tried to ask him
about himself, he seemed to somehow deflect it back to
her.

*Perhaps there is nothing else to know. Perhaps being
a sniper is all he is.*

No, that wasn't all. It couldn't be. So she hadn't had the
most fulfilling life in the world, but even she had friends.
She had stuff she liked to do. Did Lucas?

"Did you want something, Grace?" Lucas didn't turn,
his short blond hair tinted pure gold by the weak winter
sunlight coming through the stained glass.

The question shocked her. Had she made a sound somehow? Given herself away?

She put a hand on the metal banister. "How did you know I was here?"

"I heard your breathing."

Right. Okay then. Super sniper skills obviously.

She came down the stairs and went over to him, her first impulse to put her arms around him. Then she got closer and felt the tension radiating from him and crossed her arms over her chest instead.

"You heard all that?" He still didn't turn and his voice was still very, very cold.

"Uh, yes. I guess you were talking to the people after me?"

"I was."

She swallowed. "Lucas, you can't give them the money."

"I'm not going to. But they don't know that. I just need a couple of days to get the details of my other plan into place."

"What other plan?" She stared at his strong back, wanting to touch the tight muscles around his shoulders and neck, ease the tension from them. Yet something about the way he stood made her think he wouldn't welcome her touch right now.

"You don't need to worry about it." There was a fine rime of frost around the words, a warning not to push. "I've got it under control."

Grace frowned. Something was wrong; she could feel it. The way he'd suddenly gone into ice mode, the tension that was radiating from him . . . Yes, something was up. What was it?

"Are you okay?" she asked quietly.

He didn't answer, his gaze firmly on the window in front of him.

To hell with it. Something was wrong and she wanted to know what it was, perhaps help. He didn't like it when she wouldn't tell him what was up, so why should she put up with it from him?

Why do you care? You're supposed to be keeping a part of yourself back, remember?

Sure, but he'd made her happy the night before, had sat with her and talked with her, reassured her about fears she didn't even know she had. So why couldn't she give him something in return?

Taking a couple of steps toward him, she slid her arms around his waist, laying her cheek against the hot skin of his back. Instantly his whole body tensed and he moved, and suddenly she was left standing there embracing empty air.

She blinked in surprise, trying to ignore the small, sharp burst of hurt.

He'd taken a few steps away from her, his arms tight at his sides, that tension gathering around him somehow thicker, denser. "Don't." There was a whole world of warning in the word. "It's probably better if you don't touch me right now."

The hurt slid a little deeper. "Why not? What's wrong? Did I do something?"

He said nothing for a moment, his head turned away. Then abruptly he glanced at her, the look in his eyes searing, stealing her breath away. She didn't understand the expression in them, but it wasn't cold. It looked almost like . . . pain.

She took a helpless step toward him, then stopped as he tensed yet again. "Lucas," she began.

"I need to go downstairs," he said before she could continue. "Give me an hour or two." And he turned away, heading toward the elevator.

"Hey," she called after him before she could think better of it. "So I'm not allowed to run away, but you are? Is that how this works."

He came to a halt, straight backed and stiff. "If I'm going to be saving your ass I need get in some practice. Unless you have a problem with that?"

But no, that wasn't fair. She'd stripped herself bare both literally and emotionally for him, because he'd asked. Because he'd insisted. And yet he wouldn't do the same thing for her?

"Bullshit," she snapped. "This isn't about saving my life. What the hell's happened, Lucas? Why are you being so tense and weird? And why won't you tell me what's wrong?"

"There is no 'this,' remember, Grace?" The familiar ice was back in his tone. "We're not in a relationship and I don't have to tell you anything."

Oh no. *Hell* no. She wasn't going to put up with that. She wanted to know what was bugging him. She wanted to help.

Moving quickly, she went past him, then turned to face him and folded her arms, putting herself between him and the elevator, blocking it. "No, you don't get to do that," she said flatly. "You don't get to walk away and ignore me. Not after you dug around in all my issues and made me talk about them whether I wanted to or not."

He straightened, the movement subtle and yet somehow making him seem taller, more powerful. More dangerous. Silver glinted in his eyes, hard, cold. "Get out of the way."

Screw that noise. He didn't get to intimidate her. Sure, his confirmed kill count was impressive and he had skills that made him infinitely dangerous. But if he thought he could simply brush her off like an annoying fly he could think again. Goddamn arrogant, controlling men.

She lifted her chin. "Don't use that sniper shit on me and don't pretend you're not walking out because you don't want to talk. I get that. Hell, you think I wanted to talk about all that crap with my dad? I didn't. But I did because you asked me to. So, tell me what's going on. Why are you suddenly going into ice-man mode on me?"

His expression didn't relent. "Grace—"

She took a couple of steps toward him, so she was right in front of him, inches from his chest and all that hot, bare skin. Yes, he was intimidating. Yes, all he needed to do was push her out of the way. But no, she wasn't backing down. She didn't quite understand why it was important to her that she didn't. It was just that with a man like Lucas Tate, you absolutely couldn't afford to give an inch. Not when he would take every mile there was and then some.

"You told me you'd give me everything while you were here," she said, playing her trump card. "So, give me this."

Finally something flickered through his gaze, gone so fast she couldn't read what it was. "It's got nothing to do with you."

"If it's got nothing to do with me then it won't matter if you tell me then, will it?"

He said nothing, his beautiful features tense and hard. Giving her back nothing but the ice and snow of the frozen winter outside.

She didn't know what instinct it was that had her reaching out to him, especially when her touch had made him pull away earlier. But she did it nevertheless, putting her hands on his bare chest, pressing her palms against his hot skin as if the warmth of her touch could unfreeze him. And she looked straight up into those icy blue eyes.

"Tell me," she said softly. "You helped me last night. Let me do the same for you."

He'd gone absolutely still, yet the tension was vibrating off him, his eyes glittering. He looked like a man fighting something infinitely more powerful than he was and knowing he was failing yet fighting on anyway. Like holding back the tide or stopping the sun from coming up. Preventing the moon from sinking.

He was silent for so long, cold for so long, that she thought she wouldn't be able to reach him. Then just when she thought he wasn't going to say a thing, he said, "I dreamed of the horses last night."

It wasn't at all the answer she was expecting. "The horses?"

"At the ranch." His gaze was abruptly focused on hers, staring at her so intently she could barely breathe. "I dreamed about the fire I lit. The smoke and heat. The screams of the animals . . . They sound like people, did you know? They sound like people screaming." He stopped all of a sudden, and there was no warning. He reached for her, grabbing her upper arms and hauling her right up against him. Then his mouth was on hers in a kiss so desperate it stole every last breath from her body.

Lucas didn't really know what he was doing. Somewhere in between her blocking his exit to the elevator and her hand pressing down on his chest, the heat of it scorching him inside and out, he'd lost . . . something. His ability to detach himself, to cut off his emotions completely, to keep himself the fuck under control. Whatever it was, he'd lost it.

He'd thought he'd stayed cold. Sure, the nightmare that had woken him up at one in the morning hadn't helped, and because he hadn't been able to go back to sleep the subsequent hours he'd spent in the gym then pacing around in the living area, turning over all kinds of plans in his head, then sitting down to e-mail a few contacts, probably hadn't done him any good either.

But he'd thought he was fine. He'd taken that call from the asshole after Grace—the fake cop obviously having done his part to deliver Lucas's message—and given him the lowdown on what was going to happen. Two days to get the money together and then to make it to the drop-off. He hadn't given the asshole—Oliveira himself apparently—any time to respond, because he'd made his move. Or rather, he was *going* to make his move, since his real plan didn't involve exchanging money with international criminals. No, he had another idea about what he was going to do. All he needed was to wait for a couple of those e-mails before he could make it.

But he'd heard the soft sound of Grace's breathing in the silence of the room and realized she'd been there for quite some time, watching him. Listening to his conversation for sure, but definitely watching him.

He didn't like it. He was the one who watched, not the other way around.

Tension had crawled across his shoulders and back, and for some reason when her warm hands had come around his waist, touching him, they'd felt like acid on his skin, peeling him open. He'd pulled away before he'd even realized it. Which he never did. He never made any kind of physical movement that wasn't completely intentional.

Even when he'd pulled her to the floor in her studio and taken her there, that had been a completely conscious choice.

This wasn't.

It was the dream that had been the problem. For months after the fire, he'd had nightmares of smoke and flames and the sounds of animals screaming. He'd used to wake up, covered in sweat, his heart racing, fear sharp and metallic in his mouth. But once he'd started the physical and mental discipline his father taught him, riding and target practice, hard physical work to tire himself out, anything that would consume his focus and direct his attention for long periods of time, he'd gotten much better. The dreams had faded and then stopped completely. He hadn't had one since he was fifteen.

Until last night. Until he'd smelled the familiar acrid scent of smoke, felt the lick of fire against his skin, heard the screaming of horses as the stables had burned around them. He'd woken up with a jerk, once again covered in sweat, the sounds of those horses echoing in his head.

Grace had stirred beside him and he knew he'd woken her too, so he'd murmured it was nothing and to go back to sleep, while he'd gotten up, his heart pounding. He'd instinctively tried to exorcise the dream by going into the gym and working himself into a stupor with the punching bag. By the time morning had come around, he thought he'd succeeded.

Then she'd touched him, proving just how big of a lie that was.

He'd thought going straight to his shooting range would be the best way to handle it. Put some distance between himself and her, focus on the target the way he used to back in Wyoming and not on the churning mass of emotion inside him.

But she hadn't accepted that, because Grace never accepted being dismissed. She'd gotten in his face, putting herself between him and the elevator, standing there demanding he tell her what was going on. He hadn't been going to, because telling her would be tantamount to turning on that emotional tap and if he did he knew he'd never be able to shut it off. All he'd thought of doing was nudging her gently aside and out of his way.

She'd touched him again, though. Put her hand on his bare chest and pressed down, her lovely eyes full of warmth and concern. He was very good at keeping people out, at making sure they kept their distance. No one wanted to be around someone who was cold and emotionless, who never smiled and who didn't bother with small talk. But somehow Grace had gotten inside him, her warmth, her restless passion, her careless physicality. Her quicksilver emotions. And even though he knew he shouldn't tell her, he wanted to. Because there was a deep part of himself that was tired of keeping people out. Tired of being alone. Tired of having to deal with this himself.

He wanted to let someone in. He wanted to talk to someone.

So he'd told her about the dream, about the screams that were still echoing in his head, about the fear that seemed to grab him by the throat and not let go. Her eyes had gone wide, her lovely mouth in an O of shock, and suddenly talking was too much for him. There was only one way he could drown out the screams in his head and that was with her.

It wasn't a conscious decision this time. It was instinct. And a part of himself—the part that always tried to stay in control—made a desperate grab at the reins to try to pull him back.

But it was too late. Her mouth was under his and she was hot and sweet, and he wanted to lose himself. Escape the screams. Channel all the fear and pain and anger that he didn't understand, into her.

It was a violent, hungry, savage kiss. An impossible, uncontrollable kiss.

Desire raged inside him as if a dam had burst and he was overwhelmed, was drowning in the flood.

He couldn't stop himself from ravaging her mouth, pushing his tongue deep inside, as his fingers pressed hard into the fragile skin of her upper arms. The taste of her sated him and yet, at the same time, reminded him again of the fact that he was starving and desperate for more.

She melted against him instantly, her body pliant in his arms, and when he hauled her dress up above her waist she made no attempt to stop him. Not even when he shoved her up against the nearest wall, curving one hand behind her knee and hauling her leg up and around his waist, opening her up to him.

Keeping her mouth beneath his, he slid his hands

between her thighs, finding that she wasn't wearing any underwear, her flesh hot and slick beneath his fingertips. She jerked under his touch, shuddering, and he pushed her harder against the wall, crushing her there with his body, needing every inch of her up against every inch of him.

Her hands settled on his shoulders, stroking him like he was one of those terrified horses himself, trying to soothe him. But he didn't feel soothed. He only felt more desperate.

Pinning her against the wall, he ripped open the front of her dress, baring her perfect little tits, and then he tore his lips from hers, lifting her higher so her nipple was right there. Then he leaned in and covered it with his mouth, wanting the taste of her skin to explode the remains of the nightmare. Wanting her cries to drown the sounds of the horses screaming. The sound of his conscience and his own guilt screaming along with them.

She arched against him, giving him the cry he'd wanted as he sunk his teeth into her tender flesh, nipping her, then sucking hard. He pushed his hand down between her thighs again, stroking the wetness he found there, rubbing his thumb over her clit, making her even wetter, even slicker.

His name broke from her, the hands on his shoulders no longer stroking, her fingertips digging into his skin.

Yes, fuck. He wanted more of that, wanted more of her helpless ecstasy. But he had no patience, none at all. He was desperate, strung out, swamped by the emotions inside him, and with no idea at all how to handle it except this.

Taking his hand from her clit, he jerked open his jeans and grabbed his cock. Then he shoved his way inside her, hard and deep, the tight feel of her stretching around him drawing a harsh groan from his throat.

She shivered, holding on to him, her breathing loud in his ear as he kept her pinned between his body and the wall.

"It's okay." Her voice was hoarse, fingertips stroking his shoulders once again. "It's okay, Lucas. I'm here. Take whatever you want. Whatever you need."

And he did. He shoved his hand in her beautiful hair and turned his head, taking her mouth again. Sliding his tongue in deep as he thrust his cock deep inside her pussy. Pulling back, then slamming back in. Over and over. Escaping the feelings he couldn't seem to turn off. Channeling them into pleasure. Into ecstasy, because it was the only thing that made sense.

Hard. Fast. Faster.

Her pussy clenched tight around him, her mouth open and generous, letting him ravage and devour. Her body was soft and so fragile in his hands. He could destroy someone like her so easily, because he was dangerous; he always had been. He cared too much. He felt too much. Her feelings led her to creativity, to color and light and joyful passion. But his? Christ, there was only one place his feelings led him to and that was to destruction.

He slammed into her, over and over, giving himself up to the pleasure as it opened up inside him, stripping him for a few blissful moments of all thought, everything narrowing down to this moment. To her body trapped between him and the wall. Her pussy tight around his cock. Her mouth beneath his. Her hands on his shoulders, soothing, stroking.

Grace. *Grace*.

The orgasm took him without warning, exploding like an IED, fierce and bright, blowing all the thoughts out of his head, leaving him clean and empty, a few precious seconds when he didn't have to keep himself locked down or stay detached. When he could simply be.

The sound of his breathing was loud in the silence, harsh and elevated, his heartbeat so fast. He felt torn out of himself somehow, cracked open, and he had no idea how that had happened or why.

You'll never be able to get it back under control. She's ruined you.

He shut his eyes, forcing the thought away, replacing it with her musky apple scent and the salty/sweet taste of her skin.

She was stroking him again, her hands moving carefully on his shoulders and on his back. "Do you have nightmares?" she murmured. "Is that what happened?"

"I used to get them after the fire." Her touch made him shiver, but he didn't want her to stop. He didn't want to move either. "For at least a couple of years at least. I used to hear the horses screaming and the sound woke me up." It was surprisingly easy to say. "I told Dad about them in the first few weeks after the fire and I asked him why it kept happening. Why the horses sounded like people. And he said that . . ." He stopped, a shudder going through him, the words getting stuck in his throat.

Grace said nothing, her hands moving on him. There was no demand in her now, her silence an invitation that he could fill or leave empty if he chose. And a part of him wanted to leave it empty forever, to keep this particular truth to himself. Because it was terrible and he didn't want anyone else to have to share the burden of it.

But somehow he was speaking, as if the truth wanted to come out whether he wanted it to or not, drawn from him by her softness and her heat. By her gentle touch. It seemed that Grace Riley could be quiet and still when she wanted to be too.

Lucas drew in a breath. "After I lit the fire in the stables, Dad did some digging and looked at the fire department's report on my family. On the fire I lit back when I

was five. He also checked the coroner's report and . . ." He
had to force the words out. "My dad was found in bed, apparently dying of smoke inhalation. But my mom . . . she
was found in the hallway and it looked like she'd been
heading to my room. The fire there was very intense, very
hot." His voice got gravelly. "Some of the roof had come
down, pinning her underneath it and . . ." Grace's hands
didn't stop touching him, her movements slow and gentle,
weaving patterns on his skin. "She was still alive when it
happened. But she couldn't move and the fire was so hot."
It shouldn't have been so hard to say. It had happened so
long ago. "The coroner thought she'd probably burned
alive, or so Noah, my foster father, told me. He said he
didn't want to keep the truth from me, because it was a
cautionary tale. He said that I'd probably heard her, that
the horses' screams sound like people because I was still
hearing my mother screaming as she burned."

CHAPTER FOURTEEN

The view over Lucas's powerful shoulder wavered as tears filled Grace's eyes, her heart clenching tight in her chest. Tears of shock as the horror of what he was telling her finally penetrated.

She couldn't comprehend it. That a man could dump that kind of truth on his thirteen-year-old foster son.

"Why?" she asked shakily "Why would he tell you something like that?"

Lucas didn't move, his breath warm against her neck. His big, hard body was all around her, caging her, pinning her to the wall, and yet somehow it felt as if she was the one keeping him upright, not the other way around.

"It was a punishment." His voice sounded scraped raw. "I had to learn a lesson so it would never happen again. I think . . . he must have hated me to tell me that."

A tear slid down Grace's cheek and then another. She didn't stop them.

There was always going to be a reason for why Lucas kept himself so cold, so detached, and that reason was always going to be a difficult one. He'd even laid it all out for her that night of their first kiss, giving her all the reasons why he couldn't let go of his control. He'd lit fires and his family had died, but when he'd talked about it his cold voice had somehow sucked all the horror out of it. Made it seem distant.

But this . . . She was still reeling from it. He'd found this out at thirteen and had been living with the knowledge that his mother's terrible death had been his fault ever since.

No wonder he'd locked himself down so completely.

He was still inside her and of course they hadn't used any protection, but they'd already had that discussion and anyway, that seemed like the least of her problems right now. She had no idea what to say. No idea what to do. How could she make him feel better about something as horrific as that? Her own issues seemed like nothing in comparison. So her father had been a temperamental artist and had been mean to her. Balled up a few drawings. Big fucking deal.

Her heart felt bruised. Like someone had kicked it repeatedly.

"You were just a little boy." Tears made her voice thick. "It wasn't your fault. You had no idea what you were doing."

He said nothing, his face tucked into her neck. Then a shudder shook him, like he was breaking apart, so she did the only thing she could. She made her arms iron bands and kept her legs wrapped tightly around his waist. Then she held on, held him so tightly. Fiercely. And she cried for the five-year-old who'd only wanted a bike. For the thirteen-year-old whose father had given him a horrific truth to bear all on his own. For the man who'd locked himself down so totally he'd become nothing but brittle ice.

Ice that was breaking now.

So she didn't say a word. She merely held him as tight as she could, giving him the only reassurance she could: that he wasn't alone.

Eventually the shudders wracking him stopped and he was still, leaning into her. She didn't release him, kept holding him tightly as the tears streamed down her cheeks. Then after what felt like a long, long time, he lifted his head and looked down at her.

She'd thought that given how he'd shaken in her arms, he might have wept, but he hadn't. His eyes were dry, the expression on his face one she couldn't read clearly. Pain and anger and guilt shifted like the shadows of clouds on a perfect blue sea, but there was also something that looked a lot like wonder there too.

She had no idea what that meant, since there was nothing wonderful about what he'd just told her.

He said nothing, only looked at her. Then he lowered his head and kissed her again, but not with desperation or hunger this time. It was soft and warm and somehow unbearably sweet. It was a thank-you and an apology and an acknowledgment all rolled up into one.

It also told her that he didn't want to talk anymore about this. That simply telling her had taken all he had. And she understood. There was no need to go over the horror of it endlessly. It was enough that he'd told her, shared it with her, and that alone she was grateful for.

She let him kiss her for a long time, giving him her own silent acknowledgment in return, that she was glad he'd told her, that she was here for him. And when he finally broke the kiss and lifted his head, his thumb brushing away the remains of her tears, she said, "What can I do? Anything you want, anything at all, I'll give it to you."

He said nothing, his fingers gentle against her skin, the dark currents of all those emotions drifting in his eyes. Then at last he said, "I'd like to teach you to shoot."

Swallowing back more tears, she gave him a watery smile. "Okay. Then let's do this thing."

Fifteen minutes later, after they'd both showered and changed and Lucas had promised to buy her a new dress, they went down in the elevator to the basement and from there along a long concrete corridor.

He stopped at a door that had a keypad beside it, quickly entering the code. The door unlocked and he pushed it open, ushering her inside.

Grace stepped into a long concrete-block room with targets set up down one end and down the other a long counter with some stools set up behind it. Various cabinets lined the walls and Grace wondered if that was where Lucas kept his guns, but he didn't go over to them. Instead he made for another door with yet another keypad beside it, keying in the code to unlock this as well.

She followed him curiously.

This room was small, with more metal cabinets, each with yet another serious-looking lock on it.

"You ever fired a gun before?" Lucas approached one of the cabinets and unlocked it, pulling it open. Inside it were an array of pistols that made Grace blink a couple of times.

Wow, if all those other cabinets were full of guns like this one was he had a serious collection.

"No," she said. "Not even once."

"Come over here. Let me show you what I've got."

She came up beside him, looking at the guns in the cabinet, listening to him as he began to unreel facts and figures about each model. He picked each one up as he did so, flicking open the chamber, showing her the handgrip, the safety, and all kinds of other things she didn't really understand. Cartridges and calibers, plus a whole lot of numbers.

There had been tension around his mouth earlier, but now, as he talked weaponry, the tension began to ease. His shoulders got less tight too, and as he unlocked the cabinet that revealed a whole lot of rifles the dark shadows that had been in his eyes earlier faded.

She stared at him as he talked, as he became more animated. And it struck her suddenly, as he handled a rifle with calm, professional ease, showing her the various things it could do, that there was something boyish about him. Something excited and curious and interested. Like a kid showing someone his favorite toy.

It made her heart hurt. It made her feel teary all over again. And not because the boy he'd once been had gone for good, but because that boy was still there. He was bubbling up to the surface right now, giving her a glimpse of what he'd been like all those years ago. Before his father had given him a burden no thirteen-year-old kid should ever have to bear.

She wanted to tell him so. That he wasn't gone, he wasn't lost, but then Lucas had spent all his life trying to deny that boy, shutting him into a box and nailing the lid closed so he never got out. It wouldn't help to point out that Lucas hadn't nailed it shut as firmly as he could have, and she definitely didn't want him to go cold on her again. But maybe she could encourage that boy out a little more, let him play.

So she asked Lucas all the questions she could think of about the rifles. Dumb questions. Stupid questions. Ridiculous questions. Questions she couldn't understand the answers to, but she listened to them all the same, watching the fleeting glitter of excitement in his eyes as he began explaining about laser sights and listening to the raw note in his deep voice fade. As he became animated and interested, demonstrating—because she'd asked—how quickly he could take apart a semi-automatic and put it back together again.

He handed her the rifle to hold to show her how heavy

it was, and she yelped in surprise, nearly dropping the thing. His mouth twitched at that and she could have sworn it was a smile. It made her go warm all over.

At least a half hour later, after she'd asked him a completely asinine question about whether he could hit a fly on a wall from a mile away, he glanced at his watch, then at her, giving her a look that told her he knew exactly what she was doing. She smiled sweetly back and was rewarded with another mouth twitch.

Then he put the rifles away and returned back to the cabinet full of pistols, pulling one out. "Here," he said, holding it out. "Let's try you with this."

It was black and bigger than she'd thought, her head full of visions of tiny pearl-handled guns that somehow fitted easily in garters. This was *not* that type of gun. It was also surprisingly heavy.

"SIG Sauer, 9-millimeter," Lucas said as she wrapped her fingers around it. "Good gun. Not much recoil."

Grace hefted it experimentally. "Is that a good thing?"

"It is when you've never shot a gun before." He raised a blond brow in that arrogant way he had. "Two hands, Grace. You're not a TV cop."

Oh. Right.

Altering her grip, she followed him out of his armory and back into the main room, letting him position her down the end of the room where the counter was. There was a rail attached to the ceiling with a metal arm hanging down from it, the target attached to the arm. Like she'd seen on cop shows, she guessed that all Lucas would need to do would be to hit a button and the target would travel along the rail so they didn't have to go down and check it themselves.

He went over to yet another cabinet and opened it, taking out two pairs of earmuffs and some safety glasses before coming back over to where she stood.

Putting the gun carefully down on the counter, Grace took the glasses from him and frowned at them. "I get the need for earmuffs, but these?"

"Gun safety is important." He gave her cool look. "Or do you not want to do any shooting today?"

She liked that he was teasing her—and he was *definitely* teasing her. At least she hoped he was. Giving him a grin, she picked up the glasses and put them on. "There. Happy?"

"You'll do." He reached for the gun. "Now, listen carefully." And he began to explain what she needed to do with the gun. First he told her what all the parts of it were and what they did yet again; then he began to show her how it all worked.

He was very calm, very patient, and she had the sudden thought that it wouldn't matter to him how long she took to learn this; even if it took days, weeks, months, he would continue to be calm and patient.

But then that was part of who he was, wasn't it? Patience was vital to a sniper, and as he'd already told her, he was a very patient man.

As he instructed her on the proper grip, she wondered if he'd always been like that. Or was his patience cultivated, another way to put what had happened to him years ago behind him?

What does it matter? He is who he is now.

No, it didn't matter. She was only curious. As always, it was his dichotomy that intrigued her. The patience that overlaid all the fire he was underneath. He was such a fascinating man.

"Okay," he said, jolting her out of her thoughts. "Are you ready?"

She nodded and he grabbed the earmuffs, putting them on her himself and making sure they were covering her ears. Then he donned a pair before he helped her into the correct shooting stance.

The gun was heavy in her hands as she extended her arms and the target looked a long, long way away. Lucas was standing behind her and close, his body a hot wall at her back, as if he was guarding her. It made her feel protected, safe. It made her feel strong. Which was weird, since she'd never thought of herself as weak. Yet having him right there behind her added something. Like an extra layer of vibrant color on a canvas, making the picture stronger, bringing the whole thing to life.

He extended his own arms on either side of hers, his hands cupping her forearms, bracing them. Steadying her. And he was all around her, the warmth of him up her spine and across her shoulders, his fresh scent making the restlessness inside her settle.

He went still. Waiting for her.

She tried to remember what he'd told her about aiming a pistol, which she'd rather stupidly forgotten because she'd been too busy thinking about him. Blinking, she aligned the front and rear sights. He'd said something about not looking at the target but focusing on the gun instead, so she did. Then she concentrated, steadying herself.

And pressed down on the trigger.

The gun kicked in her hand, the report loud even with her earmuffs on.

Lucas didn't move, his hands dropping away from her arms now she'd taken the first shot. A bolt of exhilaration went straight through her. She'd never been particularly keen on guns and hadn't taken much interest when Griffin went to the range to practice his skills. It was simply military nonsense to her.

But she hadn't liked feeling helpless up there in the apartment. Hadn't liked feeling as if she was easy prey for anyone. No, one shot didn't make her an expert, but at least she wasn't a total newb anymore. If there was a gun lying around she could pick it up and maybe have a chance of protecting herself.

She squeezed off another few shots, trying to aim better, purely getting used to the feel of the gun in her hand and the kickback after each shot. Another couple of rounds and she'd emptied the chamber.

Putting the gun back on the counter, she pulled off her earmuffs and turned around, grinning like a maniac. "How did I do?"

Something that looked a hell of a lot like amusement glittered in his eyes. "We'll have to see the target first."

She couldn't imagine what was so funny about her wanting to know how she did, but she was glad he found it amusing. He could do with more amusement, quite frankly.

Ridiculously pleased with herself, Grace looked down toward the targets. "Push the thingy so I can see if I hit anything."

Again his mouth twitched, but he reached for the underside of the counter and must have pressed a button, the target retrieval system kicking into life, bringing the paper target slowly forward.

Breathlessly, she scanned the target for any incriminating holes.

Sadly, there were none.

"Oh." The satisfied feeling ebbed slightly. "I didn't even hit the thing."

Warm arms came around her as Lucas pulled her back against him, the length of his hard body pressed to her spine. "Don't worry," he murmured, his warm breath against her ear. "There's plenty of time to practice."

She sighed and leaned into him, relishing the feel of his arms around her and giving him back the warmth of her own body in return. "I guess no one hits their targets the first time, right?"

"Not quite no one."

"Oh, don't tell me. You did?"

"I'm a good shot."

She twisted around in his arms, looking up into eyes gone a deep, mesmerizing blue. "Show me. I want to see you shoot."

He looked at her for a long moment and then slowly, like the sun coming up after an endless arctic night, he smiled.

Grace's breath caught, every single thought emptying out of her head. Because that smile took his already intense beauty and magnified it by a thousand.

You made him smile. You did this.

"Thank you," he said, very softly.

And she didn't need to ask what he was thanking her for. She knew.

Later, as afternoon was slowly turning into evening, Lucas sat at the kitchen table, his laptop open in front of him, the plan he'd been formulating since that morning turning over in his head.

He'd left Grace upstairs in bed, having a nap, and even though his own body was desperately craving sleep, he knew he wasn't going to be able to until he set a few things in motion.

It's not that you won't be able to. You're afraid to.

But no, he'd already decided he wasn't going to think about that. About the nightmare or about the secret he'd told Grace. The truth his father had laid on him all those years ago. He hadn't wanted to tell her. Hadn't wanted her to have to share the horror of it. Or have her look at him the way she should look at him: like he was a monster.

His father, all cold reserve and detachment, had looked him in the eye as he'd told him, as if he'd wanted Lucas to know just how much of a danger he was to people. The very real and terrible consequences of his actions. And afterwards, he'd had to go and throw up, sickened by what he'd done.

No, he hadn't wanted to share that with her, but he had. And the wonder of it was that she hadn't looked at him with horror. She'd wept and held on to him tightly, as if she was afraid of letting him go.

He hadn't expected that. Hadn't expected the fierce pressure of her arms or the wetness of her tears. Or the sympathy and pain in her eyes as she'd looked up at him afterwards. He hadn't expected her to feel bad for him.

Right then, he hadn't wanted to talk about it. Just saying it out loud had been enough, and he'd been grateful that she'd seemed to pick up on it. Letting him take her downstairs to the shooting range, letting him talk about his guns.

He'd known she was encouraging him to talk, to be distracted, and he appreciated it because dealing with his weaponry was familiar. He appreciated it even more when he'd given her the SIG and taught her how to shoot it properly.

As he stood there with his arms around her, steadying her as she took aim, it struck him suddenly that he was here in the place that he came to whenever he needed to focus himself, doing one of the few things he actually let himself enjoy, with the woman who knew his secret and hadn't turned him away.

Everything fused into one special moment.

And he realized with a certain amount of shock that he was happy. That even after the nightmare, after he'd told her the truth, the pain of it cutting deep into his soul, there could be this moment. Standing in a shooting gallery with Grace in his arms as she sighted a target.

It seemed an odd place to find happiness, but that's what it felt like. Happiness and peace.

Two things you can't ever have, nor should you.

No, he knew that. He'd always known that. But surely he was allowed a couple of moments. He wouldn't have them forever, but he could let himself take them while they were here. Enjoy them in the now.

Two days he'd given himself. Two days to get his alternative plan up and running but, more important, two more days with Grace Riley.

Christ, how could she ever think she was selfish? After everything she'd given him? He was the selfish one keeping her here, and the press of his conscience told him so.

Ignoring it, he checked his e-mail, hoping he'd have a response from his military contacts. Sure enough, there was and it was good news. He would get the support he needed, as long as he had proof. Which was lucky, since there was all the proof he needed in that file his father had e-mailed him.

There was also another e-mail from Van, detailing his engagement to Chloe and how he was going to be taking over as Tate CEO and how Lucas had to get back to him and at least fucking let him know he was damn well alive.

Lucas deleted the e-mail. He didn't want to talk to either of his brothers right now. He had far more important things to do.

Hitting a button on the keyboard, he flicked the screen back to the photo he'd been looking at earlier. An Upper East Side mansion. The very same one he'd sat outside of a few days ago waiting to rescue Chloe.

Cesare de Santis's mansion.

Lucas had already put in a bit of research into the place while helping grab Chloe, figuring out what kind of security it had, how many men were guarding it, and what their movements were. Not to mention the best vantage points to take a clear shot from.

The place was well guarded. Your average stalker/burglar would never have made it past the front door. Not even if they were above average, to be fair. But Lucas was nothing like average. He was the best of the best, the elite, and he was pretty fucking sure he could get past the front door without being seen.

He frowned at the screen. Annoyingly, Van had been inside that mansion already, distracting de Santis while Lucas grabbed Chloe, and he could probably give Lucas a few pointers on what to expect inside. That would mean contacting Van, though, and that's exactly what he *didn't* want to do.

Bad enough the prick had crossed the line and kissed Chloe, but marrying her as well? Christ.

You're just pissed because you can't have what he has yourself.

Yes, he was. And maybe he needed to get a handle on that, because it wasn't as if that shit was going to change anytime soon. The past was the past and nothing was going to change it.

His mother had died a horrible death and he'd been the cause.

It's not like you deserve anything good anyway.

"What are you doing?" A pair of slim arms wound around his neck, a soft mouth brushing against his ear.

Grace had clearly woken up.

He turned and grabbed her, pulling her onto his lap in an instinctive movement that should have worried him but didn't. She sighed, settling back against his chest, her hair drifting over his shoulder and forearm, light and soft as thistledown.

She squinted at the screen. "Are you doing SEALy things?"

"Well, I am a SEAL. So, yes."

Her mouth curved. "Ah, so the rumors are true."

"What rumors?"

"That you actually do have a sense of humor."

He leaned down and nipped her bottom lip, not wanting to let on how easily she could make him smile. It had only happened in the last couple of hours too. Christ. What was she going to do to him next? "Rude," he murmured. "I may need to teach you some manners."

She went pink, amber eyes glowing. "I'm up for that. But first tell me whose place that is. You're casing it, aren't you?"

He settled his arms around her. She was wearing one of his T-shirts, a dark blue one that came down to the tops of her thighs, the fabric also revealing the fact that she wasn't wearing a bra. He approved. Perhaps she wouldn't be wearing underwear either, and if so, he approved of that as well.

"That's Cesare de Santis's mansion. And what I'm doing is technically called reconnaissance."

"Oh, I love it when you get all military on me." The soft teasing note in her voice made him want to slide his hands under the hem of that T-shirt, stroke her silky skin, tease her in return. "Can I ask why you're doing some reconnaissance?"

There wasn't any reason not to tell her, and considering it was part of getting that asshole Oliveira off her back, then she should probably know.

"I'm going to talk to him directly. See if I can get him to call those bastards off you himself."

Grace twisted in his arms, her eyes wide. "But what about the money they wanted? That guy you were talking to about needing two days to get the cash together?"

"A distraction to give me some time to plan a little personal visit to de Santis."

"Oh, right." A glint of worry flickered in her eyes. "What are you going to do?"

He studied her face. "I'm not going to kill him, if that's what you're concerned about."

She let out a little breath. "Well, okay then. Can't deny that did cross my mind."

"He's a civilian." Lucas brushed a lock of hair behind her ear. He didn't blame her for thinking de Santis's life was what he was after. Taking out the problem was what he did after all. "I don't hurt civilians. Well, not very much anyway."

She gave a shaky laugh. "So what *are* you going do to?"

"I'm going to have a discussion with him about pulling those arms dealers off your tail once and for all. It's his problem. I'm going to make sure he deals with it."

"Oh, okay." Her forehead creased. "I guess he's not just going to agree to a meeting, is he?"

"No, he won't. I'm the son of his enemy and he's already had issues with Van. I rescued Chloe from him and that's not exactly going to endear me to him."

"So how are you going to get to talk to him then?" Then she blinked and looked back at the laptop screen. "Oh. You're not even going to ask for a meeting, are you? You're going to break in."

"Yes."

She turned back to him, and this time the glint of worry was even more pronounced. "That sounds dangerous."

He lifted a shoulder. "Not really. De Santis can't do anything to me."

"You don't know that."

Shit. She was worried for him.

His heart twisted in a way it really shouldn't and he couldn't stop himself from lifting his hands and cupping her face between his palms. "It's okay, Gracie. I know what I'm doing."

"But do you have any backup? Anyone else helping you if things go wrong?"

"No. I prefer to handle this alone and I will. I can't have

anyone else getting involved and potentially screwing things up."

The worried crease between her brows didn't shift. "Lucas, this isn't a sniper mission. You don't have to do this by yourself. What about your brothers? You should call them and let them know what you're doing."

Sure, he could. But de Santis's attention was already on Van, any move Van made to help would be observed, and Lucas's plan was all about the element of surprise. He didn't want to alert de Santis in case the asshole manipulated things to protect himself. And as for Wolf. Well . . . bull, meet china shop.

Bending, Lucas brushed a kiss over her mouth. "I can handle it. I've done plenty of shit like this before and in worse situations."

Her throat moved as she swallowed. "Can't . . . can't we just, I don't know, leave? Walk away? If we stay here long enough perhaps they'll get sick of waiting and leave me alone?"

Yet he could see that even she didn't believe any of what she was saying. "We can't," he said softly, reminding her. "They're not going to stop until they get that money. And I'm not going to give it to them. Which means we have to have some other way of getting them off your back and for good. De Santis is our only option."

Her hands rose, her fingers wrapping around his wrists and holding on as if she needed to touch him as badly as he needed to touch her. "Why would he do anything you said, though? He's really going to say, 'Sure, I'll call those guys off immediately, Mr. Tate, sir'?"

He couldn't help smiling at her imitation of de Santis's voice. "Keep painting, Gracie. I don't think your acting skills are up for much."

Letting go of one wrist, she smacked him on the

shoulder. "Yeah, and I wouldn't give up sniping for stand-up anytime soon." Her mouth became soft and suddenly achingly vulnerable. "Seriously, Lucas."

He relented, stroking her cheekbones gently with his thumbs, a soothing movement that had become instinctive to him over the past day with her. "I have evidence that links de Santis with Griffin's arms dealing. All I need to do is inform the military top brass and de Santis can kiss good-bye to all the government contracts his company relies on."

"But is that enough to threaten him with?"

"He doesn't run the company these days, it's true. But he built it with his own hands and he won't want to see it lose some lucrative contracts. Plus I'm pretty sure he won't like the idea of jail either."

"So, what? You're going to threaten him with that if he doesn't call off the people after me?"

"Exactly. He created the fucking problem. He can clean it up."

Concern still flickered in her eyes. "I don't like the idea of you confronting him alone." She took a little breath. "He might try to hurt you."

Lucas felt his mouth curve in yet another smile. Jesus, what was this woman doing to him? "He can try."

She hit him again. "Arrogant son of a bitch. This isn't a joke."

"I know." He let his hands fall from her cheeks and slid his arms around her, gathering her warmth in close. "Those rumors you heard about my sense of humor? They're all lies. I don't have one. Which means I never joke."

Grace sighed, melting against him. "You're a stubborn bastard, Lucas Tate."

"Yes," he agreed. And kissed her.

CHAPTER FIFTEEN

Grace paused outside the door to the gym Lucas disappeared into every morning. He was having another session with his punching bag from the sounds of his fists thumping heavily and repetitively into the canvas. Good. He'd be in there another hour or so at least.

She continued on past the gym, going quickly down the stairs and into the kitchen. He wouldn't hear her in here, would he? If he was punching *and* she was downstairs *and* in the kitchen, which was about as far away from the gym as she could get, then he couldn't possibly.

Then again, he was a SEAL. He might have super hearing or something.

Going down into his shooting range might have been better, but she didn't have the codes for the doors and hadn't thought to ask for them. Surreptitiously grabbing Wolf's number from his phone had been about the limits of her spy skills and she'd even felt guilty doing that.

She just hadn't been able to stop thinking about Lucas confronting de Santis by himself. It was stupid to worry about him, especially when he was probably right; de Santis wasn't going to do anything to him. It wasn't as if nobody would notice if one of the Tate brothers suddenly disappeared one day. Then again, de Santis was a powerful man. She didn't know much about him, but he and his four sons had been standard gossip fodder for years. And apart from anything else, he'd been CEO of a major weapons design and manufacturing company; it wasn't like he was going to be totally squeaky clean. If he wanted Lucas to disappear badly enough then he might have the resources to make it happen *and* make it look like he had nothing to do with it.

The thought made her go cold with fear. She didn't question the emotion, didn't think too hard about the depth of it, because she was sure there were reasons for it that she didn't want to go into just yet. But she couldn't let it sit there either. She had to *do* something.

No, she couldn't be Lucas's backup. One shooting lesson didn't mean she had the skills to be able to cover him if he needed it. But she did know of a couple of people who did: his brothers.

Since his older brother, Van, had clearly enough on his plate already, Grace had decided not to contact him. But Lucas's younger brother, Wolf, might be able to help. So the night before, while Lucas had been showering, she'd quickly looked up Wolf's contact details on his phone and written them down on a piece of paper.

She pulled that paper out of her jeans pocket now, looking down at it as she quickly punched the number into the landline. It rang for a long while and she thought she might not get an answer until suddenly a deep, harsh, and very male voice said, "What?"

Grace clutched on to the phone. "Is this Wolf Tate?"

"Who the fuck is this?" If this was indeed Wolf Tate then he did *not* sound friendly.

"I need to speak with him. It's urgent."

"You'd better tell me how the fuck you got this number, honey."

She took a breath. "My name is Grace Riley. I'm a

f-friend"—she stumbled over the word helplessly—"of Lucas's."

There was a silence down the other end of the phone.

"He's protecting me," Grace went on, because she had no other choice. "My husband did a stupid thing and some bad people are after me, and Lucas is helping, and . . . I'm afraid he's going to get himself hurt. And I need to speak to Wolf, because I have to get some help—"

"Okay." The word was hard and rough as a stone. "You're speaking to him. Now, tell me exactly what's happening."

Grace sagged against the kitchen counter, a wave of relief going through her. "Oh, thank God. Okay, so here's the situation." She told him about Griffin and the arms dealers, about how Griffin had owed them money and now they wanted it back. About Cesare de Santis and about Lucas's plan to confront the guy.

Guilt twisted inside her as she did, because she knew Lucas was going to hate that she'd gone behind his back. But she also knew how determined he was when he'd decided on something, and she'd seen it over and over again in the course of the past week. If he wanted to do this alone he would, and nothing would stop him.

Anyway, it wasn't like she was going to the police or any other authorities and perhaps putting his plan at risk. She was only going to his brother. That was different, surely?

"Fucking Lucas," Wolf growled after Grace had finished explaining. "Thinks he can save the whole fucking world on his own."

Her heart missed a beat at that, because although Lucas had told her what it was about being a sniper he liked, he hadn't spoken about what had made him join the military. He'd said that taking out targets was all about protecting his buddies, protecting civilians, and even though he was extremely cold and detached, every action he took was about protecting people.

But . . . saving the world. Was that really what he was doing?

Maybe it's not the world he's trying to save. Maybe all he's trying to do is save his family.

Her throat tightened painfully, because she could see it. He'd been badly traumatized by the truth his father had told him and the only way he'd been able to deal with it was to cut himself off from his emotions entirely. But that didn't mean they'd ceased to exist. Underneath, the pain and the guilt especially were still raw. He would need to do something with that, since he wasn't a man to sit idly by, so yeah, perhaps joining the Navy, fighting a war, was his way of making amends for what he'd done as a boy.

"I don't want him to do this by himself," she said. "He needs some backup." There was a double meaning to the words there that Wolf wouldn't understand, but she did. Lucas didn't have to deal with *any* of it by himself. Not while she was here.

"Yeah, he does. Going up against de Santis without it is a dick move. . . ." Wolf paused. "I guess he doesn't know you're contacting me?"

"No. I told him he needed to get some help, but he insisted he was fine without it."

"Christ, he's a dick." Wolf sounded less than thrilled. "Put him on the phone. I'd better speak to him."

"Um, he's in the gym right now and—"

"No, I'm not."

Grace's head snapped up to find Lucas standing in the kitchen doorway, his perfect body gleaming with sweat, the cotton from his T-shirt sticking to his sculpted torso. The look in his silver-blue eyes was distinctly silver and definitely not happy. "Who the fuck are you talking to, Grace?"

"Oh shit," she murmured. "I'm busted."

Wolf, irritatingly, laughed. "Bummer. Tell him if he doesn't want to speak to me I'll call him every five minutes until he picks up his fucking phone."

She swallowed, then lifted her chin and met Lucas's cold blue eyes. "I called Wolf. He wants a word."

Lucas didn't move for a long moment, simply staring at her. Then he came toward her, grabbing the phone out of her hand. "I'll call you back," he said icily to his brother, then disconnected the call, his gaze never leaving hers. "I told you I was handling this. That I didn't want anyone else involved."

"And I told you that I was worried about you," she shot back, feeling guilty and then pissed that she was feeling guilty. "You don't have to do this by yourself, Lucas."

"There's a reason I don't want my brothers involved," he snapped. "Wolf especially is too much of a loose cannon and I can't have him doing something stupid that will draw attention."

Her guilt coiled tighter and she felt like she'd done something stupid. Which only made her madder. "You need some backup with this and I can't help you."

Lucas chucked the phone onto the kitchen counter. "You don't need to help me."

"But I want to." She took a couple of steps right up to him, putting her hands on the damp cotton of his T-shirt, unable to resist the urge to touch him. "What if de Santis manages to make you disappear? What if he hurts you? What if something happens and I never see you again?" Her heart was pounding hard, fear wrapping itself around her, and she knew she was revealing way too much about her own feelings, both to him and to herself, but she couldn't help it. "He's dangerous, Lucas. And I don't want you to get hurt."

The hard expression on Lucas's features softened a little and he lifted his hands and put his palms over hers where they clutched at his chest. "I won't get hurt."

But it wasn't simply about him being hurt. "You can't do this alone. You don't have to. You don't have to do *any* of this alone."

Perhaps he knew what she meant, because something shifted in his gaze, those dark shadows moving. "Grace—"

"Please, Lucas. Maybe you don't need backup. Maybe you're just badass enough that you really can handle it all by yourself. But please, at least talk to Wolf. At least let him know what's going on." She could feel her eyes prickle with unexpected and stupid tears. "Please don't let yourself get hurt because of me."

Lucas's blond brows drew down, his laser-sharp gaze searching her face. His palms were warm over hers, his body blazing like a furnace beneath the fabric of his T-shirt. "Don't care about me, Grace. You know that I'm not—"

"Yeah, you told me," she cut him off, her voice getting thick. He didn't need to spell it out to her. She knew what this was between them. She knew what she'd gotten herself into. "I know you can only give me what we have now. But it's too late. I care about you already." She kept her gaze on his, staring straight into his eyes, letting him see the truth. "And you might be a deadly sniper with a frankly scary confirmed kill count, but you're still just one man. Also, this isn't your fight. This was a mistake Griffin made and I don't want you to have to pay for it."

He was silent, but there was something moving in all that blue, a current of heat, though whether it was anger or something else she couldn't tell. "What about you? Does that mean you should pay for it then?"

The fear wrapped itself tighter around her, but she didn't look away. "Maybe. Maybe if I went and talked to them, told them that—" She broke off on a gasp as his fingers clenched hard around hers all of a sudden.

"No." The word was flat and iron hard. "That will not be happening."

"So it's okay for you to protect me, but I can't protect you?"

"I don't need protection."

But she could see the way the shadows in his eyes flickered. There was a reason he was being stubborn about this and it wasn't simply because he preferred being alone. And she was starting to get an idea of what that reason was.

"Maybe you don't need it," she said quietly. "But you deserve it."

An expression rippled over his face then, too fast for her to get a good look at it, but she thought it might have been shock. He released her hands, turning sharply away, and she knew she should let him go. That if he wanted some distance she needed to give it to him.

Yet he'd told her he wasn't going to let her hide from him, and that went both ways. He wasn't going to hide from her either.

She reached out and grabbed his upper arm, curling her fingers around the taut, hard muscles of his biceps and holding on tight. "I know you're trying very hard to cut yourself off. To keep yourself locked down. But you're not five anymore, Lucas. You're not thirteen either. You're not going to pick up a lighter and burn everything down if you get mad."

He froze, his head turned away from her, the tension in his arm making it feel like she was holding on to a steel bar.

Perhaps it was stupid to keep talking, to bring up the

terrible, painful past he was trying to put behind him. But she'd said too much already and she couldn't stop now.

"You're not going to hurt anyone and I think you know that too. So when are you going to stop punishing yourself for what you did as a kid? Because that's what you're doing. You're cutting yourself off, shutting yourself down. Telling yourself that it's because you like being alone, that you like the mental discipline of staying in control." She gripped him tighter, feeling his muscles tense in preparation for pulling away. "But it's not because you like it. It's because you feel you don't deserve anything more, anything better, isn't it?"

He didn't move, standing there silently, as if he was merely waiting for her to let him go.

You fucking idiot. You said too much and now you've gone and ruined it. Because it's all about what you want, isn't it?

Yes, it *was* about what she wanted. And yes, perhaps it was selfish to push this with him. Yet she couldn't seem to shut herself up.

"But you do deserve it, Lucas," she went on. "You *do.* You're a good man and you care. You care a lot. I know you try so very hard to hide it, but I can see it anyway. Getting my paintings for me, listening to me talk about my dad, telling me that I'm b-beautiful. Even the fact that you're here protecting me just because your father told you I was in danger is a sign that you care. Because you didn't have to. You could have torn that letter up and let those assholes take me. Torture me—"

He jerked away, breaking her grip with ease. Then his hands were on her hips and he was backing her up against the counter, surrounding her in the scent of clean male sweat and the spice that was all Lucas. His gaze was deep sapphire, full of anger and pain and guilt, all the emotions he hid from the rest of the world.

But not her. He didn't hide from her.

"Don't say those things." The words were hoarse. "Don't."

"Why not?" She put her hands over his where they gripped her hips, keeping that skin-to-skin contact. "I know what happened was terrible. It was awful. But you can't live your life the way you are. Keeping people out and cutting yourself off from everything that makes it worth living." This time it was her who reached up and cupped his beautiful face. Her turn to run her thumbs over the exquisite bone structure of his cheekbones and along the curve of his gorgeous mouth. "Don't you think your mother would have wanted a better life for you than that?"

Anger, pure and hot as a gas flame, leapt in his eyes. "You have no fucking idea what my mother would have wanted for me."

But she didn't look away from him and she didn't let go. If she wasn't afraid of his passion she certainly wasn't afraid of his anger. "Neither do you."

The look on his face twisted. "No. Because she died. Because of me."

Grace gripped him tighter. "Yes, she died. Coming to get you. Because she loved you. Because she wanted to save you. She loved you, Lucas. She wouldn't want this for you."

"And you would know. Having had the best parents in the world."

He was trying to hurt her, an animal in pain lashing out. But she ignored the blow, let it glance off her. "Sure, my father was an asshole and my mother let him be one, but I know enough to understand that most parents want the best for their children." Her throat closed up again, tighter this time. "They want them to be happy."

His eyes glittered, pain flashing bright. Then he bent

and kissed her, fiercely and hard. And when he lifted his head, he said harshly, "I'll call Wolf."

Then he pulled away and stalked out of the room.

Lucas went straight from the kitchen to the elevator and hit the button. The doors opened immediately, taking him down to the basement and his shooting range.

He didn't think. He went straight down the corridor, opening up the door, then shutting it hard behind him. Going into the armory, he opened up the cabinet with the pistols in it and chose one at random. Grabbing a pair of earmuffs, he then took up his position and emptied the entire clip into the target.

Reloading, he did it again.

What he really wanted was to be at an outdoor range, where he could grab his TAC-338 and settle down for a good, long shot. Where there was nothing but the target to focus on and the slow, deep-breathing exercises he practiced to get his heart rate down.

Where there wasn't a woman touching him with her warm fingers, looking up into his eyes and telling him things he didn't want to hear. Such as how he needed to stop punishing himself. That he needed to let people in.

That he needed to be happy.

Lucas raised his pistol again, taking aim, squeezing the trigger. The shot hit exactly where he wanted it to, the way it always did.

What the fuck did she know about being happy? It wasn't as if she were happy herself or as if she weren't cutting herself off too. She did the same thing he was doing in many ways. Denying herself what she wanted, because her father's voice was still echoing in her head no matter what she said.

She was a fine one to fucking lecture him about what he

deserved and she had no right at all to tell him what his mother would have wanted for him.

He shot off another round, the reports echoing despite his earmuffs.

She's right and you know it. That's why you're so fucking angry.

Another squeeze on the trigger, and this time the bullet missed the target completely, burying itself in the wall behind it.

Jesus. He never missed.

Slowly, he realized his hand was shaking. Infinitesimally, but shaking all the same. Fuck.

Ripping the earmuffs off his head, he threw them on the floor and slammed the pistol down on the counter in front of him. The smell of cordite hung heavy in the air, enough that it was usually a calming scent to him. But not now. Not today.

No, she wasn't right. She couldn't be. He wasn't a good man and he never had been, because he hadn't been a good kid. He'd been a killer right from the start.

His father had seen it and that's why he'd told him the truth about his mother. If he'd been a good kid his father would have protected him from it, wouldn't he?

Lucas put his hands flat to the counter and leaned on them, hanging his head down, his heartbeat too loud, too fast.

Happiness. What was it? Those moments he'd had with her, those moments he'd *let* himself have. But he couldn't anymore; he knew that now.

Grace had told him she'd cared about him, and that was wrong. She shouldn't. Because no matter what she said, he *would* hurt her as surely as picking up a match and torching the apartment. Because no matter what her feelings for him were, he couldn't return them. He wouldn't. And con-

tinuing on the way they were doing would only make it
worse for her.

She was creation. He was destruction. And it had to
stop.

It had to stop *now*.

*"Don't you think your mother would have wanted a
better life for you?"*

But no, he couldn't think of his mother. It was too painful. Grace had crossed a line bringing her up again and
his role in her death, and he couldn't forgive that. The
wound it had left in his soul was too deep and too raw. It
wasn't going to heal. All he could do was try to cut it out
of him and hope the infection wouldn't spread.

His phone buzzed.

Lucas glanced at it where he'd left it on the counter next
to the pistol. It was Wolf.

Lucas wanted to ignore it completely, but there was a
part of him that wouldn't let himself. That saw the fear in
Grace's eyes and instinctively wanted to ease it. Okay, so
he couldn't let himself feel for her, but he could at least
make sure she wasn't afraid.

Reaching out, he picked up the phone, hitting the answer button before he could second-guess it. "What the
fuck do you want?"

"Hey," Wolf said irritatedly, "you're the one who was
going to call me back, asshole."

"Consider this a callback then."

His brother grunted, clearly disapproving. "So what's
all this bullshit about de Santis and you going in to deal
with him yourself? Oh, and you might want to fill me in
on why you're protecting that Grace chick."

Lucas didn't want to, but he made himself. "Dad's fucking letter. That's what was in it. A mission to protect Grace.
You remember Griffin Riley? She's his widow."

Wolf muttered a curse. "What the fuck's that got to do with Dad?"

"Griffin was involved in some arms dealing. And I don't need to tell you who was paying him to tout for business."

"Jesus. De Santis, right?"

"Yes. After the letter I also got an e-mail with a file attached, and evidence in the file. There's no doubt it was Griffin and that de Santis was paying him. The stupid asshole set up a deal, took the money, but the deal fell through, and then he died. And now there's some asshole arms dealer called Oliveira who wants his money back and doesn't care if Grace doesn't have it."

Another curse. "So you've got a plan to get rid of him?"

"I do. And no matter what Grace says, I can handle it myself."

"Hey, I'm not going to muscle in on your territory, bro. Chill."

There was a silence, both of them suddenly realizing the irony of Wolf having to tell Lucas to chill out.

Christ, he was losing it. Grace wasn't his territory, not anymore.

"I'm going to pay de Santis a little visit." Lucas tried to keep his voice level and cold. "Get him to deal with his mess and maybe I won't take the evidence to the top brass. He won't want to risk his company's government contracts or a jail term."

Wolf didn't say anything for a long moment. "Fuck, if Riley was dealing in this shit then de Santis must have some military contacts in his pocket. Riley wouldn't have been able to do anything without a few people turning a blind eye."

It was true. Shit. Why hadn't he thought of that himself? This threw a wrench in his plan. How could he take the evidence to his CO if he couldn't trust that the guy wasn't in de Santis's pay? How could he trust anyone? Christ, this was bad. He couldn't take an empty threat to de Santis.

His free hand reached for the pistol on the counter in front of him and he picked it up, clenching his fingers around the grip unconsciously, the weight of the metal reassuring. "This is true." His voice sounded weird, slightly hoarse.

"I'm not going to ask if you're okay," Wolf said, annoyingly perceptive, which wasn't usual for him. "But if you want me to make a few enquiries I'm happy to."

Enquiries being Wolf speak for "smacking some heads."

Lucas dearly wanted to tell him that he had everything under control, but that wasn't something he could handle right now, not when he only had one more day before the assholes after Grace expected their money to be delivered to them.

"You can't live your life the way you are. Keeping people out and cutting yourself off from everything that makes it worth living."

He found himself snarling at the gun in his hand. Fuck, whether he wanted help or not, it looked like he wasn't going to have a choice about it.

"Fine," he said, unable to keep the word as icy as he wanted it to be. "Do what you have to do. But I'll need some trusted names within the next twenty-four hours."

"I'm on it. . . ." Wolf paused. "Are you sure there's nothing you want to tell me about you and this Grace chick?"

But Lucas was done. He didn't respond, hitting the disconnect button, then throwing the phone back down on the counter. He'd never told his brothers what his father had revealed to him about his mother, and he wouldn't. They didn't need that shit in their heads, not when they had their own issues to deal with. He wasn't going to tell them about Grace either.

She was no one's business but his.

And soon she wasn't even going to be his business.

He put on his earmuffs, then shoved another clip into the handgun. Lifted it and aimed.

No, not soon.

Now.

CHAPTER SIXTEEN

Lucas didn't come up from the basement, leaving Grace pacing up and down in the long gallery in front of the rose window, feeling like shit.

She should never have said anything to him. Should never have confronted him. Should never have told him she cared about him. Never revealed herself so completely.

But she hadn't been able to stop. Her worry for him was so sharp and not only for his physical safety. It was his emotional well-being that really concerned her, that really cut like a knife. He was so alone, so shut down. And it hurt. It hurt to see him like that. Especially when she knew now the man he was underneath that icy, frozen lake.

Yet what could she do? He didn't want to listen to her, couldn't give up the survival mechanism he'd been using for so long. And it was a survival mechanism; she could see that. Like the way she'd refused to see the reality of her marriage to Griffin, telling herself everything was fine, that they were both happy when they weren't. So she didn't have to deal with the fact that some of it had been her fault. That her refusal to talk about anything, the way she treated Griffin more like a friend than a husband, was making him unhappy.

A survival mechanism so she didn't have to see that it wasn't him who didn't seem to care that much about her or even want her. It was her who didn't want him and had never wanted him, not in the way a wife should want a husband.

Being with Lucas had brought into sharp relief what had been missing from her marriage. Yes, she'd loved Griffin. But as a friend, not as a husband. What had been missing was her passion and she'd held that back, pouring it into her creativity, into her art, rather than giving it to him. Because she was scared of giving someone everything she was only to have him turn on her the way her father had.

She stopped in the middle of the gallery and put her hands over her eyes.

Maybe she should go downstairs and try to find Lucas, apologize for stepping over the line. Tell him she wouldn't speak of it again, that perhaps they could pretend that conversation had never happened.

And then what? You told him you cared about him. He knows now. You can't take it back.

Her throat tightened.

Stupid, so stupid. She felt like she was thirteen again and showing her father her drawings, her heart thumping with trepidation and terrible hope. Desperate for him to be the loving, supportive father he'd once been before the bitterness had set in.

But of course he hadn't. And the disappointment had been shattering.

The elevator chimed and instantly her head came up, her hands dropping from her face.

Lucas stepped out of the elevator, his expression as hard and as cold as she'd ever seen it. The ice man was in full control now.

Her heart began to ache, the chill radiating from him almost palpable. God, she didn't need to see his expression to know how badly she'd screwed up; she could feel it, like an icy wind blowing straight off the Arctic.

"Lucas," she began, desperate to make things right. "I'm sorry. I should never have—"

"We need to stop."

His voice cut across her, the edge in it sharp and precise as a surgeon's knife, and at first she didn't quite understand what he was saying.

"Stop? Stop what?"

"We need to stop sleeping together." His eyes glittered, all silver, all ice. "This . . . affair we're having. It's over, Grace."

In her head she could hear the sound of heavy drawing paper being ripped slowly in two. It felt oddly like her soul being torn right down the middle.

She blinked, staring at him, trying to find even one sign of the intense, passionate man she knew lived behind that frosty silver gaze. But if he was there, there was no sign of him. "Oh," she said huskily, trying to ignore the dull ache that throbbed just behind her breastbone. "But I thought that wasn't going to happen until this situation is over."

"I changed my mind." Lucas's voice was flat. "The last part of my plan is going to need my full attention and I can't afford a distraction now."

A distraction. So that's what she was? That's what she'd become?

Oh come on. You knew this was going to come eventually. All he promised you was now. It's you who made the mistake of caring about him.

There was a lump in her throat and it hurt worse than she thought it would. A lot worse.

"If I hadn't said those things to you just before," she said before she could stop herself, "would you have ended it now?"

"No." There was absolutely no flicker of expression on his face. "What you said to me earlier has nothing to do with it."

He's lying. Of course it does.

"If I hadn't told you that I cared about you—"

"Stop, Grace." If his gaze had been an icy storm she would have frozen to death where she stood. "I told you this was only for a limited time. And now that time is up."

But she wasn't ready for it to be up. She wasn't ready for it to be over. She wanted more. Just another couple of days, another few hours even.

Now you're the one who's lying. You don't want another day or even a few hours. You want more than that.

Tears of pain were prickling behind her eyes, but she blinked them fiercely away. She suddenly didn't want to give him any more ammunition than he had already. Because hadn't she forgotten that he was deadly? He was a sniper, a precision shot. He could deal her a killing blow without her even seeing it coming.

Like now, for instance.

"So that's it?" She didn't know why she was arguing with him when every word she said revealed the true depths of her feelings. "Just 'it's over'? I don't get a say?"

"No, you don't." He might as well have been a robot for all the expression he showed, his beautiful face a mask of indifference. "And yes, just like that."

The lump in her throat was getting bigger and bigger, and her vision was wavering. It shouldn't hurt this badly; it really shouldn't. Because she'd told herself she wasn't going to fall for him, that she'd keep a part of herself held back. And she thought she had. Sure, she'd given him her passion, but nothing else, right?

Nothing except your heart.

Much to her horror, a tear slipped down one cheek, and even though she turned her head and quickly lifted her hand to brush it away, she knew he'd seen it. Because for the briefest second she thought she saw something flicker in his cold gaze. Then it was gone as if it had never been, and she knew she must have imagined it.

No, he didn't have her heart; he really didn't. She'd held that back, kept it for herself.

But the ache in her chest told her what a lie that was.

She cleared her throat, blinking furiously. "Okay," she said as if it didn't matter and didn't hurt. At all. "If that's the way you feel then."

He didn't say anything and she desperately wanted to be the one who walked away, who left the room first, but he was already moving, heading toward the kitchen without even a second glance. Leaving her standing there staring after him like an idiot.

Everything hurt. There as a great, gaping hole in her chest, and she knew if she weren't careful she was going to cry. But no, she wouldn't do that here, not where he could hear her. She wasn't going to go after him and beg him to change his mind either. That would be way too desperate, way too needy, and if she begged and he said no . . .

You'd never recover.

Swallowing hard, Grace forced herself to move toward the stairs, and a moment later she found herself standing in the little makeshift studio in front of the painting she had started only a couple of days earlier. There were streaks of reds and oranges and golds across the white canvas, the beginning she'd imagined before Lucas had burst in that day, taking her to the floor in a blaze of passion.

A shudder swept through her.

Why was she here? Painting was the last thing she felt like doing right now, especially when the last time she'd been in this room it had been with Lucas. His hands on her body, his mouth on hers, his cock inside her, lightning her up, making her blaze . . .

She hadn't meant to move toward the paint, but she found herself doing so anyway, grabbing a few tubes and a brush before coming back to the canvas in front of her. There was a feeling inside her, growing bigger and brighter, like an out-of-control brush fire on a tinder-dry plain. Painful and raw and hot, making tears leak out of her eyes and her body ache. It was anguish and desire and guilt and grief. Happiness and sorrow. It was everything and she had to get it out of her one way or another, or else it was going to eat her alive.

"You create, Gracie. You don't destroy . . ."

Grace tore the cap off one of the tubes and squeezed some fire red onto her fingers before dropping the tube carelessly onto the floor.

Then she began to paint.

Lucas leaned against the wall in the alleyway, ignoring the snow swirling in the air, and watched the chauffeur get out of the long black limo parked at the curb opposite the alley and move around to the passenger's side.

In another minute the door of the mansion should open and Cesare de Santis would come out of it, ready to go to the regular morning meeting he had with an old friend at a cafe downtown. And Lucas knew de Santis would because he'd pretty much memorized the old prick's schedule and this happened every day at 9:00 A.M. sharp.

At first Lucas had thought that getting inside the mansion and cornering de Santis there was the best idea, but then he'd hit on another plan. If he was quick he might actually be able to catch the bastard outside. Of course there would be bodyguards, but he knew how to deal with those. His SIG wasn't as accurate as his rifle, but speed was the key here, not accuracy, and it would do in a pinch.

This shit had to end here and now, and he was going to make sure it did, because if he had to spend another day in the apartment alone with Grace he was going to go insane.

Yesterday he'd thought it would be easy to tell her that it was over. After all, he'd already told her he couldn't give her anything more and she'd agreed to it. But the reality of it had been far harder than he'd thought. The shock that had unfurled over her face and the way her cheeks had lost color had felt like a knife in his heart. Then he'd seen a tear slide out the corner of one eye, and the knife had twisted, cutting deep.

It shouldn't have hurt him to tell her the truth, but it had. He'd even found himself wanting to tell her why it couldn't possibly happen between them, to justify himself. But then that would have hurt her even worse and so he'd thought that it was better that he simply walk away.

It was supposed to be a surgical, clean cut. Yet the way his chest hurt it had been more like a hacking amputation with a rusty ax.

He'd had to force himself to leave, because he knew if he didn't he'd break and go to her, take her in his arms. Kiss away the tears and promise her things he couldn't ever give her.

Wouldn't ever give her.

He was broken deep inside and the only thing holding him together was his ability to cut himself totally off from his emotions. And if there was one thing that Grace deserved it wasn't the person he was deep inside. The broken boy who'd burned his own mother to death in a fire and yet apparently hadn't learned from the mistake.

Lucas had stayed in the kitchen for a good hour after that, sitting at the table, staring mindlessly at his laptop, going over de Santis's schedule and plans of the street where he lived. He heard the moment Grace moved, her footsteps on the stairs going up and then the slam of the studio door.

And still he'd sat at the kitchen table, going over and over his plan without really thinking about it, all his senses tuned to the woman upstairs. Listening for movement. But there was nothing but silence. She'd stayed in the studio all day and hadn't come out, not even when he'd paused outside the door on his way to bed.

There had been no sound from inside and he'd almost gone in to check that she was okay. But then he remembered the last time he'd burst in on her in her studio. How he'd put his hands on her, ripped her clothes, taken her in a blaze of passion he hadn't been able to control. And he'd known right in that moment that if he went inside that's exactly what he'd do again.

He couldn't. That wouldn't be fair to either of them.

So he didn't open the door. He went on past as if there were no one in that room at all.

He'd left early that morning and there had still been silence from the studio, and he'd had a sudden fear that someone had gotten inside and taken her. But just as he'd debated whether or not to go in, he'd heard a thump and a muffled curse. Definitely Grace was in there. And she was okay.

The relief had been acute, his hand moving to the door handle to turn it and go in before he'd even realized what he was doing. But again he'd stopped himself. No, best to go now, leave and tie up all the loose ends with this situation with de Santis. So that when he returned he could tell her that she was free to go. That she was safe.

So you can discharge your duty, walk away and pretend you're doing the right thing, huh?

Fuck that. Walking away *was* the right thing. For both of them.

It sounded hollow even in his own head, but right then the door of the de Santis mansion opened and de Santis himself was coming down the stairs, flanked by two body-guards.

Lucas, in the relative privacy of the alley, pulled his SIG and aimed, waiting for the moment when de Santis was in the car, but the bodyguards were still out of it. He was only going to have a split second to take down the guards and the chauffeur, and he could not fuck this up.

De Santis got in while the two bodyguards did a reflexive check of the street. Lucas squeezed the trigger, taking bodyguard number one in the shoulder, then moved, fast and with purpose, stalking out of the alley while he fired again at bodyguard two, who was being slow to react, thank fuck. The limo was in the way, but the guy was tall and Lucas managed to get him in the arm as he reached for his piece. The chauffeur was also reaching, but by this stage Lucas was almost across the street and was able to put a bullet in the man's leg.

The three men were on the ground and de Santis was in the car, which meant Lucas had another couple of seconds to get into the limo before de Santis noticed. If, in fact, he'd noticed his bodyguards dropping suddenly to the ground at all.

The street itself was relatively empty of people and traffic, and Lucas had counted on surprise, so that if anyone happened to see a guy pointing a handgun at a limo and three men suddenly collapsing maybe they wouldn't believe what they'd seen or they'd do a double take. Of course by the time they looked again, he'd be inside the limo and no one would be any the wiser. Apart from the three men on the ground, but he couldn't do anything about that. It wasn't going to take long anyway.

Reaching for the door handle, he pulled it open and slid inside.

De Santis was sitting opposite, his attention bent on the phone he had in his hand. Obviously he hadn't noticed the sudden disappearance of his bodyguards.

"I want you to speak to Clarke, Barclay," he said without looking up. "I need an answer on the Tate question—"

"And which particular Tate question would that be?" Lucas enquired coldly, keeping his gun trained on the prick's head.

De Santis's head jerked up, the blue eyes he was famous for widening in shock as he took in Lucas sprawled on the limo seat opposite him.

But the shock only lasted a second.

"Lucas Tate," Cesare de Santis said. "Jesus Christ. Who will rid me of this turbulent family?" He did not look, unfortunately, very cowed by the muzzle of the SIG Lucas had pointed in his direction. He didn't look at the gun at all, and probably fair enough. It wasn't as if Lucas were going to pull the trigger right here in de Santis's limo, no matter how badly he wanted to. Murder, was, after all, frowned upon, and apart from that, de Santis was a civilian and, like Lucas had told Grace, he didn't kill civilians. Not even asshole civilians.

"Quoting Henry the Second isn't going to help you." Lucas met the other man's cold blue eyes. "I'm here for a very specific reason. Basically if you don't do what I want you're fucked. And not only you, but your company too."

De Santis let out a long sigh and glanced out the window. Probably checking to see where his security had gotten to. "I see," he said. "Spit it out then. Tell me what you want." Without any hurry he glanced back at Lucas, then leaned back against the seat and put his phone in his pocket. "No doubt the prettiest Tate wants something extra special."

Lucas let the insult pass over him. Instead he eyed de Santis dispassionately. The man was handsome in a heavy way, radiating a certain kind of charisma that all men used to lots of power and lots of money did. He was also quite cold.

That was fine. Lucas was cold too.

"This is about a friend of mine," he said. "You employed him as a go-between for certain arms deals."

De Santis frowned. "Arms deals? Are you sure you've got the right guy?" There was a faint edge of mockery in his tone. "With the government, right?"

Lucas said nothing. Instead he pulled out of his pocket the photos he'd gotten from the file his father had sent him and held up one in particular, of Griffin and de Santis talking on the street.

De Santis laughed. "Is that supposed to be proof?"

Again Lucas didn't respond. He pulled out a second photo, of de Santis handing Griffin a black briefcase. "If you're curious I also have pictures of Griffin Riley—the man in that picture, which I'm sure you already know—in conversation with a couple of well-known arms dealers. Plus financial records linking you to him."

The expression on de Santis's face didn't change. He tilted his head and looked at Lucas. "What do you want, Mr. Tate?"

So the guy wasn't even going to protest? Good. That was going to make things a whole lot easier to deal with. "Griffin Riley did a deal on your orders with a man called Oliveira. He took his money but neglected to supply him with the goods they wanted. Now Oliveira's men are after his widow to get that money back. I want you to call them off."

De Santis tilted his head. "Call them off? Why should I? It's not my problem. That deal was something Riley did on his own, it wasn't anything to do with me."

Lucas found himself struggling not to let his shock show. "I don't care whether it was your deal or not. You were the one who brought him into this, which means you can be the one to clean it the fuck up."

"Riley made his own decisions. I didn't force him. He

wanted money, just like everyone else. But nothing comes for free, so I made him earn it."

Lucas bared his teeth, forcing away the shock. "If you don't call them off I'm taking this information to a contact I have in the military. I'm sure the top brass will be very interested to know that DS Corp has been involved in the illegal arms trade. Especially when it comes to experimental weaponry." Wolf had called him early that morning to tell him he'd gotten the names of some Navy people de Santis had apparently paid a lot of money to in order for them to turn a blind eye. Lucas had decided not to ask Wolf how he'd known who to target or what questions to ask; it was enough that he had.

De Santis merely laughed, clearly not appreciating that he was in very deep shit right now. "I'm sure they would be interested. Except you've got nothing, Mr. Tate. A few pictures, a few financial details . . ." He lifted a shoulder. "That's not enough to—"

"Deal with your mess," Lucas cut him off, in no mood to screw around, "and I'll ensure that this information stays exactly where it is. On the hard drive of my laptop."

The other man said nothing for a moment, staring at Lucas, his gaze absolutely unreadable. "You're assuming it's my mess to clean up."

"And you're assuming I don't know you have half the military in your pocket." Lucas held the other man's gaze. "Unluckily for you, I do know. And I have proof that you've been paying a couple of the higher-ups to look the other way for years now." Wolf hadn't just gotten Lucas names; he'd also gotten a couple of very incriminating e-mails between de Santis and several commanding officers that would ensure all parties went away for a very long time.

Again de Santis showed absolutely no expression whatsoever. "So you're absolutely okay with all this apparent evidence linking me to treasonous activity. All that matters to you is that some idiot called Oliveira stop threatening some woman?" De Santis's gaze had turned sharp, probing, like a general surveying an approaching army for weaknesses.

Lucas kept his own face equally expressionless. De Santis was a predator who would exploit any chink in his armor, especially a chink like Grace. "Do you agree to my terms or not?"

"What assurance do I have that the information will stay on your hard drive?"

"Once I have proof you've dealt with Oliveira, I'll send you the information."

"Which you've made copies of, naturally."

"No," Lucas said, all ice. "I haven't. And your assurance is my word."

De Santis gave another cold laugh at that. "The word of a Tate. Jesus, if only you knew how worthless that was."

There was something in the other man's voice that Lucas knew he should be following up, but that wasn't the most important thing right now. The most important thing was Grace's safety.

"Well?" he demanded. "Do we have a deal or not?"

De Santis shrugged, then reached into the pocket of his pants and took out his phone again. "I'll be in touch, Mr. Tate. Now if you'll excuse me, I have to make this call. You've injured my security staff and they need medical attention." Punching in a number, de Santis raised the phone to his ear. "Lawson? Get me Dr. Blake. Now, please."

It was a dismissal pure and simple, and Lucas had to battle the burst of anger that went through him. He wanted to squeeze the trigger and put a bullet through de Santis's smug face anyway, but that wouldn't help Grace. He was going to have to trust that the information he had and the threat he'd just delivered would be enough to get de Santis to call off whoever was after her.

He got out of the limo and walked away quickly without looking behind him, retreating to the alleyway where he'd parked his bike. He was getting onto the machine when his phone buzzed. Hauling it out, he checked the screen.

Grace was calling him.

His chest tightened and his breath caught. Part of him didn't want to answer it, but that part was a coward, so he hit the answer button. "What is it?"

"Lucas?" She sounded hesitant, her voice a little hoarse. "Are you okay?"

He found his jaw had gone tight, tension crawling over his shoulders. "Yes." It was a struggle to keep his voice as cold as he wanted it to be. "Why wouldn't I be?"

"It's only that you weren't here and I wondered where you'd gone. And then I remembered de Santis and the drop-off and . . ." She trailed off, then cleared her throat, adding in a stronger tone, "But obviously nothing's wrong and you're fine. So that's good."

Yet he'd heard the worry in her voice. He'd hurt her yesterday, been cold and callous to her, and yet here she was, calling him to check he was okay.

"Everything's fine." He kept every scrap of feeling from the words, making them as expressionless as possible, because he couldn't afford to break or give in. "I gave de Santis the message. I'll let you know when it's all done and you're safe." If de Santis did, in fact, agree to his demand.

And what if he doesn't?

If he didn't . . . Well, Lucas would give all the information he had to the authorities and they could deal with it. Griffin's name would be mud, though, and Grace would no doubt be dragged through the media too . . . Christ. That was't a good outcome either. Then again, it was better than being dead. Wasn't it?

"Okay. . . ." There was a brief silence, and when she spoke again her voice dropped, a husky edge to it. "Thanks, Lucas. Thanks for . . . everything. I appreciate it."

It wasn't much, only a simple thank-you, and yet it stuck in his heart alongside that fucking knife that her tears had put there yesterday.

But there was nothing he could do about that. He'd made his decision, and once he made a decision he never ever went back on it.

"It was my father's directive," he said, reducing everything. Making it smaller, turning it into nothing. "Don't worry. It'll be over soon."

There was another, long silence and he could almost feel her longing like a palpable thing. And he found himself holding his breath, his fingers tight around his phone, waiting for her to say something, though he had no idea what.

But all she said was, "Okay." Her voice was small and it made everything in him draw into a tight, hard knot.

Then she disconnected the call without another word.

CHAPTER SEVENTEEN

Lucas didn't come back. Not that she expected him to, but she kept half an ear out while she worked all the same. Listening for the sound of the elevator chime or the doors opening.

Neither came.

It was okay. She knew he wouldn't return. She'd thought he might leave her with a text or something, though, just to let her know where he was and what he was doing. That he was okay. He hadn't and she'd been forced to call him, which she hadn't wanted to do. But she couldn't stand not knowing.

Hearing his voice and the cold note in it had been unexpectedly painful. Hearing the way he'd dismissed his protecting her as his "father's directive" worse. He was minimizing it, of course, and probably to protect himself. She understood that. Didn't make any of it easy to bear, however.

Grace put her phone down on the floor, then turned back to her canvas.

She felt exhausted. She'd been in the studio, working like a madwoman, for a full twenty-four hours straight. A painting hadn't consumed her this way for a very long time, and it was still consuming her. She'd slept in the studio when she was tired, stopping only for bathroom breaks and to grab coffee and a couple of sandwiches. Once or twice she'd stopped to stretch out painfully cramped muscles or to walk around as she turned something over in her head.

Every so often she would stand back to study the painting and see where she was headed with it, but viewing it as a whole was too painful, so she had to focus on small sections of it instead.

It was coming together. It was going to be amazing.

It was probably also going to kill her.

But waiting around, listening for the door, hoping it might be him and yet at the same time dreading it would be him, was too much for her. Losing herself in the painting was the only option, so lose herself she did.

Time passed; she didn't know how long.

Her phone buzzed a number of times, but since she had her fingers covered in paint and she didn't want to stop, she didn't pick it up until she'd finished the section she was on.

When she did, she saw there were a number of texts from Lucas telling her that de Santis had called off the dealers. That she was safe and that she could move back into her apartment whenever she liked, though she could stay where she was for as long as she wanted to as well. All she needed to do was text him when she wanted to move and he'd send around some people to help her with her canvases.

So, he wasn't coming back, was he? That day in the long gallery as he'd told her it was over, that was the last time she'd ever see him.

Pain and fury lodged inside her chest and she very much wanted to smash something. He was a coward. A fucking coward. Perhaps she'd pick up her paints and fling them all over the white walls, all over the white cushions of his precious fucking couch. All over the floors. Get color everywhere and permanently so he could dismiss her all he liked, but he'd never be able to get the traces of her out.

She'd done that the night she'd left, after her father had told her he'd refused to let her grandparents pay for art college. That if he hadn't managed to get them to pay for him they certainly weren't going to pay for her. So she'd gone out and spilled house paint all over his shitty car.

But that had been years ago and she wasn't a child any longer. She wasn't going to spill paint around Lucas's lovely white apartment. He'd told her it was over and so it was over. She'd accept it and move on, because she was a fucking adult. Because she wasn't destructive like her father. And anyway, did she really care that much about Lucas?

Her gaze fell on the painting in front of her, the one she'd been slaving her guts out on. And the fury rose up inside her, making her want to take to the canvas with a pair of scissors as if that would cut out the pain.

But she didn't do that either. She moved over to it instead, reaching out as if to touch the cheek of the man she'd painted on it, the hurt and the fury bubbling away inside her.

It was too personal, this painting. Too revealing. It was also too important.

No matter how bad she felt, this painting reminded her of the good too and she had to keep it. She couldn't destroy it.

It was part of her and she cared. She cared very, very much.

Too much.

She didn't respond to Lucas's texts until the end of the day, telling him in a short, no-nonsense response that she'd be ready to go the following morning and that yes, some help with the canvases would be required. He answered with a terse *Fine*.

It all seemed so anticlimactic. After the danger and the passion and the intensity, that a couple of texts was all it took to let her know that she was safe and that she was not needed any longer. She could go about her life as if nothing had happened.

The next day, as the men came to remove her canvases, Grace watched them carefully to make sure they didn't damage anything. The last painting, the most important one, she kept covered with a sheet because she didn't want anyone seeing it. She kept vacillating about whether she wanted it in the exhibition or not, but since it was supposed to be the piece that drew everything together, she supposed she was going to have to use it.

As the removal men finally left the apartment, Grace stood there for a couple of moments, looking around at the place that had been her home for the past couple of weeks. She'd thought she'd feel sad about leaving, but she didn't, and at first she didn't really understand why, since she'd felt very comfortable here, even though some very uncomfortable things had happened. Even though she'd had some of the happiest moments of her life here.

But no, she knew why.

Lucas wasn't here and without him it was just a house. A nice house, but just a house all the same.

He made it home.

Grace shook her head, denying the thought. She couldn't afford to think those things. It was over. It was done. And now she was going to move on with her life, without any stupid man cluttering it up.

Before she left she laid an envelope on the coffee table in front of the couch. An invitation to her exhibition. She had no idea if he was going to return here—if he'd ever return here—but if he did he'd see it and maybe he'd open it. Maybe he'd even decide to come.

But if he didn't then she could tell herself that he hadn't

gotten the invitation rather than he simply didn't want to
see her again.

It was a cop-out and she knew it. But the alternative was
hunting him down and shoving the envelope into his hand
herself and she didn't think she could do that. She didn't
think she could face yet another rejection from him.

Cop-outs were all she had left.

Lucas stayed away from the Village apartment. Five hours
after he'd gotten out of de Santis's limo, the asshole had
sent him a terse text informing him that he'd dealt with
Oliveira, that he wouldn't be bothering her again. De Santis
neglected to send proof, telling Lucas he would just have
to take his word that the situation had been handled.

The prick.

Lucas decided to hold on to the information he had on
the bastard in that case, and even though he'd already decided he wasn't going to see Grace again, he found himself
keeping an eye on the apartment just the same. Watching
her for a couple of days to make sure everything was okay
wouldn't be a bad idea in case de Santis was a lying sack
of shit.

The media storm about Van's relationship with Chloe
was at its height and Lucas knew several of the sharper
media outlets were trying to track him down for comment.
But no one knew where he lived, which made finding him
difficult, so he was able to evade the media spotlight. Evading Van's calls was even easier. Lucas simply didn't answer them. He didn't want to know why Van was marrying
their adoptive sister or why he'd suddenly changed his
mind and decided to give up the military, become the Tate
heir the way their father always wanted.

Lucas didn't want Van prying into his life and asking
him what the fuck was up with him either. All he wanted
was to make sure Grace was safe and then he'd be giving

up his directorship of Tate Oil and heading back to base, like he'd always planned.

Wolf called him a couple of times, but Lucas decided he wasn't going to answer him either. Lucas didn't know what his brother would be asking him about and he didn't want to know.

Instead he hung out around the apartment, watching out for Grace and making sure there was no one shady around. He thought she might leave immediately, but she didn't. A day passed and then the removal men arrived. They parked in the basement and he was able to find a vantage point so he could see them remove all the paintings one by one. The last canvas they carried down was covered by a white sheet—the one she'd been working on, he guessed.

He didn't want to see it. He really didn't.

Not long after the removal men had gone, he returned to another vantage point where he could check the front door of the building, and soon enough the front door opened and Grace stepped out. Tall and elegant, her purse slung over one shoulder. She wore jeans and one of her paint-spattered T-shirts, that black leather trench coat belted around her narrow waist. Her hair was pulled up and coiled in a messy bun on her head, though not with a paintbrush this time. Standing on the top of the steps, she blinked, as if the weak winter sunlight was too bright, and hunched her shoulders.

His chest hurt, like he'd broken a rib, a dull, aching pain. He couldn't seem to drag his gaze away from her. Even on a dull gray day with snow in the air, wearing a black trench coat, she burned like a bonfire. Her hair the color of summer, her skin pink from cold. He couldn't quite see from where he stood, but he knew that her eyes would be gold.

He wanted to close the distance between them. Wanted to put his arms around her, hold on to her bright flame, let her burn him to ash and fuck everything else. But he couldn't. He had nothing to offer her, nothing to give her but a few more days of hot sex, and he knew—he *knew*—that that wasn't what she wanted. The tear that had slipped down her cheek the day he'd left had told him everything he needed to know about that.

She'd started to care and he couldn't have anyone caring about him. Especially not when he couldn't care about her in return.

But you do care about her.

Maybe he did. But he shouldn't. He should pack that emotion away, put it back in the box it had escaped from, and never let it out again.

That's impossible. . . .

Lucas ignored the thought as Grace stuck her hands into her pockets and started down the stairs. She didn't take a taxi, she headed straight for the subway, and he followed, telling himself he only wanted to make sure she got home safely, that it had nothing to do with not wanting to let her out of his sight.

It was almost a disappointment when she arrived home without incident, disappearing into her building. He'd already made sure that her apartment would be as she'd left it. Turned out that Oliveira and his men had broken in and made a bit of a mess in their efforts to locate her, but Lucas had had some Tate employees come in and straighten it out. She probably wouldn't even notice.

He waited outside the building, feeling a bit like a dog beside the grave of its dead master; then because he needed not to feel that kind of shit, he returned back to the Village to make sure Grace hadn't left anything behind.

It was curiously quiet without her vibrant presence, the emptiness echoing around him. The faint smell of turpentine and paint lingered in the air, but he didn't go up to the studio where she'd been. He suddenly didn't want to be anywhere near that room. It was too full of passion, of heat, of the memories of her silky skin under his hands and the softness of her hair wound around his fingers, her cries in his ear.

Even here was too much, standing in the long gallery with that weak sun shining through the stained glass, casting colors all over the white cushions of his couch. There was a gold stain on one of them, where he'd spilled her nail polish . . .

Memories flooded his head, hot and dirty and raw, and he had to take a couple of breaths to force them away. He couldn't be thinking about this. He *shouldn't* be thinking about this. Not about her. She was out of his life and that was the best thing all-round.

His gaze settled on a white envelope sitting on the coffee table. Frowning, he moved over to it and picked it up. His name was written on the front in a sprawling, untidy script. Grace's handwriting? It had to be. No one else could have put that envelope there.

Opening it up, he slid out the piece of paper inside and unfolded it. More of that untidy, sprawling handwriting covered the page. On it was a date and a time, and an address. The art gallery where she'd first approached him. And underneath that she'd written:

Lucas, I know you're not interested in art, but you told me once you might be interested in mine. So if you are, take this as an invitation to my exhibition. It'll be my very first one ever and you know how much this means to me. I'd love it if you would be there, but if not . . .

She hadn't added anything more, just let the sentence trail off. She hadn't even signed the note.

He wouldn't go of course. He couldn't. A clean break was better, even though it would probably hurt her if he didn't go. But what would be the point? He still couldn't offer her anything, didn't want to offer her anything, and anyway, he was a SEAL through and through. He wasn't giving up the Navy for anyone. Grace had already lost one husband; it would be cruel of him to let her have him, only to leave on a deployment he might not come back from.

Excuses, excuses. . . .

They weren't excuses. They were facts. That's all there was to it.

Taking his phone out of his pocket, he texted the housekeeper who looked after this place to make a special dry-cleaning trip for the couch cushions, adding another note to look out for paint stains in the front left bedroom. Then he turned and left the apartment, leaving Grace's note sitting on the coffee table.

He wasn't going to go to her exhibition, but he kept an eye on her for the next day or so, waiting outside her apartment so he could see when she went out and following along at a safe distance when she did. Nothing ever happened to her and he didn't see anyone shady following her either—no one except him at least.

It was starting to look like de Santis was as good as his word. But of course as long as the incriminating information Lucas had on de Santis stayed on his hard drive and wasn't sent to his military contacts then Grace would remain safe. It wasn't something he was comfortable with, not when de Santis was such a fucking traitor, but if it kept Grace safe then he wasn't going to argue.

Since when has she become more important to you than your country? You could pass the intel along and let the authorities protect her.

He could, but something inside wouldn't let him. He didn't want her safety to be in anyone else's hands, only his. Which, of course, meant something. But he didn't want to think about what it meant, so he didn't.

He simply watched her, telling himself it was only about her safety. Only that and nothing more.

Despite all of that, the night of the exhibition came around a day or so later, and he found himself outside Grace's apartment, watching as she came out of the building, heading straight for the cab that had pulled up to the curb.

His breath caught, because she was looking stunning tonight. She was in a flowing strapless dress of emerald green that wrapped tightly around her breasts and hips before flaring out into long, fluttering skirts that swirled around her legs, all silky and liquid. She wore no jewelry except her bracelets and the stunning veil of her hair, let loose down her back like a waterfall of red-gold.

His hands itched, wanting to reach for her, to pull her into his arms. But he kept them shoved deep in the pockets of his jeans. Shit, she was amazing. Flamboyant and bright and so achingly lovely. He really should have given her something before he'd left. Some nice polish and a necklace or maybe a bracelet to add to her collection. A special piece so that she had something of him to wear on her special day. Though really, why he should want her to have something of him he had no idea.

This was *her* day, not his, and there was no reason to want to involve himself. No reason he should be part of it.

She got into the taxi and he got onto his bike, following along behind the cab as it made its way through the evening traffic to the gallery.

Fifteen minutes later, he'd parked the bike and was standing opposite the gallery, watching the crowds begin arriving to her show. And there were actual crowds. He knew nothing about the New York art scene, but he was sure an unknown wouldn't get anything like the turnout Grace was getting. The gallery owner must have had a lot of contacts in order to bring in this many people.

He leaned against the streetlight, not sure what he was doing, since she was in the gallery now and nothing was going to get her there. It had been at least two days since de Santis had called off his dealers and Lucas had seen no one, so it was likely she was safe. How long was he going to keep following her?

He needed to end this shit right now, get back to base.

Yet he didn't move as more people flooded into the brightly lit gallery.

Music drifted across the street, the sound of laughter and conversation rising above the traffic. Looked like a goddamn party.

You could go in, just take a look. She'd never know you were there.

The thought wound through him, insidious. There *were* a lot of people there and she'd wouldn't spot him if he was careful, though why he would go in he didn't quite know. It would only be to support her, but if she didn't know he was there what would be the point?

Does it matter if she doesn't know? This isn't for her; it's for you.

Fuck, that was true. If he went inside it *would* be for him. It would be one last moment of connection to her, where he would be surrounded by her color and warmth and vibrant spirit. His last chance to be near her . . .

What a pathetic piece of shit he was. He should be turning around and getting on his bike and getting the fuck out of there, heading back to base and what he knew. What was safe. For him, for her, for everyone who knew him.

Yet that wasn't what he did.

He had no idea what made him cross the road and approach the entrance to the gallery. The asshole on the door made a big deal of the guest list, asking pompously whether he was on it or not, but Lucas just stared at him. "I was invited," he said coldly. He didn't want to give his name because he didn't want any media attention. He also didn't want Grace finding out he was here.

The man made spluttering sounds, but Lucas simply stared him down until finally the idiot, totally intimidated, jerked his head toward the door.

Lucas stepped inside.

And realized for the first time that Grace wasn't just good.

She was a genius.

CHAPTER EIGHTEEN

Grace stood in the corner of the gallery, one hand holding a glass of champagne, the other her little green silk clutch. It was a stupid accessory and she couldn't understand why she'd brought it with her. It took up one hand, making it impossible to hold a drink and eat an hors d'oeuvre at the same time. Not that she wanted to do either of those things, truth be told. Not when she was so goddamn nervous.

The gallery was packed and she was sure it was all a mistake. Craig had told her he'd managed to rustle up a crowd, but she hadn't realized it was going to be such a big crowd. She'd asked him why there were so many people and he'd just smiled and touched the side of his nose, telling her the answer to that question was on a need-to-know basis only.

Maybe he'd paid for everyone to be here. She was an unknown after all.

She'd spent most of the evening being led around and introduced to a lot of people, gallery owners, critics, collectors, and a few other artists. She barely remembered their names, their faces a blur. After almost two weeks of being locked away in an apartment with only Lucas for company, she found all the people, all the attention, a little overwhelming.

Apparently, people were liking her work. Apparently,

they were liking it a lot. And she didn't know quite how to handle that.

Craig had wanted her to go stand near the painting she'd done in a frenzy those last couple of days in the apartment. The one that tied her whole "urban heroes" collection together. But she didn't want to. In fact, she didn't want to even go near it, because she knew that if she did people were going to ask questions about it. Questions she didn't want to answer.

She took a nervous sip of her champagne and looked down the crowded gallery to where that painting had been positioned. Craig had hung it on the back wall at the end, by itself. The other paintings were apparently supposed to draw you in, he'd said, and that last painting was the reward. The essence of the entire collection.

He'd wanted her to explain it to him, but she hadn't been able to and she still couldn't.

There were a lot of people in front of it and someone was gesturing, pointing out something.

Her throat got tight, and even though she didn't want to look, she couldn't help herself.

A man lay on his side on a wide white bed. He was naked, a white sheet winding around his beautiful body. Color fell over his skin, red and gold, shining on his blond hair and over the exquisite bone structure of his face. He was facing the viewer, the deep azure of his eyes almost mesmeric.

He should have been a cliche, nothing special. A male model advertising aftershave or linen sheets or perfume. But the way the light fell on the man's body, on his face, caressing every part of it, making him glow, took the painting beyond cliche. As did his expression and the look in his eyes. It was fierce, intense. Hunger and passion and heat, yet there was tenderness at the same time. One corner of his mouth was almost turned up, as if he was on the point of smiling, and you just knew if you waited a moment he *would* smile and it would be glorious.

Grace swallowed and tore her gaze away from it. She knew exactly what that painting represented

The painting represented the missing pieces of herself, the parts she'd always held back, kept safe. Passion and, more important, love.

She took another sip of her champagne, distractedly scanning the crowd, helplessly looking among all the people, unable to stop herself.

He wasn't here; of course he wasn't here. Not that she expected him to be, and maybe that was a good thing. He would have hated to see himself in that painting, the essence of who he was displayed for the world to see. The essence she saw every time she looked at him.

Maybe she shouldn't have done it. Ever since she'd left the apartment and gone back to her own pokey little place, the paintings crowding in on her, she'd debated whether including the piece in the exhibition was the right thing to do.

Looking at it hurt, because she missed him so badly. And in the few days before the exhibition, she'd had to cover it with a sheet so she didn't see him. So she wouldn't be reminded of those precious few days with him. Not enough to build a relationship, yet apparently quite enough to fall in love.

But she'd decided that she couldn't not include the piece. She wanted the world to see the man he truly was, the man she'd come to know that week in his apartment. Passionate and intense. Protective and caring. A man who felt so much. A man who felt too much.

It was necessary to include the piece in the show. Vital. Because he was one of the heroes. He was the man she loved.

Her throat constricted like someone was strangling her and she had to take another sip of her champagne.

This exhibition was supposed to be her crowning glory, the point she'd been working toward for years, her very own New York show. And she was supposed to feel good about it. Thrilled. Excited. She was supposed to be pinching herself and unable to believe it was really happening. Her big "fuck you" to her father.

But her father was dead and so was her only other main supporter—Griffin. She hadn't spoken to her mother in years and the only other person who meant anything to her wasn't here either.

So she didn't feel thrilled or excited. She didn't want to pinch herself. She didn't even feel good. All she could think was, 'what's the point'? What was she trying to achieve? Proving that she was good enough to people who were dead and to one man who didn't care. Great. Wonderful.

If this was her crowning glory then why did she feel like utter shit?

"Grace." Craig appeared beside her. "You should be down the end next to that painting. What are you doing hiding away in the corner?"

"Just taking a break." She tried to smile but knew it wasn't convincing.

Craig didn't seem to notice. "So exciting!" He clutched her arm. "Do you see the red dots all around? People love your work. I knew they would, I *knew* it." Flashing her a glance, he jerked his head toward the painting of Lucas on the back wall. "They all want that one, though. Are you sure that's not for sale? I've had some major offers on it."

"No." She didn't even have to think about it. That painting wasn't for sale and it never would be. "I'm not selling. I don't care how much they offer for it."

Craig shrugged. "All right. I did tell them that, but you know some people. Think they can buy anything if the money's right." He gave her a grin. "They all want to know who modeled for you too."

"No one," she said automatically. "I made him up." Lucas Tate wasn't as well known in the media as his brother, but he was still recognizable. So it was interesting that no one had recognized him in her painting. Then again, maybe it wasn't so surprising, since the man he was in the painting wasn't the man everyone knew.

Craig gave her a skeptical look but didn't comment. "Are you ready for your close-up? I'm going to announce you soon."

Ah, yes. He wanted her to give some kind of speech. Unfortunately, she had no idea what she was going to say. Perhaps she could simply sidle away and pretend she wasn't here?

Over by the door to the gallery, there was a small kerfuffle.

She turned her head to look, frowning as she spotted a police officer talking to the man at the door. The doorman was pointing in her direction and sudden foreboding clutched at her, though she had no idea why.

The police officer looked at her, nodded to the doorman, and then started heading in her direction.

"How odd," Craig murmured. "What are the police doing in my gallery?" He made a tsking sound. "If Sebastian has been doing coke in the men's room again I'll kill him."

But Grace wasn't listening. The foreboding was winding deeper, pulling tighter as the cop approached them. She couldn't have said why, but there was something familiar about him, something that made her feel cold.

"Can I help you, Officer?" Craig asked smoothly, the very epitome of the urbane art gallery owner. "Is there a problem?"

But the officer ignored Craig completely, focusing on Grace instead. He was wearing sunglasses, which was weird, mirrored aviator shades that reflected her pale face back to her. "Grace Riley?"

Was it . . ? No, it couldn't be. Not the fake cop who had nearly gotten her to open Lucas's front door. Lucas had dealt with him, hadn't he?

"Yes," she said, trying not to sound hesitant. "That's me. What can I do for you?"

"I need you to come with me please, ma'am."

Craig frowned. "Now? Can't it wait? I'm just about to do a big announcement."

The officer didn't even turn his head. "Now, ma'am."

The foreboding sunk sharp claws into her. "Um, it won't take long," she said, prevaricating. "Can you give me five minutes?"

"Ma'am," the officer began.

Craig's hand tightened around her arm. "I'm sure five minutes will be enough, Officer. This is very important." He began to tug her down toward the back of the gallery, where Lucas's painting was.

And then it seemed that a lot of things happened all at once.

The officer's hand whipped out all of a sudden and Craig fell to the floor. Grace opened her mouth in shock only for the officer to reach out and grab her, jerking her up against him.

For a second all she could do was stand there, staring in horror at Craig lying on the floor bleeding from a head wound, the cop's fingers holding her painfully in place.

"You stupid bitch," the cop growled in her ear. "You should have come with me when I told you to."

Her brain wouldn't work and nothing was making any sense at all. Why would a cop have hit Craig? Why was he holding her now? What the hell was happening?

You know what's happening. It's the same cop who turned up at the door, who Lucas apparently dealt with.

Cold shock was beginning to work its way through her,

flooding over her skin, freezing her blood, her lungs, her heart.

The people around her were beginning to notice Craig now, more heads turning to look at the man on the floor, the ripple of shock moving outward over the crowd the way it was moving outward over her.

"Don't make a fucking sound," the cop said savagely, and began to move, pulling her toward the gallery door.

Through the shock and the fear, Grace was aware of one thing and one thing only. It looked like Cesare de Santis had not been as good as his word and had not called off his dogs after all. And that once she was pulled through that door she was dead. It would be over.

So Grace did what any sane person would do. She fought.

She jerked away sharply and it appeared he hadn't been expecting her to, because she managed to pull herself out of his grip. But he was fast, grabbing her again, this time around the waist. She dropped her glass, the smashing sound drawing attention, then tried to elbow him in the face, kicking out behind her with her sharp heels.

He cursed savagely and for a brief moment it felt like she was winning, that she was going to get away. Then something cracked across her cheek and pain exploded through her, making her gasp and tears start in her eyes. She stumbled; then an arm was gripping her far too tightly around her waist and something hard and metallic was jammed against the side of her head.

"Move again, you little bitch," the cop said pleasantly, "and I'll blow your ugly fucking head off."

Lucas felt tension prickle across the back of his neck even before he heard the gasps of shock. He'd felt it before that too. A gradual tightening in his gut that he'd learned over the years never to ignore.

He'd been down near that painting she'd done, the one everyone was staring at, unable to process it. Intellectually, he knew that the painting was of him, but he didn't recognize himself. The man was a complete and utter stranger to him.

He'd stood there in the well-dressed crowd, in plain jeans, sweater, and leather jacket, unseen because if he didn't want to be noticed then he made sure he wouldn't be. He had his shades on for added protection and he kept his head down and his shoulders hunched. People ignored him, brushing past him like he wasn't even there.

But he heard them talk about the painting, about the use of light and color, and about how she'd managed to capture such an intensity of emotion. They were right, she had, and the longer he looked at the face of the man in the picture, into the man's blue eyes, the more he wanted to look away.

He didn't know what disturbed him so much about it, because even though it was of him it really wasn't. He'd never let that kind of emotion show on his face; certainly he never let himself feel it. That had to be something she'd imagined, surely?

The crowd around him swirled, but he didn't move, staring at the picture, unable to pull himself away from it. It made his chest get tight, made it difficult to breathe. Made him . . . Christ, he didn't know what else, but he should be turning around and walking out of this goddamn place before Grace spotted him.

That's when he felt it, the tension, like an icy current in a warm tropical sea. Then came the gasps of shock. He didn't turn, scanning around for a place to stand where he'd be unnoticed and yet have a prime view of the gallery. He didn't want to draw attention to himself, not until he'd figured out just what the hell was going on. There was a small alcove off to his right, where the lighting didn't quite

reach, so he made for it, sliding into the shadows as the
sound of crashing glass rose above the crowd.

Something was happening in the middle of the gallery,
the sounds of violence, a woman's scream, a man cursing.
Shock was rippling outward through the crowd, people
backing frantically away from whatever was going on.

Another cry. He recognized it. *Grace*.

His whole body went tight, every muscle clenching, and
it was all he could do not to burst into action right there
and then. But years of military training held him still
because he had no idea what was going on and he didn't
want to move until he did.

He spotted her as the crowd began to move away, standing in the middle of a rapidly widening circle. A cop had
his arm around her, holding on to her tightly, and his other
hand was holding something up to her head. Holy fuck.
The muzzle of a gun.

His heartbeat began to get faster and faster, a voice in
his head screaming at him to take action, because she was
in danger. It took everything he had to ignore the voice,
because he couldn't, not yet. Someone was holding a gun
to her head, point-blank range. One move and it would all
be over.

She was absolutely white and there was a cut on one
cheekbone, a rapidly darkening bruise. The fucker was
starting to walk her back out of the gallery, while people
stood around watching in shock. No one did anything. No
one said anything.

A cop. The guy was a cop.

Oh fuck.

It was the guy he'd had in his shooting gallery. The one
he'd sent back to the asshole's employer—Oliveira—to deliver the message about the drop-off. The drop-off that
never happened because fucking de Santis was supposed

to call the prick off. Yet it looked like Oliveira hadn't gotten the message.

Lucas's heart raced faster, the look of shock and fear on Grace's vivid face hurting him like a sliver of glass sliding beneath his fingernails. A sharp, agonizing pain.

The SIG was in his hand before he'd had a chance to think about it and he was aiming at the guy dragging Grace out of the doors. One chance, that was all Lucas had, and it had to be a head shot, an instant kill. Easy. At least, it should be.

But this wasn't his rifle, and as he raised his gun to aim his hand was fucking shaking like a leaf and his heartbeat wouldn't slow down. He tried to make it, tried to will himself into that calm space where there was only the target, only the sound of his heartbeat in his ear. All his awareness focusing in on that sound, getting slower and slower, counting the beats. *Forty, thirty-nine, thirty-eight . . .* Except his heartbeat wasn't getting any slower, because all he could see was her face. All he thought about was that if he fucked this up she would die. One shot and she was dead. His Gracie . . . dead on the floor . . .

It was going up now, his heart rate getting faster and faster, his hand shaking like an alcoholic going through withdrawal. Where the *fuck* was his detachment? Where was the ice? All he could feel was rage exploding through him. Rage at himself for not taking that prick out when he'd had him trussed up in his shooting gallery. Rage at the prick for taking her when none of this had anything to do with her. Rage at her for making it impossible to detach himself the way he should. The way he needed to able to so he could protect her.

Rage at her for making him care.

The gun in his hand shook and he was breathing so fast, like all the oxygen in the room had been sucked out and he was slowly suffocating.

One shot, that's all he needed to make, and it was an easy one. The guy was right there. But shit, she looked so pale and there was blood on her beautiful skin, her little purse had fallen out of her hands, and Lucas could see the tremble in her fingers.

Gracie . . . His beautiful Gracie . . .

Then she gave the minutest shift of her head and looked right at him, and he thought that maybe she was simply looking into the crowd in front of him. But then her eyes widened, gold flaring bright in her gaze. She'd seen him. She knew he was there.

He couldn't squeeze the trigger; he couldn't fire. Not with her looking at him, making him feel like she had her hand around his heart and was holding it so tightly he couldn't breathe. He couldn't risk her life on a shot he might not be able to make. No, he was going to have to let that asshole drag her out of the gallery and hope like fuck he could end the prick outside.

Fuck. *Fuck*.

Yet weirdly, the fear in her face began to ebb and she mouthed something at him, and it sure as hell looked like she was saying, *It's okay*. Which wasn't true, because it wasn't okay. She was going to die because he couldn't keep his fucking heart rate down.

Because he cared too much. That had always been his problem, hadn't it?

He cared too fucking much.

Across the room, being dragged away by some asshole with a gun to her head, Grace smiled at him, breaking his heart into a million pieces.

Then came the muffled sound of a gunshot and everything went to hell.

CHAPTER NINETEEN

She'd felt him from across the crowded gallery, through the shock and the fear and the pain. She knew that prickle of awareness so well. It had been what had driven her from this gallery the very first day two weeks ago, when she'd spotted him staring at her from across the street. That day all she'd known was that someone had been watching her. Now she knew it meant that Lucas was here.

So she'd looked at the patch of shadow near the painting of him, her gaze unerringly drawn. He was there; she could see him. Feel him. Tall and dark and powerful, standing motionless with his arm extended, a gun in his hand.

She couldn't make out his features because he was too far away, but that didn't matter.

He was here. Despite everything, he'd come.

Something inside her had settled in that moment, the fear falling away from her, the pain too. His hand was shaking, she could see it tremble, and she knew that because of that he wouldn't be able to make the shot.

But strangely, that didn't matter.

All that mattered was that he'd come. That he'd seen the painting she'd done of him. That he'd seen the man she saw when she looked at him.

Her love on canvas.

And right now, knowing he was here, that he was with her, well . . . it seemed as good a place as any to end it.

Except just as she was bracing herself to pull away for the last time, because she'd be damned if she let this asshole choose when and where he was going to shoot her and if she was going to die she was going to die at least trying to escape, there was a sudden spray of red all over her and it sounded like the entire gallery of people began to scream. Then the arm around her fell away and so did the gun at her head, and abruptly she was standing by herself, covered in blood and shaking like a leaf. At first she thought she'd been shot and that the pain hadn't hit yet, that this was death and she didn't quite realize it.

Then a giant man appeared suddenly in front of her. He was dressed in jeans and a T-shirt, a black peacoat flung over the top, had a short black Mohawk and the strangest eyes she'd ever seen: one blue and one green. He was glaring ferociously at her as if this were somehow all her fault, which was slightly alarming considering he was holding a vicious-looking handgun in one hand.

"Are you okay?" he demanded in a deep, gravelly, and somehow familiar voice, completely ignoring the screaming chaos of people around them.

"Um . . ." she said stupidly.

"Fucking hell," the man muttered, and stepped toward her, reaching out, running his hands over her in a completely impersonal way.

She felt cold and she knew she was probably going into shock. Why was there blood everywhere? Was it hers? Had she been shot or not?

Then the giant was abruptly jerked back as someone pulled him violently away by the collar of his coat. There was a brief altercation and Lucas was standing in front of her instead, his warm fingers gripping her upper arms so tightly it hurt, his eyes gone gas-flame blue. "Grace." His

voice was cracked and raw. "Grace, are you okay?" He
gave her a little shake. "Fucking answer me!"

"Get her out of here," the giant said in that deep, gravelly voice. "Jesus Christ, I knew you were in trouble, you
dumb shit." He didn't seem to be speaking to her, but to
Lucas. "You should have told me. Then we could have handled this situation a whole lot better and with a whole lot
less fucking drama."

Lucas didn't appear to be listening; he'd begun running
his hands over her the way the giant had done, only gen-
tler, more careful. "Talk to me, Gracie," he murmured.
"Tell me you're okay."

"I'm okay." God, she sounded like a little girl.

"What a fucking mess," the giant said. "Get moving,
Luc, and get her somewhere safe. Jesus, how many times
do I have to say it? Oh, and don't take her on your fucking
bike like that. Here's the keys to my car." He pulled some
keys from the pockets of his jeans and held them out.

This time Lucas turned and met the other man's weird
eyes. He said nothing, just stared at him long and hard.

"Yeah," the man said. "I get it. But no thanks required,
bro."

Lucas gave one short nod; then he grabbed the keys and,
without a word, turned back to her and swept her up into
his arms.

She blinked, wanting to protest that she could walk very
well on her own, thank you very much, but then she tasted
something metallic on her lips and she knew it was blood.
Not her blood. And she began to shake even harder as the
full realization of what had happened began to sink in.

That cop had put a gun to her head. He'd been going to
kill her. Yet he hadn't. For some reason, he was dead and
she was alive, and now she was in Lucas's arms, being carried out of the gallery and into the freezing night outside.

It was very cold and her gown was sticking wetly to her

and she didn't want to think about why that might be. But Lucas's body was hot and hard against her, the reassurance of his solidity holding the panic at bay.

He carried her over to a plain-looking black Toyota that had been parked haphazardly at the curb, unlocking it, then bundling her inside. Then he rounded the side of the car and got in, sticking the key in the ignition and turning up the heating full bore.

He didn't say a word, reaching over for her seat belt and buckling her in before starting the engine and pulling away from the curb. She could hear sirens as they drove, a cop car or two flashing past in the night.

She wanted to ask where they were going, but she didn't want to open her mouth and taste that blood again, so she stayed silent, shivering despite the rapid way the car heated up.

Every so often she stole a glance at Lucas. His face was hard and set, his knuckles on the steering wheel white. He looked like he was barely holding it together, which for some reason made her feel better.

They didn't drive far.

Barely five minutes later they were driving down a small, narrow road and down into an underground car park. She tried to get out and walk herself, but Lucas wasn't having any of it, picking her up and carrying her over to the elevator.

They went up to the top floor, into an unfamiliar apartment. This one was decorated much like the apartment in the old church, plain white walls and very little furniture. It felt colder than the one with the stained glass, emptier somehow. In summer it would probably be lovely, with skylights letting in the sun, but right now, in winter and at night, those skylights let in nothing but darkness.

Lucas carried her down the hall and into a bathroom. It was large and white tiled, with a massive shower. She blinked as he strode to the shower and turned it on before coming back to her. Then with gentle insistence he turned her around and took hold of the zipper at the back of her dress, beginning to pull it down.

"What are you doing?" Her voice was croaky. "I can undress myself very well, thanks."

Lucas said nothing and he didn't stop, unzipping her dress, then tugging it down so it pooled at her feet. His hands moved to the strapless bra she wore underneath, beginning to unhook it.

"Lucas," she murmured softly as the fabric began to loosen.

"I just have to see you." There was a raw note in his voice, almost desperate sounding. "I just have to see you to make sure you're okay."

"I am okay."

"Let me, Gracie. Please." He unhooked her bra without waiting for an answer, his fingers lightly brushing down her back, making her shiver.

So she let him. Let him touch her, let him ease down her panties, then kneel at her feet to take her shoes off. Then when she was naked, she let him take her to the shower stall and she thought he'd leave her then, but he didn't. He kicked off his boots and, still fully clothed, got in with her.

"Okay," she said shakily, putting her hands on his chest because she couldn't bring herself to stop touching him, watching as the sweater he wore became wet, sticking to his sculpted torso. "Now you're being ridiculous."

But he said nothing. Instead he pushed her gently against the white-tiled wall and kept his hands on either side of her head, looking down at her, his intense blue gaze running all over her while the water darkened his blond hair.

"You smiled at me," he said, like an accusation. "You fucking smiled at me."

She stared back at him, seeing the tension in the lines of his beautiful face. He was angry and scared, and it made her heart contract painfully in her chest. That was for her, wasn't it? "Yes. I did."

"Why? I couldn't make the shot. I couldn't save you and you fucking smiled at me."

Ah, so that was what this was about.

The shock that had her in its grip began to ease, the cold ebbing away with it. The water going down the drain was red, but she didn't look at it. She only looked at him, at his intense, gorgeous face. At the fear and anger and pain that burned in his eyes.

She reached out and touched him, stroked along one perfect cheekbone. "Why couldn't you make the shot?"

"I couldn't slow my fucking heart rate. It wouldn't go down, no matter how much I tried, and my hand was shaking, and I tried, Gracie, I tried so fucking hard. . . ." He trailed off, the shower stall loud with the sound of his ragged breathing, his whole body vibrating with tension. He was visibly trying to get himself under control. "You nearly died." He sounded hoarse now. "If I'd taken that shot and missed you would have been killed." His lips peeled back in what was almost a snarl. "But you smiled at me. You were going to die and you fucking *smiled*."

Her heart ached and ached, for the pain and fear she saw in his face. For the vulnerability he was showing her right here in this moment.

She spread her fingers out along his cheekbone, feeling his warm, wet skin. "I smiled because you got my invite. Because you came. Because I didn't think you would and you did."

"I don't understand why that fucking matters."

She looked him straight in the eye. "You understand."

"No." A muscle jumped in his jaw, she felt it against her fingers, and there was denial in his blue gaze. "I told you. You can't care about me. You can't. That shot? I couldn't take it because my heart rate wouldn't slow down. Because I couldn't turn off all the fear. Couldn't turn off all the anger. I cared too much, Gracie. And because of that, you nearly died." He took a shuddering breath. "I can't let that happen again. I can't."

There was so much desperation in his eyes it made her hurt for him. But the curious calm she'd felt back in the gallery when she'd first seen him in the shadows was returning, bringing with it a kind of deep certainty.

She reached up with her other hand, taking his face between her palms, holding him. "Did you see my painting?" She didn't bother explaining which one she meant, but she didn't have to. Emotion flared in his gaze; yes, he'd seen it.

"It's of you," she added quietly.

His denial was instant. "That's not me."

"Yes, it is. That's the man I see when I look at you."

He started to shake his head, started to pull away, but Grace wasn't done.

That calm had her in its grip, that deep certainty. The knowledge that she was done with running and hiding. With being afraid of rejection and being vulnerable. With being scared of giving someone her soul and having it thrown back in her face.

She was done with being afraid, period.

She wanted Lucas Tate. She'd wanted him the moment she'd first met him. But shutting herself away wouldn't get her what she wanted and neither would denial. Neither would pouring everything into her art and telling herself that her work was all she needed. Because if that had been enough she would have finished that goddamn painting two weeks ago.

It hadn't been enough. She needed more than that. She always had.

She needed him, and that painting in the gallery was living proof.

So she held on to him, tightened her fingers so he couldn't pull away, and she faced her fear. "Don't you walk away from me," she ordered. "Don't you dare be a coward now."

He could have pulled out of her grip so easily. He was so much stronger than she was. But he didn't. He remained motionless, the water soaking his sweater and his jeans, sliding over his perfect golden skin.

"That painting," Grace said fiercely, "is my heart." He began to shake his head, but she wasn't finished. "I know I wasn't supposed to feel anything for you, but I'm done pretending that I don't care. Done pretending that you don't mean anything to me." She was holding him so tightly now, staring into his eyes. "I *love* you, Lucas Tate. And that painting is everything that's been missing from my life. All the pieces of me I've been holding back. It's love and it's passion and it's tenderness. It's vulnerability. *My* vulnerability. It's the man I love. It's *you*."

He didn't want it to be true. He didn't want her to say those things to him. But her fingers were holding on to him and he didn't want to pull away. Her amber eyes were so bright, her hair wet and sticking to her elegantly shaped skull, the apricot gold darkened and licking like flames against her pale skin.

All the blood from the asshole who'd nearly killed her had washed away now, and apart from the bruise on her cheekbone, she was uninjured.

It should have made him calmer, but he wasn't.

He felt frantic. Desperate. Outside himself.

Wolf's sudden appearance made no sense at all and

Lucas still didn't know how his brother had managed to turn up precisely at the right time or why, but he had. Shooting the fake cop in the head without hesitation, leaving Grace standing there covered in blood but free.

Lucas didn't know why he was standing there fully clothed in the shower stall either. He'd only meant to take her back to his SoHo apartment, the one that was officially his, show her the bathroom, and leave, let her wash off the blood on her own.

But once he'd touched her he hadn't been able to stop, and before he knew it he was standing there in the shower, with her backed up against the white tile.

Wrong. It was wrong. He should be leaving her, not letting her touch him. Not letting her tell him that the painting she'd done of him in the gallery was her heart. Not letting her tell him that she loved him.

Because he knew he didn't deserve it. He *knew*.

"You can't love me," he said in a voice he didn't recognize as his. "I don't want you to love me."

"I don't care." The look on her face blazed. "And if that makes me selfish then too bad. I love you and I'm not taking it back."

The desperation inside him twisted tighter and he didn't know why. He wanted to push her hard against the tile, cover her mouth with his, invade her, conquer her. Take what she wanted to give him, because he wanted it so desperately too.

But he couldn't. Feeling anything at all held the potential to destroy and he was nothing if not destructive. Besides, his soul had been scarred by fire, it was never going to heal, and she deserved so much more than a heart made of nothing but ashes and smoke.

"I will never love you back," he said fiercely, holding her gaze. "Never, Grace. I can't. Is that what you really want?"

"No, of course that's not what I want, you fucking idiot!" She pulled his head down farther, so they were nose to nose, the glorious color of her eyes so close to his he could see the bright golden specks like glitter in them. "But I'm prepared to wait until you do."

He felt like he couldn't breathe, like he was suffocating. "You don't understand. I *can't.* Caring about *anything* is destructive. It kills, Grace. *I* kill. And you're . . . Jesus, you're life and color. You're joy and you're fucking creation. You're the opposite of me in just about every way there is, and there is no way I should even be touching you, let alone anything else."

"Is that what you think?" She was so close, all he could see was her eyes, brilliant and gold and full of fire. "That because you got angry once and lit a fire that killed people *all* feeling is bad? That *you're* bad?"

His jaw was tight as if it were going to crack. "Dad told me I needed to—"

"I don't give a fuck what your father told you. *My* father told me I was a talentless waste of space and I believed for years that somehow I was the reason he'd turned into such a bitter old man." She looked so fierce, like a warrior. "Until you. *You* made me feel like I was worth something. *You* made me feel beautiful. *You* made me understand just how much of myself I was holding back and *you* made me stop being so fucking afraid." Her fingers tightened on him. "None of what we shared together was destructive, Lucas. Your passion, your intensity, your goddamn *feelings,* helped me create, don't you see? Without you that painting would never have existed."

It wasn't like that. It wasn't. "You would have died," he said raggedly. "Because I couldn't slow my heartbeat enough to save you. Because I cared too much about you. In the same way I got too angry with my parents. With my foster father. It's destructive, Grace. I'm destructive."

The expression on her face was almost impossible to look at, the emotion in it so bright it was like staring directly into the sun. "How many people have you saved, Lucas?"

The subject change was so abrupt, he didn't understand what she was talking about. "What?"

"I know your confirmed kill count. But what about a count of all the lives you've saved?"

His arms were shaking. His bruised and battered soul was shaking. "That's not . . . That's . . ."

"That's not what? You told me you saved lives, that's what a sniper does. He takes one life to save many, right?"

"Yes, but—"

"But what?" Her hands were sliding up his chest and around his neck and she was holding on to him, winding herself around him like a vine. All slick bare skin and soft, feminine heat, and yet somehow so strong. "You don't destroy, Lucas Tate. You protect. And I think you've been so busy protecting people from yourself that you don't know any other way to be." Her voice lowered. "But you don't have to do that anymore. You're not dangerous. I know who you are and you don't destroy people. You save them."

He couldn't speak. Because it didn't seem possible that she could see him like that. And yet he remembered the painting in the gallery, the one he couldn't look at.

That painting is my heart. . . . It's you.

And it became clear to him, blindingly, why he'd always found it difficult to look at the sketches of him she'd drawn, why he could hardly even look at that painting.

It was because he wanted to be that man in the painting. He wanted to be the man she saw. The man who saved people. Who looked at her with hunger and passion and intensity and most of all *love*.

He wanted to love her. He had since the moment he'd met her.

The thought was a sledgehammer breaking down walls, the ice around his scarred soul cracking, then thawing, melting under the heat of the emotion swamping him.

And he found he'd buried his face in her neck and his arms were around her, holding her as tightly as she was holding him, and somehow they were sitting on the floor of the shower with the water pouring down onto them and she was in his lap. Still holding him. Keeping him together.

She didn't say a word, her legs wound around his waist, her arms around his neck.

So he let it all go, the ice and the snow. Let it all melt away, until there was nothing freezing him in place or holding him back anymore. Nothing to stop him from turning on that fucking tap and letting all the feelings come flooding out.

Her. He wanted her. All the time. Everywhere. For however long she wanted. For a day. For a week. For a year.

Forever.

It was Grace. It had *always* been Grace. And he'd never been in love before, but he knew that this was what it felt like. This desperation. This hunger. This need. Maybe that's what all of this had been and he'd never known it, never understood.

Well, he understood now and he wanted it. All of it.

"Take me, Gracie," he whispered, not hiding his desperation. "Take me, *please*."

But her hands were already there, wrestling with the wet denim, undoing the button and tugging at the zipper. Opening up his jeans and getting him out, her fingers on his skin making him shudder. Then she was lifting herself up and sliding down, her slick flesh parting around him, enclosing him as tightly as her arms had seconds earlier.

So fucking hot. So fucking good.

He gripped her and she bent her head, covering his

mouth with hers as he thrust up inside all that tight, wet heat. There were fire bursts in his head and she was a living flame between his hands, moving on him so fluidly, so perfectly. Not even the water flowing around them could put her out.

Nothing could. She was fire and lightning. She was sunshine. She was everything.

And as she took him deeper, faster, harder, all he could do was whisper the same phrase over and over again in her ear. "I love you, Gracie. Oh God, I'm so in love with you."

CHAPTER TWENTY

Grace opened her eyes and for a second she couldn't work out where she was. She wasn't in her bedroom in her apartment or in the bedroom in Lucas's apartment with the stained glass in it.

No, this room was kind of cold looking. White walls with nothing on them. Dark wood floor. A plain dresser against one wall and not much else.

She frowned and rolled over.

And her heart began to swell up, becoming large and painful, pressing against her ribs, making them ache.

Because Lucas stood naked near the window. His back was to her, the skylight above his head shining gray morning light all over his golden skin. He should have looked pale and washed out, yet he didn't. The way the light fell illuminated all the sculpted lines of his beautiful body, the exquisite width of his shoulders, the elegant play of his lats, and the strong column of his spine. The muscular curve of his truly fabulous butt and long, athletic legs . . .

Her heart swelled up even more.

After what had happened in the shower last night, after she'd taken him the way he'd asked her, they'd dried each other off and then gone to bed. But not to sleep. In fact, she didn't think they'd slept for hours, unable to stop touching each other, reaching for each other.

I love you, Gracie.

She hadn't expected that. She really hadn't. But somehow she'd broken through all his ice and reached the man buried underneath it. The bright, vital passionate man he'd been all along. The man she'd always known was fire.

Lucas stopped speaking, turning to put the phone down on the dresser next to him. Then he turned back to the window, looking out of it.

Unable to resist the urge, Grace slipped out of bed and went over to him, slipping her arms around his waist, laying her head against him, pressing her cheek against his back. The feel of his smooth, warm skin against hers was a glory she didn't think she'd ever get sick of.

His hands came down to rest on hers where she'd laid them on his taut stomach.

"How long have you known that I was awake?" she asked quietly.

"Since the moment you woke up." There was a warm thread running through his voice that thrilled her utterly. That was for her; she knew it.

"What gave it away?"

"Your breathing."

"Again? Okay, I must remember to stop breathing so I can get past your super sniper powers."

"Don't you dare." His hands tightened on hers. "Wolf called. He handled the situation last night. The press were told it was a random attack. Drugs, the usual shit."

She swallowed, a lingering remnant of the fear of last night washing through her. And he must have felt it, because he suddenly turned around, sliding his arms around her and drawing her close. There was no silver at all in his eyes. They were glowing, a deep, true blue that took her breath away.

"The cop," he said. "It was the guy I had in the basement. That I sent back. I thought he was just a cog in the machine, but apparently he was Oliveira himself."

She swallowed, staring up at him, seeing shadows in his gaze. But she knew what they meant. "You couldn't have known who he was, Lucas. And you couldn't have known he'd come after me. You couldn't have killed him either."

He said nothing for a long moment. "De Santis gave me his word he'd called them off. I even followed you for a couple of days after you left the apartment to make sure you were okay."

Her heart lurched a little in her chest. She hadn't known *that*. "You did?"

"I wanted to make sure." His hands spread out on her hips, stroking her, his gaze searching her face. "Wolf was able to find out a little more about what happened. Apparently, Oliveira was concerned about more than simply money. He wanted to make an example of you, a public show of what happened to people who betrayed him. His power base was probably failing and he needed something to shore it up and you just happened to be his unlucky choice of method." Lucas's thumbs moved caressingly. "I'm sorry, Gracie. I should have—"

But she reached up and laid a finger across his beautiful mouth. "No. There's nothing you should or shouldn't have done. And short of following me around forever there wasn't anything you could have done to stop it."

He sighed and kissed the tip of her finger. "Wolf wouldn't tell me how he knew. He just told me he had sources tell him that something was going to happen and decided to come check on us."

"That seems like . . . very good timing."

"A little too good, yes."

"Hmmm." She leaned into his warmth. "Is it worth calling your other brother to find out what's going on?"

"Probably." He lifted his hands, running his fingers gently through her hair, and it felt good, making her want to purr like a cat. "I need to talk to Van about a few things anyway."

"What things?"

"Me." He combed his fingers through her hair again. "And you."

She shivered. "What about me and you?"

"That we're together. And that I should probably stop being a hypocrite about him and Chloe."

"Oh really?"

"Yes, really." Then Lucas Tate smiled, a smile she'd never seen before. Bright. Fierce. Sexy. Thrilling. "If he can have what he wants, then so can I." His hands slid down over the curve of her butt, squeezing her gently, making her shiver. "I'm afraid it means you're not ever going to be getting rid of me, Gracie. I'm going to be around permanently, whether you like it or not."

Her throat closed, a bubble of happiness nearly cutting off her speech. But she forced herself all the same, because there was at least one question she wanted to know the answer to. "What about the Navy? Will you go back to base?"

Lucas's smile deepened, became something even more beautiful if that was possible. "No," he said slowly. "No, I think I'm done with that. I might give civilian life a try for a change."

Her breath caught as a relief she hadn't known she'd feel flooded through her. "Oh, well, are you sure? A sniper in a suit sounds dangerous."

Lucas gave a laugh that brushed over every nerve ending she had, rough and sexy and soft as worn velvet. "I'm not dangerous," he murmured. "Not anymore. But I'll settle for being just a little bit wicked."

Wicked, yes, she thought that maybe he was.

Then his hands slid a bit further over her skin and there was no maybe about it.

Wicked was exactly what he was.

"You're an asshole." Van's voice down the other end of the phone line sounded aggrieved. Which, to be fair, he had every right to be.

"Yeah, I know," Lucas said, pointing to the place he wanted the two removal men to put the large canvas they were both carrying. "And like I said, I'm sorry for being a dick about it. In my defense, it was my own shit. Not yours. I'm happy for you and Chloe, I really am."

And he was now he had Grace. Now he'd realized what it was he'd been missing all this time.

The men stood the canvas against the wall, then went out, while Lucas tilted his head back and eyed the ceiling. Grace wanted a skylight put in for a bit more light and he wondered whether or not two might be better.

It was a week after her exhibition and they'd both decided that there was no point living apart, that they both wanted to move back into the apartment in the converted church together. Lucas already had a cleaning company and a dry cleaner on speed dial because he had a feeling he was going to need both quickly and often. Grace wasn't the tidiest person around when it came to either her paint or her nail polish. Not that he minded. He was sure his tidy streak could work both ways.

Van made a noncommittal noise. He and Chloe had apparently retreated from New York to Wyoming without telling anyone, purely to get away from the media circus the news of their engagement had generated. "So are you going to tell me what your shit is?" He sounded less aggrieved now, which was good.

Lucas knew he should have called him before, but what with chasing up any loose ends that Oliveira had left behind in order to make sure Grace was completely safe, not to mention dealing with the fallout of what had happened at the exhibition, he hadn't had a moment. Though perhaps that was more because he'd been avoiding the issue. Calling up his brother to apologize and admit he'd been an asshole wasn't easy.

"Not yet." One day Lucas would tell Van and Wolf about his mother, but that day wasn't today. It probably wouldn't even be tomorrow, or maybe not until even next year. But he would. Eventually. "I will at some stage."

Van made a growling sound but didn't press. "Fine. So what? You're shacking up with this Grace chick then?"

"You can call her Grace, you know."

"Okay, okay. You shacking up with Grace?"

"Yes."

"Good." His brother didn't sound at all surprised. "Since you're not re-upping, I'll expect you at work tomorrow then, bright and early. A director's work is never done, you know."

"Fuck you," Lucas said succinctly.

Van laughed. "Nine A.M., asshole. And I'm going to need a debrief about this de Santis shit, since I've got some intel to pass on. . . ." He paused. "By the way, I've been calling Wolf for days now and he's fucking avoiding me, the prick. You know what's going on with him?"

"No. And you're not the only one who's been calling either." Lucas had been trying to get in touch with his younger brother, but the last time he'd spoken to Wolf had been the day after Wolf had put a bullet through Oliveira's skull. "He's not answering his phone."

"Fuck," Van muttered. "He's still in New York, though, right? He's not back on base, I've checked."

"Christ knows." Lucas turned as the door of the studio opened and a familiar tall, slender figure slipped in. All thoughts of Wolf vanished from his head. "I've got to go," he said to his brother.

"Hey," Van said, right before Lucas disconnected. "You sound happy. Are you?"

Lucas smiled, but it wasn't for his brother. It was for the woman who was coming toward him, amber eyes full of warmth, her lovely mouth turning up in a grin that was just for him. She had a paintbrush in her hair and an armful of paint tubes and there was nothing he wanted more than to pull her down on the floor and revisit a few special memories associated with this particular room.

"Yeah," he said, and there was no trace of ice in his voice at all. "I am."

"You are what?" Grace asked as he disconnected the call without waiting for his brother to respond, and put his phone back in his pocket. "And who was that?"

"It was Van. I just told him I was happy."

Grace's smile was as bright as the summer sun. She dumped the paint on the floor and came over to him, sliding her arms around him, pressing her beautiful body up against his. "Good." She rose up on her toes to brush his mouth with hers. "So am I. I even thought I might call my mother, which means I must be *very* happy."

"If I can call my brother then you can definitely call your mother." He lifted his hands and pulled the paintbrush out of her hair, watching as the little bun uncoiled down her back in a beautiful red-gold fall of silk. Then he tangled his fingers in it, gently tugging her head back so he could look into her eyes. "Did Craig get back to you about extending the exhibition?"

"Yes." Her gaze glittered with excitement. "By another couple of weeks. Plus he's had requests for my work from lots of different collectors, so I'm going to be kind of busy for the next six months."

"Unsurprisingly."

"Why unsurprisingly?"

"Because you're a fucking genius, that's why."

Color flooded through her lovely face. "I wouldn't go that far."

"I would." He shifted his hands so his thumbs could stroke along her high, angular cheekbones, tracing the soft skin. "I think I know why your father was so much of a prick to you, Gracie."

Her forehead creased. "Oh?"

"He was jealous."

"Jealous?" she repeated, blinking. "No. He was really good. How could he—"

"He took one look at your drawings and balled them up. Threw them away. There's only one reason he would have done that. Plus . . ." He held her gaze, looking into her eyes. "I know nothing about art, remember? But the moment I stepped into that gallery, I knew you were something special. I knew you weren't just good, you were brilliant."

Her cheeks were pink with pleasure and her eyes were full of gold and fire, the colors of his soul. The colors of his heart. "Well, that's as may be." Her voice was a little thick. "But I still can't hit a fly on a wall from a mile away with that stupid gun."

He smiled. "It's true. You're good with a paintbrush, Gracie. But I'm a better shot."

"That's not the only thing you're good at either." She grinned, then wound her arms around his neck, arching her body into his. "I can think of several other things you can do very well."

She wasn't wrong. There *were* a number of other things he was good at.

He had over two hundred confirmed kills. Could slow his heartbeat to thirty beats per minute. Could stand motionless for hours in order to remain hidden. Could take an impossible shot and hit his target every time.

Yeah, he was the best in the business.

But most of all, he was the best at loving Grace Riley.

And that was the only thing that mattered.

EPILOGUE

Wolf Tate slid his Glock into the waistband of his jeans as he walked quickly down the street, leaving the screams and shouts still echoing from the gallery behind him. It was cold out, snow in the night air, his breathing fogging heavily in front of him.

A cop car whizzed past him, but he didn't glance after it. He didn't need to. Lucas had gotten Grace away and Oliveira was dead, and he'd played his part. It was all good.

At the end of the block, he rounded the corner to where a long black limo sat at the curb. Without hesitation he reached for the door handle and pulled it open before sliding into the warm, dark interior.

A man sat opposite him, his blue eyes as chilly as Lucas's could be. "Oliviera?" the man demanded.

"Dead." Wolf sat back on the cushy leather seats. "Just like you asked."

"Good," said Cesare de Santis. "And the rest of his men?"

"Dealt with."

"What about your brother and the woman?"

"They're out of your hair." Wolf allowed himself a smile. "And don't worry, the intel Lucas has on you is going to stay on his laptop, just like I promised you. I'll make sure of that."

De Santis did not look convinced. "You've promised me things in the past that you haven't delivered on, Tate. I haven't forgotten."

Wolf decided he was sick of smiling. He leaned forward, nice and slow, because there were a number of other things he was sick of and this prick sitting in front of him was just one of them. But first, there was the little matter of payment.

"I did what you fucking asked me to do," he said. "On a number of occasions. Now it's time for you to pay me what I'm owed."

De Santis gave an exaggerated sigh. "Ah yes. The money."

Wolf laughed. "I don't want money and you know it."

The other man's eyes got colder, because he knew what Wolf wanted. Oh yes, he did.

Wolf decided that perhaps he had another smile left in him after all, and this time it was feral, white, and sharp with teeth. "Money's for assholes, de Santis," Wolf said. "What I want is your daughter."

Read on for an excerpt from the next book by

JACKIE ASHENDEN

THE UNDERCOVER BILLIONAIRE

Coming soon from St. Martin's Paperbacks

She swallowed, resisting the urge to pull her hand away from his. Not wanting to give herself away more than she had already.

Oh come on. He already knows. You've never been very good at hiding how you feel.

She looked away, letting her hand rest in his and trying not to pay any attention to her racing heartbeat. "Okay," she said, her voice sounding far more husky than she wanted it to. "Let's have that coffee then and we can talk."

But he didn't let her hand go. Instead she felt one long finger catch her beneath the chin, turning her head back to meet his gaze. "Hey, what's up?" he murmured. "You're blushing."

No kidding. She tightened her jaw and steeled herself to give him a steady, level look back, as if nothing was wrong, nothing at all. But that stare of his was mesmerizing. She'd always loved how he had one blue eye and one green. Heterochromia it was apparently called, or that's what he'd told her when she'd asked about it once. Not that it mattered what it was called. She just found it beautiful, that crystalline blue matched with the leaf green, the colors vivid through his long dark lashes . . .

His mouth curved. "Liv? You can answer any time."

Oh, right. He'd asked her a question and now she was simply staring at him like a lunatic.

A question he already knows the answer to, come on.

A wave of sudden annoyance caught at her, partly driven by her own helpless reaction to him, because yes, of course he knew. He must. He wasn't stupid, no matter that he always talked his own intelligence down, and neither was she.

"You know why I'm blushing already." The words were out before she could stop herself.

His eyes widened, which made a small part of her suddenly very satisfied that she could surprise him. Because really, she was getting a little tired of being the only one who was flustered. She didn't like how out of control it made her feel, and come to think of it, she was starting to feel a bit peeved that she didn't rock his world in quite the same way as he rocked hers.

She stared back at him, making no move to pull away. There was no point now, not if he knew how he affected her anyway.

"Yeah," he said slowly, searching her face. "I guess I do."

"So why ask me then?"

He didn't let go of her hand and that finger under her chin stayed exactly where it was. Her heartbeat was banging like a damn drum in her head, and she wanted to pull away with just about every part of her.

But something small and defiant and stubborn held her still.

"Maybe I wanted to check something." The finger beneath her chin moved, trailing very lightly down her neck. Goosebumps erupted all over her skin and it was all she could do not to gasp or take a quick step back.

"Check what?" Shivers of excitement were chasing all over her skin and her voice sounded husky. And it annoyed her. What was he doing? What was he looking for? An admission that she was attracted to him? If so, why?

His finger paused in the hollow of her throat and she knew he could feel her pulse. And that it was fast. Too fast.

His gaze held hers, intense all of a sudden. "It's been six months since I've been with anyone, Liv."

Wait, what? Was that an . . . invitation?

No, it couldn't be. He didn't feel that way about her. He was her friend and he'd never done anything to make her think he felt anything more for her. She didn't want to go there, she just didn't.

Swallowing, she said, "I thought you wanted to talk about your father?"

"Yeah, well, maybe I changed my mind." His finger moved lightly on her skin in a gentle stroking motion, while his gaze dropped down to her white nightgown. "Maybe I want to do something else."

Something else . . .

Olivia jerked away from him before she was even conscious of doing so, taking a couple of steps back to put some distance between them. She was breathless, her heart raging behind her ribs, her pulse rocketing and her skin strangely hot and tight. "I don't . . . know what you're talking about." Her voice sounded all thick and unsteady.

Wolf stared at her for a long second. "You know what I'm talking about, Liv. I think we both know what I'm talking about."

"Yes, and I thought I was your friend." She couldn't get her breathing under control or her heartbeat. "Was that why you brought me here? To . . . to . . ."

"To what? Fuck you?"

She'd long gotten used to Wolf's filthy mouth, but hearing that word in conjunction with herself made a hot, electric thrill shoot straight down her spine.

He couldn't mean it, though. He just couldn't. The whole thing was too weird. The kidnap, the hustling into the hotel and then the strange questions he'd asked her. Not to mention the look on his face when she'd stupidly thought the champagne and the candles had meant something else.

She couldn't afford to believe he could mean it.

"No," she said flatly, hating the way the word came out so shakily. "You don't want that. It doesn't make any sense. You said this wasn't a date."

The intensity of his gaze felt like it was burning right through her. "It's not. I never fuck on a first date."

Again that hot thrill, and this time moving lower, between her thighs. Her brain was going places she didn't want to go, sending images she didn't want to see rioting through her mind. Wolf naked. Wolf touching her. Wolf fucking on the first date. Wolf fucking her . . .

"No," she said again, shaking her head violently. "No."

There was a tense, heavy silence.

Then he was moving toward her, fast and fluid, and she only had time to stumble back a few steps, before he was right there in front of her. He grabbed her hand and before she could stop him, he'd brought her palm flat to his chest, right over his left pec, pressing it down onto his skin. "You want me, Liv. I know you do. I can see it in your eyes."

She froze, what little breath she had left rushing out of her.

He's right. You do.

But not like this. Something wasn't right. She could feel it.

He made no move to do anything else, merely held her hand against him, that intense uneven gaze holding hers.

The heat of his body was blistering. Hard, hard muscle. Tanned skin slightly roughened with hair. The steady, slow beat of his heart.

She'd been so good, so careful. She'd never imagined touching him or anything else, because she wasn't a masochist. It was bad enough being hopelessly in love with him let alone to fantasize about anything else.

But now she *was* touching him and it was . . . .

No. No, she couldn't do this. It was too close to what she desperately wanted and it was becoming obvious to her that she was simply a convenient body. He didn't want *her*. If in fact it was actually sex he wanted in the first place.

She jerked her hand away from the furnace of his naked chest.

Only for him to take one step even closer, his other hand sliding into her hair, his big palm cradling the back of her head, his fingers pressing gently against her skull. Then before she could react, he lowered his head and that wide, beautiful mouth was on hers.

Shock held her utterly still.

Wolf Tate was kissing her. Wolf Tate was kissing *her*.

If she hadn't been able to breathe before, now it was as if all the air in the entire world had been sucked away and there was no relief to be found anywhere.

His lips were . . . .soft. She hadn't expected that. He was so hard everywhere else, and yet there was nothing unyielding about the mouth brushing gently over hers. Nothing forceful. His breath was warm and somehow she couldn't stop shivering as he brushed his lips over hers again, a butterfly kiss.

He made a sound, rough and approving, inhaling as if her scent was something he liked. Then his tongue touched her bottom lip, gently coaxing.

Wildfire was kindling in her veins, a rush of intense heat sweeping over her, scorching her.

She felt dizzy. This was her first kiss. With the only man she'd ever wanted it to be with. The only man she'd ever wanted to touch, ever wanted to have touch her.

It's not real and you know it.

Doubt was a small, hard kernel of ice sitting in her gut, impervious to the flames. There was too much that was strange about this whole situation, too much she didn't know and she couldn't kick the feeling that Wolf wasn't telling her the whole story.

Which meant she couldn't give herself over to this kiss. She couldn't let him do anything more. Another woman might have thrown caution to the winds and take what she wanted, even if this was all she'd ever have, but Olivia wasn't that woman.

Her whole life was about caution. About watching and waiting, and thinking things through carefully. And as much as she wanted Wolf Tate, she'd already told herself she would never have him, not the way she wanted him. It was something she'd come to terms long ago. Because he didn't want her. Not really. He wasn't in love with her the way she was in love with him and if she let herself have this, only to find out that it wasn't real . . .

Well. She'd never recover.

Looking for more hot billionaires?

Don't miss the next novel
in the brand-new Tate Brothers series

THE UNDERCOVER

BILLIONAIRE

Coming soon from St. Martin's Paperbacks